all my bests

BRITNEE MEISER

ALADDIN
NEW YORK LONDON TORONTO SYDNEY NEW DELHI

This book is a work of fiction. Any references to historical events, real people, or real places are used fictitiously. Other names, characters, places, and events are products of the author's imagination, and any resemblance to actual events or places or persons, living or dead, is entirely coincidental.

ALADDIN

An imprint of Simon & Schuster Children's Publishing Division

1230 Avenue of the Americas, New York, New York 10020

First Aladdin paperback edition November 2024

Text copyright © 2024 by Britnee Meiser

Cover illustration copyright © 2024 by Ali Mac

Also available in an Aladdin hardcover edition.

All rights reserved, including the right of reproduction in whole or in part in any form.

ALADDIN and related logo are registered trademarks of Simon & Schuster, LLC.

Simon & Schuster: Celebrating 100 Years of Publishing in 2024

For information about special discounts for bulk purchases, please contact Simon & Schuster Special Sales at 1-866-506-1949 or business@simonandschuster.com.

The Simon & Schuster Speakers Bureau can bring authors to your live event. For more information or to book an event contact the Simon & Schuster Speakers Bureau at 1-866-248-3049 or visit our website at www.simonspeakers.com.

Designed by Heather Palisi

The text of this book was set in Adobe Caslon Pro.

Manufactured in the United States of America 1024 BID

2 4 6 8 10 9 7 5 3 1

Library of Congress Cataloging-in-Publication Data

Names: Meiser, Britnee, author.

Title: All my bests / by Britnee Meiser.

Description: First Aladdin paperback edition. | New York : Aladdin, 2024. | Audience: Ages 10 and Up. | Summary: When Immie and Jack start high school, they wonder if their friendship can endure the changing social dynamics and the realization that they want to be more than friends.

Identifiers: LCCN 2024000133 (print) | LCCN 2024000134 (ebook) | ISBN 9781665948210 (pb) | ISBN 9781665948227 (hc) | ISBN 9781665948234 (ebook)

Subjects: CYAC: Friendship—Fiction. | Interpersonal relations—Fiction. | Family life—Fiction. | High schools—Fiction. | Schools—Fiction. | Romance stories.

Classification: LCC PZ7.1.M46914 Al 2024 (print) | LCC PZ7.1.M46914 (ebook) | DDC [Fic]—dc23

LC record available at https://lccn.loc.gov/2024000133

LC ebook record available at https://lccn.loc.gov/2024000134

For my mom,
who gave me everything I need

all my bests

PART ONE

Immie

~~Dear Jack,~~
~~I'm still really mad at you.~~

~~Dear Jack,~~
~~Do you miss me as much as I miss you?~~

~~Jack,~~
~~I can't believe you're dating her. HER!! How could~~
~~you do this to~~

~~Dear Jack,~~
~~What happened to us?~~

Dear Jack,

    I'm not writing you this letter to tell you that I forgive you. I'm not even writing it for you—I'm writing it for me.

    I've spent so much time thinking about you lately that I forgot to consider what was best for me. And now that I'm finally thinking about ME, I realize that you weren't. Not recently, at least. Maybe not ever.

    We haven't talked in two weeks. I know some of that is my fault. You tried to talk to me after the bonfire, but it was too late, and I was angry. Then you stopped trying. That's on you. ~~Why couldn't you just see how much I wanted you to~~

You were my best friend, Jack, and you hurt me. You should have never stopped trying.

I've had a lot of time (A LOT) to think about what happened between us, and while I still don't forgive you for the way you treated me, I've accepted that _we_ aren't supposed to be a thing. As friends or more. I wish that meant I was no longer hurting, but you yanked my heart out of my chest and stomped on it with your soccer cleats. That's going to take some time to heal. Even then, it will scar.

I still miss you. It sucks, but it's true. I think part of me always will. We have a lot of history, and it all lives in my head rent free. So I thought, maybe if I could get it out, it would be a little easier to manage. Things always make more sense when you see them from the outside, don't they? Like seeing a butterfly pressed in glass, I could look at how we were, figure out where we went wrong, and finally have some peace.

Oh, guess what song just came on the queue? "How's It Going to Be." Remember what you said when I played it for you? Probably not, but I do. You said it was "too angsty."

TOO ANGSTY???

I never told you this before, but the first time I heard "How's It Going to Be," I cried. That's because it's a song about loss. I was listening to the lyrics, and before I knew it, I was thinking about you and what it would be like if you weren't in my life.

How _would_ it be if you didn't know me? Well, it would

be horrible ~~agonizing~~ devastating. No one to explore the woods with. No one to talk to when Mom was in one of her migraine moods. No one to eat the banana-flavored Laffy Taffys, so they'd just sit there in the candy dish until they mysteriously fused to the bottom and I'd have to use a knife to scrape them out. I had absolutely no interest in a life like that.

Do you understand now why I got so upset when you took off your headphones in the middle of the second verse? This song, which you dismissed as "too angsty," is what made me realize my true feelings for you, and you didn't even bother to listen to it the whole way through. That's what I think about now when I hear it.

Rejection

~~loss~~

Heartbreak.

I know I'm probably not making a lot of sense. Elijah told me the other day that I ramble when I get worked up. I can't help it. I've got so many feelings, and they're all fighting to come out. But I know you'll never read this, so it doesn't matter if I'm making sense, and anyway, love rarely makes sense.

Yeah, I said it.

I did love you, Jack. That's the point. But you didn't love me back.

THAT'S the point.

This is a love letter and a goodbye letter.

This is our history out of my head.

This is me, letting you go.

Along with this letter is the portable CD player I bought from eBay. Inside the player, a CD with the words ALL MY BESTS written on top in black Sharpie. I have burned eighteen songs onto this CD the way they did it before streaming, when music was tangible and playlists were special gifts, like carving out a piece of yourself track by track, line by line, until you've created a perfect specimen.

These songs dropped me right back in the middle of all our big moments and allowed me (or forced me, depending how you look at it) to live them again. It was hard, but I had to do it. I HAD to figure out which moments were most important to our story.

Maybe no one will ever listen to it. Or maybe someone someday will stumble upon our spot and feel what I felt—what you never did. And I'll be forty, doing whatever I'm going to do with my life, and I'll inexplicably have a feeling that I'm not alone anymore. And maybe I won't, like, know it consciously, but somehow my _soul_ will know that someone is listening to all my bests.

Spoiler alert: "How's It Going to Be" is the last song on the playlist. I didn't know it at first, but this song has always been about the future.

My future.

Without you.

TRACK ONE

"We're Going to Be Friends"—The White Stripes

This one's obvious, isn't it?
From the very beginning, you were there.
I never stood a chance.

*M*y name is Imogen Marie Meadows. I'm seven years old.

I can do long division and spell "facade" and "rutabaga."

I love to draw pictures and collect taxidermy butterflies.

I know all about in vitro fertilization.

I do not know anything about my father.

This is what I'm ready to tell the boy who's zooming toward me on a skateboard—this, and nothing else. I'm used to people asking questions about me, because my mom and I move around a lot, so I've come up with a script that perfectly *encapsulates* me. (That's a word I just learned—"encapsulate": to express the essential features of something succinctly.)

Then he falls off his skateboard and into my front yard.

I stand still on my porch, watching and waiting. But the boy doesn't get up. He doesn't even move, just lies there with his face in the grass. Did I just witness someone *die*? Now *that* would be an interesting addition to my script. I look around for Mom, or one of the movers, but everyone is inside the house, unpacking our furniture. Guess it's up to me to investigate.

I take a sip from the glass of lemonade I'm holding, then slowly walk toward him.

"Hey," I whisper.

No answer.

"HEY! Are you dead?"

Finally, he turns his head to look at me, squinting through the bright light of the summer sun.

"Not dead," he says weakly.

"Hm." So much for my fun new anecdote. "Okay. I guess that's good."

"You guess?" He pushes himself off the grass to sit upright and takes off his helmet, revealing a shaggy head of bright blond hair. He looks at the glass in my hand. "Hey, is that lemonade?"

"No," I say quickly, tucking my long black hair behind my ear.

"Can I have some?"

I make a face. "You can't just ask strangers for lemonade."

"Sure you can," he replies. "Haven't you ever seen a lemonade stand before?"

"Do I *look* like a lemonade stand to you?"

"Okay, okay. Jeez." He stands up, dusts himself off, then looks around for his skateboard. It's in the neighbor's yard. He sighs.

"You better go get that," I say, trying to urge him along. I'm ready to get back to reading my book and drinking my lemonade in silence.

"Yeah." He doesn't move, just stares at his skateboard wistfully. "You know, I think I'm done with skateboarding. I stink at it."

I nod. "You can say that again."

"Okay." He cups his hands around his mouth. "I STINK AT IT!"

A giggle escapes my lips, surprising both of us. He cocks his head at me, smiles a little.

"It's okay. You can laugh," he says. "I laugh at myself all the time." Then he looks back at his board. "I don't even like skating, anyway. I only do it because of my older brother."

"Is he as bad as you?"

He shakes his head. "No, he's good. Michael is good at everything." A pause. "He's not going to like it when he finds out I busted his board. Maybe I can blame the new scratches on our cat Tina."

"What did Tina ever do to you?"

He gives me a knowing look. "Have you ever had your sister put catnip in your pocket when you weren't paying attention?" He winces at the memory.

"I don't have a sister," I say with a frown. "Or a cat."

"Consider yourself lucky."

He goes to the neighbor's yard to get the skateboard, and I see my chance to get away. I walk around the side of my new house, cut across the backyard, and step past the tree line. There are woods behind my house, which Mom already said I can't explore alone. She didn't say anything about hanging out on the edge, though. That's where, earlier today, I found the Tree.

The tree has these huge, exposed roots that I can crawl under like a dugout. It's the perfect place to disappear. Under the tree, I try to get back to reading, but I can't focus. I keep thinking about what that boy said: *Consider yourself lucky.* Is it lucky to be lonely? It's never really felt that way.

"So what's your name?"

The sound of his voice makes me jump. I look up to find him with his skateboard in his hands, grinning at me from the other side of the roots.

"How did you find me here?"

"I followed you."

"That's creepy."

His smile falls. "Was I not supposed to? I thought we were talking."

"We *were*. And now we're not," I say, returning my attention to my book.

He lingers there, not saying anything. I sigh and put the book down.

"You're distracting me."

"Sorry." He crouches down. "But come on. You're really not going to tell me your name? We're practically neighbors."

"Fine. My name is Imogen Marie Meadows. Happy?"

"Imogen? That's a weird name."

"My mom calls me Immie."

"That's a weirder name." He puts the skateboard down by the trunk of the tree and crawls under the roots to sit next to me. "I'm Jack."

"Well, Jack, you're being kind of rude about my name."

"Oh." His eyes widen. "Sorry, I didn't mean to be. I just meant that I haven't met anyone named Immie before."

It wasn't the first time someone made fun of my name. Kids at my last school called it a grandma name, which is funny, since I actually *was* named after my grandma. Once, Timothy Kline said Imogen sounded like "emoji." I responded by hissing at him and stomping on his foot, and I got sent home early. I still don't regret it. Nobody disrespects Grandma Imogen like that.

"I forgive you."

"Hey." He points to a doodle of a butterfly in the notebook by my feet. "Did you do that? It's really good."

I feel my cheeks heat up. "You ask a lot of questions," I say, flipping the notebook closed. "I don't even know you."

"Not yet," Jack says. "But we're going to be friends. I can tell."

My first-grade teacher once wrote the word "prickly" on my progress report. *Immie doesn't play well with others,* she added underneath. Mom was upset with me when she saw it. She thought I wasn't being nice to the other kids in my class, but that wasn't fair. I *tried* to be nice, at least at first. Then I brought my favorite taxidermy butterfly in for show-and-tell. Rebecca Miller in the front row said, *Ew, she brought a dead body in!* and Timothy Kline called me a weirdo, and that was it. I was on my own after that.

"Immie?" Mom calls.

Jack and I poke our heads out from behind the tree's roots. Mom is standing on the back porch with her hands on her hips. Her blond ponytail is messy, and her white T-shirt is wet under the armpits.

"Who's your friend?"

"Cookie Monster," I call back. "And he's hungry!"

"Very funny." She crosses her arms. "What's your name, little man?"

"Hi, Immie's mom!" Jack waves to her. "I'm Jack Marshall. I live right over there." He points to the left.

"Nice to meet you, Jack." Mom smiles. "Do your parents know you're here?"

"They like it when I play outside during the day," he says, not exactly answering the question.

Mom pauses, then says, "All right." She won't ask any more questions—yet. She's too busy unpacking our old things into our new life.

"Why do they like it when you play outside?" I ask.

Jack grabs a tuft of grass and starts yanking on it. It seems like he doesn't want to look me in the eye. "My house is kind of busy. I have four siblings, and my parents just found out they're having twins."

"Wow." I do the math in my head—seven people living under one roof, plus two more on the way. I can't imagine what it would be like to have such a big family. "That's the opposite of my house."

"Really?" He looks at me with interest. "How many siblings do you have?"

"None. It's just me and Mom."

"That sounds great," he says. "You get to have all of your mom's attention."

12

"I guess." I don't tell him the truth, which is that a lot of the time, Mom's attention is focused on grading papers and writing lesson plans.

"Where's your dad?" Jack asks.

I should have known that question was coming next.

"I don't have one."

"What do you mean?" He stops tugging on the grass. "Everyone has a dad."

"Not everyone," I correct him, thinking about a girl in my class last year who had two moms. "Not me. I was conceived through IVF."

"Con*ceived*?" Jack scrunches up his forehead. "IVF? What does that mean?"

"It means . . ." I make my voice sound serious. "It means I hatched from an egg."

Jack narrows his eyes. "No way, you're lying."

"I'm not! One day Mom decided she wanted a baby, so she went to the egg store and picked me out of all the other eggs. She said my egg was light blue and sparkly."

"Oh, yeah." Jack nods like it makes perfect sense. "So that's why your eyes are that color."

I burst out laughing. "I didn't really come from an egg!"

Jack shakes his head and looks at me with interest. "You're kind of weird, huh?"

I narrow my eyes at the word.

"Don't worry. I like it."

"Really?"

"Yeah," he says, like it's obvious. When Timothy Kline

called me a weirdo, he said it like a bad thing. I never knew weird could be good.

"So, what is I-F . . ." He trails off.

"IVF?"

"IVF," he repeats. "What is it really?"

I take a deep breath, preparing to say my speech. "My mom gave an egg to a scientist, and the scientist mixed it with a sperm in a lab, and that's how I was made. Then the doctor put me inside my mom to grow, and then I was born, just like you."

Jack watches me tell the story with a blank expression on his face. When I finish talking, his eyes light up with understanding. "So you did hatch from an egg!"

"Not that kind of egg."

"Oh." He nods, but I can tell he's still confused. I don't know how to clear things up for him. I'm just repeating what my mom only recently told me. I tried asking follow-up questions: If she gave the egg, where did the sperm come from? And what *is* a sperm, anyway?

I open my book again, feeling strange, like maybe I revealed too much.

"I think I'd like to get back to reading now."

"Okay," Jack says. "Can I keep sitting here with you?"

"You just want to sit there while I read?"

"Yeah," he says. "I don't want to skateboard anymore, but I don't want to go home yet either."

That's when a little white butterfly flutters in and lands on the toe of Jack's sneaker. A good sign. Maybe Grandma

Imogen sent it. I think of her, smiling with a butterfly perched on her wrinkled hand, and feel a pang of sadness.

"Sure, you can stay."

Jack grins, pleased, then leans back on his hands and closes his eyes. He stays like that for a while, until the butterfly flies away, and then says, "This is a good tree. We should name it."

"Name it?" I furrow my brow. "Name it what?"

"Hmm." He considers. "How about . . . Queen LaTreefah?"

I fiddle with my glass of lemonade, letting the ice cubes clink together inside, and I consider. The tree already feels like *mine*. Do I want to share it? I twist the glass too fast, almost spilling the whole thing, but Jack saves it just in time.

"Hey, you lied!" he says, licking some of the splashed drink off the back of his hand. "This *is* lemonade."

"Yeah, it is," I say. "You want some?"

He looks at me curiously. "I thought you said you didn't give your lemonade to strangers."

"I don't," I say. "But we're not strangers anymore. And I guess this can be our tree. But that's what we're going to call it. Our tree."

He smiles wide. "See? I told you we were going to be friends."

I give him a warning look. "Don't get any ideas. It's *just* a lemonade."

"Too late," he says. "I've got plenty of ideas."

I roll my eyes, trying to hide my smile. Maybe a friend wouldn't be so bad after all. Especially a friend like Jack.

TRACK TWO

"Wrapped Up in Books"—Belle and Sebastian

We were starting high school, so I knew some things were going to change. I just never imagined one of those things would be us.

SEVEN YEARS LATER

When the bell rings at the end of fourth period and I take my first step toward the door, there it is: the Squeak.

I guess my hope that the squeak would magically disappear during the lecture on proper paintbrush care was wishful thinking. It's just my luck that the shoes I bought for the first day of high school *specifically* to make me look cool and mature are having the opposite effect. I pull my phone out of my bag and type a new message to Jack.

Immie: I made a horrible mistake

Jack: ?

Immie: My new boots. They've been SQUEAKING all morning

"Did you see Vanessa's teeth?" Hannah says, catching up to me as we round the corner out of Ms. Moser's art classroom.

"She got her braces off over the summer, and now she looks five years older."

I run my tongue over my two front teeth, freshly self-conscious about the kiddish way one kind of overlaps the other. "Does that mean you're going to stop calling her Vampira?"

Hannah cackles. "I didn't call her Vampira because of her teeth. I called her that because she stole my calculator in the sixth grade."

"That doesn't even make sense."

"It does," Hannah asserts, bumping shoulders with a slow walker as she passes by him in the hall. "Stealing my *brand-new* pink calculator was total demonic behavior. Guess you just had to be there."

"I *was* there," I remind her. "We both had sixth-period math with Mrs. Hess."

Hannah furrows her brow. "I don't remember you being there."

"I sat in the back." I shrug and look down at my phone, where there's a new message from Jack.

Jack: I'm sure it's not that bad

I frown. I first told him about the boots this morning, when his older sister Carrie, a senior this year, drove us to school. Even then he said I was being dramatic.

He has *no* idea.

Immie: Wrong

Immie: Every step I take sounds like I'm stomping on a clown's nose

Jack: That's kinda funny

"I thought you moved here in the seventh grade?" Hannah glances at me, flicking her long dark braids over her shoulder.

I shake my head, still focused on typing my reply. "Not seventh grade. *When* I was seven."

Immie: FUNNY?

Immie: I'm going to be known as squeaky shoe girl for the next four years and you think that's funny???

"Dang," Hannah says. "Either I'm oblivious, or you have powers of invisibility you've never told me about."

The truth is, since the day Mom and I moved to Storm Valley, Pennsylvania, it's been all Jack, all the time. That hasn't left me a lot of time for other friends. The only person who ever came close to getting me like he does was Grandma Imogen, and she died right before we moved here, so it was kind of like Jack filled the hole that she left. Sometimes I even think she sent him to me.

"Thank god for art class." Hannah adjusts her tote bag on her shoulder. "Otherwise, I would have never been able to force you into being my friend."

"You didn't force me," I say, grinning, even though she did, a little. One thing about Hannah is that she loooves to talk while she paints. Since we were seated next to each other in the art class we both took over the summer, I went from not knowing her at all to knowing everything about her in a couple of weeks. (I could tell you all about the summers she spent in Jamaica with her granny, or the drama between her favorite beauty YouTubers, or the time, when she was twelve,

18

she saved her cousin Norbert from an aggressive scurry of chipmunks after he got his head stuck in the tree hollow where they were nesting. Now he owes her free ice cream for life.) And it turned out it wasn't so terrible, getting to know someone who wasn't Jack, especially considering that someone was a girl. For the first time, I had a friend to talk to about Regency romance movies and Jacob Elordi's abs.

My phone buzzes in my hand.

Jack: It's the first day of high school, Outie. Everybody's way too focused on themselves to notice what your shoes sound like

Jack: Just be yourself

"By the way." Hannah pulls the syllabus for our new art class out of her tote bag. As we get closer to the cafeteria, I can hear the buzzing chatter growing louder. "What do you think about this midterm project? It seems kind of intense to me."

I groan. "Can we not think about that yet?" The midterm project—that, yes, the teacher introduced on the *first day*—is called Who Am I, and it's due in December, right before the holiday break. It can be in any medium, or mix of mediums; the only guideline is that it has to attempt to answer the question "Who am I?"

High school is the start of a really beautiful transformation process, Ms. Moser said. *You're growing, changing, evolving from the children you have been into the adults you'll become. Every day is a chance for self-discovery, and that's why this project is not about the answer. It's about the attempt.*

Whatever *that* means. I just know that the thought

19

of revealing any part of my ooshy-gooshy inner self to my classmates or teacher makes me want to die.

"I haven't thought much about it," I say, typing my response to Jack. "I'll probably just paint something."

Immie: Wrong again, Monty. First impressions stick

I smirk down at my phone, using my nickname for Jack to fight fire with fire. As a kid, he'd eat whole packs of shredded Monterey Jack cheese, scooping it out with his hands like it was a bag of chips. Over time, Monterey Jack morphed into Monty, and Jack *hates* it.

Hannah and I find an empty table on the far side of the cafeteria that's a little too close to the trash cans, but it's better than sharing a table with a bunch of people I don't know.

"I'm going to text Alex and Zoya to tell them where we are," Hannah says when we sit down. "I'm so excited for you guys to meet."

I focus on unzipping my lunch box instead of replying. I'm not exactly thrilled about having to meet new people. I just want Jack. This is the first time in the history of us that we don't have the same lunch period, and I already miss him.

"You're going to love them," Hannah continues.

I grab my ham and cheese sandwich and scrunch up my face.

"Don't be such a Debbie Downer! Yes, you're different from them. But different doesn't have to be a bad thing." Hannah fixes her brown eyes on me. "You and I are different."

"Not that different," I say. "We're both . . . artsy."

"Yeah, but other than that, I'm pretty much normal. You, on the other hand—you talk about taxidermy and decapitated queens, like, a lot more than the average person."

"Marie Antoinette's last words were *I'm sorry, I didn't mean to,* because she stepped on the executioner's foot. How ironically tragic is that?"

Hannah looks at me like I have two heads.

"Hey, you're the one who was always talking to me," I remind her. "I was perfectly happy painting landscapes in silence."

In the empty spots next to us, two lunch trays are dropped onto the table with smacks that make me jump. I look up to see Zoya and Alex. Zoya takes the seat next to Hannah; Alex, next to me.

"What are we talking about?" Zoya says, removing the lid from her yogurt cup.

"How it's fun to make new friends," Hannah says brightly, and I resist the urge to roll my eyes. "Speaking of which . . . Immie, meet Zoya and Alex. They've heard a lot about you."

"Hi," I say, my voice flat. I take a bite of my sandwich and get a large glob of mayonnaise. I try not to gag as I swallow it down.

"The famous Immie." Zoya puts her elbows on the table and leans forward. She's all angles, sharp cheekbones, light brown skin, and long, glossy hair. She looks like a model. "Has anyone ever told you that you look like a Tim Burton character?"

"Um." I tuck a strand of hair behind my ear. "No?"

I should've known the cafeteria's hideous fluorescent lighting wasn't doing me any favors. It washes me out, making my already pale skin look practically translucent against my black hair, like I'm Victor from *Corpse Bride*.

"She means that as a compliment," Alex says next to me, as if sensing my discomfort.

"I do," Zoya assures me. "I love his movies."

"Okay."

"You're friends with Jack Marshall, right?" she asks.

"Jeez, Z," Hannah mumbles. "Let the girl breathe."

"Yeah." I'm glad to be talking about Jack. "We've been friends forever."

"Jack's great," Zoya says. "He and Serge have been attached at the hip lately."

I already know from Jack that Serge is Zoya's boyfriend. He's also Jack's closest friend, aside from me. They've been playing club soccer together for years and were the only two freshmen boys to make varsity at tryouts over the summer.

"He's so funny," Zoya adds. She glances at Alex, who seems to be focused on mixing granola into her yogurt.

"And nice," Alex says from behind her thick red hair. She's tiny and round-faced, and sort of reminds me of a nervous little bird.

"Immie is funny and nice too," Hannah says. "Even if she's quiet about it."

I groan. "Thanks, Mom. But I can make my own friends."

"Speaking of moms," Zoya says, fixing her amber eyes onto mine again. "Yours is principal at the middle school, right?"

I take a sip from my water bottle, feeling like a bug under a microscope. "Yeah. Why?"

"I don't know, just . . . isn't that weird? Having your mom be in charge at home *and* at school?"

"Not really. I didn't see much of her. And she's only been there for a year. Before that she was an English teacher at Greenfield."

The whole truth of it is that I was glad she got the job. When I found out she was applying for principal positions, I was worried we'd have to move again. I remember the look on Jack's face when I told him it was a possibility. It was like all the color drained from him at once. *But you can't go,* he said. *Not now.*

I might have to, I said.

Fine, he replied. *Then I'll come with you.*

"Ah." Zoya nods. "Well, better you than me. If my mom was my principal, I just know she'd be watching my every move."

"Mine too," Alex agrees. She looks at me for the first time since sitting down. "And what does your dad do?"

"No clue," I said. "I've never met him."

Zoya is immediately intrigued. "Why not?"

Hannah frowns at her. "Way to be nosy, Z."

"It's fine," I say. This is just a part of the speech. "My mom had me through IVF. It's always been just the two of us."

"IVF," Alex repeats. "That's like, implanting a fertilized egg into the woman's uterus, right?"

I finish my sandwich and yank open my snack-sized bag of chips. "You got it."

"So she just used a sperm donor?" Zoya says, looking at me with genuine interest. "Or someone she knew?"

I pop a sour cream and onion chip into my mouth. "Sperm donor, I think."

"You think?" Zoya says, surprised. "You mean you've never asked?"

"I'm sure I have," I say, though now that I think about it, I'm not sure at all. "It just never seemed very important, knowing the answer."

"Really?" Zoya says. "I'd be dying to know."

Hannah elbows Zoya. "You're moving from nosy to obnoxious now."

"I agree with Zoya," Alex says. "I'd be curious too."

I feel a twinge of irritation. "What difference does it make? Either way he's not in my life."

"I think there's a difference," Alex says.

"A big difference," Zoya agrees. "What if there's a whole story behind it? What if they were in love?"

Zoya's elbow knocks her spoon off the table, and it thankfully ends her inquisition. She bends down to pick it up. "Hey," she says when she sits up again. "Nice boots."

Eighth period, study hall. It's a random mix of kids from all four grades, which is perfect, because I don't know a single person. Even better, there's a Be Quiet rule. I can just sit at my desk and draw without having to play nice with anyone.

I open up my sketch pad and get to work. Five minutes ago, I didn't know what I wanted to draw, but now the strokes just come flowing out of me. It's a sneaker—Jack's sneaker, I realize halfway through—with a black swallowtail perched on the toe. The perspective is from down below, like a smaller bug looking up in wonder at the big, beautiful butterfly. I'm layering in blades of grass as tall as trees when I feel my phone buzz in my pocket—four quick, rapid pulses, the signature text vibration Jack made for himself.

Jack: Am I still coming over for dinner

Immie: Duh. I haven't seen you in years

Jack: I know. I think I forgot what you look like

Jack: You have blond hair, right? And huge clown feet? Like, we're talking really big feet. Scary big

I laugh into my lap and look up. That's when my heart skips a beat.

Across the room, a boy with dark, curly hair is watching me. *Smiling* at me. When I meet his eye, he gives me a small wave. I look to my left, at a girl hunched over her calc homework, and to my right, at an empty desk. When I look back at him, he gives me a little nod, like he's saying, *Yes, you.*

I drop my gaze and try to get back into my sketch. Why is he smiling at me like that? Did he hear my squeaky boots when I walked into the room? He probably did—he's probably laughing at me. *Ugh.* I'm shoving these boots to the back of the closet the second I get home.

I glance up—

He isn't there.

"Hey," whispers a voice.

I turn to my right. The boy is sitting at the empty desk.

"What are you drawing?"

I cover my sketch pad with my hands. "We're not supposed to talk."

"We're not," he replies. "We're whispering."

I raise an eyebrow. "Are you trying to be funny?"

"Maybe." He puts an elbow on his desk. "Is it working?"

I look down at my hands instead of responding. If I just ignore him, maybe he'll go away.

"Did you know you bite your lip when you draw?"

I frown, cover my mouth. "Stop looking at my lips."

He laughs a little, and it accentuates the dimple on his left cheek. "I wasn't. I was looking at you."

"That's not really any less creepy."

"Creepy?" He shakes his head. "Aw man. I'm really blowing this, huh?"

I have to stop myself from hissing at him the way I used to do when I was younger. If I wanted someone to go away, hissing at them almost always did the trick. I consider what Jack would say if I told him I'd hissed at an upperclassman on the first day of school. *When I told you to be yourself, I didn't mean the part of you that's a cat.*

"I was curious about what you were doing there." The boy nods toward my sketchbook. "I mean, I don't think I've ever seen somebody so focused on anything." He leans in, whispering, "Did you even notice that Dave just broke up with Laura?"

I furrow my brow. "Who?"

"Laura Brown, the girl who was sitting here ten minutes

ago," he says. He leans back in his chair, looking impressed. "She started crying and then ran out of the room. Legitimately *ran*."

I blink at him. "Look. It's cute that you think you can waltz over here and strike up a conversation—"

"Waltz?" he repeats, amused. "Do I waltz?"

"—but you should know, I'm not interested. It's been a long day full of new people and forced conversations, and I'm all talked out. I don't *want* to meet anyone else."

"Whoa," the boy says, leaning back. "Well, I can see why so many people want to talk to you," he adds. "You've got such a cheery disposition." He presses his lips together like he's trying not to laugh.

I'm doing my worst—Mom would be *so* proud—but he's still here with an unforced lightness about him, and I have to admit, I'm intrigued. I try to tone it down a bit when I say, "You don't know me."

"And I guess I never will," he says. "It's too bad. I don't have any friends in this class."

My thoughts flash back to first-grade show-and-tell, to Timothy Kline and Rebecca Miller, to feeling alone. They wrote me off without even bothering to get to know me first. If I do the same to this boy, I'm no better than them.

I roll my eyes. *Fine.* I'll bite. Then I pick up my sketch pad and shove it in his direction.

A surprised smile crosses his face. "Seriously?"

"Take it before I change my mind."

He takes the drawing from me and studies it. For so long,

in fact, that I start to worry the sketch is total crap, and he's just biding his time while he racks his brain for something nice to say.

He looks up at me. "You're really good."

I snort. "You're just saying that."

"No, you really are," he insists. "And *phew*, am I relieved. You were going so hard over here. It would be kind of embarrassing if you weren't."

The corner of my mouth turns up. "Okay, give it back." I snatch the book out of his hands.

"What's your name, Picasso?"

"Immie."

"Immie," he repeats. "I'm—"

"Elijah," says the teacher. Every head in the room looks up and over at us. I sink down in my seat.

The teacher's eyes dart back and forth between us. He holds up a finger to his lips. "Save it for the bell, huh? You got ten more minutes."

"Yes, sir," the boy—Elijah—says. "Sorry."

Everybody returns their attention to their phones and their worksheets. But not Elijah. He's still looking at me.

"See you around, Immie," he says. Then he stands up and walks back to his seat.

TRACK THREE

"Call Me When You Get This"—Corinne Bailey Rae

School was keeping us busy, forcing us to spend more time apart. But when we were together, none of that mattered. Everything was the same as it always was. Or so I thought.

The following week, I wake up from my accidental nap on the couch to the smell of teriyaki sauce and the sizzle of sautéed chicken. I sit up, rub my eyes, and look into the kitchen, where my mom is standing over the stove in sweatpants, swaying her hips to a sunny R&B song.

"What is this?" I sit down at the kitchen island and point to the speaker in front of me.

Instead of answering, Mom starts singing along as the chorus breaks out, using the wooden spoon as a microphone. "'I just want you to know, how I'm touched deep in my soul, just being with you . . .'"

"I like it," I say, smiling.

"This is Corinne Bailey Rae," Mom says, lowering the wooden spoon and continuing to cook the chicken like nothing happened. "She's one of my favorites."

One thing about Mom is she has great taste in music. I always tell her she could have been a singer in another life, or one of those people who finds new talent for record labels, but she always shakes her head at the idea and says something like, *Things happened the way they were supposed to, Imogen.*

She's about to shake some red pepper flakes into the pan when I yell, "STOP!"

Mom jumps, accidentally sending flakes flying through the air.

"Jack can't do spicy, remember?"

"Geez, you almost scared me to death! Forgive me for forgetting the preferences of our perpetual dinner guest. Can't you two spend *one* meal apart?"

"We already do that every day," I say, patting her on the shoulder before going to get the broom. "At lunch."

She puts her hand to her chest and gasps dramatically. "Are you okay? Can you stand?"

I roll my eyes. After sweeping up the mess, I pick up my phone to send Jack a quick text: Where are u??

"Seriously, though," Mom continues. "A little distance is healthy, Butterfly. You should make some more friends. Take advantage of new opportunities and don't just hide out in the woods with Jack all the time."

Just then Jack sends me a reply.

Jack: Just got home. See you soon

I like the message, then lock my phone and place it face down on the counter. When I look up, Mom is watching me.

"Imogen, did you hear a word I just said?"

"*Yes*, Mom," I groan, sitting back down. "You think Jack and I spend too much time together. And I respect your opinion. Even though you happen to be wrong."

She shakes her head, turns her attention back to the food on the stove. "This is what I'm talking about. You need to branch out."

I prop my elbows on the counter. "For your information, I've *branched out* quite a lot already. I sit with Hannah and her friends Zoya and Alex at lunch. And . . . last week, when we met, they actually had a lot of questions about my dad."

She freezes mid-sauté. "Oh?"

"Yeah." I feel nervous all of a sudden, and I don't meet her eyes. "They were asking who he is and stuff."

She puts the wooden spoon down. "And what did you say?"

"The usual. IVF and all that."

"Okay." She crosses her arms and eyes me curiously. "So what's this about? Were they mean to you?"

"No. It was more like they were wondering why I wasn't curious about him." I watch her turn off the burner under a pot full of broccoli in boiling water.

"Why would you be?" Mom says. "He was just a donor. Never your dad."

I nod. That's what she always says, and up until now, it's always been enough. This time, though, something is different. I haven't been able to get Zoya's words out of my head all week.

What if they were in love?

"That's what I told them," I say, twirling a section of hair around my finger. I have to tread carefully here. "It's like he's not even real. He was just, like, a list of facts on a piece of paper in a sperm bank."

"Well, not exactly," she says.

My head snaps up. "What do you mean, *not exactly*?"

She sighs, long and loud. "Am I not enough?"

"Mom, come *on*. Don't take it there."

"You're the one who took it there."

"It's not, like, *important* to me," I say, even though I'm not sure if that's true. "It's just, you know. It's part of my history."

She doesn't reply, just continues to stir the broccoli in with the chicken. Suddenly the midterm art project pops into my head. *Who am I?* How can I try to answer that if there's a question mark where half of my genes are supposed to be?

"I can handle the truth, whatever it is," I add. "I'm in high school now! Practically all grown-up! Look how tall I am! Check out my motor skills and my vast vocabulary. It's *prodigious* how *unequivocally sagacious* I'm becoming."

I pat my head and rub my stomach at the same time, trying to make her laugh, but she holds up the spoon like it's a stop sign and shakes her head.

"That's enough," she says. She's got a look on her face like she feels a migraine coming on.

"But—"

Just then the doorbell rings.

"Oop. Jack's here!" Mom says. "Better go let him in."

"Saved by the bell," I mutter. Then I jump off my stool and run to the foyer.

I open the front door a crack. "Password?"

"Lima bean."

"Nope. Two more guesses, traveler."

"What? Yes it is."

"No, it's *not*," I insist. "We changed it last week. After the—"

"Oh yeah. Big blue moon. Still can't believe it wasn't actually blue, by the way."

I open the door wide. Jack is standing there in his soccer hoodie and a pair of basketball shorts, his hair soaking wet from, I assume, a post-practice shower.

"Hey, Outie," he says with a smile. "Long time no see."

"Actually, my belly button has inverted now, so you can retire that nickname."

"Oh really? I think I'm going to need to see proof before that happens."

I grin and practically tackle him into a hug, breathing in a whiff of his green apple shampoo. His presence is pure joy compared with the tension I just sliced my way through in the kitchen with Mom. "Missed you."

He hugs me back, and for the first time all day, I feel like I can relax.

"Ooh, how about this?" I point the remote at the TV and click on the movie description. "'*Love on the Moors* is a period drama about missed connections and unspoken love—'"

"Pass," Jack says. He's sunken into the couch next to me, his socked feet propped on the coffee table, his long legs parallel to mine. It's amazing how much he's stretched out since we've met. I've grown, *obviously*, but my spurts haven't kept up with his.

I glare at him. "You didn't even let me finish reading it."

"You don't have to finish reading it. I already know what it's about."

"Do not."

He gives me a look like, *Get real*. "It's just like the movie we watched on Friday—"

"No. *Pride and Prejudice* is a classic!"

"—a bunch of people in stuffy outfits standing around, talking about the weather as a metaphor for their feelings."

"But that's what makes it great! It's angsty!"

"It's boring," he counters. "Why can't they just say how they really feel?"

I stick my tongue out at him. "Because. Not everybody is as bad at keeping secrets as you are."

I like to tease him about it, but honestly, it's one of my favorite things about him. I never have to wonder how he feels about anything. I know he'll always tell me the truth.

"I'm just saying." He shakes his head. "It feels like a cop-out. If they told each other the truth right away, then they'd have to actually come up with a plot."

I shake my head and continue scrolling through our movie options. "Why do I even invite you over here?"

He gives me a sly smile. "Because of the Skittles."

I raise an eyebrow. "Excusez-moi?"

He pulls two packs of Skittles out of his sweatshirt pocket—one sour, one wild berry. I gasp, delighted.

I reach for the wild berry and then stop myself. "Wait. This isn't a bribe to get me to agree to watch a superhero movie, is it?"

"Of course not," he says. "Skittles are for pure intentions. Now, if I'd brought Starbursts . . ."

I laugh and take the wild berry.

"Plus," he says, ripping open the sour Skittles and shoving a handful into his mouth, "it's the least I can do, since, you know—your mom gives me free food all the time."

"It's not free," I say, making a tiny tear in the bag of wild berry. "It's a bribe to keep you hanging out with me." I pour a single Skittle into my hand and pop it in my mouth.

"Oh yeah?" He laughs. "Well that's a bribe I'll accept." Then he gives me a knowing look. "Even though I hear you don't need me anymore. You're Miss Popular now."

I frown, still sucking on the Skittle. Me, Miss Popular? I could hardly think of anything worse.

"Who told you that?"

"Serge. Zoya said you guys are eating lunch together."

I return my attention to the TV. "I have lunch with Hannah, who sits with Zoya," I say, scrolling through the movie channels. "And Zoya and Alex are kind of a package deal. Like Tweedledee and Tweedledum."

"They're not so bad."

I wrinkle my nose. "What? They're nosy and gossipy and—" I look at him. "How do you know what they're like?"

"They both came to watch us practice today. Serge pretended to be embarrassed, but I know he liked having someone cheer him on."

"Yeah?" I feel a weird pang of something like jealousy. I should've been there. Not Alex. *Me.* "Would you like that too?"

He shrugs and looks away, and I wonder if I've now gone and embarrassed *him*. "Well, yeah. Who wouldn't?"

"Me," I say instantly. "I don't like people watching me do anything."

"That's because you're you." He sits up straighter. "You'd be happy living in a hut in the woods with your books and your sketch pad, never seeing a single person ever again. Like a hermit." He hunches his back and hooks his arm as if he's holding a cane. *"Git off my lawn!"*

"Not true." I giggle, nudging his calf with my bare foot. "I'd miss you."

His eyes meet mine, and his playful smile relaxes into something softer—something more sincere. "I'd miss you too."

We scroll through channels for a minute, until I get tired of looking and settle on a rerun of a sitcom.

"I love this episode." I pull the blanket off the back of the couch and wrap it around me like a cloak.

"Of course you do. You love all the episodes where the whole family is together."

"Well, yeah. They're the funniest. Plus, it's nice. Or, I don't know—comforting."

"What's comforting about everybody being all up in each other's business all the time?" Jack says, his tone somewhere between skeptical and amused.

I roll my eyes. "Of course you don't get it. Your life is basically one big episode of this show."

"Exactly. I know what I'm talking about." He leans back on the couch until he's lying down. "*This* is the life, right here. You can stretch out on the couch, watch whatever you want on TV, and you don't have to share a wall with a sister who talks on the phone as much as she breathes."

"I share a wall with my mom," I point out. "And she falls asleep with her bedroom TV on a lot."

He smiles. "Still. If I could trade places with you, I would."

I don't know how to respond. It's not exactly a secret that Jacks prefers the calm of my house to the chaos of his own. It's why he's over here all the time and not the other way around. I always try to tell him how lucky he is to have a big family that cares about him, and what I wouldn't give to have the same. But he never listens.

That's when my thoughts jump to my biological dad and the conversation my mom and I had in the kitchen.

He was just, like, a list of facts on a piece of paper in a sperm bank.
Well, not exactly.

Not exactly? What isn't she telling me? Is my bio dad someone she knew? Do I have a dad out there, waiting for me to find him? Or a whole entire family I never knew about?

When the show goes to commercial, Jack sits up. "You're coming to the game on Wednesday, right?"

"Of course. Wouldn't miss it."

"Good." He puts the half-eaten bag of Skittles on the coffee table. "I'm kind of nervous."

"Don't be. You're really good," I remind him. "That's why you made varsity."

37

He keeps his eyes straight ahead and puts his hands in his sweatshirt pocket. "Yeah, I guess."

"What's the worst that could happen? You make a mistake, and you redeem yourself next game." I give him a reassuring pat on the arm. "This is just the first one."

"Right," he says. "It's the first one. And first impressions stick—or so I've been told."

"That only applies to squeaky boots," I say. "And seven-year-old boys who fall off their brothers' skateboards to get my attention."

"Right. I *definitely* did that on purpose."

"Doesn't matter whether it was on purpose or not," I say. "It worked, didn't it?"

He smirks and opens his mouth like he's about to say something clever, but then the show comes back on. He closes his mouth, changing his mind.

"Yeah," he says after a moment. "Yeah, I guess it did."

We settle into a comfortable silence, and everything is exactly the way it's supposed to be.

TRACK FOUR

"Ghost of a Good Thing"—Dashboard Confessional

When I remember what you said to me that day under the tree, I think of this song. It's the moment I realized that maybe I couldn't tell you everything.

On Saturday, I sleep in until ten. When I come downstairs, bleary-eyed and still in my skeleton pajamas, I hear Mom listening to an angsty love song in the kitchen. *"You're chasing the ghost of a good thing, haunting yourself . . ."*

Mom is sitting at the kitchen island with her hands crossed in front of her. She looks perfectly put together in a simple blouse and jeans, but her eyes tell a different story.

"Morning," I yawn as I pull my hair up into a messy bun. "What are you doing?"

"Imogen." She turns off the radio and smiles at me. It's so big and forced, it honestly scares me a little. She taps the stool next to her. "Come sit with me."

I don't move. "What's going on? Did someone die?"

Her smiley expression falls, replaced by a frustrated crease between her brows. "Don't be ridiculous. Come on, sit. I have something to give you."

I do as I'm told. She reaches for my hand, but I pull away.

"Mom, stop!" I cross my arms. "You're being so weird. Just tell me what's going on."

She sighs, pinches the bridge of her nose. She must be fighting a migraine.

"Why aren't you in bed?" I ask. "Did you take any medicine?"

"I'm fine," she says with a wave of her hand. "Fine. I don't have a headache—I just . . ." She drops her hand and looks at me earnestly. "I've been thinking about what you said. About your sperm donor."

My heart starts to beat faster.

"You're right, you're getting older. And whether I like it or not, he's part of your history. You deserve to have a piece of him if that's what you really want."

Here she reaches for something in the center of the island. I don't register what they are until they're right in front of me.

"CDs?"

"Five of them," Mom says.

I sort through the stack. The CD cases are all clear, the CDs themselves the blank ones people used to burn songs on. There are words written on them in black marker. *SUMMER '06 MIX. SONGS FOR FEELING SAD*. One just says my mom's name: *NORA*.

I look up at her. "What are these?"

"I'm not going to tell you who your biological father is," she says, running a hand through her graying hair. "I'm the one who raised you. I'm your mom *and* dad in all the ways that count." She picks up *NORA* and cracks a small smile. "Also, he deserves his privacy. This was the arrangement we agreed upon."

My jaw drops a little. "So you did know him?"

She sighs and nods.

"Was he your boyfriend?"

"I'm not telling you anything else. It's not my place."

"Then whose place is it?"

"These are his CDs," she says instead. "Mixes he made for me a long time ago. It took some digging, but I found them in storage. I think everything you need to know about him, you can find out in here." She puts *NORA* back on top of the stack. "Music was pretty important to him."

I look down at the stack in wide-eyed wonder. Here is something my dad once touched. Here is a piece of him, which means a piece of me, too.

"Thank you." I put down the CDs and lean forward to give her a big hug.

"You're welcome," she says, stiff underneath my arms. Mom isn't really a touchy person. She says hugs make her feel awkward.

I let her go and reach for the CDs again. "Do we have a CD player?"

"I don't think so," she says. "But we can get one."

I run up to my room and put the CDs on my nightstand. Then I grab my phone from my bed and text Jack.

Immie: Emergency meeting!!!!

Immie: Tree. Ten minutes

I brush my hair and teeth, splash some water on my face, and slip on my sneakers without bothering to put on socks first. Eight minutes later, I'm down the stairs and out the door.

When I get to our tree, Jack is already there, sitting on the ground and scrolling his phone.

"You're late." He tries to make his voice sound serious, but he can't hide his playful smile. I don't think Jack could be mad at me even if he tried.

I step over the roots of the tree, some of which are still thicker than my whole body, and sit down next to him. "No, you're just freakishly early. What were you doing, waiting by the door?"

He looks at me. Strands of his shaggy blond hair are stuck to his forehead with sweat. "I just got home from soccer. I was in the driveway when you texted."

"Ah," I say, flicking a piece of grass out of his hair. "That explains the smell."

"You know you love it," he says, lifting his arm and leaning into me. I laugh and push him away.

"How was practice?"

His mood deflates like air out of a balloon. "Fine."

"Are you still pouting about your game on Wednesday?"

The boys' soccer team lost their first game of the season. Even worse, Jack sat on the bench the entire time. I made a sign with his jersey number on it in big glittery letters—LET'S GO #18!—and it stayed rolled up between my knees the whole time. His parents, seated in the bleachers next to me, were all quiet and straight-faced. Twice his dad took a phone call out in the parking lot.

"No," he says, his voice grumbly. "And we're not talking about me. We're here because *you* called an emergency meeting."

"Right." I nod. "I did do that, didn't I?"

His forehead creases with concern. "Everything okay?"

"Um." My heart is pounding fast. I feel nervous and excited and *weird*. "It's nothing bad. Just—my mom just gave me some CDs that used to belong to my dad?"

He sort of frowns. "What?"

I nod. "CDs he made her. Mixes, or whatever. They're called, like, *Sad Songs* and *Summer Songs*. One of them is just my mom's name."

He shakes his head, struggling to understand. "Why would he make her CDs? Is that, like, a sperm donor thing?"

"No, doofus. And he wasn't just a donor," I say. "Apparently, they knew each other. They were *friends*. Or maybe something more—I don't know. She won't tell me."

"Whoa." He runs a hand through his sweaty hair. "Intense."

"I know."

We're quiet for a moment. I hear chirping cardinals and tweeting wrens, the wind whooshing through the leaves on the trees, and I wonder if my dad is out there somewhere, and what he's listening to.

"Are you okay?" Jack's brown eyes are wide, worried. "I mean, why'd she give you those CDs if she wasn't going to tell you anything else about him?"

I fidget on the ground, and my knee brushes against his. When we were little, this place used to feel huge. Now, admittedly, it's getting cramped. I wonder how many years we have left until we outgrow it completely.

"She said everything I needed to know about him, I'd find out by listening to the music."

"I'm guessing you've listened."

I shake my head. "I don't have a CD player."

"Oh," he says. "Well, what are you going to do?"

I shrug. "Buy one? And then listen, I guess. And then go from there."

"Meaning?"

"Meaning . . ." I fix my gaze on a little ant scurrying past my shoe. "What if she's wrong, and the music isn't enough?"

"Immie." His voice is cautious. "Do you ever think that, if she didn't tell you his name, maybe it's for a good reason?"

"Like what?"

"Like . . . I don't know." He's got a guilty look on his face. "Maybe he's a bad person."

A bad person. What does that even mean? I imagine a Disney villain with a handlebar mustache. A guy who steals ice cream from little kids or an angry, red-faced man yelling at a waiter. None of it makes any difference.

"So what? He's still my dad."

"But what if you don't like what you find out about him?" He continues like he doesn't hear me. "What if you're disappointed?"

"I won't be disappointed," I say, defensive. "I'll know the truth, and that will be good enough for me."

He nods but doesn't say anything, which irritates me. What is he thinking that he's too chicken to say out loud?

"What?" I press. "You really don't think I deserve to know who he is?"

"That's not what I meant," he says. "Just be careful. Please?"

"Of course." The ant has made its way onto my sneaker. I flick it off without a second thought. "I always am."

He chuckles. "Right. That's why you have three broken bones under your belt."

"Hey, let's not forget the broken pinky was because of *you*."

"Oh. So it's my fault you can't catch a basketball?"

I give him a shove, already smiling despite the weirdness that just passed between us.

TRACK FIVE

"Fight Test"—The Flaming Lips

My mom, my life, the universe—everything was getting confusing. And worst of all? I couldn't talk to you about any of it. I didn't realize it at the time, but it was the beginning of the end.

I use Mom's credit card to buy a portable CD player from eBay. It gets delivered to our house the following Wednesday, on an afternoon when the sky is bright blue and the clouds look like fluffy Pomeranians. I meet the delivery woman at the front door and tear the package open with my bare hands right there on the porch.

The player is silver and surprisingly heavy. Inside, someone forgot to remove an old Christina Aguilera CD. I run up to my room and toss the old CD on my bed, then replace it with the CD marked *SUMMER '06 MIX*. Instead of listening in my room, I grab a blanket and head out to the backyard.

I lie down in the yard and look up at the sky. I'm nervous. Mom said everything I needed to know about my dad I would find out from his music, but what if Jack was right, and I don't like what I find? Maybe that's been her plan all along.

I take a deep breath. There's only one way to find out.

I slip the headphones over my ears, press play, and close my eyes.

"Oh, and what about the one that has that funky, kind of beachy guitar? It goes something like, 'You're really lovely, underneath it all.'" I try to sing the chorus melody.

"That's by No Doubt," Mom says, running a brush through her hair. "It was Gwen Stefani's band before she went solo."

I'm standing in the doorway of Mom's bathroom, watching her get ready for a board meeting after listening to *SUMMER '06 MIX* twice all the way through. "I love that one. And the 'Don't go chasing waterfalls' one. Oh, and the one you played in the kitchen. That's on there too."

"Uh-huh," she mumbles as she applies some nude lipstick. "Lots of good stuff."

"I *know*," I gush. "I love everything, really. And there are actually a couple songs I knew already too. Like the one that Napoleon Dynamite dances to—you know that movie, *Napoleon Dynamite*? It's one of Jack's favorites; he's made me watch it like a million times—"

"Oh." She looks at me through the mirror. "Am I still giving you a ride to the soccer game? If yes, you need to be ready in five."

I shrug. "Jack said I don't have to come."

Mom raises an eyebrow. "Why?"

"I think he's embarrassed."

The boys' soccer team lost their first two matches. Today is the rivalry game, and instead of feeling psyched about it, Jack is all kinds of tense. I tried to cheer him up on the ride to school, reminding him that he's been on the bench both games, so technically, *he* didn't lose anything. He told me that didn't help at all.

"Poor kid. His time will come, though. Are his parents going to be there?"

I shake my head. "They almost never make it to his games. That's why the first one was such a big deal to him."

"Then maybe you should go." She walks past me into her bedroom, and I spin around to face her. "He'd probably appreciate your support."

She picks up a gray blazer draped over the end of the bed and puts it on. I'm about to push back—I was kind of hoping to stay home and listen to another mix tonight—when my phone buzzes in my pocket. It's a text from Hannah.

Hannah: Just got to the game with Alex and Z. You coming?

"Fine." I reply with a quick "ya" and pocket my phone. "I'll go. But he owes me."

"Immie." Mom's looking at me in that annoying way, like I'm one of her students. "You already know Jack would do anything for you."

A few minutes later we're getting in the Honda, Mom in her gray pantsuit and sensible heels and me in jeans, a dark green STORM VALLEY THUNDERCATS hoodie, and my white sneakers. As I'm buckling in, I look at the dashboard and remember that the car has a CD player.

"Wait!" I jump out before she can stop me and run up to my room to grab the *SUMMER '06 MIX* from the portable player. When I hop back in the car, Mom sees what I have in my hand and frowns.

"It's a five-minute drive to the high school."

"Which means we have time for at least one song," I say, already putting the CD into the stereo. "Two if we're lucky and hit all the red lights."

She shakes her head and backs out of the driveway.

"Hold on," I say as Mom pulls up to the curb by the entrance of the stadium. "The song's almost over."

"Immie, I'm going to be late."

"Please! Just twenty more seconds. This is one of my favorites."

She sighs but puts the car in park anyway. "Please don't make me regret giving you these CDs."

Instead of responding, I pretend I'm holding a microphone and sing along. "'I don't know where the sunbeams end—'" Then I put the pretend microphone in front of Mom's mouth. "Come on, sing! 'It's all a mystery . . .'"

Mom pushes the fake microphone away from her face. "No thanks."

I groan. "You're no fun."

"Excuse me. I'll have you know that I saw the Flaming Lips sing this song live."

Huh. I'm impressed. "You did?"

"Yep. A group of us went to their show in New York right after the album came out." She stares out the windshield, smiling at the memory. "It was Halloween."

"Wow." I shift in my seat to give her my full attention. She almost never talks about her past, so I need to soak up every single second of this conversation. "Tell me more. Were you wearing a costume?"

"Oh yeah." She laughs. "My friends and I were Josie and the Pussycats." She sees the confused look on my face and adds, "They're a band from an old comic."

I try to imagine it: a twenty-something Mom at a concert in New York City with all her friends. It's hard for me to do. What was her life like before I came along, and she became Mom?

"I used to love this band," she says. After a few moments, she clears her throat and then adds, "Your . . . um, your dad did too."

It's the first time she's ever called him my dad and not the sperm donor. She's got a pained look on her face, which I don't think is a coincidence.

"Really?" I say. "Did he go to the concert with you?"

She doesn't respond, which I take to mean yes.

"Was he your date? What was his costume?"

Her voice is stern. "You know I'm not telling you that."

"Mom, that's not fair! You're the one who brought it up in the first place."

She looks straight ahead. "I'll pick you up after the game."

I bite the inside of my cheek. There isn't any point in arguing with her. When she puts her foot down, she might as well be wearing heels of steel. I listen to the closing lyrics of the song—*It's all a mystery*—and feel like the Flaming Lips are speaking directly to me.

50

"He doesn't just belong to you," I say. "Whether you like it or not, he belongs to me, too."

"Immie—"

I get out of the car and slam the door.

Inside the stadium, the game has just started, and the stands are packed. I take a few deep breaths, and then I spot Hannah, Zoya, and Alex near the top of the bleachers.

"We saved you a seat," Hannah says when I walk up to meet them, giving me a hug. I sit down in the empty space between her and Zoya. I notice Zoya has a handmade sign for Serge: #2, I ♥ YOU!

"Did I miss anything?" I scan the field for Jack but don't see him until my eyes hit the sidelines. On the bench again. I wince.

"Yes," Hannah says, looking down at her phone. Her glittery silver eye shadow catches the light and pops against her dark skin. Makeup is her favorite form of art.

"Look at this text I got from Bethany!" She holds her phone up to my face to show me the message, sent fifteen minutes ago.

I miss you sm!!!

"But what does it *mean*?" Hannah practically groans.

"I think it means she misses you?" I say.

"*So* much," Zoya adds, making kissy faces.

Hannah met Bethany the last week of our summer art class and has been crushing hard ever since. It's sort of cute to see her so smitten, even though personally, I would rather eat rocks than let myself be turned to mush by one person.

Just wait, Hannah said when I told her as much. *Someday, you'll lock eyes with the right person, and then you'll see.*

"Then she should come to the game," Hannah grumbles. She locks her phone and puts it in her pocket. "Instead she says she's got too much homework."

"Maybe she does," I say. "I definitely do."

"And yet, you're here."

Before I can confess that my mom basically had to force me to come, suddenly Zoya jumps up. "WOO!" She holds her sign up high in the air. "Did you guys see that? He stole the ball! LET'S GO, SERGIO!"

Zoya is a loud talker at normal volume, so it's no surprise her screams carry all the way to the field. When the ball is kicked out of bounds by another player, Serge turns and blows her a kiss. She pretends to catch it.

"Ugh." Hannah stands up. "Your happiness is too much. I need nachos. Snack bar trip, anyone?"

"I'll go," Alex says, standing up on Zoya's other side. It's the first time she's spoken since I arrived.

Across the field, the away team bleachers erupt into cheers, while a collective groan runs through our side. The Greenfield Generals have scored the first goal.

"Here we go again." Zoya slumps a little in her seat.

"Coach Berotti should put Jack in," I say, watching him on the bench. He's slumped forward with his forearms resting on his knees, totally immersed in the game.

"It's too bad he plays striker," Zoya says. "I don't see Coach benching Elijah. He's too valuable."

Imagine my surprise when I found out that Elijah, the sophomore who called me Picasso in study hall, is also the soccer team's star player. And as lead striker, he's in direct competition with Jack—a fact I learned not from Jack, but from his dad at last week's game. I'm pretty sure Jack has no idea Elijah and I know each other, and I haven't exactly found a natural way to bring it up.

I watch Elijah jog down the field, trying to think about the fact that he's Jack's competitor, and *not* about his cute dimple. "How valuable can he be if we haven't won a game yet?"

Just then a player from Greenfield gets in Elijah's face. Elijah pushes past him, and the player loses his balance and falls. The referee blows a whistle, holds up a yellow card, and points to Elijah. The other player stays down, clutching his ankle and screaming in agony.

"Oh come on!" Zoya yells, while people around us start booing. "He's faking it!"

Another player helps the injured Greenfielder limp off the field. On our side, Coach Berotti is talking to Elijah—scolding him. I look for Jack at his spot on the bench, but he isn't there. He's hanging by the fence, talking to a girl with long red hair. He says something clever—which I can tell because of the sly expression on his face—and the girl throws her head back and laughs. That's when I realize who it is.

Alex.

"How is she allowed on the field like that?" I say, to no one in particular.

Zoya follows my line of vision. "She's the coach's daughter. Didn't you know?"

"Oh." I watch her hand Jack something—a drink—and I frown. I would've gotten him a drink if he'd asked me to. "No. I didn't."

"Immie," Zoya says innocently. "What's up with you and Jack?"

I tear my eyes away from the two of them to glance at her. "What do you mean?"

"Nothing. Just . . . I see how you look at him."

I narrow my eyes at her. "I look at everyone. I'm looking at you right now."

"Yeah, but not like *that*."

I laugh, because she's ridiculous, and then glance over at Jack and Alex again. I feel a tinge of annoyance at the fact that she's still there, on the other side of the fence, laughing with him. What could they be talking about? What's so *funny*?

"You just did it again," Zoya observes.

I whip back around, feeling like I've been caught, but caught doing *what*, I'm not really sure. "Are you trying to imply that I've got some big, secret crush on him or something?"

"I never said *big*."

"We're just friends," I assure her. "We grew up together. I've seen him pick his nose and smelled his dirty laundry. He's like . . . a brother."

"I have a brother," Zoya says. "And I definitely don't want to hang out with him every day."

I'm about to argue some more when Zoya continues. "All I'm saying is that if you like him, you should go for it. Serge and I think he likes you, too."

I feel my face get hot. "What? That's ridiculous." I shake my head. *Completely, utterly ridiculous!* She doesn't know me that well. Who does she think she is, making all these assumptions? "Did Jack say something to Serge?"

"Not really," Zoya says. "But he doesn't have to. Serge says it's the *way* he talks about you that gives him away."

I stare at her. "Like how?"

"Like you couldn't do anything wrong even if you tried. Like you're the best thing since sliced bread."

I look down at the fence again. Alex is gone, but Jack is still there. He meets my eye, smiles, and waves. I try to return the smile, but I'm pretty sure it comes out as a grimace.

"If you like him," she says again, "you should tell him. But don't wait too long." Her voice turns serious, like a warning. "Trust me."

Geez. Two freshmen manage to date more than two months, and they think they know everything about *love*. Please.

A shadow falls over us. I look up to see Alex holding a bottle of Gatorade. Hannah is behind her, munching on nachos.

"You okay, Immie?" Alex says, sitting down.

"These nachos are just what the doctor ordered," Hannah says. "Why does artificial cheese taste so good?"

Suddenly Zoya looks out at the field and gasps.

"Oh!" She jumps up just as Serge gets control of the ball and passes to another player, number 5. "Yes! YES!" She picks up her sign and starts jumping up and down. "Great pass, Serge!"

That's when the referee blows his whistle. Elijah and the same Greenfielder, whose ankle seems to have magically healed, are in a screaming match again. Number 5 tries to mediate, putting his arm on Elijah's shoulder and pulling him back, but Elijah shrugs him off, making him stumble. Coach Berotti starts flailing his arms on the sidelines, yelling at Elijah to get off the field. After what feels like an eternity, but was probably just a few seconds, he finally listens.

"Oh my god," Zoya says. "He's taking Elijah out."

The crowd around us is in an uproar. By benching Elijah, Coach is removing the highest-scoring player from the field. Everybody stands up and starts screaming that he's making a huge mistake.

Well, everybody but me. I stand up and look at Jack.

TRACK SIX

"September"—Earth, Wind & Fire

Three words (?): ba dee ya.

*T*his song again?" Jack groans, looking up from his cell phone.

We're in the last row of Jack's family minivan on our way to an apple orchard. We've only been in the car for twenty minutes, but it's the third time "September" by Earth, Wind & Fire has come on the radio.

"They want to make sure we know what day it is," I joke. "In case we forgot."

Jack's family always goes apple picking on the first day of fall. This year, his older siblings couldn't make it, so they had extra room in the van and invited me to come along. Even though Jack is less than thrilled about being here—apparently some boys from the soccer team are going go-karting today—I couldn't be more excited. It's my chance to have my very own sitcom family moment.

"Real original." Jack leans forward. "Mom, can you maybe change the station?"

"No!" His six-year-old sister, Marigold, slams her little fists down on the seat in front of us. "I like it!"

"'Do you remem-ba,'" Noah, Marigold's twin brother, sings next to her. Those are the only words he knows, so he just sings them over and over. When the song gets to the chorus, the twins both start singing "ba-dee-ya" and dancing in their seats. I sing along with them, which makes them giggle and clap their hands in delight.

"Oh god, make it stop," Jack says, throwing his head back.

"Don't be such a grump." Deb, Jack's mom, looks back at us from the passenger seat while his dad, Frank, stays silent behind the wheel.

"Yeah, Monty. Don't be such a grump." I shake his shoulder, trying to get him to join in. "'Ba-dee-ya—'"

He ignores me. He's too busy smiling at something on his phone.

"Hey." I crane my neck to get a better look. "Who are you texting?"

He quickly turns his phone away from me, but not before I catch a glimpse of the screen—he's in a group chat called Thundercraps. I frown. What does that mean?

"Just the guys from the team," he says, and then pockets his phone. What are they talking about that's so top secret?

Since the game against Greenfield, he's been in his group chat constantly. Probably because he's the new MVP. With just two minutes left in the game, the coach finally took Jack

58

off the bench, and he ended up scoring the winning goal. I can still picture it: the team rushing the field, rushing *Jack*, crowding around him, shaking his shoulders, patting him on the back. Jack was beaming, his excitement so captivating, I couldn't look away. I remember wishing I could be down there with him, smiling and laughing and hugging. I didn't even care that he was probably really sweaty. Ever since then, he's been getting almost as much playing time as Elijah. With the two of them on the field, the team has been unstoppable. They've won every game.

Jack's younger sibling Carter, seated by the window next to Marigold, looks up from their cell phone. "Are we almost there?"

"Five minutes," Frank says. "And I want phones away when we get there."

"Great," Jack replies, sarcastic. "Just long enough to hear this song a fourth time."

I watch him out of the corner of my eye. In the last week, his popularity status has shot up exponentially. Everyone— teammates, students, even some teachers—is suddenly paying attention to him. They fist-bump him in the hallway or steal nervous glances as he passes by, like he's someone to be admired instead of overlooked, the way it's been our entire lives. I'm happy for him, but I feel sort of nervous, too. It's like the peaceful little snow globe we existed in has been smashed open, and the rest of the world is rushing in.

"'BA-DEE-YA, DEE-YA, DEE-YA,'" Noah and Marigold shout over each other as the song fades out. They're still going when the next song starts to play. I recognize the opening notes right away: "It Ain't Over 'Til It's Over" by Lenny Kravitz, the last song on my dad's *SUMMER '06 MIX*.

I don't even realize I'm quietly singing along until Jack looks at me and asks, "What is this song?"

"Oh." I haven't wanted to talk to Jack about my dad's CDs. I still feel weird about the way he reacted, and I'm worried that if I bring it up again, it will just be more of the same. I almost feel guilty, like by not confiding in him, I'm doing something wrong. But I'm not, am I? After all, it's my life. It doesn't have anything to do with him.

"Nothing. Just something my mom used to like."

At the apple orchard the air smells crisp, like fall, even though it's seventy degrees and sunny outside. I see rows and rows of trees lined up on the left, lush with red and pink apples ripe for the plucking. Off to the right are tables and stalls, cute wooden things with hand-painted signs that say APPLE CIDER DONUTS and APPLES: 99¢ PER LB. The tables are already packed with people—families, it seems to me—and little kids run around in the grass, their fingers and faces sticky with cider.

"Mom." Marigold tugs on the hem of Deb's cardigan, her eyes fixed on the barn straight ahead. "Sheep!"

"Those are goats." Jack's hood is up, and his hands are in his pockets. "But nice try."

I smack Jack's arm with the back of my hand. "I'm changing your nickname from Monty to Moody."

"Fine with me." The corner of his mouth turns up. "Goutie."

My jaw drops. "*Goutie?* That doesn't even make sense."

"Sure it does."

"I do not have gout!"

"Goats!" Noah shouts. "Let's go pet the goats!"

Deb and Carter take the twins to pet the animals, while Jack and I go with Frank to get some apple cider doughnuts.

"This is so cute," I say, looking around. "I wish my mom and I did more things like this."

The sun moves behind a cloud, causing the temperature to drop and casting Jack's face in shadow.

"She's busy," he says. "That doesn't mean she loves you any less."

"I know." I cross my arms against the new chill. "But still, it would be nice if she could prioritize me a little more. Like how your mom is always volunteering for stuff at school."

"She does that because she doesn't have anything else to do," Jack says. "She's a stay-at-home mom. We *are* her job."

Frank buys us each one doughnut and gets two for himself. They're warm and delicious.

"Can Immie and I go pick some apples?" Jack asks after he eats his.

"Yeah," Frank says. "Just not too many. You know the rest of the crew will want to get some too, and the last thing we need is a surplus of rotting fruit."

"That's the *last* thing we need?" Jack leans on the table. "I would've guessed the last thing we need would be, like, a zombie apocalypse, or Pringles cans for hands. But you're right. A surplus of rotting fruit? That would be way worse."

Frank takes a bite of his doughnut, ignoring him. "Immie, you can pick as many as you'd like."

I grin. "Thanks, Frank."

We get baskets from one of the stalls and walk over to where the trees begin. As soon as we're out of Frank's eyeline, Jack pulls his phone out of his pocket. I frown at him.

"Who's Miss Popular now?"

"What?" he says, his eyes on the screen as he types out a message.

"You've been glued to your phone all morning."

He looks at me. "Is it bugging you?"

"No," I lie. "It's just . . ." I cross my arms. "Different."

He smiles to himself, then locks his phone and puts it back in his pocket. "Okay, it's gone. You, Goutie Marie Meadows, officially have my undivided attention."

I roll my eyes. "From Moody to Snooty."

"Where should we start?" he asks, dropping his hood and spreading out his arms. "The world is your orchard."

I can't help but laugh. "That depends. What's your favorite kind of apple?"

"Guess."

"Easy," I say. "Granny Smith. You love sour stuff."

He smiles. "You're right, that was too easy. Yours is harder." We pick a row with no other people in it and start walking. "You like sour too, but not as much as me. You'd rather eat something sweet. But not *too* sweet either. And I know you don't like Red Delicious apples because of the thick skin. You used to spit it into a paper towel at snack time."

"That's right," I say, reaching for an apple. "I had a very refined palate in second grade. Lunchables or nothing." I

62

examine it on the branch, then decide it's a little too red for my liking and let it go.

"I also know you like stuff that's crispy," he continues, not looking at the apples, but right at me. "Crispy chicken sandwiches, crispy French fries, potato chips—you enjoy a good crunch. I'll bet that applies to apples, too. That's why I'm going to lock in my final answer as . . ." He pauses to start a drumroll on his thighs. "Honeycrisp."

I clap. "Bravo. Truly."

He grins. "Thank you."

I pause, eyeing another apple. "How do we know which ones are good ones?"

"I dunno." He reaches for the same apple and plucks it from the tree. He tosses it up in the air and catches it. "I think it's a gut feeling. Like, you just know."

He offers me the apple. My fingers brush against his when I take it from him.

"I'm glad we got to do this," I tell him. "It feels like I've hardly seen you since your big game."

"I know, I'm sorry. I've been really busy."

"Too busy for your best friend." I try to say it in a playful way, but it comes out sort of accusatory.

"Don't be like that," he says. "Now that Coach has me starting as winger, I've had to practice a lot more. Plus there's all the team-bonding stuff."

"Is it everything you thought it would be?" I stop to pick another apple.

"What?"

"You know." I inspect the apple for bruises instead of looking at him. "Being on the soccer team, having all these new friends."

"Oh yeah," he says. "I'm like Lionel Messi, but better."

I shoot him a look. "Be serious."

He sighs. "Fine. In some ways, I guess it is. And in other ways . . . no."

I put the apple in my basket and keep quiet, waiting for him to say more.

"Ever since that game, it feels like the pressure has been turned up, and now everybody is expecting something from me." He pauses to kick an apple that fell from a tree. "Coach, the team, my parents, even random kids at school—they all expect me to be scoring goals left and right. But I don't know if the Greenfield game was just a fluke. And I really don't want to let anyone down." He glances at me. "Especially not you."

I soften. "You could never let me down. You're, like, my favorite person on the whole entire planet."

He smiles. "Never? You mean it?"

"Duh." I nudge him. "You could be arrested for murder, and I'd still come visit you in jail every week."

"Good to know." He chuckles. He looks down, puts his hands in his sweatshirt pocket. "I guess I'm just afraid that if I mess up, it's all going to go away."

We've caught up to the apple he kicked, so he kicks it again, and we watch it roll through the grass.

"I think everybody's afraid of that," I reply. "In their own way."

"Not you. You're not afraid of anything."

I think about Jack's phone, buzzing like crazy in his pocket. *I'm afraid of losing you,* I almost say. *I'm afraid you're going to leave me behind.*

A breeze lifts my hair off my neck and sends goose bumps down my arms. I'm only wearing a T-shirt, so I shiver.

"You're cold. Here."

He pulls his sweatshirt off over his head and hands it to me. It's his dark green soccer hoodie with his last name on the back. When I put it on, it smells like Tide detergent and cologne, and it's warm—like him. "Thanks."

Then I see something in the distance.

"What's that?" I point across the orchard, toward the gathering of people.

Jack holds his hand over his eyes, shielding them from the sun. "I dunno." He looks at me. "Let's go find out."

We walk to the other side of the orchard. At the break in the trees, across a dirt path, there's a small farmhouse. A dozen or so people are wandering through the front yard, browsing stacks of furniture and tables covered with trinkets.

I gasp. "A yard sale!"

"Sweet," Jack says. "Do you think they have socks?"

I wrinkle my nose. "I hope not."

We cross the path, onto the lawn, and an old woman in a sun hat smiles at us. Jack waves and smiles back.

"All prices are negotiable," she says. "Just come and find me."

Jack nods. "Awesome. Thank you, ma'am."

I stifle a laugh. He's such a people pleaser.

We pick a row of tables that isn't too crowded and start

walking through. It seems like a lot of knickknacks from the eighties and nineties—glassware, picture frames, children's toys. My mind flashes, briefly, to the last time I was at a yard sale like this, looking for long-lost treasures with Grandma Imogen. Yard sales and flea markets were her favorite.

"Look at this." Jack is holding up what appears to be a tiny radio, attached by a key chain to some even tinier CDs. "They've got Avril Lavigne, *NSYNC, Alicia Keys—"

"Oh," I say, leaning over to inspect a small glass dolphin. "Speaking of Alicia. Did you hear about what happened at lunch yesterday?"

"You mean Serge's homecoming proposal to Zoya?" He puts down the radio, then picks up something furry that looks sort of like an owl, but more cursed. "Yeah."

Serge asked Zoya to homecoming with a bouquet of roses and four guys from concert choir. They showed up at our lunch table to sing an a cappella rendition of "If I Ain't Got You" by Alicia Keys—their song, apparently—and Zoya started *crying*.

"It was so extra," I say, remembering her heaving sobs. "She cried so hard, you would've thought somebody died."

"She's dramatic, that's for sure." Jack puts down the cursed owl. "But it's kinda nice, too, right? I mean, she really loves him."

"She loves the attention," I say, without really thinking about it.

He doesn't respond right away, but I can feel his eyes on me.

"What?"

"It still surprises me sometimes. How cynical you can be about other people."

"Wow, okay. Sorry I'm not the kind of girl that breaks down into tears over a big homecoming proposal."

He smiles down at the ground, and his shaggy hair falls into his eyes. "Nope, you're definitely not. Anybody who knows anything about you would know your homecoming proposal should be way more subtle."

I feel a strange little flutter in my chest.

"That's true." I pick up a ceramic cat and try to keep my voice casual. "Any kind of spectacle would be way too embarrassing." I show him the cat. "This looks like Tina."

He takes the cat from me, inspects it. "Eh. Kind of. Tina's scragglier." He puts the ceramic cat down. "So nobody's asked you?"

"Huh?"

"To homecoming," he says. His attention is focused on a one-eyed Mr. Potato Head. "Nobody asked you to be their date?"

I let out a cackle. "No! No way."

He shrugs. "Crazier things have happened."

I pick up an animatronic jack-o'-lantern, flip the switch on. Nothing happens, so I put it back down. "No, I know. I just mean . . . I wouldn't go with a date. Nobody's asked me, or anything, but even if they *did*, I'd say no." I look at him. "I'm going with you. Obviously." The fact that this isn't a given, that Jack thinks someone might have asked me and I didn't tell him, is a little stab to my gut. It means things are changing. Will I look up one day to see that these little fractures between us have become gaping craters? I push the thought away.

"Me?" He sort of laughs. "Outie, you're gonna have to buy me dinner first."

"Not like *that*." I feel my cheeks get hot. "It's our first high school dance. We *have* to go together, you know—as friends." I walk around to the next row of tables, and a thought occurs to me. "Unless . . ." I look at him across a stack of vinyl records. "You were thinking of asking someone else?"

In sixth grade, Jack started walking with Courtney Beaver to math class. I had music class with Courtney, and she was an insufferable know-it-all. *Actually, Imogen, it's pronounced ar-PEH-jee-oh, not ar-PEG-ee-oh*. Whatever. I tolerated her for Jack's sake, until one day when he asked if she could sit with us at lunch. *Absolutely not*, I said. *Veto*.

Veto? he replied. *You can't veto a person*.

Sure you can, I told him. *I just did*.

A few months later, when I admitted I thought Stephen Cahill from language arts had nice eyes, Jack's response was immediate. *Veto. He chews gum and sticks it under his desk*.

Since then, we've been exercising the power of veto whenever one of us was into someone the other deemed unworthy. Come to think of it, though, I haven't had to veto one of Jack's crushes in a while. As far as I know, he hasn't had any.

"Well, now that you mention it," he says, and my heart, for some reason, does a somersault. "I *was* going to ask Margot Robbie, but turns out she's busy that night."

"Ha-*ha*," I say dryly, though secretly, I'm relieved.

Something two tables down catches my eye. I walk toward it, away from Jack.

"Oh my gosh." I pick it up carefully. A blue morpho butterfly, wings spread, mounted between two pieces of glass. I know it's real because of how delicate it looks, with cerulean wings so vibrant and thin they look like tissue paper.

"It matches your eyes," Jack says over my shoulder.

"It's beautiful." I run my finger lightly over the glass. "These are rare. I've never seen one up close before."

"You mean you don't have this one in your collection?"

I shake my head. I have twenty-eight different species of butterfly and moth, but the blue morpho isn't one of them. I look on the bottom of the frame for a price and wince.

"Forty dollars." I put the butterfly back where I found it. "Too much."

"The lady said prices are negotiable."

"Mom gave me ten dollars to buy some apples," I tell him. "That's all I've got."

"Hmm." He looks at it thoughtfully. Then he starts scanning the yard until his gaze falls on the front porch. "One sec."

He walks across the yard and up the steps to the porch, where the old lady is knitting in a chair. I watch her smile in recognition, then listen carefully as Jack starts to speak. I take a couple of steps toward them, trying to eavesdrop, but I can't hear anything. Eventually, I see the woman nod and shake Jack's hand. He shakes back enthusiastically—so much so that I worry he's going to shake her fragile little arm right off her body.

He walks back over to me.

"Well," he says. "Ready to go?"

I look around. We still haven't checked out half the tables. "Um. Yeah, I guess."

"Cool," he says. "Don't forget your butterfly."

My eyes widen. "My . . . what?"

A corner of his mouth turns up. "The blue guy. The little Immie."

"Monty. Stop messing around."

"Outie," he says, mocking my serious tone. "I'm not. The corpse is yours."

"But you don't have forty dollars."

"Would you stop worrying? The lady and I worked out a deal." He picks up the butterfly and holds it out to me. "It's yours."

Finally, I let myself smile. "You bought me taxidermy?"

Jack hates my taxidermy butterflies. The first time I showed him my collection, he called it creepy, and every time he's been in my room since, he fixes his gaze squarely away from the shelf where I keep them all.

"Would you just take it? I don't like holding dead things."

I do as he says and then throw my arms around him, careful not to damage the glass. "Thank you."

When he hugs me back, I feel his phone buzz in his pocket, but I let it go this time.

TRACK SEVEN

"With Arms Outstretched"—Rilo Kiley

I never knew what was really going through your head in the days leading up to the dance. If you'd told me, maybe things could've turned out differently. Then again, there were a lot of things you weren't telling me back then.

A few days before homecoming, I'm walking out of Ms. Wendt's classroom with Jack after a particularly tough exam on the Revolutionary War when I see Elijah lingering across the hall. Jack says hi to him, they talk for a second about soccer, and then Elijah turns to me.

"Hey."

"Hi."

He smiles at me. "Can I talk to you?"

Immediately Jack tenses up. "I gotta get to Spanish," he mumbles. He quickens his pace and walks away from me without another word.

Before I have time to process what just happened, Elijah closes the gap between us, falling into step with me.

"Picasso," he says. He's tall, over six feet, and has to sort of crouch to talk to me.

"Elijah," I say, watching the back of Jack's head until it disappears.

"How's your day going?"

"Um." I adjust my grip on my book bag, feeling awkward. "Fine."

"Good," he says. "Glad to hear it."

"Can I help you with something?"

He smiles like he knows something I don't. He's got a nice smile, which I silently scold myself for noticing. *He's Jack's soccer rival,* I remind myself. *Resist his charms!*

"Maybe. That depends."

"On what?"

"On whether or not you have a date for homecoming."

I stop in my tracks and narrow my eyes at him.

"So," he says when we start walking again, casual as ever. "Do you?"

"Um." Jack and I agreed to go together, but it isn't technically a date, is it? I throw the question back at him. "Do you?"

"Nope."

"Excellent. Glad we cleared that up." We reach my locker, and I bend down to put in my combination. He leans into the locker next to mine.

"I was actually wondering . . . if you maybe wanted to go with me."

"Me?" I say with a raised brow. "Um, don't take this the wrong way, but I think you've had one too many soccer balls to the head."

He laughs. "I promise you, I'm perfectly lucid."

"Why would you want to go with me?" I fumble with the lock, messing up my combination. "You hardly know me."

"I know enough," he says. "You interest me."

"I *interest* you?" I laugh, messing up my combination again.

"So? What do you think?"

In my silence, I watch Elijah open one of his notebooks to a free page. He pulls a pen out of his pocket and scribbles something down.

"Here's my number," Elijah says, tearing off the corner of the paper and handing it to me. "Take some time. Think about it. I'm not going to ask anyone else."

"Uh. Okay."

"I better get back," he says, looking over his shoulder at the hallway, which has begun to clear out. "I'm probably going to be late."

"Where's your class?"

"Ms. Wendt," he says, referring to the history classroom I just came out of.

"This is a little out of your way."

He shrugs, and I smile despite myself.

"Wait!" I yell when he starts to walk away.

He stops, turns back around.

"I . . . Actually, I can't."

I'm thinking of Jack, and the blue morpho butterfly, and the cozy feel of his sweatshirt against my skin. "I'm sort of already going with someone." And then I add, for some reason, "My friend."

"Well, then. Maybe next time." He turns around, doubling back the way he came.

Saturday afternoon, Hannah, Zoya, and Alex come over to my house to get ready for the dance. I put on the getting-ready playlist I made earlier in the day and pour seltzer water into Mom's champagne glasses to feel fancy.

"To the best night ever!" Hannah says, holding up her glass.

"To the best night ever," we repeat, and then clink. I feel the sting of the bubbles at the back of my throat, and I hope, with all my heart, that the toast comes true.

Last night, at the football game, Jack was in a mood. It turns out he thought I was going to homecoming with Elijah instead of him. Apparently one of his teammates was spreading the rumor. I cleared it up for him and assured him that *he's* the one I want to go with, and it ended up okay. Still, there's a lingering feeling in the back of my mind that the whole misunderstanding wouldn't have happened if he hadn't been so unavailable lately. We were supposed to hang out on Thursday—ice cream and a movie, like old times—but he said he was too tired. Despite how hard I'm trying, we're more disconnected than ever.

I hear the song coming through the speaker, Rilo Kiley's "With Arms Outstretched." *"If you want me, you better speak up, I won't wait."* It's what I want to say to Jack.

"Immie, what's up with your bedspread?" Zoya asks, studying my light blue comforter. "Are those floating heads?"

"*Decapitated* heads," I correct, pushing the thoughts out of my mind. "It's Marie Antoinette! See the fancy hairstyles?"

"Who's Marie Antoinette?" Alex asks.

"Oh, here we go," Hannah says, throwing back a big swig of her seltzer.

"The *let them eat cake* lady, right?" Zoya asks. "The queen of France?"

"She never actually said that," I tell them. "She was actually—"

"No!" Hannah says. "Please, no history lessons. We're not at school yet."

"Fine." I cross my arms. "I'll just talk about girly things, like clothes and makeup."

Hannah nods once. "Thank you."

I roll my eyes.

After that, we get to work, styling our hair and applying makeup side by side in the long mirror over my dresser. I'm not very good at being *glam*—I don't usually wear makeup or do anything to my hair other than brush it—so Hannah gives me sharp cat eyes with her liquid eyeliner, and Zoya pins my hair into a loose updo, letting tendrils hang down and frame my face.

"*Voilà.*" She takes a step back to survey her work. "A masterpiece."

"What do you guys think?" Hannah looks at us through the mirror. She's holding up two pairs of earrings. "Hoops or studs?"

"Studs," I say, walking to my closet, where my dress is hanging up. "I like the way they match the sparkles on your skirt."

I hide behind the closet door to change, stepping into my dress, pulling it up, and slipping my arms through the spaghetti straps. I lean my head out. "Can someone zip me up?"

Alex walks over. "This looks great on you," she says, pulling up the zipper and attaching the clasp.

"It does," Zoya agrees. "Teal is your color."

"Thanks." I look at myself in the mirror, and I'm surprised by what I see—still me, but shinier, sharper. The dress fits perfectly—it's tight around my waist and then flares out around my hips into a puffy tulle skirt that falls just above my knees. I do a little spin and the tulle lifts into the air, and I feel like a ballerina.

"This *is* kind of fun," I say. "I'm starting to get why some people are so obsessed with this stuff."

"Stick with us," Zoya says. "We do supermodel sleepovers all the time."

I look at her through the mirror. "Supermodel sleepovers?"

Zoya nods enthusiastically. "We do each other's hair and makeup, get all dressed up, and have a fashion show."

"Usually in Zoya's basement," Hannah adds. "It's the biggest. Plus, her mom has the *best* closet. It's like a time capsule of vintage designers."

"That sounds . . . fun?" I say, not sure whether it actually does or not. "I've never been to a sleepover."

All three of them stop what they're doing and turn to face me.

"Never?" Zoya says, shocked.

I shake my head, feeling weirdly vulnerable. I used to have sleepovers with Grandma Imogen, but I don't think that really counts.

"Well," Zoya says. "That's a problem that will be remedied *tonight*!"

"Tonight?" I repeat, uncertain. Still, I'm sort of touched that Zoya cares so much about giving me this experience.

"Ms. Meadows!" Hannah yells. She grabs Zoya's wrist, and they hurry out of the room, leaving me and Alex alone.

Alex picks up a brush and starts running it through her hair. The soft red waves look elegant with her black satin mini dress. I catch her eye in the mirror.

"Hey," she says. "Can I ask you something?"

"Sure."

She hesitates a moment. "Do you—I mean, are you and Jack, like . . . a thing?"

"Oh!" I wasn't expecting that. "Um. No. We're just going together as friends."

"Cool." She looks down at her lap. "So you wouldn't mind, then, if I asked Jack to dance?"

I open my mouth to respond, but no words come out. *Jack already has someone to dance with,* I think. *Me.* But of course that isn't true. We're only going together as friends. Slow dancing, or anything that veers even slightly romantic, isn't part of that. But still.

He shouldn't dance with anyone but me.

"I don't know," I say finally. "That might be weird, right? I mean, he is *my* date." I feel my face get hot. "You know?"

She smiles but doesn't say anything, just continues brushing her hair.

Hannah and Zoya come running back into the room with

smiles on their faces. "Your mom says it's okay!" Hannah says excitedly. "We're all sleeping over here tonight!"

I snap out of my discomfort with Alex to face a new, more pressing problem.

"Here?"

"Oh, I can't," Alex says, putting the brush down. "I have to go to my mom's."

"Boo," Zoya says. "Next weekend, then. We can do my house."

I don't know what to say. My gut reaction is to be annoyed—they planned a sleepover at my house without even asking me!—but I don't really *feel* annoyed.

I feel nervous.

Then I notice Alex and Zoya standing in front of the shelves where I keep my taxidermy butterfly collection. Zoya's head is cocked to one side; she's looking at a purple emperor that I inherited from Grandma Imogen. The deep purple of the butterfly's wings matches her dress.

"These are kind of weird," she says with a frown on her face. I can see it reflected in the glass.

I smile, privately, just for me and Grandma. "Thank you."

I slip my feet into the silver strappy heels my mom let me borrow from her closet. Then the doorbell rings.

"Immie!" Mom calls from downstairs. "The boys are here."

TRACK EIGHT

"Dreaming of You"—Selena

You probably knew this one was coming, and that's because we HAD a moment. You can pretend it didn't happen, but I know what I felt. And I know, when I looked in your eyes, that you felt it too.

The school cafeteria is transformed for homecoming. Right outside the doors there's a photobooth with a bunch of props, and we pose for a few pictures before going in. For the last one, Jack puts his arm around my shoulders and pulls me close. It's weird to see him so dressed up, with his crisp button-down shirt and tie, and his slicked-back hair that accentuates his jawline. My first thought, when he showed up at my door, was that he looked *good*. Really good. It gave me a weird, fluttery feeling in my chest.

Inside, the room is draped in streamers and pulsing with energy. The overhead lights are off, but the room glows, lit by thousands of twinkle lights hanging from the ceiling. The tables and chairs are gone, stacked together and pushed to the far ends of the room, and in their place, packs of students dance to a Cardi B song. We're barely inside for a second before Zoya takes Serge's hand and drags him onto the dance floor.

"This is her favorite song," Hannah explains, watching Zoya move through the crowd. Then her eyes go wide. "Ah! It's Bethany. Alex, dance with me so she doesn't think I'm a dateless loser."

Alex frowns. "We're not losers just because we don't have dates."

"Oh whatever. Come on." She grabs Alex's hand and off they go.

I turn to Jack, still a jumble of excitement and nerves. "Ready?"

He takes a breath and smiles back at me. He seems a little nervous too.

"Ready."

On the dance floor, I start to do my signature shoulder shimmy, and then I stop myself. What if my moves are embarrassing? Jack and I have danced side by side at every middle school dance, but this time feels different. We're in high school now.

I start to sway my hips and bob my head in a way that feels less natural but might come off as more mature. Across our dance circle, I see Hannah make a face.

"Are you okay, Immie?" she shouts. Everybody turns to look at me.

I stop dancing, resist the urge to drop to the floor and crawl away. "Fine. Just, um—I had something in my shoe."

The Cardi B song fades out, and the DJ's voice comes through the speakers. "All right. We're gonna slow things down now."

A song I don't recognize starts to play. It's from the nineties—it has to be—with dreamy piano and twinkling chimes that sound like starlight. I can't decide if I think it's corny or romantic or both, but either way, it makes me feel a little like I'm under a spell.

All around the room, couples start to pair up. I see Serge and Zoya, Hannah and Bethany—oh, there goes Alex, running off the dance floor. Then Jack takes a step toward me.

"Did you bring your steel-toed shoes?"

I blink, dazed. "What?"

"Um." He clears his throat. "You know. Do you want to dance?"

A wave of nausea washes over me. For a second, I really think I might throw up.

"Oh—yeah. Yes."

I extend my arms as far as they'll go and slap my hands on his shoulders. He puts his on my waist so lightly I almost don't feel them.

"Is this okay?" he asks.

"Yep," I say, hoping he can't see how red my face probably is. "Definitely. Yes."

We start swaying. I try to relax. I tell myself there's no need to be nervous—we're friends. Friends dance together *all* the time. The song gets to the chorus: *"Cause I'm dreaming of you tonight . . ."* I wince. Why does it have to be so romantic? I want to say something to break the ice, but I can't think of anything. On second thought, I'm not even sure if I remember how to speak.

Jack beats me to it. "Question. Would you rather have your hands and feet switched, or your ears on your elbows?"

I have to cover my mouth to stop from laughing too loudly and wrecking the ambiance.

"Personally, I think it would suck to have feet for hands, purely because you can't hide that," he continues. "Although, hands for feet could actually be handy—ha, *handy*." He takes a moment to laugh, pleased with himself. "You could pick stuff up with them like a monkey."

"Wow," I say. "Jack Marshall, ladies and gentlepeople."

He grins. "You love it."

"I love *you*" is what comes out of my mouth; then I realize what I said.

We've never told each other that before. I feel Jack stiffen, feel his sway falter, and for a few seconds, we fall out of rhythm with the song. It's so awkward, trying to get our bodies in sync again, that I genuinely wish an alien spaceship would send down a beam of light to abduct me.

"Ears for elbows," I say quickly, trying to save face. "No question."

"Respectable choice," he says. He seems nervous again. "Hey. You, um, you look really pretty. I, um—I don't know if I said that before."

He didn't—back at the house, when he saw me come down the steps, all he said was *cool dress*. I didn't want to admit it, but it stung a little.

"Thanks," I say, heart pounding. Across the dance floor, through a sea of bodies, I spot Elijah dancing with some girl. He must feel my eyes on him, because he looks up, smiles, and gives me a little nod. I smile back, then return my attention to Jack.

"You clean up pretty nice yourself. Is that a new shirt?"

"Thanks. Um, yeah." He clears his throat. "I got it at the mall with Serge and Ben after soccer on Thursday."

My heart practically contracts. Thursday. The night he was supposed to get ice cream and watch a movie with me.

"I thought you were too tired to hang out on Thursday," I say, trying to keep my voice casual.

"I was. But I needed to get stuff for the dance, and Ben was already going to the mall." A pause. "It wasn't a big deal."

"Okay," I say, still swaying to the music. "So . . . why didn't you tell me?"

"I don't know." He frowns. "I don't tell you every time Mom stops at the creamery for milk after she picks me up from practice, do I?"

I furrow my brow. "What?"

"It was just, like, an errand," he says. "I didn't know I had to tell you."

"You don't *have* to tell me anything," I say. It's not like Jack to cancel our plans so he can hang out with other people, and it's *definitely* not like him to lie about it. We never lie to each other—it's kind of our thing.

"Come on, Outie," he urges. "I wasn't *keeping* it from you."

"Really?" I don't dare look at him. "Because it sure feels that way."

"Well, if that's how I made you feel, then I'm really sorry."

He sounds sincere enough. I sigh, relenting, and look up at him.

"I didn't mean to hurt you. I just wasn't thinking." He smiles cautiously. "See? I really was tired."

An unruly piece of hair has broken free from its hold and fallen over his eye. I reach out, brush it away. He doesn't flinch.

"It's just that you've been so busy lately," I say, moving a little closer. "I'm happy that you've got this good thing going with the team, but I really—" I hesitate. Suddenly I feel incredibly vulnerable. "I miss you."

He adjusts his grip on my waist, and I become hyper-focused on the places where he touches me.

"You don't have to miss me," he says. His voice is quiet. "I'm right here."

My heart starts to pound. All of a sudden it feels like there's an electric current running between us. I look into his eyes, wondering if he feels it too, and I think he does, because his hands move from my waist to the small of my back so he can pull me closer. Instinctively I lean into him, wrapping my arms around his neck so we're just inches apart. I feel his breath on my ear, and I shiver.

And then the song ends, transitioning into "Shake It Off" by Taylor Swift without missing a beat. All around us the dance floor comes to life again. I step back, feeling flushed.

"I—"

He lets go of me.

"Sorry," he cuts me off. "I just need to . . . um, I'll be back."

He turns around and walks off without so much as a glance, leaving me there, alone. I watch him push through the double doors and disappear into the hallway. I continue to watch the doors after he's gone, too shocked to move.

What just happened?

"Girl," Hannah grabs my arm. "What was *that*?"

"He just left," I say, still watching the doors.

Hannah shrugs. "Maybe he had to go to the bathroom or something."

I shake my head, confused. "He was . . . we were . . ." I shake my head again. I have no idea how to describe what we were, to Hannah or myself. "He seemed fine a minute ago."

More than fine, I think. He seemed . . . different. In a good way.

I wander off the dance floor and find a free table near the doors. I sit down, letting my tulle skirt poof out around me.

It was like the energy between us had shifted. One minute we were arguing, and the next, we were—what?

Slow dancing, says a voice in my head. *Really* slow dancing, the way couples do.

But we're not a couple, argues another voice, the more rational of the two. *We're best friends, and we really missed each other. Our dance was basically a glorified hug.*

So that's it. Hannah's right, and I'm overthinking it.

Right?

"Immie?"

I look up, and there's Elijah. He looks dreamy in light blue pants, a white shirt with a big collar, and a silver chain around his neck. Paired with his dark curly hair, he looks like he stepped straight out of the 1970s.

"Wow," he smiles at me, and there's that dimple. "You look gorgeous."

I blush at his compliment. Sure, it might be forward, but considering the jumbled confusion happening inside my brain right now, it's kind of a relief to know exactly how he feels.

"Thanks."

He points to the empty chair across from me and raises his eyebrows. "Can I sit?"

I glance toward the door. Still no sign of Jack.

"Go for it."

He picks up the chair with one hand and flips it around, then sits down and leans over the back. "Are you having fun?"

I shrug. "Yeah, I guess."

The corner of his mouth turns up. "Yeah, sitting here all alone looks like a blast."

"I'm just waiting for Jack."

"Right." The way he says it, drawing out the *i*, makes me wonder what he's thinking—what he *saw*. "You and Marshall. Is there something there?"

"No," I say quickly—maybe a little *too* quickly, judging by the look Elijah gives me. I clear my throat and try again. "No. There's nothing. It's just . . ."

I wince. Elijah is being honest, so I might as well be too.

"There was a moment. On the dance floor."

"Ah." He nods. "A moment."

"Yeah. There was a moment, and then he ran away. Like . . . like I was disgusting, and he couldn't get out fast enough."

"Oh, I doubt that," Elijah says. "Maybe you just scare him."

"*Scare* him?" I nearly laugh. "No. We've been best friends since we were seven."

"There you go," he says. "You've always been just friends, until tonight, when you had your moment. Now the line is blurred, and he's freaked."

I furrow my brow. "What are you, some sort of love guru?"

He smirks. "Something like that."

I lean forward, put my chin in my hands. "I don't want him to be freaked," I say. "What do I do?"

I look behind him at the doors, where Jack has just appeared. Elijah sees me looking and follows my gaze.

"Be honest with him," Elijah says, standing up. "Then at least you won't regret the things you didn't say. Trust me, that's way worse."

"You would know?"

"Oh yeah," Elijah says without shame. "It's why I always lay everything out on the table. And why I'm not going to stop shooting my shot with you." He winks, and I roll my eyes but smile—I can't help it.

"Good night, Immie," he says, and then disappears into the crowd.

I look back at the doors and see Jack walking toward me. Right away I can tell something isn't right. He looks pale and sort of frazzled. His tie is loose around his neck, and the top buttons of his shirt have come undone.

"Hey," he says when he gets close. His voice sounds strained, tense. I stand up. My legs feel a little wobbly.

"I don't feel well," he says. "I think I need to go home."

TRACK NINE

"Complicated"—Avril Lavigne

Carrie played this song one morning in her car, and I must have listened to it a hundred times since. It wasn't just you that was making things complicated. It was Mom, too. I felt suffocated by all the secrets.

*T*he next day, Jack texts and says he's feeling better, so he comes over after dinner to do some homework. We sit at the kitchen table, speaking very little except when one of us needs help with a math problem. We don't talk about the dance, or the way he put his arms around me, or the fact that he got his sister to drive him home right after. We don't talk about last night at all. It's excruciating. By the time we finish our homework and Jack goes home, I've basically convinced myself that the sparks I felt between us were all in my head.

"That was weird," Mom says, putting on her rubber gloves by the kitchen sink. "Right?"

"*Mom.*"

"What?" She turns on the faucet. "You barely said two words to each other. It's not exactly like you."

I'm annoyed both because she's bringing it up and because

she's right. "I know," I say with a groan. I close my textbook, gather my folders, and shove them all in my book bag. "Something happened at the dance last night."

She nearly drops the plate she's scrubbing. "*What?* What happened?"

"Ugh. Nothing that bad, Mom. Relax." I zip up my book bag and carry it over to the door. "It's just—Jack and I danced together. *Slow* danced." I walk back into the kitchen, sit down at the counter. "And then right after, he sort of . . . ugh. He ran away." I put my head down on my arms and wish I could banish the memory to the far, far recesses of my brain.

When I peek up at Mom, she looks at me with a raised brow. "*Ran* away?"

"I wish I was exaggerating."

"Well." She turns back to the dishes. "Did he come back?"

"Just long enough to tell me he needed to go home."

"Hm." She's quiet, scrubbing at a tough stain. "Maybe he was sick."

I put my elbows on the table, rest my chin on my hands. "That's what he said."

"But you don't believe him?"

"I don't know." I keep thinking about what Elijah said, about how Jack was probably freaked out by our moment—or whatever it was—on the dance floor. But if that's true, why hasn't he said anything to me? We tell each other everything—always.

Except, says a voice in my head, *for your true feelings about your bio dad.* But that's different. That doesn't have anything to do with him. "It seemed like there was something he wasn't telling me. But maybe I'm overthinking it."

She turns off the faucet, turns to face me. "He's your best friend. If there's something going on, he'll tell you. Otherwise, don't worry about it."

"That's easy to *say*."

"Well." She pulls off her rubber gloves slowly, one finger at a time. "I'm glad you had the girls over last night. They seem like a lot of fun."

"Oh no." I sit up straighter. "Where are you going with this?"

"I'm not *going* anywhere. I'm just saying. I think it's good you're branching out. Jack doesn't have to be your whole world anymore."

"Mom. Seriously?"

"You worry about him a lot," she says. "What he's doing, how he's feeling, whether I've made him enough food. It's not healthy, to be so wrapped up in one person so young."

"I'm not *so* young," I say. "And what would you know about it, anyway? You have no idea what our friendship is like."

"I know more than you think." She turns her back to me to put the gloves away.

"What does *that* mean?"

She sighs, turns to face me again. "I know that you've been stressed out, not seeing as much of him lately. And that's not good. Because guess what?" She looks at me across the counter. "That's life. People grow up, and they get busy. Things *change*.

It's normal. And it's not going to go back to the way it was."

Her words sting like a paper cut to the heart. "Stop it!" I practically jump out of my seat. "Just stop it."

"I'm just saying—"

"Well, stop! Stop saying anything. I don't want to hear it."

She holds up her hands in surrender. It occurs to me just how tired she looks. "Fine."

I go to my room without saying anything else. Inside, I'm fuming. I slam the door and get a little rush of satisfaction when I hear her yell "Hey!" from downstairs. What Jack and I have is special. And nothing—not soccer or school or even time itself—can change that.

I reach for the CD player, remove *SUMMER '06 MIX* and put *SONGS FOR FEELING SAD* in its place. I put my headphones over my ears, crawl under the covers, and press play.

By the end of October, things are mostly back to normal between Jack and me. Or as close to normal as they *can* be, considering I don't see much of him outside school. Between soccer practice and preparing for the team's contribution to the annual Halloween carnival, he's busier than ever. That's why, when we do get the chance to hang out, I try my best to keep things light. I pretend I'm not still thinking about his hands on my waist, and he pretends there was no weirdness between us at homecoming, and the world continues to spin.

"So that's it?" Hannah says to me one day in art class. "You're just going to pretend it never happened?"

"No," I say, tying my hair back with a scrunchie. I don't like when it hangs in my face while I paint. "I'm just not making a big deal about it. Obviously, it wasn't a big deal to him."

She swivels on her stool to look at me directly. "You don't really believe that, do you?"

I don't reply, just pick up my brush and swirl it around in apricot-orange paint.

"Girl, be serious. I *saw* it. The whole school saw it."

"And?"

"*And* . . . there was some serious heat between you two."

"You don't know what you're talking about," I say, pointing my brush at her. "You were just feeling all mushy from your dance with Bethany."

"It *was* a great dance." She smiles, remembering. "But no. I know what I saw. You and Jack, crushing on each other."

"No way," I insist. "I could never. He's . . ." I struggle to come up with the words. How do you describe someone whose existence is woven so deeply into your own that they feel less like their own person and more like an extension of yourself? "Well, he's Jack. Talking to him is the same thing as, like, breathing."

Hannah snorts. "Right. And you *don't* have a crush on him."

"I don't!" I say. "And he doesn't either. If he did, why would he run away and then never bring it up again?"

"I don't know." She swivels back toward her canvas. "Because he's a boy, and they're oblivious about this stuff? Or maybe he's waiting for you to say something first?" Hannah guesses, mixing pink and purple paint. "Yeah, maybe he's embarrassed about running off to the bathroom, and needs reassurance that he didn't make a fool of himself."

"I dunno." Jack makes a fool of himself in front of me constantly, and on purpose. He's the least self-conscious person I know. "I doubt it."

"But it's possible." She puts her brush lightly on the canvas and starts to make small upward strokes. "Like I said: oblivious."

I focus on the butterfly wing I'm painting. If Hannah's right, and he's just waiting for reassurance from me that things are still normal between us, then that should be good news. Instead, it frustrates me. Why do I have to be the one to decipher how he feels? Why can't he just tell me how he feels, the way he's done our whole lives?

Ms. Moser stands up at her desk. "Hey, listen up, everyone." She waits until the room is quiet and then continues. "Before I lose you to your muse, I want to urge you all to start working on your midterm projects. They're due in a little over a month, which might not seem that soon, but I promise you, the deadline will be here before you know it."

I sort of hide behind my canvas. I've been so focused on everything happening with Jack that I haven't even thought about the midterm. *Who am I?*

I have absolutely no clue.

After school, I begin the Search.

I figure if I have to make an art project telling people who I am, then first, I need to find out where I come from. That means uncovering my dad's identity is now officially a school requirement.

That's how I'm justifying it to myself anyway.

The whole truth is that I'm sick of all the secrets. Lately it feels like everybody has them. Mom won't talk about her past, Jack won't talk about his feelings, and my dad—well, he's nothing *but* secrets. I can't do much about the first two—at least not now—but my dad's identity is public domain. The answer is out there whether Mom gives it to me or not. And it would be nice to get an answer for a change.

I start small: scrolling through my mom's social media friends and tagged photos, searching for someone around her age who kind of looks like me. When that goes nowhere, I switch to snooping in her bedroom. I figure I have an hour or two before she comes home from work, catches me, and shuts this whole thing down.

I move quickly but carefully, rifling through drawers and peeking inside shoeboxes, looking for pictures, ticket stubs, old receipts. I don't find anything. My mom, it turns out, isn't a very sentimental person. Nothing in her room is out of place.

I pick up a framed photograph of Grandma Imogen from my mom's dresser and look into her eyes the way some people look at a mirror. That's when it hits me. If I want to figure out who my dad is, I'm going to have to get creative.

An hour later, I'm lying on my bed with my laptop open on my chest, listening to "Complicated" by Avril Lavigne (again) and surveying my brand-new social media profile. I'm a forty-two-year-old woman named Kristen Robertson, I have twenty-six friends—some people really will accept anyone—and I live in West Mifflin, Pennsylvania, my mom's hometown. My profile picture, a friendly-looking brunette with a bob, is AI generated. Aside from the hand, which is admittedly a little smudgy, the profile looks real enough to fool anyone who isn't a chronically online teenager. Hopefully that means it'll get past my mom.

"*Why'd you have to go and make things so complicated?*" Avril sings. I type my mom's name into the search bar, wondering the same thing. I find her profile right away. We have eight mutual friends—I already sent requests to as many of her former classmates as I could—and we're both members of a group called Oddly Satisfying.

I type up a message, trying to make myself sound like a mom. Hey girl! Long time no see. Had lunch with Jodi last week and we were reminiscing about old times . . . Hope you're doing well!

I cringe, press enter, and send the message. I take a deep breath. She's still at school—she had a board meeting tonight—so it could be a while before she sees it.

And then the little green light appears next to her profile picture—she's online. A moment later, the message is marked as read and three little dots appear.

She's typing.

Nora Meadows: Hi there! I'm so sorry, did we go to high school together?

My eyes widen. I sit up straighter and compose a response.

Kristen Robertson: Yes. I was two years below you. Jodi and I were close friends

Nora Meadows: Oh, great! Sorry again, my memory isn't what it used to be.

Nora Meadows: How is Jodi? Haven't spoken to her in a while. Life keeps getting in the way.

Kristen Robertson: Oh, you know. Same old Jodi. But I want to know how YOU are. Did you end up marrying that guy you were dating?

Nora Meadows: Who, Rob?

I gasp. *Rob?*

Nora Meadows: No. We split up.

I deflate. False alarm.

Kristen Robertson: No, that's not who I was thinking of. The other guy, the one with the dark hair

I smile, feeling clever. I didn't inherit my black hair from my mom.

Nora Meadows: Max?

Max.

Nora Meadows: Nope, never been married. It's just my daughter and me.

Kristen Robertson: Your daughter with Max?

The three little dots appear and then disappear on the screen. My heart is pounding. Could this be it? Could it really be this easy?

The dots appear again.

Nora Meadows: How do you know Jodi?

Uh-oh.

Kristen Robertson: We had art class together

Nora Meadows: Jodi never took art.

Nora Meadows: I'm talking to her right now. She says she's never heard of you.

Nora Meadows: Who is this?

I slam the computer shut.

Well, there goes that. Still, it wasn't a total loss. Now I know about Max.

I lie back in bed and stare at the ceiling, thinking. Max could be my dad, but there are a million Maxes in the world. How will I figure out which one is *the* one?

I open my laptop up again and visit my mom's profile page. She's got four friends named Max, and one of them is a woman.

It's a start. Three Maxes, three potential dads. My very own *Mamma Mia!*

I feel my phone start to buzz and glance at the screen—my mom is calling. My pulse quickens. There's no way she knows what I've been up to . . . right? She's smart, but she's not psychic. At least I don't think she is.

"Hey, Mom," I answer the phone, trying to sound cheery and not at all suspicious. "What's up?"

"Hey, Butterfly." She sounds normal, if a little tired, but that's not so unusual after work. "I'm on my way home. What are you feeling for dinner?"

"Dunno," I say, clicking on the first Max's profile—Max number 1. He's got a head of swoopy gray hair, and he's holding a Dachshund. "How about Italian?"

"Great. We'll order a pizza." She sighs. "I'm not feeling much like cooking. I've had a day."

"Oh no." I try to keep my voice casual. "What happened?"

"Overbearing parents. Underpaid faculty." I can picture the look on her face, the disdainful eye roll that I very much *did* inherit. "The usual."

"Sorry."

I relax a little. She doesn't sound like she suspects anything. I click on Max number 1's personal information and find out he's from Seattle, is a Pisces, and went to the same college as my mom. I go to his profile photos and linger on a close-up, trying to decide if I can see myself in his face.

"Anyway, I'll be home soon. Love you."

"Love you too."

I hang up the phone and click over to the next photo.

TRACK TEN

"Secret Smile"—Semisonic

*After you smiled at me in the haunted house,
I heard this song and thought it was a sign.
How pathetic is that?*

By Halloween, I've created extensive fact sheets for all three Maxes. The data I gathered is split into two categories: More Likely to Be My Dad and Less Likely. For example, Max number 2 is a financial planner. That's less likely. He enjoys music (more likely), especially jazz (less likely). Max number 3, according to some old, tagged photos, spent the summer of 2000 following the band Phish on their cross-country tour. That's definitely more likely. But he got married in 2004, which means he probably wasn't burning CDs for my mom in 2006. Less likely.

When I compare the facts, Max number 1 has the most information in the More Likely to Be My Dad category. But does that mean he *is* my dad?

I'm still working on that part.

After school I do the only thing I can think to do—the one

thing I haven't done—and put *NORA* into the CD player. It's the only CD I haven't listened to yet, because I've been waiting for the right time. Upon reflection, I'm not sure there really *is* a right time to get to know your mom through someone else's eyes. Listening has got to be like ripping off a Band-Aid.

I get in bed, pull the comforter over my head, and press play. I'm not listening to enjoy, but to learn. Why did he choose these songs? Were they her favorites? Songs that reminded him of her? Something else entirely? And what do the songs say about their relationship? Maybe he was apologizing or reminiscing or confessing a crush.

Maybe he was saying goodbye.

The opening notes of the first song come through the headphones: mid-tempo alt-rock, I'm guessing late nineties. The intro is cool and aloof—just a little dramatic, like she is. So far so good.

Then the lyrics start, and the plot thickens.

> *Nobody knows it but you've got a secret smile*
> *And you use it only for me.*

Hmm. A secret romance? Maybe *that's* why my mom won't tell me his identity—because nobody else knows either.

The comforter gets yanked off my head, and I scream, because a decaying zombie is standing over me. Then the zombie starts peeling off its skin, and I realize it's my mom, taking off a mask and laughing hysterically.

"You should've seen your face," she gets out between guffaws. She mimics me, widening her eyes and opening her mouth.

"Nice," I say, removing my headphones and sitting up. "Traumatizing your own child. *Really* nice."

She shrugs, pleased with herself. "I thought so." Then she looks at the CD player, and her smile dims.

"I'm listening to *NORA*," I tell her. "You've got a secret smile, and you use it only for him, huh?"

She crosses her arms. "Don't read too much into it, babe."

"Whatever you say."

She ignores me. "Do you need me to give you a ride to the carnival? Or are you going over with Jack?"

"Jack is already there. He had to stay after school to help set up the haunted house."

Every year, Storm Valley hosts a Halloween carnival in the field behind the high school. The festivities are usually limited to things like bobbing for apples, pumpkin ring toss, and— the star attraction—a hay maze. But this year, the boys soccer team is taking it up a notch and hosting a haunted house to raise money for new uniforms to wear to playoffs.

Ever since they qualified, the boys have basically become local celebrities. The whole school—no, the whole *town*—is excited. There are signs everywhere wishing them luck. In the halls at school, in people's yards, in shop windows downtown— their team photo even made it onto a Main Street billboard. Jack seems thrilled about the attention. I'm trying to be thrilled too, but it's hard to share him with the rest of the world. I just want all the *hoopla*—one of Grandma Imogen's favorite words—to be over so I can have my best friend back.

"Gotcha," Mom says, walking toward the door. "In that case, get your costume on and meet me downstairs in ten. I've got a party to get to."

She shuts the door behind her, and I fall back into bed with a groan. I've been so preoccupied with the search for my dad that I forgot to come up with a costume. What can I throw together in ten minutes?

When I get to the haunted house, I can hardly believe my eyes. For the last few weeks, Jack, Serge, and the entire soccer team have been incredibly tight-lipped about their plans, which I just assumed meant they didn't have any. I thought, at best, I'd show up to some oversized cardboard boxes glued together and draped in sheets.

Instead, an inflatable structure looms at the back of the carnival, positioned perfectly in front of the moon. It looks like a haunted house straight out of a storybook—purple brick walls and a black pointy roof, cobwebs in the windows, even an iron fence around the outside. There's a line to get in, and as I approach the back of it, I hear an ear-piercing scream come from somewhere inside.

"Immie!"

I turn my head to see Jack coming through the front door. He's dressed in a lab coat and black gloves, and his already unruly hair has been teased and sprayed to look like a mad scientist who just walked out of an explosion. I feel a flutter of excitement in my chest, like butterflies furiously flapping their wings.

I laugh. "Wow, look at you."

"Look at *you*," he says, smiling. "You're wearing my sweatshirt."

"Oh yeah." I shrug, trying to act casual. "I didn't have a costume, so I thought I'd just be you."

"Well, you failed," he says. "You look nothing like me. Thank goodness."

Before I have time to process what he could possibly mean by "thank goodness," he gestures to the house behind him. "What do you think?"

"I'm impressed," I say. "Really. I didn't know you had it in you."

He crosses his arms triumphantly. "I'm going to choose to take that as a compliment."

Elijah walks by in a long black robe. He's got a scary mask in one hand and a corn dog in the other. "Picasso," he says with a smile and a nod.

I roll my eyes. Jack's smile falters.

"Picasso?"

I shake my head. "It's just what he calls me."

He snorts. "Well, isn't that adorable."

I look at him, curious. Do I detect a hint of jealousy?

"You should be careful," he says, his voice flat.

"Careful about what? He's just being friendly."

He gives me a Look. "Really."

All of a sudden it seems extremely important that Jack knows I'm telling the truth. "It's not like that."

"Mm." He nods. "Whatever you say."

Three girls leave the haunted house, and the line moves forward. They walk past Jack, exchange glances, and giggle.

"Why do you care, anyway?" I ask before I can stop myself. "I *don't* like him, but if I did, why would it matter to you?"

I expect him to use his power of veto, the way he's always done before. Instead, he says, "It doesn't matter," and I'm taken aback.

Why *not*?

An awkward silence hangs in the air. These have been happening more and more lately. I blame soccer. The Jack I know would make some kind of joke out of it, but *this* Jack has been so busy with his teammates that it's like he forgets how to talk to me sometimes.

We get to the front of the line, where Serge, dressed like the Joker, is working the cash box. Zoya is behind him, sitting on a bale of hay and scrolling her phone. The light from her screen illuminates her drawn-on whiskers and bunny-ear headband.

"Hello, Imogen." Serge smiles mischievously. "Ready to be terrified?"

"I'm looking forward to it." I hand him a five-dollar bill.

"Watch out for the guy hiding in the toy box," Zoya says with an edge in her voice. "He made me spill my Frappuccino."

We step through the front door—into the *foyer*—where there's an inflatable chandelier, an old wardrobe, and a rickety-looking chair. Everything is covered in cobwebs. It takes a moment for my eyes to adjust, and I realize there's a giant spider hanging from the ceiling.

"Nice touch," I say, looking up at it.

The wardrobe opens slowly with a creak, and someone with a Ghostface mask wiggles their fingers at me from inside. I take a step closer to Jack, my heart pumping with adrenaline.

"Remember the haunted house we went through last year?" My voice cuts through the quiet.

"How could I forget?" He pushes his hair out of his face and smiles. "The executioner touched your arm, and you told him off in the middle of the torture chamber."

"No," I correct. "I simply reminded him that actors weren't supposed to touch the guests, and that if he didn't knock it off, I had grounds to sue."

He chuckles. "I'm pretty sure you made him cry."

"Good. Consider it karmic justice."

We pass through the doorway into the next room. The walls are inflatable, but the rooms have all been filled with real furniture.

"Where did you get *this*?" I point at a large golden mirror with a crack down the middle.

"The junkyard," he says proudly. "Ben took his dad's pickup truck, and a few of us went scavenging. Pretty cool, huh?"

"Yeah." I try not to feel bothered by the fact that this is the first I'm hearing of it. "Sounds like fun."

He snorts.

"What?"

He bats at a toy spider hanging from a string, and I have to dodge out of the way so it doesn't hit me. "Your words said fun, but your tone implied root canal."

I scoff. "My tone? What is this, an interrogation room?"

"Actually. . ." He gestures to the bookcases. "It's supposed to be a study."

I roll my eyes. "Funny."

The next room is a baby's room, complete with the toy box Zoya mentioned and an old, scratched-up crib that's definitely haunted.

I walk right over to the toy box and open the lid. "Gotcha!"

But the chest is empty. I turn back to Jack. "Huh."

That's when a figure jumps out from behind the door, wearing a pink, blood-stained dress and a mask that looks like a scary doll. I scream, recoiling into Jack.

"Yes!" The scary doll shakes his fist in the air. "That's ten screams. Nick owes me five bucks. Marshall, you're my witness." Then he runs off, presumably to find Nick and rub his nose in it.

I look down at my hand, which has somehow ended up in Jack's.

"Oh," I blurt out, letting go of him. My heart is pounding, but not from the fear. "Sorry, I—"

Jack stops me. He grabs my hand again and intertwines his fingers with mine, giving them a little squeeze.

"It's okay," he says, giving me a small smile. All of a sudden, the lyrics to the first song on *NORA* pop into my head: *you've got a secret smile, and you use it only for me.* "Right?"

When we were kids, we used to hold hands all the time—crossing the street, jumping on Jack's trampoline, running through the woods—and then middle school happened. All of a sudden, holding hands meant something different. Something more.

I don't remember the last time Jack and I held hands, but I know it didn't feel like this. *This* feels like sparks—no, like fireworks. *No.* Like heat and light themselves are emanating from the space between our palms.

Maybe it's just because I've missed him, but it definitely feels like more.

I want to ask Jack what it all means—we've been friends for seven years and now we're holding hands in a haunted house and I feel all warm and fuzzy inside, sort of like how I feel when I find a new taxidermy butterfly, only better, and *tinglier*, but it's also a little weird, like I'm Eve eating the forbidden fruit, like it's wrong and right at the same time, and it makes me feel excited and dangerous and alive, and does he know what I mean? Does he feel it too? Is this the start of something new?

"Right," I reply.

And then we walk, hand in hand, out of the haunted baby's room.

We wind up in a hallway lined with creepy, old-timey portraits. The portraits have eyes that seem to follow us, but they don't scare me. Right now, my heart is beating so fast that it feels like *nothing* could scare me.

Something moves at the end of the hallway. One of the portraits is coming to life—two guys on the soccer team, dressed in shirts with frilly collars and coated in paint, lean out of the frame like they're going to crawl right through it. But when they see Jack, they immediately start ragging on him for being on a date, and Jack drops my hand. He tells them—quite forcefully, if you ask me—that I'm *not* his girlfriend and then storms off.

I glare at his teammates. "Breaking character? Real mature. You *will* be hearing about this in my Google review."

I catch up with Jack in the next room, but we're silent for the rest of the haunted house, and there is decidedly no hand-holding or even the casual touching of two humans sharing the same space. He's so distant that you'd think I'd caught the bubonic plague or something. When we finally walk out into the chilly autumn air, I stop and turn to him.

"Jack."

Maybe I'm feeling fragile from the jump scares and emotional roller coaster we just went on, or maybe I'm just done dancing around things, but I blurt out, "I miss the way things used to be. Back when we could disappear under the tree for hours, and nobody would care."

Jack looks surprised for a second, but then his brown eyes soften, dropping their guard. "Yeah. Me too," he says. "But at least we can disappear next weekend. You're still coming to the cabin, right?"

Jack's family is taking a trip to their cabin upstate, and they invited me to come along. I've been to the cabin like a dozen times before, but for some reason, this trip feels more significant. It will be the first time since high school started that Jack and I will get to spend all weekend together.

Serge walks up to us, shining a flashlight under his chin. "Muahahaha!" he bellows in a deep voice. "Jack Marshall and Imogen Meadows, your time is up." He drops the flashlight. "Seriously, though, Jack. Break is over."

Jack turns to me. "Sorry. I get another break in an hour. I'll come find you then?"

I nod and he walks away. I feel that same hollow ache in my chest as when he let go of my hand in the hall. Not long ago, he wouldn't have to walk away from me at all. We'd leave this house, go get some caramel apples, maybe do the hay maze, and then carpool home, knowing that the next day would be more of the same. In that story there would be nothing—not soccer or high school or even time itself—that could tear us apart.

For a while after he's gone, I stand there as people come and go from the haunted house.

I hear Zoya's voice at the soccer game: *What's up with you and Jack?*

I hear Elijah's voice at homecoming: *You and Marshall. Is there something there?*

I hear Hannah's voice in art class: *There was some serious heat between you two.*

They were right. This whole time, they were right.

I, Imogen Marie Meadows, am crushing hard on my best friend.

"Sparks"—Coldplay

After you told me you liked this song, I listened to it over and over. I thought maybe you were trying to tell me something. Especially after what happened in the cabin.

*E*arly Saturday morning, a week after the Halloween carnival, I toss my overnight bag into the trunk of the Marshall family minivan and climb into the last row with Carrie and Carter. Jack sits in the middle row with Marigold and Noah, and his parents are up front. Jack glances back at me and smiles his secret smile.

All week at school, I've been searching for that smile, dissecting it, trying to figure out if it could mean what I think it means. Does Jack like me as more than friends too? Or were the sparks I felt in the haunted house all in my head? Maybe Jack only held my hand because I screamed, and he wanted to comfort me the way any good friend would.

I've been looking for a sign one way or another—watching him across the room in social studies, brushing arms in the hallway to see what he'll do, even asking him his opinions on other single girls in school (*Vanessa looks pretty today, doesn't she? Isn't Ellory Adams so funny?)*—but so far, I've gotten a whole lot of nothing from him. And until I get *something*, there's no way I'm telling him how I feel. It's humiliating, how obsessive I'm becoming. It's like I'm turning into Zoya.

"Why not just tell him?" Hannah said in art class yesterday, right after I told her the truth and made her promise not to say a word to anyone—*especially* Zoya.

"Because," I said, in the middle of painting a still life of plants on the windowsill. "Telling him is going to change everything, whether or not he feels the same way. I'm not sure I'm ready for that yet."

"Girl, you like him. Everything already has changed," Hannah replied. "You can't hide how you feel forever." Then she dipped her paintbrush into the cerulean blue I mixed myself, smearing a little red in it.

"Actually," I said darkly. "You can."

I spend the two-hour drive to the cabin listening to my dad's CDs. I know all the songs by heart, so I skip around based on which ones best match the vibe. Every now and then I give the CD player to Jack so he can hear my favorites.

At one point, he takes off the headphones mid-song. "I don't really like this one."

I put the left headphone up to my ear and gasp. "What? Jack, 'How's It Going to Be' is a masterpiece."

He shrugs. "It's just too angsty."

One song he really likes is "Sparks" by Coldplay—he likes it so much, I catch him listening to it on his phone. I lean forward so my lips are by his ear. The music plays softly: *"My heart is yours, it's you that I hold on to . . ."*

"Third Eye Blind is too angsty, but this song isn't?"

"It's not angsty," he says, removing an earbud from one ear. "It's emotional."

When we get to the cabin, two other cars are already there. Elise, Jack's eldest sister, and her fiancé, Brad, drove up last night from Philly. Michael, Jack's older brother, came from Penn State with his roommate. Carrie discovers Garth, the roommate, when he and Michael come to help us bring our bags inside, and she throws a fit.

"You guys wouldn't let me bring Lucy, but you let Michael bring *Garth*?" she says in disbelief, her hands on her hips.

"Uh, duh," Michael says. "Garth is way more fun. Can Lucy identify forty-seven different kinds of birdcalls?" He hefts her suitcase out of the trunk and throws it at her feet.

I look at Jack, eyebrows raised. "Can Garth?"

Behind him, Garth cups his hands over his mouth and tilts his head back, making a birdcall into the sky.

"Garth is his friend," Deb says. "They're not dating each other."

Carrie stands her bag upright and lifts the handle. "He could be. You didn't know when I first got together with Lucy."

Michael starts making kissy faces at Garth, who pretends to swoon.

Frank hands Jack his bag. "No girlfriends."

I don't know why, but hearing him say it in such a definitive tone makes my pulse quicken. I'm not Jack's girlfriend, but if I ever were, does that mean I'd be disinvited from these cabin

112

trips? And what other Marshall family gatherings would I have to give up?

Carrie scoffs. "Brad's here!"

"Brad is your sister's fiancé, Carrie," Deb says. "He's like family."

"But Immie's here!"

I suck in a breath and glance at Jack.

"Immie is family," Deb says. She puts an arm around me and gives me a little squeeze, and I really hope she can't feel how fast my heart is beating. "Now stop it, Carrie. You can survive two days without Lucy."

"This is so unfair." Carrie grabs the handle of her suitcase and storms off, struggling to drag the wheels over the stones.

We empty the bags out of the car and go inside, where Elise and Brad are making breakfast. The smell of eggs and bacon wafts through the cabin and makes my stomach grumble.

"Carrie, Carter, Immie, Jack, you've got the bunk beds," Deb says. "Michael and Garth have the couch, Elise and Brad are in the guest room, and the twins are with us." She nods, responding to herself. "Great. Everyone's got somewhere to sleep."

I follow Jack and Carter to the bunk bedroom. We walk in to find Carrie's stuff splayed out over the bottom bunk on the left side. Carter turns to look at us. "Usual spots?"

"Sounds good to me," Jack says, lying down on the other bottom bunk. I toss my bag on the bed above his, climb up the wooden ladder, and collapse on top of the quilt. I stay quiet, listening for the sound of Jack's breathing.

We eat breakfast until we're stuffed, and afterward, Michael says he wants to go fishing. Jack, being a chronic Michael-pleaser, agrees to go along.

"You hate fishing," I say to him when we're alone in the bedroom. Tina is in my arms, purring while I give her gentle pats. I don't want him to go, but I don't want to *tell* him that either, so I'm grasping at straws.

"No I don't," he says, booping Tina on the nose with his finger. She opens her eyes wide, like a warning, and then slowly closes them again. "Come with. You don't have to fish."

I shake my head. "If I see a fish get pulled up on a hook, I'll start crying."

He chuckles. "It's cute how much you love animals. Even gross ones like fish and bugs."

"Especially bugs," I say, though my brain is repeating the word "cute" on an endless loop. Cute. But cute like, *friend* cute, or crush cute? I'm already tiring myself out with all this over-thinking.

When I sigh, he raises his eyebrows, looks at me curiously. "You okay?"

"Oh yeah," I say, trying to sound upbeat. "Totally, totally fine."

I force a smile. It's going to be a long weekend.

After dinner, I follow Jack into the living room, where a few of his siblings, plus Garth, are hanging out. I take a seat on the couch next to Carrie. Jack sits on the floor by my feet.

"You guys playing?" Carrie says. She's leaning over the coffee table, setting up a murder mystery game. "It's up to eight players."

"Definitely," I say. "I love games like this."

"Look out," Michael says to Garth. He's leaning over the fireplace, stoking a small flame with a poker. "Immie's way competitive."

I put a hand over my chest, feigning offense. "I am not!"

They all get a good laugh out of that.

"Remember when she broke Boggle?" Carrie says, shuffling cards. "And that thing was *indestructible*."

"Or when she cracked that vase with the Yahtzee dice?" Carter adds, looking up from their phone.

"I once saw her hit a mini-golf ball into the clown's mouth from four holes away," Jack says. "We didn't get a free game, though. We got kicked out."

I hold up my hands. "I'll be a good sport this time, I swear."

Carrie explains the rules of the game: We're at a Regency dinner party, and one of us is a murderer. We have to strategically form alliances and share information until someone correctly guesses who the murderer is. Players will be randomly murdered throughout the game. If you're murdered, you lose. If you guess wrong, you lose. The winner is the last person standing.

"Yes." I bounce eagerly in my seat and rub my hands together. "Let's go."

On the other side of the coffee table, Garth scootches away from me.

"Okay, then." Carrie shuffles the envelopes marked CONFIDENTIAL and passes them out to us randomly. I open mine and sigh—I'm the Countess Druann VanDerseps, wife of the count. I wanted to be the murderer.

I peek over at Jack and see that he's the count. I smile to myself. Jack is my *husband*. Is this a sign?

The game starts with some casual dinner party conversation. I learn basic information about everyone, like Elise is a potato farmer with three children, and Michael is a retired detective. When it's my turn, I tell them I'm Jack's wife, and everybody laughs. Everybody except Jack.

"Aw gross." Jack leans away from me like he's physically repulsed.

I frown at him. "Gross? I'm not *gross*." I nudge him with my foot. "Jerk."

"I didn't say *you* were gross," Jack replies, not quite looking at me. "I said being married to you would be gross."

"That's not better," Carter mutters.

"Oh yeah?" I cross my arms. Before I realize what's coming out of my mouth, I blurt out, "I bet *Elijah* wouldn't think it's gross."

Jack stiffens slightly. He looks down at his cards. "Good one. Is it my turn?"

At the first sign of gossip, Carrie's face lights up. "Elijah Whitehouse? What's happening with you and Elijah?"

"Oh, nothing," I say, feeling smug. "But he asked me to homecoming, and—"

"He *did*?" Carrie practically gapes. "And you turned him down to go with my blockhead brother?"

"Elijah would ask a trash can to homecoming if he thought he'd get something out of it," Jack mutters, aggressively shuffling his cards.

"What does *that* mean?"

"Nothing," Jack says. "My turn. I own—"

"No, no," I interrupt him, angry now. "First you said I was gross, and now you're comparing me to garbage."

"No I'm not."

"You kinda are," Elise agrees.

"I'm *not*." Jack groans. "I'm saying . . ." He drifts off, looks at me with pleading eyes. "I'm saying I don't like him, okay?"

"Since when?" Jack told me about all the extra practices he's been doing with Elijah to improve his game. "You said he's a good soccer player. That he was helping you work on your passing."

"He was," Jack says. "And that's exactly my point. He thinks, because he's older and cooler, that he can do whatever he wants. *With* whoever he wants."

"He's hot." Carrie shrugs. "It tends to happen."

"And also, his soccer cleats are this obnoxious neon yellow color. We have all-black cleats, but he just *has* to have the brightest pair on the turf."

"Okay, now it sounds like you're jealous," Carrie says.

My breath catches in my throat. Jealous? Is it possible? Next to her, Carter laughs.

Jack rolls his eyes. "Are you done?"

Carrie smiles innocently. "For now."

He turns to me. "I'm sorry, okay? I didn't mean to say you were gross garbage. Really. You're the opposite of that."

I nod. I still feel stung, but I don't want to harp on it anymore. Not in front of his older siblings, who love to tease him.

Jack sighs, looks at his card, and starts to read. "I own a newspaper in London famous for its sensationalism. Recent headlines have splashed my wife—" He glances at me. "My wife's name about because of . . . her affair."

"Oof," Michael says in a goofy, old-timey accent. "You're a dirty cheatah, Countess."

"Of *course* I had to cheat," I say. "I have a husband who thinks I'm gross garbage!"

"No," Jack says. "You have a husband who thinks you're dramatic."

"It's not dramatic. *You're* a love murderer!"

Jack laughs. "Are you seriously accusing me of being the murderer before the first round is even over?"

"No. That's not—"

"It sounded like an accusation to *me*," Carrie says.

"Me too." Michael smirks. "Immie's out."

My jaw drops. "What?"

"Wait," Jack says. "I—"

"I wasn't accusing him! This is sabotage!"

"Sorry, Immie," Carrie says. "Be more careful with your words next time."

"Look." Elise picks up a card and shows it to us. "You would've died at the end of this round anyway."

"Ugh!" I toss my cards up in the air, and they rain down across the coffee table.

"There she blows," Carter mumbles. I shoot them a glare and stand up.

"You're all working against me because you're afraid I'm going to beat you, and it's *sick*," I say, walking away. "You're sick people."

"Aw, Immie, don't be like that," Michael calls out after me. "You can't win every time."

"YO." Jack has his hands around his mouth like a megaphone. "Immie's right. I'm the murderer."

I stop in my tracks. "Seriously?"

He nods.

I smile wide. "Ha! Take that, suckers!"

"Liar," Carrie says to Jack. "You're just protecting your girlfriend."

My smile falls.

"Shut up," Jack says to her.

"Ooh, sensitive subject?" Carrie sneers. "So what, you guys kiss or something?"

"No," he says.

I cross my arms, hoping nobody can hear the rapid beating of my heart. "And you say I'm the sore loser, Carrie?"

"I didn't lie, anyway," Jack says. "Check my cards." He puts them in the envelope and throws it at her like a Frisbee. The corner of the envelope collides with her cheek.

"Ow!" She puts her hand on her face. When she pulls it away, there's a speck of red on her finger. "You psychopath. You made me bleed!"

"Oh god, Carrie," Michael groans. "I think you'll survive."

She gets up from the couch and runs out of the room. Jack and Michael exchange a glance. "Luce," I hear Carrie's voice echo from the bathroom. "I hate my stupid family, I want to—" Her voice cuts off when she slams the door.

We all look at each other, unsure what to do.

"That was fun," Garth says, nodding. "Let's play again."

I wake up in the middle of the night and can't fall back asleep. I lie in the dark for a while, self-conscious about every single breath I take, until I hear someone rustling around in the kitchen. As quietly as I can, I climb down the bunk bed ladder. That's when I notice Jack isn't in his bed. Tina is in his place, sprawled out on top of the covers, paws twitching in her sleep. I tiptoe across the creaky wooden floor and out of the bedroom.

Jack is standing over the sink, putting water in the electric teakettle. I can hear the music coming through his headphones even though he's all the way across the room.

"Sorry," he says, pulling his earbuds out of his ears. His T-shirt and flannel pants are rumpled, his hair messy from sleep. "Did I wake you up?"

"No." I shake my head. "I was up. Are you making tea?"

"Hot chocolate. You want one?"

"Okay," I say. "Thanks."

I move to the island and sit at one of the bar stools, watching him get another mug from the cabinet and fill it with hot chocolate mix. When he's done, he leans into the counter. I breathe in the piney scent of the bodywash he used during his shower after the board game debacle. When I realize I've closed my eyes, I fake a cough so he doesn't think I'm a total weirdo for huffing his boy smell. That's not something Friend Immie would do.

"You're wearing my sweatshirt," he says casually. I can't tell if he's bothered that I still haven't given it back.

"It's comfortable," I say, running my fingers through my hair. "That's the only reason."

"Well, I'm glad it's being put to good use."

I laugh awkwardly. I don't know what he means by that, and it's awful, not knowing. It's completely unfamiliar.

The electric teakettle beeps. Jack picks it up and fills our mugs with water, then grabs two spoons and a bag of mini marshmallows. As he moves around the kitchen, I notice his shoulders—have they always been so broad? And since when has his jawline looked so defined? He's always been cute—like a puppy, or a rosy maple moth—but tonight, cute doesn't seem to do him justice.

All of a sudden, Jack is *hot*. Better-than-Jacob-Elordi hot.

We relocate to the living room. It's dark, but dim orange embers still glow in the fireplace. I sit down on the couch while Jack picks up a couple of fresh logs from the basket and adds them to the stack.

"So." He picks up a knitted blanket and sits down next to me on the couch. "Are you still mad at me?"

"Yes," I say immediately, stirring the hot chocolate mixture until it thickens. "You called me gross."

"Outie, you know I don't think you're gross," he says. "I was just being dumb."

I shake my head. I don't know what he thinks about me

anymore. I know I should drop this—it was a *game* after all—and yet I can't. "But *why?*"

He picks up his mug and starts stirring the spoon, clinking it against the sides. I think he's doing it so he doesn't have to look me in the eye.

Jack offers me some of the blanket, and I scooch closer to him, careful not to spill my drink. His leg is warm against mine, and even though I'm feeling grumpy, I have to resist the urge to snuggle closer.

"I'm sorry," he finally says, and I can tell, by the way he tries to meet my eyes, that he means it. "I really am."

I pick up the bag of mini marshmallows and pour some into my mug until they cover the hot chocolate like a fluffy duvet. It's an apology but not an explanation, and I'm about to keep pushing when I realize: this is the longest we've been alone all day. I don't want to waste time fighting.

"You're off the hook this time, but you better watch yourself, punk," I say, letting it go. I shift in my seat and pull the blanket up to my chest. "I hope your siblings don't hate me for ruining the game."

"They could never. They love you," he says, and then adds, "And I do too."

I chuckle and lean into him. He's talking about friend love, about family love, and I wonder if this could be enough for me. "Duh." I say, noticing how warm his body feels underneath the blanket. "I know that much."

"I don't think you do."

I look up. The expression on his face is serious, dimly lit by the glow of the fire. I feel a shiver run down my spine, but it's not from the cold.

"Jack," I blurt out. "Why did you hold my hand in the haunted house?"

I'm so close to him that I can feel his heart beating. It's a relief to know it's going just as fast as mine.

"Because." He's looking away from me, but his voice is soft. "I wanted to."

"Why?"

Jack seems to consider for a moment. And then, with no warning, he puts his hot chocolate down on the coffee table. When he turns back to me, he reaches out and brushes my hair out of my face. Instead of dropping his hand, like he'd usually do, his hand lingers on my cheek and then moves to the back of my neck.

I freeze.

I've never been kissed before, but I've seen enough romance movies to have an idea of how it's supposed to go. But this is me. And that's Jack. Is this really happening?

Before my brain can figure it out, my body takes over, I close my eyes, and—

"You are so busted."

We jump apart, and I spill my hot chocolate all over Jack's sweatshirt. I look up, stunned.

Carrie is standing in the doorway with one hand on her hip and a smug look on her face.

TRACK TWELVE

"Paper Bag"—Fiona Apple

My feelings were clear, but yours were more confusing than ever. The search for my dad was a welcome distraction.

When I get home from the cabin the next night, I shut myself in my room with my laptop, determined to figure out if Max number 1 is my real dad once and for all. I need a distraction from thinking about Jack.

Last night, after Carrie interrupted our . . . what?—almost kiss?—she went into the kitchen, and Jack ran after her without a word. I sat there for a minute in Jack's sweatshirt, covered in hot chocolate, listening to the muffled sounds of their voices in the other room. I kept waiting for him to come back and tell me that everything was going to be okay, to reassure me that what happened between us—or, what almost happened— wasn't a mistake. That he felt it too. He liked me too.

But he didn't. In fact, he didn't come back at all. And when I woke up this morning, his bed was already empty. All day, I felt like he was avoiding me. The one time I managed to get him alone—in the living room, while Carrie went to the bathroom during a commercial—he spent the whole time texting in his group chat. If it weren't for the giant stain on his sweatshirt, I might have started to wonder if last night was just a dream.

I spend a couple of hours scouring the internet, looking for fatherly clues. A lot of what I find is promising: Max number 1 and my mom lived in New York at the same time. He's liked the Facebook pages of a lot of the bands featured on the CDs. And, thanks to Max's Facebook friend Krista, there's an old, tagged picture of Max number 1 and my mom, who is *not* tagged, at a party—*kissing*. There's no denying that this is the Max she told Kristen Robertson about—that they were together.

But is he my dad?

I open up Google and type in Max number 1's full name, then start scrolling the results to see if anything new has come up since the last time I looked. It's all the same headlines—Facebook and LinkedIn profiles, yellow pages, obituaries—and after a while, my eyes start to glaze over.

I pick up my phone and type out a new message to Jack.

Immie: I feel kinda weird about the way we left things. I thought something was happening and then Carrie came in and screwed everything up, and you haven't really talked to me since then, and now I just feel confused. So what's the deal? Do you like me or?????

I read the message back and cringe. There's no way I'm sending that. I delete it all and try again.

Immie: Hey. I know you're prob going to be busy this week because of playoffs, but if you have a free minute maybe we could talk? In the tree, like old times.

I press send, then fall back on my bed and stare at the ceiling. A song from *NORA* is playing through my laptop speakers—"Paper Bag" by Fiona Apple. The lyrics, like practically everything else these days, remind me of Jack. *"Hunger hurts and I want him so bad..."*

I haven't been to the tree in weeks. Maybe even months. We used to hang out there almost every single day, even when it rained or snowed, and my mom would have to drag us into the house. It's weird how something can be such a huge part of your life, and then one day, without even realizing, it becomes part of your past.

My phone buzzes with Jack's signature vibration. I sit up so fast it makes my head spin.

Jack: Idk if I'll have time

I stare at the screen. I wonder if he'll have time for me again after soccer season is over, or if this is how it's always going to be from now on, seeing him every now and then, whenever he can squeeze me in.

My phone buzzes again.

Jack: But I'll let you know ☺

Half an hour later, I'm lying at the end of my bed, upside down, with my head hanging over the side and my palms touching the carpet. My eyes are closed for maximum concentration. I'm listening to my dad's CDs, thinking about what I know of him for sure. I know he was in my mom's life in the early 2000s. I know he had great taste in music.

And, I realize with a jolt, as "Fight Test" starts to play through my headphones, I know he and my mom went to a Flaming Lips concert together on Halloween. *Right after the album came out,* she said. "The album" must mean *Yoshimi Battles the Pink Robots.* But when did it come out?

I flip my legs over my head and kind of cartwheel off my bed, landing on my knees with a thud. My mom yells from downstairs, "You okay?"

I run to my door, open it a crack. "Yeah!" I reply, and then close it just as fast. I hurry to the bed to pick up my phone so I can look up the album. *Yoshimi Battles the Pink Robots,* release date: July 16, 2002.

"Two thousand two," I say to no one. If Max number 1 is my dad, he was at this concert.

Veins coursing with adrenaline, I open up my laptop and log into Kristen Robertson's account. I have three new friend requests from my mom's mutuals, and I accept them just because.

Max number 1 is still in my recent searches. I go to his profile and start to type out a message.

Kristen Robertson: Hi there. You don't know me, but we have a mutual friend.

I'm hoping you can help me figure something out. Were you at the Flaming Lips concert in New York City on Halloween in 2002?

I take a deep breath, trying to calm my racing heart. I read over the message once, then two more times. It's as good as it's going to get, but still, I hesitate. After I send this message, there's no going back. What if he *is* my dad? What if he *isn't*? Things are going to change either way.

I press send. And I wait.

"My Number"—Tegan and Sara

The world came crashing down, and you broke your promise when I needed you the most. I don't know if I'll ever forgive you for that.

Can I heat up these Bagel Bites?" Zoya says, looking through my freezer after school on Friday. "I'm, like, starving."

"Make some for me, too," Alex says, eyes closed. Hannah is painting her lids with glittery green eye shadow, her makeup spread out all over the kitchen table. I've got my getting-ready playlist on, and a song by Tegan and Sara is blasting through the speaker. *"Promise me you'll never go away, promise me you'll always stay..."*

"Just make the whole bag," I say. When I told my mom the girls were coming over after school to get ready for the soccer game, she went out and bought enough snacks to feed us, plus Jack, plus the rest of the soccer team, including JV. I told her she went way overboard, but she didn't care. She was just excited I had new friends to feed. "Hey, I'm going upstairs really quick, to change."

"Change into what?" Hannah says, focusing on Alex's left eye. "Aren't we all wearing our sweatshirts with turtlenecks underneath?"

"Yes." I roll my eyes at the fact that Hannah wants us to dress the same. "But my sweatshirt is upstairs. Be right back."

By *my* sweatshirt, I actually mean Jack's sweatshirt, but I don't want to tell them that and then have it turn into a whole thing. In an hour, Jack and the rest of the team will face the Sugar Hill Falcons in the semifinal round of playoffs. If they win, then it's hello, finals. I want Jack to know that—even though he never texted me back about a time to talk—I support him. Maybe seeing me wear it will give him a confidence boost.

When I walk into my room, I hear a plinking noise coming from my laptop, and my heart nearly stops.

I have a new message.

I run to my desk, fumble twice typing in my password. I get it on the third try, and my eyes go wide. *There it is.*

It took five days, but Max number 1 has finally responded.

Max number 1: Hi, Kristen. Flaming Lips/Beck? No, I was not at that show. I wanted to go but tix sold out! Think I ended up going to a metal show at Rough Trade instead, ha.

Max number 1: Why do you ask?

It's hard to describe the feeling that washes over me. Disappointment? Maybe a little. Embarrassment? Definitely. And something else, too—something like relief. Nothing against Max number 1, it just never really felt like he was my dad. I know it doesn't make sense, but I just have this idea that when I see my real dad, something will click.

129

The computer plinks again. Another message from Max.

Max number 1: I see you're friends with Nora. Is this the "mutual friend" you were talking about?

I consider my options. I could close out of this conversation right now, but then I'd be back to square one in this whole investigation. *Or . . .* I could see if he knows anything.

Kristen Robertson: Yes, I am friends with Nora. A group of us went to that show together and I was trying to remember the name of the guy she was with. I know you two went out around that time. Thought it might have been you ☺

Max number 1: Sadly, not me. Maybe Jax, or Rob, if he was in town.

Rob. The name is like a light bulb in my brain. I open up my chat with my mom and scroll up. There it is: Who, Rob?

She said they broke up, so I didn't give him another thought. Why would she date Max after Rob, but use Rob as a sperm donor?

Kristen Robertson: Oh right, Rob. He was her ex?

Max number 1: Yes, I forgot about that. They dated in high school.

Max number 1: They were just good buddies when Nora and I went out. He'd stay with us when he wasn't touring.

Kristen Robertson: Touring?

Max number 1: He played guitar for a bunch of bands. One of them even took off for a little while.

Kristen Robertson: Which one?

Max number 1: Honeydust

Honeydust.

Why does that sound familiar?

I close my eyes. I picture words, bouncy and bright. I picture sunshine on faded cotton.

Then I open my eyes with a gasp.

I leave my computer on my desk and walk briskly to my mom's room—she won't be back from work for at least another half hour. Downstairs, I hear the microwave beep, hear Zoya call my name. I ignore it all, making a beeline for Mom's dresser, searching through the drawers where she keeps her T-shirts. I find what I'm looking for in the middle drawer, all the way at the bottom. A faded yellow shirt with the word "honeydust" across the front in psychedelic letters, on top of a neon sun. On the back, a list of tour dates, starting in June 2004.

"Oh my god," I say, feeling breathless as I hold it in my hands. I saw this shirt the first day I searched Mom's room, but she has a lot of old band T-shirts, so I just lumped it in with all the others. I had no way of knowing it would be the key to everything.

I take the shirt back to my room and sit down at my desk. I exit out of my conversation with Max number 1 and open a new tab. In the search bar, I type *honeydust rob*.

The first thing that pops up is the band's Wikipedia page, which has a list of touring members. *Rob Stanley, guitar*. I immediately search his name.

There are two photos at the top of the page. The first is a group photo that looks like it was taken in the early 2000s. Three men and two women, probably in their late twenties, are arranged on a street corner, all looking at the camera. My attention is drawn to the guy on the far left, to his straight black hair and long, wiry frame. Things about him seem familiar: the shape of his eyes, the soft slope of his brow, even, weirdly, the apples of his cheeks. I don't know why, but it scares me.

The second photo is a portrait of him. He's older—his hair is shorter, his face a little sharper—but looking at his eyes still feels like looking in a mirror. He's smiling at the camera with his mouth open, like whoever took the picture caught him on the verge of laughter. I look at the two photos side by side, and I think, *This makes sense.*

There he is. My dad.

I hover my mouse over the first photo to check the source: honeydust's Wikipedia page. The band even took off for a little while. I wonder what Max meant by that. I hover over the second photo, which links to the website for my mom's hometown newspaper.

I click.

The first thing I see, at the top of the page, is *OBITUARIES*. The second thing is my dad's picture.

The room goes still.

I hear a sound, like a high-pitched ringing, that wipes every single thought from my head. I scroll down the page on autopilot. The article was posted in April of last year.

I start to read.

ROBERT E. STANLEY, 45, passed away peacefully on Wednesday at his home in Brooklyn, NY. He was born on March 3, 1979, in West Mifflin, PA, and was a 1997 graduate of Valley View High School. He was a masterful guitar player who spent most of his career touring with a variety of rock bands all around the world and will be remembered for his many contributions to the music community.

It takes me a while to read the whole thing; the words keep getting jumbled together. I learn that he is survived by his wife and stepson, two sisters, and both of his parents. I learn that his passion was helping others achieve their dreams in the arts. I learn that he had a generous and loving heart. That he will be missed by all who knew him.

I scroll back up to his picture. The longer I look at it, the more his face morphs into mine, until I can no longer unsee the resemblance between us, and I have to look away. This is my dad, even though it doesn't say so in his obituary. This is my dad, and he's dead. I don't know how I'm supposed to feel.

"Immie?" Hannah calls out from the bottom of the steps. "Do you have any makeup remover? Alex sneezed and got eye shadow on her forehead."

I close my laptop, hide the honeydust shirt under my bed. If there's a time for grieving, it's not now.

The sky is spitting mist when we get to the game. Still, the bleachers are packed, and we have to climb all the way to the top to find empty seats. I use the sleeve of Jack's sweatshirt to wipe the seat dry, but when I sit down, my butt immediately feels damp through my jeans. I grit my teeth. It's going to be a long, cold couple of hours.

"Glad we did our makeup for *this*," Zoya says bitterly. She's trying and failing to cover her head with her arms.

She and Alex decide to go look for ponchos in Alex's dad's office. As they leave the stadium, the soccer team emerges from the locker room, huddled together with long sleeves on under their jerseys. Jack is at the back of the pack, keeping his head down. Around me, the crowd woos and roars with applause.

"You okay?" Hannah nudges me. "You've been quiet."

I look down at the ground. I don't know how to answer. Nothing in my life has changed, and yet, everything feels different. An hour ago, I thought I had a dad out there somewhere, living his life, listening to nineties alt-rock, and maybe, just maybe, thinking of me. Now I know I don't. I'll never meet him, never get to know him, never send him links to my favorite songs. And maybe I *wouldn't* have, anyway, but still. It was a possibility.

"I don't know," I say finally. "It's about—"

I stop before I finish the sentence. Once I say the words, they're out there. I can't take them back. Hannah will be the first one I've told, when Jack didn't even know that I was looking for my dad. Really looking for him. That shouldn't feel like a betrayal, not when Jack has been ditching me like he has been, but it does.

The ref blows his whistle, and the game begins. "Nothing, I'll tell you later," I say.

I scan the crowd below until I see Jack's parents—or, the backs of their heads. Next to Frank, I notice a blonder, shaggier head of hair. *Michael.* He must've driven down from Penn State to surprise Jack.

It doesn't take long for Sugar Hill to score the first goal. I hardly notice when the ball hits the net. The spotlights through the misty rain create a foglike effect on the field, making it hard to see what's happening anywhere. There's a part of me that's glad Jack isn't playing. This whole thing seems like a broken bone waiting to happen.

Alex and Zoya come back with ten minutes left in the first half.

"Where *were* you?" Hannah says, snatching the poncho from Alex's outstretched arm. I take one too, even though it's kind of pointless. My sweatshirt is soaking wet.

"Sorry." Alex sits down next to me. "It took forever to find them."

"Also, we stopped at the snack bar." Zoya holds up a bag. "Twizzler?"

Hannah, sliding the poncho over her head, frowns at her.

Just then the rain takes its first victim. One of the juniors who gave Jack a hard time about holding my hand in the haunted house slips, lands on his arm, and lets out a wail. They pause the game until they're sure nothing's broken. And then—

"Jack's going in!" Alex says excitedly—a little *too* excitedly.

He runs onto the field, and my heart does a nervous little leap in my chest. For a moment, I almost don't recognize him. Where's the gangly boy next door who ate shredded cheese by the handful and spent hours watching me read? This boy looks confident, more mature, like he's got the crowd wrapped around his finger and the whole world at his feet. I feel a surge of longing for him, followed closely by a wave of fear. The soccer season is almost done. After that, what's going to happen to us? Our friendship was forged in the dark, watching movies with the curtains drawn or hiding out in our place beneath the tree. With all these spotlights shining on him, will he still be able to see me?

"Not the Same"—Ben Folds

Nothing was the same after that.

"Well," Hannah says while we wait outside the stadium. "That was a bummer."

The boys lost the game, but that wasn't the worst part. The worst part was when Jack got hit in the face with the ball and benched with a bloody nose.

"At least it stopped raining," I say, trying to find a positive. I glance toward the locker room—toward Jack. He's been in there with the team for a while now. "How long do you think they'll be?"

"My dad is probably giving them a pep talk or something." Alex looks up from her phone. "I can go see. I should take the ponchos back, anyway."

We hand her the ponchos, dripping wet from rain. She only takes two steps before Hannah points across the parking lot.

"Look, there they are."

We turn to see a pack of soccer boys leaving the locker room with gym bags slung over their shoulders. I spot Serge and Elijah, but no Jack.

"Here we go." Zoya plasters a smile on her face, holds up her hand, and yells, "Sergio!"

Serge, mid-conversation with Elijah, turns and spots us. They both start to walk over.

"Ugh, they're going to be unbearable," Hannah observes. "Maybe you should do something funny to lighten the mood."

"Like what?" Zoya says.

"I don't know. Trip or something."

Zoya's jaw drops. "What? That wouldn't be funny."

"It might," I say. "As long as you don't get seriously hurt."

She puts a hand on her hip, narrows her eyes. "Oh, but if I get a little bit hurt, that would be fine?"

I shrug. "Well . . ."

"Picasso," Elijah says, stepping onto the curb. I don't know if it's the way he's looking at me, or the fact that Jack is still nowhere to be found, but I'm nervous.

"Poor babe," Zoya coos to Serge in a high-pitched voice that makes me wince. She throws her arms around him. "You did so good."

"Nah," he says, hugging her back. "We were off our game. It's all right."

"It's not your fault." I point up at the dark, damp sky. "The weather was terrible."

"Seriously," Elijah agrees. His curly hair is wet with sweat and rain. He has to keep pushing it out of his eyes. "The fog was so bad. Couldn't see a thing."

"Coach is going to dispute the refs," Serge says. "They should've postponed the game. Andrew has a sprained wrist. And Jack—"

My heart nearly stops. "What? Is his nose broken?"

"No," Serge says. "It was a gusher, though. Gonna bruise for sure."

I glance at the locker room again. Maybe he's getting checked out by first aid or something. I pull out my phone, send him a quick text: Waiting for you by the exit.

"Hey, guys?" Hannah says. She's hugging herself and bouncing up and down. "Not to be dramatic, but I'm hungry, and I'm about to freeze to death. Can we go?"

"I'm having a bonfire at my place. There will be snacks," Elijah tells her. "You should come, if you don't already have plans." Here, his gaze shifts to me.

"Yes!" Hannah says immediately. "I love bonfires. They're so warm."

Out of the corner of my eye, I spot a familiar head of shaggy blond hair across the parking lot. "There's Jack," I say, taking a step toward him. "I'm just going to—"

I stop talking when I see who he's with. Alex and Michael. The three of them seem to be laughing, which is strange, considering the mountain of gauze taped to Jack's nose and the fact that he just lost the biggest game of the season. Then I see Alex lean in for a hug.

Why are they hugging? Why is he hugging her and not me?

"I have to get going," Elijah says, snapping me out of it. "Gotta get the fire pit ready, and all that good stuff. I'll see you guys in a bit? Immie?"

I nod. Over his shoulder, I see Alex jog back in our direction. Jack isn't with her. He walks off with Michael without so much as a glance my way.

"Yep," I say, forcing a smile.

Elijah smiles back, and then he and Serge do that bro-handshake-hug thing guys always do. Then he walks off.

"Sorry," Alex says when she catches up to us. "I got held up talking to my dad."

I frown at her. "You mean Jack?"

She actually has the audacity to look surprised. "Yeah, I saw him on the way out. I just wanted to tell him good game."

"Mm." I cross my arms. "Did you tell him all his friends are over here, or did you conveniently leave that out?"

She looks at Zoya, and something unspoken passes between them. Then she turns to me. "Yes, Immie. I told him *you* were over here. But he didn't want to come."

My stomach drops. He didn't want to come?

Hannah raises her brows. "Hoo boy."

Zoya glances nervously from Alex to me and back again. "Did he say why not?" she says.

Alex shakes her head. "He just said he was riding back with his brother."

For a moment, an awkward silence hangs in the air.

"He doesn't see his brother very much," I say finally, heart pounding. "He probably just wanted the quality time. It's not a big deal."

Zoya and Hannah nod while Alex avoids my gaze altogether. I feel a little bad about snapping at her, but not bad enough to apologize. I pull the sleeves of Jack's sweatshirt down over my fingers, wrap my arms around myself. *It's not a big deal.* I'm not really sure who I'm trying to convince.

"So?" Zoya says, a little too chipper. "Are we ready to go?"

It turns out Elijah's house is only a few blocks away from mine. When we pass through the gated fence and into the backyard, most of the team is already there. Everyone's huddled around the fire pit or hanging out on the patio, eating snacks and drinking soda out of plastic cups. I scan the crowd for that familiar flop of blond hair, but I don't see it.

I pull out my phone, hoping for a text from Jack explaining his whereabouts. There's nothing, so I send one of my own.

Immie: Are u coming to Elijah's bonfire?

"Are those the broccoli bites from A and M Pizza?" Hannah points at the snack table, mouth agape.

"Yep," says a boy's voice. I turn—Elijah is walking toward us. "We got all the apps."

"Ohmygod!" Zoya grabs Serge's hand and starts pulling him toward the table. "Those fried pickles are calling my name."

"Wait!" Hannah hurries after them. Alex gives me one quick, uninterested glance and then follows Hannah without a word. I sigh. That's going to be a problem, but one for later. First, I need to find Jack.

I turn to Elijah. "Thanks for inviting us," I say with a smile.

"Thanks for showing up," he says.

A breeze picks up, going right through the fibers of Jack's sweatshirt. I shiver.

"You cold?" he says, gesturing to the orange glow down the yard. "There's a fire for that, you know."

I nod. "Fire is good." And then I wince. *Smooth, Immie. Really smooth.*

We walk toward the fire pit, where a dozen or so kids are hanging around, sitting in lawn chairs or roasting marshmallows. The heat is nice, but it only helps a little.

"My sweatshirt is wet from getting rained on at the game," I explain, still shivering. "I'll be fine as soon as it dries."

"I can throw it in the dryer, if you'd like," he offers. "You can borrow something of mine in the meantime."

I glance around again. How would Jack feel, knowing I was trading his sweatshirt for one of Elijah's? I glance at my phone, hoping for a response to my text, but there's nothing.

"Sure." I'm cold, and Jack's not here, so he's not going to see anything at all. "Thanks."

I follow Elijah to the patio, past a group of kids arguing over who gets the last mozzarella stick. He slides open the glass door and steps inside, then gestures for me to come in.

It's quiet inside the house. The glow of the TV in the next room illuminates the kitchen just enough for me to follow Elijah without tripping over anything. He turns on a hallway

141

light and leads me to a slim door, behind which a washer and dryer are stacked on top of each other. He looks at me expectantly.

"Oh," I say. "Right." I hurry to take off my sweatshirt and hand it to him. I have a turtleneck on underneath, but I still feel weirdly exposed. I cross my arms self-consciously.

He tosses the sweatshirt in the dryer and presses a few buttons, and the machine whirs to life.

"Half an hour," he says with a nod. "Let me grab you another one from my room."

He opens a door to the left of the washer-dryer and turns on the light. My first thought, at seeing inside Elijah's bedroom, is shock. It's *pristine*. The bed is made, the desk is organized, the shelves and dressers are shined to perfection. Pretty much the opposite of Jack's room, which is guaranteed to have no less than three piles of dirty clothes on the floor at all times.

I hover in the doorway. "Wow. I think your room is cleaner than mine."

He bends over to slide open a dresser drawer. "Cleaning sort of relaxes me. Is that weird?"

I shake my head. "Not at all. Just different from your average teenage boy, I guess."

He chuckles, rifling through the drawer. "Who wants to be like everyone else?"

I smile; then the feeling of something brushing against my calf makes me jump. I look down to see a chunky black lab looking up at me and wagging its tail.

"That's Biscuit," Elijah says. "He's a good boy."

"Is that so?" I say, bending down to scratch him behind the ears. "Are you a good boy?" He opens his mouth like he's smiling, letting his tongue loll out. "Aw. Yes you are!"

"Oh man. You know the way to his heart." Elijah walks toward me with two sweatshirts—a black one and a light blue one. "Which do you want?"

I purse my lips, weighing my options, then decide on the blue. "Good choice," he says. "Blue looks nice on you."

I feel myself blush, hurrying to put on the sweatshirt so he doesn't notice. Then I look down to see the design on the front. It says STRAWBERRY LAKE AND BEACH.

He puts the black sweatshirt back in the drawer, then walks over to the doorway and turns off the light. For a second, we both hover there, inches apart.

"Well?" he says, and it's only then I realize that I'm in the way. "Should we get back to the party?"

"Yeah." I keep my focus on my feet instead of his dimple. "Um. Thanks for letting me borrow this. I'll give it back as soon as mine is dry."

"No worries," he says. "It looks better on you, anyway."

I follow him back outside, where I immediately spot Hannah, Zoya, and Alex near the snack table. Hannah and Zoya are looking at me, eyes wide. Alex's eyes are narrowed.

"That's not what you were wearing five minutes ago," Hannah says coyly.

"It's Elijah's," I say, grabbing a paper plate. "It's no big deal. He's letting me wear it while mine dries."

"Jack's not going to like that," Zoya says, almost as an aside.

I get a slice of cheese pizza and frown. "Why would he care?"

Suddenly Zoya looks guilty, like she got caught. "You know, aren't the two of you, um . . ." She drifts off, takes a bite of her mozzarella stick.

I turn to Hannah. My eyes are daggers. "You *told* them about the cabin?"

"The *cabin*?" Zoya's jaw drops. "What happened at the cabin?"

"I didn't say anything." Hannah picks up a broccoli bite and pops it in her mouth. "Everybody figured there was something going on."

My stomach drops. "What do you mean, everyone?"

"Andrew and Sean *saw* you holding hands in the haunted house," Zoya interjects. "Thanks, by the way, for telling us about that. I had to hear about it from Ben. *Ben*, Immie!"

In the yard, Ben turns and looks at us. Hannah shakes her head, waves him away.

"Now *what* happened at the cabin?" Zoya looks at me expectantly.

"Um." I hesitate. "Jack and I almost kissed."

Zoya gasps. Next to her, Alex hardly flinches.

"Almost?" Zoya says. "What does that mean?"

"His sister sort of interrupted us," I tell her, and then take a bite of the cheese pizza. It's cold.

"Okay. So why didn't you want us to know?" Zoya says, looking hurt. "Did you think we wouldn't keep your secret or something?"

"No," I say, even though that *is* part of it. Zoya has a bigger mouth than a megaphone. "I guess . . . I don't know. I just didn't think about it."

Alex lets out a small, mean little laugh. I spin to face her directly.

"Alex, do you have something to say?"

"Nope." There's a hardened look in her eye unlike anything I've seen from her before. "But even if I did, I doubt you'd listen, anyway."

Zoya and Hannah exchange a glance.

I put down my pizza, suddenly not hungry. "What's your *problem*?"

"What's yours?" Alex snaps back, holding her ground. So she does have a backbone after all.

"Girls," Zoya says, holding out her hands. "There's no need for this tension. We're all friends here."

"Are we?" Alex says, crossing her arms. "Because if you ask me, Immie doesn't know the first thing about being a friend. All she cares about is herself."

"Alex." Zoya sighs. "Come on."

I let out a scoff. "Oh yeah? Well, if you ask *me*, all you care about is trying to steal Jack from me."

For a second, everybody is quiet. I see Hannah wince.

"See what I mean?" Alex looks at Hannah and Zoya. "Even now, it's all about her."

"You're not denying it," I point out.

"Because it's ridiculous. I would never do that to my friend. And for the record, I *told* you I wanted to dance with Jack at homecoming, and then what did you do? *You* danced with him instead. So who really did the stealing, huh?"

I notice people around us turning their heads in our direction, listening in, but I don't care. My blood is boiling, my adrenaline pumping. I'm on a roll now, and I can't be stopped. "He never would've gone with you. He'd never *like* you. There's nothing special about you *at all*."

Zoya's mouth drops open. "Immie."

"What?" I snap at her. "All you guys talk about is who's dating who, and what you're going to do this weekend, and what's on sale at Sephora. It's boring. You're *boring*. So excuse me if I don't always listen to what you have to say."

All three of them are quiet. Alex puts her hand on her hip and lifts her chin in the air slightly, looking vindicated. Zoya looks like she might cry. I hear someone nearby say "yikes."

"I thought we were friends," Zoya says finally, her voice shaky. Then she runs off. Alex follows her.

I turn to Hannah. Her mouth is pressed into a thin line.

"I didn't mean you," I tell her. "You know I don't think that about you."

"I actually don't," Hannah says. "I knew you didn't always jive with Alex and Z, but that was *mean*, Immie . . ." She shakes her head. "A kind of mean I didn't know you had in you."

"But, Hannah. You know they—"

"They have their issues, sure." She cuts me off. "But so do you. So do we *all*. And we love each other anyway. That's literally all being a friend is."

"I know," I say. My voice sounds small.

"Do you?" She gives me a stern look. "You've always kind

of marched to the beat of your own drum, and I thought it was cool. That's *why* I wanted to be your friend. I thought you were this, like, icon of independence." She laughs, but there's no humor in the sound. "But now I don't think that. I think you're afraid."

"*Afraid?* Why would I be afraid?"

"You tell me." She looks across the yard, where Zoya is crying in a corner, and Serge and Alex are trying to comfort her. "Later. You can tell me later. Right now, I need to go be with my friends."

She walks away. I watch her go, feeling small and embarrassed and alone.

That's when I see him.

He's by the fire, talking to a guy on the team and running a hand through his messy blond hair. I'm so relieved that I think, for a moment, I might cry.

I practically sprint over to him. "Jack!"

He turns to me, looking surprised, and I don't even give him a chance to say anything—I just tackle him in a hug.

"Immie." He hugs me back. "Hey."

"I've been waiting for you," I say, still hugging him. "Didn't you get my text?"

He shakes his head. "My phone is sort of broken."

I let go of him reluctantly. "Oh, weird. How'd you break it? You know what, tell me later, it doesn't matter. Better your phone than your nose." He's removed the gauze, and I can see the black and blue of a gnarly bruise starting to form around the bridge. "Does it hurt?"

He shrugs. "It's fine." Then his gaze falls to my sweatshirt.

"It's Hannah's." I say quickly. There's no reason to tell him it's Elijah's—it would just make him think it means something it doesn't. "I was wearing yours, but it got soaking wet at the game, so she let me borrow it."

We're not hugging anymore, but Jack's arm is still slung around me, and I press my cheek into his shoulder. I feel so comfortable here. It doesn't matter that my dad is dead, that my mom's a liar, or that my friends hate me. Everything is going to be all right. Jack and I are going to be all right.

The party chatter fades to a distant hum, and a feeling of calm passes over me. I close my eyes, listening to the crackle of the embers in the fire, feeling the breeze tickle my cheeks and the rush of blood pumping through my veins. Suddenly I'm transported to that night in the cabin. I see Jack's lips, slightly parted, feel his hand on the back of my neck and the warmth of his breath as he leans toward me. Just two more seconds, I think—two more seconds and his lips would've met mine, and everything would have been different.

It's not too late, says a voice inside my head. We're here now, together again. We could make it right. I could kiss him, and everything can be like it was, only *better*.

With my eyes closed, and his arm still slung over my shoulder, I lift my chin and purse my lips. I go on my tiptoes, trying to fill the space between us.

And I wait.

And wait.

I open my eyes.

My face is an inch from his, but he hasn't moved. All the warmth is gone from him. Instead he looks . . .

Scared?

"I can't." He whispers. He drops his arm, takes a step back.

I open my mouth to speak, to ask him why not—*why not?*—but no words come out.

"I'm sorry," he says. His breathing is heavy; I watch the rapid rise and fall of his shoulders.

I shake my head. I don't understand. I look past him, toward the fire, and I notice that a small crowd of people is watching us—my former friends among them. Hannah, Zoya, and Alex see me look at them, and they all turn away, as if to say, *You're on your own.*

The surge of embarrassment is nothing compared to the realization that Jack doesn't want me. I can hardly wrap my head around the words. He doesn't want me, and my friends hate me, and my dad is dead, and I am alone. Completely, utterly, eternally alone.

That's when one thought overshadows all the others: *Get out of here.*

So I do. I walk away from Jack and leave the bonfire as fast as I can. Once I'm through the gate, I start to run. I run for three blocks, not stopping until I get to my front yard. I linger there for a second, breathing hard, and look down the street at Jack's house.

The kitchen light is on, but the rest of the house is dark. I wonder if the Marshalls are in the living room, watching a movie as a family like they do most Friday nights. If it were any other Friday, Jack might invite me over to join, or he might ditch his family and come to my house so we could have our own movie night. He'd want to watch something action-packed or suspenseful or maybe some dumb comedy. I'd fight him on it, because that's what we do, we poke and joke and argue until we find common ground. There's no common ground to be found here, though. Not this time. Not anymore.

I turn away from his house, from the memories, from everything that might have been, and I go inside.

I open my bedroom door to find my mom, sitting on my bed with the honeydust T-shirt in her hands.

"Are you Kristen Robertson?" she says, her voice calm.

I stay in the doorway, my fingers still grazing the knob.

"My old friend Max called me and said someone named Kristen Robertson reached out to ask him who I was with at a Flaming Lips concert twenty years ago." She tilts her head a little, as if gauging my reaction. "An honest conversation goes two ways, you know."

I shrug. "Fine. I made that account. So what?"

Her face goes blank with surprise. "So what? Immie, you reached out to my friend, pretending to be someone else, because you wanted information you knew you wouldn't get from me. That's not okay."

My hand falls from the doorknob. "Yeah? Well, keeping my dad a secret from me isn't okay either. He's *my* dad. I deserve to know who he is." I stop, correct myself. "Who he *was*."

150

"He was not your dad," she says, and her words hit like a punch to the gut. "I'm sorry, but he wasn't."

"Well then, who is?" I don't mean to shout, it just sort of happens. If I don't shout, I might cry.

She shakes her head. "That's not what I—" She sighs. "Technically, he was your biological father, yes. But he was never going to be your dad. That was part of the agreement we had when he donated the sperm in the first place."

I cross my arms. "What agreement?"

She doesn't say anything right away. She just looks at me, and for the first time, I see the pain in her eyes. She really doesn't want to talk about him.

"Whatever you think I can't handle, I can," I say. What I don't say: *He's already dead. How much worse could it be?* "Please."

"Come sit by me." She pats the bed. I groan, but I do it.

"I was thirty-two," she says, tucking a strand of hair behind her ear. "I wanted to be a mom. But I had been so focused on my career that I hadn't prioritized a relationship. At that point, Rob had been my best friend for years."

"And your boyfriend, too," I add. "Right?"

"We dated in high school." She waves it off. "We were so young, it doesn't count."

Jack pops into my head. I expect to get hit with a fresh wave of pain, but instead I just feel numb, like the whole thing was a dream.

"Anyway," she continues. "He never wanted to be a dad. Honestly, he wouldn't have been very good at it. All he wanted to do was travel and play music." She pauses to look, pointedly, at the shirt in her lap. "But he had a good heart. No information sheet about anonymous donors could promise me that." Mom gives me a wry smile. "And he knew how much I wanted to be a mom. He agreed to donate his sperm so I could try IVF, but only on the condition that, if it worked, he wouldn't be part of it."

"By *it*," I repeat, "you mean my life."

"This is why I didn't want to tell you about him." She closes her eyes and pinches the bridge of her nose. "I knew you wouldn't understand. I should've never given you those CDs."

"I understand just fine," I say. "You didn't tell me about him because you didn't want me to know him."

"It's not about want. You were never *meant* to know him." Her voice is firm, as if there's a difference. "You were never meant to be part of his life."

"But that decision shouldn't be up to you." My feelings are starting to come back, and one stands above all the rest: anger. "It should be up to me and him."

"You're *my* child, Immie." She reaches for my hand. "Mine. He was just a sperm donor."

"But that's not fair!" I yank my hand away. My eyes burn with rage and tears. "You didn't even give him the chance to get to know me. Maybe he would've liked me. Maybe he would've changed his mind."

She shakes her head.

"And now he'll never get to know me, because he—" My

voice breaks. "Because he's dead." I start to cry. "It's messed up. It's so messed up."

"Immie." She tries to hug me, but I push her away.

"You're so selfish," I say through my tears. "You didn't care about giving me a real family."

She rears back like I slapped her. "Immie, we *are* a real family."

"No we're not. We never take weekend trips or have family meals at the dinner table like Jack's family. You've never chaperoned a single one of my field trips, or gotten to know my friends' parents. You're always working, and I'm always by myself."

She's not looking at me anymore. When she speaks, her voice is timid. "I'm doing the best I can."

"Exactly! And that's why real families have *two* parents."

I regret it as soon as it comes out of my mouth.

"I'm sorry." I grab her hand and look at her with pleading eyes. "Mom. I didn't mean it."

She continues to stare at the floor, unblinking. Her hand is limp and lifeless in mine.

"I'm sorry," I repeat, on the verge of tears again. It's all I can think of.

She gets up and walks out of the room. I stare at the empty space in the doorway, hating her, hating Jack, and mostly, hating myself.

"Fine," I say, quietly at first, and then louder. "Fine!" I get up, cross the room, and slam the door. I don't need her. I don't need *anyone*.

I grab the CD player from the nightstand, get in bed, and pull the covers over my head. I want to disappear for a while, so I press play. "Not the Same" by Ben Folds comes on. *"You were not the same after that . . ."*

My thoughts threaten to shift to Jack, but I don't let them. I turn the volume all the way up, close my eyes, and let the music take me away.

TRACK FIFTEEN

"Maps"—Yeah Yeah Yeahs

I debated adding this song to the list, but in the end, I knew I needed to be honest. Even—and especially—if it hurt.

I stay in my room all weekend, keeping my head under the covers and my phone turned off. I don't want to see anyone or talk to anyone or think about all the people I've hurt. All I want to do is sulk. So that's exactly what I do. I alternate between watching *Gilmore Girls* on my laptop and looking my dad up on the internet, reading every single thing I can find. I listen to honeydust's record—they just had one—and pay close attention to the guitar parts. I realize I feel closer to him listening to the music he chose for my mom than the music he made for himself, and I wonder if that's strange.

I finally turn my phone back on late Sunday night. Not so much because I want to return to reality, but because I need to set my alarm for school in the morning. I expect my screen to light up with dozens of texts and missed calls—from Jack, from Hannah, maybe even from Elijah—but there's nothing there. Not one single notification from anyone.

Not even Jack.

Maybe he's mad at me for running away. Maybe he's embarrassed. Still, I don't understand why he wouldn't want to make things right between us. The Jack I know hates conflict. He wants everyone to be happy all the time. Especially me.

Although . . .

If I really think about it? Recently, that hasn't been true. Ever since school started, Jack has been distant and unavailable, taking longer to respond to texts, canceling plans, and spending all his free time with the soccer team. I haven't been a priority.

This is what hurts me the most: not the rejection or the waiting or even the embarrassment. It's the realization that my best friend is gone, and in his place is someone I don't know at all.

Monday morning, I text Carrie and tell her I'm taking the bus to school. It's only the second time I've ridden the morning bus this year, and after I climb the steps to find no empty seats and everybody staring at me, I'm reminded why. Still, I'd rather ride on top of the bus like it's a skateboard than ride to school with Jack.

I spend the first two periods of the day mentally preparing myself to see him in social studies. I think about what I might say if he approaches me. *What's the matter with you? What did I do wrong?* Or the classic: *How dare you?* I'm so out of it that my math teacher has to call my name three times before I hear him. He asks for the answer to problem number 4, and that's when I realize I forgot to do the homework.

When the moment I've been waiting for finally comes, all my preparation has been for naught. Jack walks right past me and doesn't say a word. The pain of it makes me want to throw up. He sits in his seat and keeps his head down, and I make it my mission to fix my gaze away from him for the entirety of the class's forty-nine minutes. I can't cry at school. I just can't.

When the bell rings, I make sure that my bag is already packed so I can book it out of the room. But he was ready too. He catches up with me.

"Hey, Immie. Can we talk?"

"No." I shake my head, ignoring how cute he looks in his cream-colored sweater. In this moment, I want to hurt him like he hurt me. "Just—no. I need space. From you. To figure things out."

He looks at me, long and hard, and my heart, or whatever was left of it, disintegrates into dust.

"Fine," he says. "If that's really what you want."

I nod. *Is it?* "It is."

He nods too. "Okay, then."

And then he tears his eyes from mine and walks away, and I swear it feels physical, like the tight-knit fabric of our friendship is ripping at the seams, growing wider with every step he takes.

I don't go to art class. Instead, I go to the nurse and pretend I have period cramps. She gives me medicine and lets me lie down for a while. When she sees me cry, she assumes it's just PMS. I don't correct her.

I leave the nurse's office at lunchtime, but I don't go to lunch, either. I go to the art room, while Ms. Moser has a free period. I ask if I can stay and work on my midterm project through my lunch period, and she agrees. I spend most of the time sketching out a concept for a painting of a swallowtail butterfly, but it's no good. At the end of the period, I crumple up the sketch and throw it in the trash.

When the bell rings at the end of the day, and I'm on my way to the bus, I realize I forgot my supplies in the art room and have to double back. I find the paints and wrapped canvas at my station where I left them, glance up at the clock, and wince. If I don't run, I might miss the bus. I gather my supplies, hurry out of the room, and bump right into Elijah.

"Whoa." He laughs, putting a hand on my arm to steady me. "You okay?"

"Yeah, fine, sorry." I smile apologetically and step around him. "I've gotta catch the bus."

"Buses already left," he says. "I just came from that way."

"Oh." I stop in my tracks, adjusting my grip on the canvas so I don't drop it. "Well. Guess I'm walking."

"Guess so." He closes the distance between us. "You want some company?"

I raise an eyebrow. "Really? You're walking home too?"

"I am now." He takes the canvas out of my hands and smiles, flashing his dimple. "Come on."

I follow him out the doors that lead to the student parking lot. It's a whole other world back here: upperclassmen linger in and around their cars, talking and kissing and yelling out windows and honking their horns at whoever is in their way. Elijah navigates it with ease. Several people say hi or hold out their hands for a fist bump.

One of the junior guys on the soccer team rolls down the window of his truck and leans out. "Yo, Whitehouse. You coming?"

"Not today," Elijah calls back. I see him tilt his head a little in my direction. The guy's eyes dart between us, and he does a little catcall whistle. Elijah flips him off.

"You have a lot of friends," I observe.

"Nah," he says. "I'm just friendly."

We leave the parking lot and turn left, starting our ascent up the hill that leads to the intersection that will take us to our neighborhood. Immediately I become short of breath.

"I've never walked home before," I say. The air is so cold I can see my breath. "This hill is a lot steeper than it looks."

"Tell me about it. We have to run it for soccer drills sometimes."

"That sounds terrible," I say. "Exactly why I don't play any sports."

He laughs. "You've never played a sport?"

I shake my head. "My mom tried to get me into field hockey when I was little, but I hated it. I always ended up sitting in the grass and talking to bugs instead."

"Talking to bugs, huh?" He has an amused look on his face. "What did you say?"

I shrug. "Anything, really. They were pretty much the closest things I had to friends, at the time." *And might be again,* I think, but don't say. I change the subject. "Thanks again, for letting me borrow your sweatshirt on Friday. I'll make sure I get it back to you."

"Don't worry about it," he says. "I've got a million of them."

I nod, not sure what to say to that. I settle on "Cool."

"You took off without saying goodbye," he says, so casually that it's hard to tell if he's bothered or not.

"Yeah." I look down at the ground. "Sorry about that. I . . . had to go."

"I was looking for you. To, uh, give you your sweatshirt back, but your friends said you'd gone. So I gave it to Marshall."

My heart contracts in my chest. So Jack knew I gave his sweatshirt to Elijah to dry. I wonder if he knew I was wearing Elijah's sweatshirt, too. *I hope he did,* I decide. I hope it made him jealous. I hope it hurt him.

"That's fine," I say, holding my head high. "I didn't want it anymore."

"Oh?" Elijah looks at me. "Why's that?"

"Because we're done," I say, testing out the words in my mouth. "I mean, we never really started, but—whatever was going on between us, it's done."

"Ah." He nods. "Sorry."

"No you're not," I say, pretty much without thinking.

He cracks a smile. "No. I'm not."

I glance at him again, and I'm overcome, weirdly enough, with relief. Here's a boy—a cute, charming boy—who's willing to walk home with me in near-freezing temperatures and carry my clunky canvas up a steep hill, just to prove to me that he likes me. No mixed signals, no ulterior motives, just the truth, laid plain for me to see like cards spread out on a table. It's kind of amazing, how easy it can be.

We reach the top of the hill and start our descent down the other side, talking about school and soccer and my favorite dead queens.

"Anne Boleyn had a big mouth," I tell him. "She would've loved social media."

"Sounds like someone else I know," he responds with a playful smirk. I smack him on the arm.

By the time we reach the intersection at the bottom of the hill, the ache in my chest has gone from a sharp pain to more of a dull throb. Elijah, surprisingly enough, is even more fun to talk to than he is nice to look at. When we turn onto his street, I realize I don't *want* to stop talking to him just yet. I think about the long, lonely afternoon I have ahead of me, and the pain in my chest comes back.

"What do you have going on tonight?" he asks, as if reading my mind. I wonder if he thinks I'm some sort of social butterfly with tons of friends.

"Nothing," I say. "Homework. *Gilmore Girls*. The usual." Then I wince. There I go again, determined to make myself sound like the least cool person on the planet.

"You want to see something?" He looks excited. Giddy, almost. "It's at my house. Feel free to say no."

Maybe I should say no. Maybe I should be smart about

going over to an older boy's house by myself, especially considering that boy has been very clear about his crush on me. What would my mom say?

"Okay."

When we get to his house, I follow him up his driveway. I cringe a little, thinking about the last time I walked up this driveway, and how it ended up being one of the worst nights of my life.

Instead of going inside, he pulls open his garage door. I don't know what I expect—a sculpture or a drum kit or even a dead body. What I don't expect is a car.

"This is my baby," he says, tapping it on the hood. It's a vintage-looking Jeep, light blue with a black interior.

"This is yours?" I'm surprised. "I figured you'd have a Mustang or, like, a Range Rover."

"So you think I'm a dad having a midlife crisis?" He laughs. "It's a ninety-eight Jeep Cherokee. My dad and I have been fixing it up."

"Wow. I didn't know you were into cars."

He's turned away from me, so I can't see his face when he says, "There's a lot you don't know about me."

I blink, a little startled. He's right. I've been so busy obsessing over Jack that I haven't made much space in my head for anybody else. I think about what Alex said at the bonfire: *All she cares about is herself.* That's when shame washes over me like a wave.

He leans my canvas carefully against the wall of the garage and opens the passenger-side door. "After you."

I get in. The Jeep has an earthy smell, a mix of pine and moss and used car. Elijah climbs in the driver's side and presses a button, turning on the radio. A classic rock song starts playing loudly through the speakers, making me jump. He turns down the volume.

"We've been working on it for a year now," he says. "It should be ready to go by the spring, when I get my license."

"I like it a lot," I say. "Especially the color."

"Yeah?" He says. "Well, you look good in it. Blue's your color."

I feel myself blushing. I glance at him out of the corner of my eye, taking in his dark curly hair, his sharp jawline, his cool disposition, and I picture it—me in the future, sitting in this seat, looking at him just like this, feeling totally comfortable.

"Thanks for walking home with me," I say in an effort to lower my heart rate. "You saved me the embarrassment of sprinting through the halls."

He smiles. "For you, any time."

"*Any* time? Even at two o'clock in the morning?"

His smile turns playful. "Especially at two o'clock in the morning."

I suck in a breath and start choking on my own spit. I lean forward and rummage through my bag to find my water bottle. Also, so I can hide my face from Elijah.

"Sorry." My voice is scratchy. I drink some water and compose myself. "That was embarrassing."

"Don't be," he says. "And seriously. When I get my license,

163

I'd be happy to give you rides home so you never have to sprint to the bus again."

My mind goes, immediately, to Jack. He definitely wouldn't like it if I started riding home with Elijah. He wouldn't be too happy about today, either, if he ever found out. But what does it matter? We're not, and were never, together. I can do whatever I want.

"I'd like that," I say. "Thanks."

The song on the radio ends, and "Maps" by the Yeah Yeah Yeahs comes on in its place.

"I love this song," I say.

"Yeah?" He turns it up and Karen O's hypnotic voice fills the car. *"Wait, they don't love you like I love you."* "Me too. The Yeah Yeah Yeahs are great."

"I only know this one song," I say, embarrassed. "It was on a CD my dad made for my mom when they were younger."

"That's so cool," he says. "What other songs are on it?"

"Oh, lots of stuff from the nineties and early two thousands. TLC, No Doubt, Sugar Ray—"

"Oh man. My dad is obsessed with Sugar Ray," he says. "What is it with dads and grungy sunshine rock?"

I force a laugh and shrug. *What is it with dads?* I don't know how to answer.

"Seems like yours has great taste in music," he says, and I realize, too late, what I walked into. What I have to say next.

"Yeah. I think he did." I keep my attention fixed on a hangnail on my thumb. "He—he died last year, though."

I feel the energy in the car shift, feel Elijah's eyes on me.

"Sorry if I made it weird," I say quickly. "I—I just found out, so I don't really know how to talk about it."

"No," he says. "No, I just—I'm so sorry, Immie. That really sucks."

"It's okay," I assure him. I feel weirdly apathetic toward the sympathy in his voice, almost like it doesn't belong to me. "I never met him."

He nods. "Still. That's gotta be weird for you."

I glance at him, curious. "What do you mean?"

He hesitates. "I just mean, like—it's gotta be complicated, mourning a guy you never knew, when he's *supposed* to be the guy you know best. There's not much of a playbook for that, is there?"

I blink, dazed. I can't believe it—Elijah has just casually put into words the feeling I've been struggling with since I read the obituary.

"No, there's not," I say, my voice a little stronger. "It's like, my mom thinks because I didn't know him, I shouldn't be so sad. But that's exactly why I *am* sad." I tuck a strand of hair behind my ear, struggling to say what I mean. "Not because he's dead, exactly, but because I'll never get to know him."

"That makes complete sense to me," he says. "But I mean, even if it didn't, so what? He's your dad. Nobody can tell you how to feel."

I feel strange relief at the truth of it, like a weight has been lifted from my chest. Elijah is right. Even though it didn't say so in his obituary, and no matter how much my mom insists otherwise, Rob Stanley *was* my dad. I'm allowed to be sad that he's gone. I'm allowed to grieve the relationship we'll never have. I'm allowed to feel whatever I want to feel.

"Thanks," I say to him. "You're kind of the first person I've been able to talk to about this."

"You can talk to me about anything," he says. Strangest of all, he actually sounds like he means it.

"Really?"

"Yeah." He shifts in his seat to face me. "C'mon. You know how I feel about you."

I look into my lap, bite the inside of my cheek. I know he thinks I'm *interesting*, that he likes the way I look in the color blue. But does it go deeper than that?

The song on the radio changes to something slower and softer. When I look up, my hair falls into my eyes, and Elijah, very gently, reaches forward and brushes it away. His hand lingers there, grazing my cheek, my chin. He turns my face toward his.

That's when time slows down.

"Immie." His voice is soft, his eyes locked onto mine. Up so close, they look more hazel than brown, flecked with bits of golden amber. I need to remember that detail for later, when I try to paint them.

"Can I kiss you?"

I blink. I feel frozen, like a deer in headlights. What I do next is crucial: either I run, or I get hit. I weigh the options: if I run, it probably wouldn't be the end of the world. I don't think Elijah would make me feel bad about it. Then again, running

166

would mean the closing of a door, and I don't know if I want to do that now, when I've only just begun to glance at what's inside.

So I close my eyes.

And I get hit.

Elijah presses his lips to mine. They're soft and warm, the way I always thought Jack's might be. I think it feels nice, so I relax into him. His fingers move to the back of my neck, and I feel a little tingle in my chest, like a tiny, hopeful fluttering. We stay like that for a second, or a minute, or an hour, I don't know, but all of a sudden it's over. He pulls back, but he keeps his hand on my neck, and my skin feels like fire under his touch.

I start to laugh—I can't help it. I feel giddy and a little breathless. I just had my first kiss. I, Imogen Marie Meadows, just had *my first kiss*.

And then my heart sinks.

I just had my first kiss. My first first that isn't with Jack.

The song on the radio changes again, and I recognize it immediately. The cowbell, the signature horns, and finally, tragically, the lyrics: *Do you remember the twenty-first night of September?*

Elijah laughs. "Wow." He takes his hand off my neck and changes the radio station. "What a mood killer."

Jack. I picture the look on Jack's face earlier today when I told him I wanted space, how shocked he was, how crushed. How would he look if he knew I filled that space with Elijah— with Elijah's *mouth*? It would devastate him. He would never forgive me.

I will never forgive me.

"Tap at My Window"—Laura Marling

I was working on mending my friendships. Little did I know, you were working on my friendships too.

When I walk into art class the next day, Hannah is already there, setting up her station. I put my book bag down on the floor and sit on the empty stool next to her.

"I know you're mad at me," I say. "And you have every right to be. But I kind of did something insane, and . . ." I swallow my nerves. *Just say it.* "I'd like to talk about it with my best friend."

Hannah arches an eyebrow. "You've never called me your best friend before."

"I know," I admit. "I'm working on being more open with my feelings."

"Mm." She remains stone-faced. "How's that working out for you?"

"I'm *sorry*, Hannah," I say. "What I said at the bonfire was awful. It was uncalled for, and—"

"Zoya cried for almost an hour," she says, propping her

wrapped canvas on the easel. It's a half-finished painting of a landscape at sunset. "And Alex doesn't want anything to do with you."

I fidget in my seat. This is going to be harder than I thought.

"I made a mistake," I admit. "What I said—it wasn't even really about them. It was about me, and this—this tendency I have, to try to prove that I don't need other people. But it's not true. I do need other people. I need *you*. And—and I need them, too."

She sighs and swivels her stool toward me.

"Go on."

I take a deep breath, preparing to say what I rehearsed in my head all last night and this morning. "I've never had a friend group like this before. My whole life, I've spent so much time alone, or with Jack—" My voice breaks a little when I say his name. "Because being with him was kind of like being alone. And that was easier, for me, than putting myself out there, trying to make real connections with people. Because, historically, that never really went well for me."

She crosses her arms.

"You were right," I say. "I *am* afraid. I'm afraid of letting my guard down and getting hurt. I'm afraid people will look at me, and all they'll see is this, I don't know, this *weird* girl with the bug collection, and they'll just write me off. So I tell myself I don't need them, and I write them off instead."

Finally, Hannah nods. "Okay," she says. "Now we're getting somewhere."

"I took you for granted," I say. "And Zoya and Alex, too. I treated you like disposable friends, when really, you're the most loyal friends I've ever had."

Even more loyal than Jack, it turns out, though I don't say that part aloud. I tuck a strand of hair behind my ear, look down at the floor. "I'm sorry I didn't realize it sooner."

When I look up at her again, the anger is gone from her face.

"The important thing is that you realize it now," she says. "That counts for something."

I smile, relieved. "So you forgive me?"

"I forgive you," she says with a decisive nod.

"And Alex and Z? Do you think they will too?"

"Yeah," she says, but her voice wavers, just a little. "Z is easy. She's more confused than anything. And Alex, well . . ." She trails off. "Alex is harder. But if you tell her what you just told me, I'm sure she'll come around."

I nod. I can accept that. "Okay."

"Now." She leans in, her eyes bright with mischief. "Tell me about this insane thing you did."

I feel a wave of nausea pass through me. "Um. I sort of . . ." I lower my voice to a whisper. "Kissed Elijah."

"*What?*" She practically squeals. A few people around us turn their heads our direction.

"Hannah?" Ms. Moser says from her desk. "Immie? Everything okay over there?"

"Fine," we call back in unison. I look at Hannah with wide eyes. "Shh!"

"What do you mean, you kissed Elijah?" Her voice is low, but her tone is just as urgent. "The last time we talked, you were trying to kiss Jack." She sees the horrified look on my face and grimaces. "Sorry. But you know we all saw it."

I put my elbows on the table and my head in my hands. "I know."

"It wasn't *that* bad," she says. "Only the four of us knew how big of a deal it was. Everybody else probably thought you were just in a fight, or something."

"Well, we're not in a fight," I say, peeking at her over my hands. "We're not anything anymore."

"Hannah, Immie," Ms. Moser says from behind us. "There's a lot of talking and not much painting going on over here."

"Sorry, Ms. Moser," I say again. "I'm kind of having a crisis." I turn back to my project and mouth to Hannah, *I'll tell you later.*

Ms. Moser gives me a sympathetic look. "Put it in your art," she says. "That's what it's there for."

At lunch, I tell Zoya more or less all of what I told Hannah in art class, leaving out the part about me kissing Elijah. If I tell her, I know she'll tell Serge, because she's terrible at keeping secrets from him, or anyone, for that matter. If Serge knows, it will definitely get back to Jack. I can't apologize to Alex yet, because she has a quiz bowl meeting during lunch, and this is something I have to do in person.

Zoya forgives me, and we spend the rest of lunch talking about the holidays. Hannah is going to Jamaica for Christmas, and Zoya will be at her aunt's upstate, but they'll be back in time for New Year's Eve, so we make plans to go see the annual bologna drop downtown. It's Storm Valley's very own Times Square ball drop situation, except here, a giant papier-mâché bologna gets dropped in the middle of Main Street. *Much* more festive.

Alex avoids the lunch table all week. Zoya makes excuses for her—quiz bowl, dentist appointment, studying for a test in the library—but we all know the real reason she's staying away.

By Friday, I decide I can't wait any longer to apologize, and I make it my mission to track her down. I look for her during homeroom and between classes, but I don't find her until after school lets out. I spot her bright red hair as she's walking to the bus, so I rush through the front doors to try to catch her on the stairs. When I see Jack walking beside her, I stop, letting everyone else stream out around me.

They're looking at each other, smiling like they don't have a care in the world, like they're better off without me. When Alex throws her head back, laughing hysterically at something Jack said, I think about how that used to be me, how nobody could make me laugh as hard or as often as Jack did. And when Jack laughs in return, I know exactly how it sounds, even though he's too far away for me to actually hear. It sounds like music.

Like *home*.

My eyes start to burn. I spin around and apologize to students whose faces I can't see as I push past them toward the bathroom. I make it there before anybody can see me cry.

TRACK SEVENTEEN

"Chiquitita"—ABBA

The ultimate breakup song. That's what Mom says. She's partially right—it's good for a broken heart. But I learned it can bring people together, too.

When I finally leave the bathroom, I run into Elijah and Andrew, one of the older boys from the soccer team. When Andrew offers me a ride home, I robotically accept without thinking about it. Elijah gets in the back with me, and I'm worried, at first, that he'll want to talk to me, and that I'll have to try to be flirty and witty when all I really want to do is break down. He surprises me, though. He doesn't say a word the entire way.

When we get to my house, I say thank you to Andrew and Elijah and get out of the car. Elijah gets out too.

"It's okay," I say. "You don't have to walk me to my door or anything."

"I want to talk to you for a minute. Andrew's gonna wait."

My stomach drops. "Okay."

I walk to the porch and sit down on the front steps. He sits next to me, looking straight ahead.

"What was that back there?"

"What do you mean?"

"I saw you looking at Marshall in front of the school."

I hesitate. "I don't know what you're talking about."

He looks down and picks at a thread on his jeans. He looks sad and vulnerable, and it makes me want to die.

"I like you, Immie," he says. "There it is. I like you. I really do."

"I like you too."

He smiles, just a little. "But you like Marshall more."

I don't answer right away. What I feel for Elijah and what I feel for Jack are like night and day. You can't compare them—you shouldn't even try.

He nods, seeming to take my silence as its own answer.

"That's what I thought."

He starts to stand up, but I grab his arm, pull him back down.

"Wait," I plead. "Listen. It's been him for so long. And you—you came out of nowhere."

"No." He shakes his head. "I've been right here the whole time, waiting for you to figure out your feelings. And I thought, when we kissed, that you *did* figure them out. I thought—" He rubs the back of his neck, kind of laughing to himself. "I thought you picked me."

That's when I realize it. I'm doing to Elijah exactly what Jack did to me. I'm stringing him along while I try to get my life together, because I know he won't go anywhere.

And that, I've learned all too well, is not fair.

He stands up again, and this time, I let him. "When you figure out what it is you want," he says, "give me a call, okay?"

When I go inside, I head straight for my bathroom and turn the shower on, setting the water as hot as it will go. I peel off my clothes and stand underneath the stream for a long time.

I change into sweatpants and shut the curtains against the afternoon light before I get into bed. I'm only there a few minutes when my door opens.

"Immie." My mom turns on the light. I cover my eyes with my hands.

I groan. "Why are you home already?"

"The middle school had a half day today. Who was that boy?" I feel the bed shift under her weight as she sits down. "The one you were talking to on the porch."

"Elijah," I say into my hands. "He's on the soccer team."

"Why did he bring you home?"

"*Because*, okay?"

"Hey." Her mouth is a hard line. "Watch how you talk to me."

"Sorry." I roll my eyes.

"Excuse me?" She's angry now. "You can't just show up here in some random boy's car and then get an attitude when I ask you about it. You're my daughter. I'm allowed to know who you're with."

"I'm surprised you even care." My eyes start to burn. I keep my gaze fixed away from her.

She looks surprised. "Of course I care."

"Really? Because you've hardly said two words to me all week." I feel my eyes well with tears. I try to blink them back, but one escapes, and I hurry to wipe it from my cheek before she sees. "You have no idea what's been going on."

She must see, because she sighs, softens. "Move over."

I hesitate.

"Come on," she says, nudging me. Then she climbs into bed next to me, and I scooch over as far as I can without falling off.

"I'm sorry I've been distant," she says, pulling the comforter up over herself. "What you said really hurt me."

"I know." I still won't look at her. "I know it was horrible, and that's why I apologized right after I said it. You didn't have to punish me forever."

"It wasn't about punishing you. It was about . . ." She trails off. "I guess I just didn't know what to say. I felt like I failed you, and I was ashamed."

Her words take me by surprise. I thought she was furious at me. It never occurred to me that she might have been keeping her distance because *she* didn't want to face *me*.

"But you didn't." I turn to look at her. "You couldn't. You're the best mom—you've given me everything I need."

"Except a dad."

"No." I shake my head. "I never felt like I needed a dad. I just wanted to know who he was." I shift so I'm sitting upright. "It's for the same reason I like to read history books. It's just that this time, it's my own history I'm learning about."

"You have to understand. Everything I did—the reason I

didn't want you to know who he was—it's all because I wanted to protect you."

"Protect me from what?"

She hesitates. "From heartbreak."

"Because he died?"

"Because . . ." She looks at me apologetically. "Because he wasn't a happy person."

There's an inexplicable chill in the air. Suddenly I feel uneasy.

"What do you mean?"

She puts her hand on my leg and pats it reassuringly. "Are you sure you want to hear this?"

I nod, even though actually, I'm not sure.

"He struggled with depression for most of his life," she says. "Got diagnosed in high school and went on medication, which helped. But in his twenties, after he started touring all the time, he wasn't so good about taking it." She takes a deep breath, for strength. "He'd stay with me when he wasn't on the road, and I could tell he wasn't well, so I'd help get him back on track. But then he'd tour again, and the cycle would start all over."

"Why was he depressed?" I pull the covers up to my chin.

"I don't think there was a specific reason, Im," she says. "Some people just have a harder time with life."

"So that's why he died?" I ask. "Because he was depressed?"

"In a way. He had a habit of self-medicating with alcohol. It . . . started to get out of hand right around when you were born. He actually tried to come see you once, a few weeks after

177

I got out of the hospital. But he'd had a lot to drink, and he was yelling in the street, and—" She shakes her head. "I told him afterward that was it. I said he needed to clean up his act, and get sober, or else I couldn't be around him anymore."

"Oh." My heart is pounding. "So . . . so he didn't?"

"No, he didn't." She looks at me sadly. "He was my best friend for sixteen years. I was devastated when I heard what happened to him. For a while, I even blamed myself for not trying harder to help him. But I had to do what was best for you—and for me. You understand that, don't you?"

I nod. "You can't force people to do what you want them to do," I say. "I get it."

And then I start to cry again.

"Oh, shh." She puts her arms around me and starts to rub my back. "Don't cry, Butterfly. It's okay."

For a minute I just let myself sob into her chest. It feels good to be held by her like this—I can't remember the last time it happened, or if it ever has.

"What's going on?" she says when I calm down. "Why the tears?"

"It's Jack." I sniffle. "I think—I think we're done."

She leans back to look at me, a concerned crease in her brow. "What do you mean, done?"

I tell her everything. I don't leave anything out—not the almost kiss in the cabin, or the almost kiss at the bonfire, or even the actual kiss in Elijah's car. By the time I'm done talking, the tears have dried on my cheeks, and I can breathe through my nose again.

"I'm sorry," she says. "I'm sorry you're hurting, and I'm sorry you've been going through it alone."

I lean into her. "I just wish I never tried to kiss him. I should've known it was going to be a disaster."

"No." She rubs my arm. "You should always tell the people you love how you feel. Otherwise, you're lying to them."

I realize she's right, and I wonder when, exactly, Jack and I started getting so comfortable lying to each other. We never used to keep secrets. We never had to, because we had nothing to hide. Now we're basically living separate lives.

"I just can't imagine my life without him," I say, and for some stupid reason, my eyes fill with tears again. "This week has been horrible. I can't feel this way forever."

"You won't," Mom says, wiping my tears. "If this is really the end for you and Jack, you'll learn how to be without him. It will get easier and easier, until one day, you'll realize you haven't been thinking about him at all. You'll have new friends—you *already* have a new crush—and this heartbreak will feel like a distant memory. And you'll be grateful for it."

"Grateful?" I almost laugh at the idea. "Why would I be grateful I lost the best friend I ever had?"

"Because. You survived it," she says, and the confidence in her voice makes me think she's speaking from experience. "Grief doesn't have to be all bad. It teaches us things about ourselves we wouldn't have learned before, and it makes us stronger."

I don't respond. I don't want to be stronger because Jack isn't in my life. I want to be sad. I *choose* to be sad.

"Do you want to know what I think?" she says when I don't answer.

"Okay."

"I don't think this is the end."

I sniffle again. "You don't?"

A small smile creeps onto her face. "We're talking about the boy who used to sit in our backyard for hours just to watch you read."

I roll my eyes. "We're not little kids anymore, Mom."

"I *know*," she says. "That's kind of the point, isn't it? You're not kids anymore. Your relationship is changing. You have to figure out how you fit into each other's lives now that hormones are involved."

"Ew. Stop."

"I'm just saying." She nudges me. Then her smile falls, just a little. "You know, after I broke up with Rob—um, your sperm donor—I thought we'd never be friends again. But then we spent the summer apart, and when school started again in the fall, we found our way back to each other. And then we were best friends for *sixteen* more years."

"Did he lead you on only to reject you in the most humiliating way possible?"

"No. He did something worse."

My jaw drops. "Really? What did he do?"

She smiles, small and secret.

"Fine," I groan. "Well, will you at least tell me how you found your way back to each other?"

"You already know the answer to that." She leans around

me to gesture toward the CD player on my nightstand. She doesn't know it, but the CD inside is *NORA*. "With music."

I almost laugh. *Music*. Of course.

Then she sits up straight. "I have the best idea." She gets out of bed and leaves my room without another word.

"Where are you going?" I call after her.

I hear her footsteps move down the staircase, then into the living room. She opens a cabinet and starts rummaging through it. A click, a scratch. And then, turned up so loud it echoes throughout the entire house, a song I've never heard before.

"Immie, come down here!"

I get out of bed and follow the music down the stairs. It's classical guitar, and I think piano, too.

"What is this?" I yell, walking into the living room.

"This, my dear, is *the* best breakup song of all time." She holds the remote up to her mouth like a microphone and starts to sing along to the lyrics. "'Chiquitita, tell me what's wrong . . .'"

"This isn't on any of the CDs," I say.

Mom dismisses my words with a wave of her hand. "He was too pretentious for ABBA," she says. "Just one of the many reasons we weren't right for each other." She holds out her hand to me and sings some more. "'How I hate to see you like this . . .'"

I sit down on the couch and watch her performance, equal parts embarrassed and amused. The chorus hits, and she starts dancing around in her sweatpants, swinging her messy ponytail to the beat.

"Come on," she says. "Dance with me!"

I shake my head. "No thanks."

"Come *on*." She dances around the coffee table and tries to pull me off the couch. When that doesn't work, she pokes me in the side, where she knows I'm ticklish—I squeal and roll away from her. She keeps trying to tickle me until I finally give in and get up. The song gets louder, more intense, and she screams along to the lyrics. "'You and I know how the heartaches come and they go . . .'"

Maybe it's her off-key singing, or the clunky way she dances to the upbeat tempo, but soon I'm laughing. I'm having *fun*. I'm not thinking about Jack or my dad. I'm dancing to the song, listening to the lyrics, giving myself over to the strange sensation of hope.

"'You'll be dancing once again, and the pain will end . . .'"

TRACK EIGHTEEN

"How's It Going to Be"—Third Eye Blind

Well?

Ask two people to paint an apple, and you'll get two different-looking fruits. The core parts will probably be the same: the color, the shape, the stem. But the details, and the intention behind them—that's where the differences will be.

Ask two people to preserve a memory, and the same thing happens. That's because memory is a workable thing, kind of like art. You can mold it and shape it, build it up or beat it down. The important bits will stay the same, but the details are going to change depending on who is doing the remembering, or when, or why.

So how do you accurately and honestly preserve a memory?

Well, you can't. But you can try.

This is what I'm thinking about while I put the finishing touches on my midterm art project. *Who am I?* I'm the cinnamon roll smell of Grandma Imogen's kitchen on Saturday mornings. I'm the warm paper of Mom's lesson plans fresh out of the copier and the satisfying slice of the paper cutter in the teachers' lounge. I'm the secret thrill of the folded notes Jack passed me in school. I'm every melody from my dad's burned CDs. I *am* my memories.

"I think you need one more crack here." My mom leans over the kitchen table and points to a section of acrylic. It's been a week since we danced around the living room to ABBA.

I take the chisel and the hammer and smack the acrylic sheet until another crack forms.

She nods. "That's it. Perfect."

I take a step back and remove my protective goggles—she made me wear them—to study the project as a whole. I smile, satisfied. "It's done." Then I collapse into a chair. "Thanks for helping me."

"I just held the pieces in place while you glued." She sits down in the chair across from me. "You did it all. And you did *good*." She reaches across the table to squeeze my hand.

I look at my project again. The idea came to me last minute, when I was already midway through a canvas painting. Over Thanksgiving break, Mom and I pulled a bunch of bins out of storage, bins that contained boxes of memorabilia and old pictures. Five nights of cutting, pasting, arranging, and shaping later, and I ended up with what I believe is my best attempt at answering the question. It didn't turn out exactly the way I planned, but that's okay. Nothing ever does—especially not me.

My eyes linger on a yellow Laffy Taffy wrapper, and my heart sinks just a little. It would be easy to blame Jack for everything that happened between us—to say that he changed. But that wouldn't be totally fair. I changed too. That's one thing this project taught me. Pulling all my memories out of those dusty old bins, spreading them out side by side and logging them like an archivist, made me realize that I'm *always* going to be changing. And nothing—not Jack or my butterflies or my dad's identity—can truly define me. I'm many things at once, and I'm everything in between.

"So what now?" Mom says. "Should we go get some milkshakes to celebrate?"

"Can we go in a little while?" I look out the window at the setting sun. I've got twenty minutes, maybe, before it gets dark. "I just have one more project to finish."

I carry the shoebox and Mom's biggest garden shovel out to the tree. It's cold outside, so cold it could snow, and I worry that the ground will be too hard to dig into.

When I get to the roots, I hesitate. I haven't been here in a long time. It feels haunted to me now—like betrayal and loss. But the sun is sinking behind the horizon, elongating the shadows of the trees. I have to do this now, before it's too late.

I drop to my knees and start to dig. The ground is still soft, and I have a shoebox-sized hole in no time. I put the box in, but instead of covering it with soil, I remove the lid for an open-casket viewing. I want to see inside one last time.

The CD player that has been my closest companion the last few months.

A CD with "ALL MY BESTS" written across the front

in black Sharpie, along with a track list explaining the song choices.

A handwritten letter folded four times.

The letter was Mom's idea. She told me to put all my feelings down on paper and then burn it or shred it or stick it in a drawer somewhere, but I chose to bury it in here for symbolic reasons. She doesn't know about the music. That's between me and whoever might find this box one day.

I sit in silence, in the shadows, letting the breeze tousle my hair and rustle the leaves around me. I sit for what feels like a long time, knowing that when I close the lid on the box, I'll be doing the same thing to Jack, and to the girl I was when I loved him. Maybe my mom is right—maybe it won't be forever—but for now I'm accepting the fact that it could be. I'll walk away knowing I've given him all my bests. Now I've got nothing left.

I put the lid on the box and cover it with dirt until it disappears. I wipe the dust from my hands. A clean slate.

My name is Imogen Marie Meadows. I'm fourteen years old.

I can tell you Marie Antoinette's last words and how to draw the perfect liquid cat eye.

I love to draw pictures, collect taxidermy butterflies, and have supermodel sleepovers with my friends.

I used to be completely devoted to Jack Marshall, but we grew apart.

You can't preserve a memory, I think again as I walk away. All you can do is hold each other tight while the moment lasts and then know when it's time to let go.

My phone buzzes in my pocket. I pull it out, look at the screen, and smile.

"Hey," I answer. "What's up?"

"Hey," Elijah says. "I was just thinking about you."

PART TWO
Jack

Immie,

Bet you weren't expecting to hear from me. Or
maybe you were. Maybe that's why you buried your
box under the tree, because you secretly hoped
that one day, I would go back there and find it. I
may not be as smart as you, but I know you. And
you never could resist a good symbolic gesture.
Ha, remember that time a wasp got in your room
and stung you, and then you stuck its decapitated
head on a toothpick and left it on your windowsill
"as a warning" to the other wasps? I have to
admit, I feel a little bit like that first wasp. I stung
you, even though I didn't mean to. Now it's off with
my head.

   Anyway, I listened to your CD. And the first
thing I want to say is that I'm sorry. I know you don't
want anything to do with me, and I don't blame you. I
messed everything up. There's nothing I can say that
will undo that. All I can do is try to explain and hope
that, at the end of it, you'll understand. Maybe you
can even forgive me.

   You told me once, when you were drawing, that
butterfly wings are symmetrical, like two equal parts
of a whole. It's sort of the same when it comes to
stories, don't you think? You can't have one side

without the other to fill in the blanks. It's only when you have both that you can see the complete picture.

You told me your story—your truth. Now it's my turn. And it starts like this.

Immie Marie Meadows, I love you.

TRACK ONE

"Nobody Gets Me But You"—Spoon

Seven years later and it's still true.

You know the feeling you get when you come home from school after a really long day, and you're starving, but you figure there's not gonna be anything good to eat because—the last time you checked—the only stuff in the fridge was, like, mayonnaise and leftover green beans, *gross* stuff, but *then* you open the pantry and find it freshly stocked with BBQ Pringles, Swedish Fish, and all your other favorite snacks?

It's like, at first, the world is dark and hopeless, and you think you're gonna starve, and then bam! Everything you ever wanted is right in front of your face, and you'll never go hungry again.

That's exactly how it feels when I see Immie Meadows.

I see her before she sees me. I'm skating past dead Mrs. Lieberstein's house when she walks out the front door, carrying a glass of . . . what? Water? I'm too far away to tell, but it looks ice-cold and delicious.

There's a moving truck in the driveway, and I watch her step aside so two big guys can carry a couch up the porch steps and through the doorway. When she does, a gust of wind brushes her dark hair out of her face, and I can see her more clearly. She looks about my age—seven—or maybe a little older. Is she my new neighbor?

I try to do a little ollie on my skateboard (okay, my brother Michael's skateboard) but mess up. I'm no good at skating, it's true. I thought, if I practiced hard enough, maybe Michael would want to hang out with me again. We used to do fun stuff together all the time, but now that he's in middle school, he's always busy. *And* moody. If I learned to skate, we could ride our boards to the playground, or to Dairy Queen for cookie dough ice cream, or anywhere really. Things could go back to the way they were.

I get back on the board and try again. Now there's even more at stake. If I do this right, maybe *she'll* notice me.

Except I don't do it right. I lose my balance and fly off the board, landing face down in her yard. It knocks the breath out of me.

Is it possible to die of embarrassment? I don't know, but I stay where I am and keep quiet just in case.

That's when I hear a voice. It's small and squeaky, like a mouse.

"Are you dead?"

One glass of lemonade and two hours later, I have to go home for dinner. I don't *want* to. I want to stay with Immie underneath the tree, where the rest of the world doesn't matter. I know that when I go home, I'll be in for another night of chaos: overhearing Carrie video chat her friends on full volume, or Elise crying over her boyfriend, also on full volume, or Carrie *and* Elise screaming at each other about who stole the other one's makeup. I'm seven years old. There's no reason I should know what contouring is, but I do. I really do.

"You can come back tomorrow if you want," Immie says, peering at me over her book. Her eyes are the color of blue raspberry Jolly Ranchers, my favorite flavor. "I'll probably just be reading some more."

So I do. I come back the next day, and the next day. Both days Immie has a different book. It's not something I'm used to. I'm not really a reader, but Immie? She reads with her whole body, scrunching her eyebrows and looking all serious when she learns something new, or leaning in when she gets to a really good part. A couple of times she catches me watching her and says, "What?" but I just shake my head and look away. She doesn't even know that when she reads, she goes someplace else.

On the third day, Immie's mom invites me to stay for dinner. It turns out she's a really good cook. She makes me the tastiest bowl of spaghetti I've ever had (just don't tell my mom), and after dinner she lets me and Immie watch whatever we want on the TV.

Whatever we want! I can hardly believe it. But I guess that's the thing about being an only child. You get to watch whatever you want, whenever you want. You don't have to share the remote—or the couch—with six other people.

"So how come you've been coming over here so much?"

Immie says, hugging a pillow and looking at me curiously. "Don't you have any other friends?"

I look down at my lap, feeling a little embarrassed but not wanting to show it. I've got some friends at school, kids I eat lunch with and partner up with for projects, but outside school, I never see them. Last month I was invited to Karly Webster's pool party, but I couldn't go. My parents were too busy to drive me.

"Not really," I admit. I'm worried she'll think I'm pathetic, but she just nods, pointing the remote at the TV and turning it on.

"Me either," she says. "Nobody gets me."

"I do," I say without thinking. She doesn't respond, just smiles into her lap.

We scroll through the shows and settle on *Avatar: The Last Airbender*, a show I actually love, even though I would have watched anything to stay by her side.

On the fourth day, Immie shows me the butterflies.

"Wait here. And *no* peeking."

Immie opens her bedroom door just a sliver and slinks inside, closing the door behind her. "Are you ready," she says from behind the door, "to be *amazed*?"

"Amazed? What do you have back there, a two-headed unicorn?"

"You mean a unicorn with one head isn't good enough?" She opens the door. "Anyway, it's better than that." She steps to the side, letting me through.

At first I don't know what I'm supposed to be looking at. Most of the room is still filled with boxes, but there's a bed, a tall dresser, a table with a mirror—she's even got one of those giant blow-up chairs, purple and sparkly.

Then I turn around and notice the shelves—or, what's on the shelves.

"This," she explains, looking proud, "is my taxidermy butterfly collection."

I move closer. The shelves on the far side of her room are lined with dead bugs displayed in glass cases. Most of them are butterflies, but there are some other bugs too—moths and even one beetle. Their wings are spread out like they're flying, which is the creepiest part somehow.

I must have a bad look on my face, because Immie's excitement dims.

"You don't like it?"

"To be honest, it's kind of creepy." I can't look away from one of the butterflies, big and dark, that has a design like owl eyes on the back of its wings. "Why do you have these?"

She sees me looking at the butterfly and takes it down from the shelf. "Most of them were my grandma Imogen's. She had a lot of weird stuff like this." She smiles down at it. "But the butterflies were her favorites."

"Okay," I said. "But why do *you* have them?"

"*Because.* I think they're beautiful." Immie puts the bug on the shelf and takes a step back. "Did you know most butterflies only live to be like a month old?"

I move away from the shelves slowly, like if I move too

fast they might come alive to attack me. "No, I didn't."

"It's sad that they only get to be here for that long," Immie continues. "At least when they're preserved like this, their beauty can live on forever."

I make a face. "But they aren't really living on. They're dead. If you took them out of the glass they'd probably turn to dust. Poof."

I can tell Immie is disappointed by my reaction. She sits down in the purple blow-up chair. "Sorry if you're freaked out."

The last thing I want to do is hurt Immie's feelings. In fact, I'd do just about anything to make her happy. But something about these bugs really does give me the heebie-jeebies. Dead bugs aren't beautiful. *Alive* bugs aren't even beautiful.

"I'm not freaked out," I lie. "I like that you're a big weirdo."

Then I smile, because the second part is true. I've only known her for a few days, but already Immie Meadows is the best friend I've ever had. She's smart, cool, funny, brave—all the things I want to be. Best of all, she likes me for me. She's the one person who doesn't think I'm too much.

TRACK TWO

"Slow Burn"—Kacey Musgraves

This song perfectly captures how I felt that day. Relaxed, optimistic, happy to be alive. Now that I think about it, I don't think I've felt that way since.

SEVEN YEARS LATER

I'm standing in the center of the Storm Valley High School soccer field, waiting to hear if my life is over.

The first time I saw this field, I was nine. Michael made varsity as a freshman, and my dad brought me to the team's first home game. The turf was brand new, the boundary lines coated in fresh paint, and the stands were packed with people in Storm Valley green. The Thundercat mascot pumped up the crowd so much, the air felt electric, like the whole stadium was alive.

Right away, I was hooked.

I remember watching Michael dribble the ball up and down the field, amazed by his control. He never let anybody take it from him, no matter how hard they tried. When he passed the ball to number 7, and the player scored, the roar that rippled through the crowd was . . . what's the word?

Exhilarating.

It was the first time I felt part of something bigger than myself. I shot a quick glance at my dad—he was looking out at the field with so much pride. I knew right then I wanted to be on that field one day too.

It's not even that I loved soccer, at least at first. It's more that I wanted to feel the rush of keeping the ball in my possession as I ran it down the field, or the excitement of scoring a goal for my team. I wanted to hear that goal punctuated with cheers from the crowd too. But mostly, I wanted my dad to look at me the way he was looking at Michael.

"All right, boys, listen up." Coach Berotti puts his clipboard under his arm, claps his hands, and rubs them together. "It's been a great week. I saw a lot of guts out there on the field, and some real sportsmanship, too. I wish I had varsity spots for all you." He grabs the clipboard and squints at it. "If you don't hear your name called, don't be discouraged. Take this time to hone your skills, strengthen your weak spots, and try again next year."

"Good luck, bro," Serge says to me under his breath. We've been playing club soccer together since sixth grade, and I know he wants to make varsity just as bad as I do.

"You too," I say, and mean it.

Coach Berotti clears his throat. "All right, here we go. Smith. Whitehouse . . ."

Down the line, Andrew Smith fist-bumps Elijah Whitehouse. I'm not surprised Elijah made it. He was lead striker last year, taking the place of my brother when he graduated. He's the new highest scorer on the team.

"Snyder. O'Leary. Adeyemi . . ."

When my brother was a junior, he set the school record for most goals scored in a single season. Elijah tried to beat it last year but didn't even come close. There's no doubt in my mind he'll try again. But now Michael's record is my score to beat.

"Codispoti. Cruz . . ."

I started playing soccer because of Michael, but then something unexpected happened. I *liked* it. Even better, I was good at it. I could spend hours kicking a ball around without realizing any time had passed at all. After a while, it didn't feel like Michael's thing anymore. It felt like mine.

Last year, when Michael went to college, he tore his ACL and ended his soccer career. My dad was crushed. I, on the other hand, was hyped—not about the injury, but about the implication. It was my chance to finally step out from under his shadow. I could make my parents proud, not just as Michael's little brother, but as my own person.

"Hobson. Talbert . . ."

I started practicing harder and longer than I ever had before. I played in the rain, the fog, the snow. I spent every day of summer break dribbling up and down my street with one goal in mind: be good enough to make varsity. Sometimes Immie would sit in her front yard reading her books or drawing her pictures, and I'd ask her to pretend to be a goalie so I could work on my shooting. For a while she played along, even though she hates sports. Then one day the ball hit her in the face and gave her a nosebleed. I never asked her again after that.

"Dobies . . ."

My thoughts turn to Immie. This morning, when my mom was backing the car out of the driveway, I heard Immie calling out to me. I looked in the direction of her voice, and there she was, in her pajamas and slippers, running through the street.

Obviously, I got out of the car.

"Monty," she said, pausing to catch her breath. Her hair was wild, and she had a big grin on her face. "I just . . . wanted to wish you . . . good luck."

And then she threw her arms around me. It took me a second to realize I wasn't dreaming, but then I hugged her back. I remember that her hair smelled like peaches.

"Moreno."

I snap out of it and look at Serge. His eyes are wide, like he's in shock.

"Dude!" I whisper, shaking his arm.

"Did he say my name?" Serge says. "He said my name, right?"

"Marshall."

I look at Coach. Am I hearing things, or did he say my name too? He looks back at me and gives me the slightest nod.

A smile spreads across my face.

I did it.

Serge and I look at each other and start laughing. Coach shoots us a warning look, and we quiet down, but inside, I'm screaming and sprinting around the stadium. I don't even hear the rest of the names. All I can think is that I did it. I *actually* did it.

I picture Immie's face smiling at me in the driveway, her

skeleton pajamas and her wild black hair. When I left her there, all I could think about was how scared I was of disappointing her. For once, I want *her* to be impressed by *me*.

"If you heard your name, congratulations, you're a Thundercat." Coach Berotti takes off his hat, letting his mullet fly free. "Welcome to the Storm Valley varsity soccer team."

Serge's girlfriend, Zoya, is hanging out by the front gate, talking to Coach's daughter. When she sees us walking toward her with our bags slung over our shoulders and smiles on our faces, she lets out a high-pitched squeal.

"Ohmygod!" Zoya runs through the gate and jumps into Serge's arms. I look away, trying not to think of Immie.

"You made it?" she says, and looks at me. "Both of you?"

"Yeah, girl," Serge replies. "You're looking at the only two freshmen on Storm Valley varsity."

She squeals again, right in his face, and gives him a long kiss. I exchange a glance with Coach's daughter, Alex, and we smile awkwardly.

Serge pulls his phone out of his pocket and answers it. "Hola, Mamá. ¿Estás aquí?" He looks at me. "She's here."

Zoya turns to me. "We're all going to Hearth's tonight. Are you coming?"

"Oh, I uh . . ." I look at Serge, and then Alex, who gives me a small smile. "I can't. I've got plans."

"With Immie?" Serge wiggles his eyebrows suggestively. He pronounces "Immie" like it's spelled with ten *I*s.

"Yeah?" I say, my heartbeat picking up. "We're just hanging at her place, like always."

"Immie Meadows?" Zoya sounds interested. "Is she your girlfriend?"

"No," I say quickly, at the same time Serge says, "He wishes."

I try to laugh it off while internally fighting the urge to kick Serge across the field like a soccer ball. "I wish I had a hamburger. I'm starved."

"Mm-hmm." Serge adjusts his bag over his shoulder. "Whatever you say, brother. Let's go."

I follow Serge out to his mom's SUV and climb in the back seat.

"Thanks for giving me a ride home, Mrs. Moreno."

"Of course, honey," she says in her thick accent. She smiles back at me warmly. "Congratulations, boys! I'm so proud of you."

She puts the car in drive, and Serge waves goodbye to Zoya, who's blowing him kisses on the other side of the window. They've been a couple for three months now. When are they going to stop being so obsessed with each other?

I think about Immie, hear Serge's voice in my head. *He wishes.*

I sigh. Serge is wrong. There's no point in wishing for something that won't ever come true. Immie will never feel that way about me. I'm nothing special, and she's . . . well, the *most* special.

I've pretty much had a crush on her for as long as I can remember. I know, I know. Idiotic, right? I almost told her once, last year, when her mom was looking for a new job and she thought she was going to have to move again. I remember saying that she *couldn't* go—we'd just turned thirteen; we were about to start eighth grade; everything was *just* getting good. She said she might have to.

"Fine," I replied immediately. "Then I'll come with you."

She smiled, small and sad. "You'd do that for me?"

We were sitting in our spot under the tree. I sat up straight, looked her dead in the eye. "I'd do anything for you."

She looked down at the ground, let her long black hair fall over her face. "Why?"

My heart was beating fast. If she knew the way I felt, and she felt the same way, maybe she'd try to talk her mom out of moving. This was my chance—possibly my only chance.

"Because—"

Shouting in the distance made us both stop and turn our heads. It was a girl's voice, and it sounded familiar.

"I think that's Carrie," I said, already moving to crawl out from under the tree. Immie was right behind me.

We walked around the side of the house until we could see them. Carrie and Lucy, who'd only been going out for a few weeks at that point, were having an argument in the driveway. "You don't love me!" Carrie practically wailed. I couldn't hear Lucy's response because she was talking at a normal volume. Then Lucy tried to reach out to Carrie, but Carrie pulled back, shaking her head.

"My heart is *broken*," she said between sobs. "*You* broke it."

"Blech." Immie scrunched up her nose. "If you ever hear

me talking like that, tie me up and send me to the FBI, because aliens have taken over my body."

"They're always fighting," I replied with a shrug. "It's nothing new."

"That's because love makes you do embarrassing things," Immie said. "And that's why I don't want any part of it."

"I don't think it works like that."

In fact, I knew from experience that love wasn't something you chose. It was something that happened to you.

"Whatever," Immie said with a wave of her hand. "I'm hungry. Want to raid the pantry?"

Needless to say, the moment had passed. And I've never dared to bring it up again.

In the car, Serge starts browsing radio stations. He stops on the sound of an acoustic guitar.

"Aw yeah." I watch the back of his head as he nods along to the beat. "This is my song."

I laugh. "Is this Kacey Musgraves?"

"Heck yeah, dude. She's *amazing*. Voice of a freaking angel." The chorus hits, and he starts to sing along off-key. "''Cause I'm all right with a slow buuuurn . . .'"

I lean back in my seat and roll down my window, looking out at the fields as we drive past. It's a view I've seen a million times before, but today there's something different about it. The clean rows of wheat underneath the clear blue sky look like a postcard.

I smile, content. It's finally starting to sink in. My dream of making the varsity soccer team as a freshman has come true, because I *made* it come true. No wishing, just hard work. In a little over two weeks, I'll be on the turf for my first game, and I'll be so good that my parents will have no choice but to pay attention.

For the first time in my life, *everyone* will pay attention to me.

When we pull up to my house, I thank Serge's mom for the ride again and watch the car as she drives it away.

That's when I see Immie. Two houses down, standing in her front yard with a bag of snacks on one arm and a blanket rolled up under the other. She's holding a can of BBQ Pringles. My favorite.

"Oh my goodness," she calls out. "Is that David Beckham?"

"Do you think high school is going to be a lot different than middle school?"

I'm lying under the tree with my hands behind my head. Immie is next to me, sketching in her notebook. Every now and then, her bare foot grazes my shin.

"Maybe," I reply. "But probably not. Still all the same people, learning the same things."

"But we don't have any classes together."

"We have one."

She stops sketching and looks at me, surprised.

"I signed up for honors social studies," I say.

Her jaw drops. "You what?"

I prop myself up on my elbows. "I had to. You weren't going to drop any honors classes, and social studies was the one that seemed like it would suck the least."

She laughs. "I don't know about that. It's a lot of reading, and you hate reading."

"But you don't," I say. "You can just tell me what I need to know."

She swats me with a Twizzler, but I can tell by the look on her face that she's happy, and that's all I need. I'll read the textbook cover to cover if it means getting to see her smile at least once during the school day.

"Well, be careful what you wish for," she says. "Now that you've got your new soccer friends, you might not want to hang around me as much." She puts the tip of the Twizzler in her mouth and bites down.

I laugh under my breath. She really doesn't have a clue how I feel about her.

"Wrong," I say, sitting up. "A bunch of sweaty guys packed onto buses and in locker rooms? I'll want to be around you even more."

She offers me the bag of Twizzlers, and I take one. We already finished the Pringles and the sour gummy worms.

"What did it feel like?" she asks. "The moment you found out you made the team. What was the first thing that popped into your head?"

You, I want to say, but don't.

"At first I wasn't sure I heard right." I take a bite of the Twizzler. "But then, when I realized it wasn't in my head, I was happy. And, like, relieved. I could go home and tell my parents something that would make them proud—something that *I* did."

Immie shakes her head. "Your parents are proud of you. They're just . . ." She chews, searching for the word. "Busy."

"Ha. Yeah. So busy they hardly notice I'm there."

"Well, what did they say when you told them you made the team?"

"Nothing." I glance down the street at my house. "I haven't told them yet. Mom's at Marigold's ballet class, and Dad is off selling somebody a house."

She shakes her head, eats more Twizzler. She probably doesn't know what to say, and I don't blame her. She has no idea what it's like to feel invisible in her own family. She's her mom's *entire* family. I try not to get jealous, but I do sometimes. What would it feel like to know that someone loved you more than every other person on earth?

"So, what are we watching tonight?" I say, changing the subject.

Her eyes light up. "Well, a new Victorian romance just started streaming. *Or* we could watch that horror movie with that guy . . . what's his name? The one with the hair?"

"What about the new Superman movie?"

She shoots me a skeptical look. "Monty, be serious."

I smirk. She hates superhero movies with a fiery passion.

"Oh." She reaches behind her. "I almost forgot." She hands me a bag of banana-flavored Laffy Taffys. "Your congratulations-on-making-the-team present."

"Aw." I take the bag. "But what if I hadn't made the team?"

"Then they would've been your sorry-you-didn't-make-it consolation prize."

I smile. Once, a long time ago, we were eating a bag of Laffy Taffys on her living room floor. When we got to the last two—strawberry and banana—Immie pulled them both out of the bag and said, *Ew, banana*. So I took the banana. She looked at me, shocked. *You* like *banana?* I told her it was my favorite, but that was a lie. Really, I thought banana was just all right. I'm not sure why I did it. I think maybe I just didn't want her to feel bad about taking the strawberry.

"Thanks, Outie." I pull the bag open. "You're the best."

TRACK THREE

"Animal"—Miike Snow

From the first day of school, something wasn't right. I was getting everything I wanted, but I didn't feel happy. I felt like a fraud. I was a sheep in werewolf's clothing, or whatever that expression is.

*M*onday morning, I wake up at eight thirty for my first day of Hell Week.

It's tradition that the week before school starts, the soccer team has two practices a day: one in the morning and one in the afternoon. It's a week that's designed to push us to our limits— or so Michael says. More importantly, it's the week that will determine who gets to start in our first game next week.

I show up to practice ready to give it my all, to prove to Coach Berotti that even though I'm new, I can pull my weight on this team. But he isn't there. He's home sick, so Coach Robbie, the assistant, is in charge. Right away I can tell this is bad news for me. Coach Robbie graduated the same year as my brother, which means to the upperclassmen he's more of a peer than a coach—and it's pretty clear who his favorites are.

"Yo, listen up!" Elijah says when we're all gathered around

the benches. "Warm-up lap and then stretch lines on the turf. Let's go!"

Elijah has been cocky from the start. He knew he'd make the team, so he phoned it in during tryouts, acting all buddy-buddy with Coach Robbie while the rest of us killed ourselves on the field. At least today he's actually putting in some effort.

He leads the pack during the warm-up lap, but I make sure to stay right behind him. I want him to know that I'm coming for his striker spot. At some point I guess he notices, because he starts to speed up. So I match his pace. Serge, who's right next to me, shoots me a confused look. Still I don't slow down. I keep right at Elijah's heels the whole way around the track, even when we break apart from the rest of the group. We finish nearly a quarter mile ahead of everyone else.

At the finish line he gets his water bottle from the bench and takes a long swig.

"Nice hustle, Marshall," he says, still catching his breath. "You almost beat me."

"I could've beaten you if I wanted to," I say with a grin. "I let you win."

He chuckles like he doesn't believe me and returns his attention to his water bottle. Serge catches up with a suspicious look on his face.

"What was that about?"

I shake my head instead of responding.

"Don't piss him off, man," Serge says quietly, so Elijah can't hear. "He's teacher's pet around here. If you get on his bad side, he'll make both our lives a living—"

"Moreno, Marshall."

I turn around at the sound of Elijah's voice. He's taller than me, which is annoying. I have to squint into the sun to look at his face.

"The ball bags are in the storage closet in the gym. You two need to go get them."

"What?" I say. "Coach didn't tell us—"

"It's a freshman rite of passage to carry the ball bags during Hell Week," he says. "Sorry. I don't make the rules."

You kind of do, I want to say, but the look on Serge's face is a silent warning not to protest. I clench my jaw, nod once. Elijah walks away.

The rest of the day doesn't go much better. I'm kept out of the morning 2v2s, and in the afternoon scrimmage, I'm assigned as a fullback even though I tell Coach Robbie I want a shot at striker or winger. Then there's Elijah. Making me run for balls and fill the water cooler, and then *accidentally* knocking over the cooler right before I can refill my bottle, so I have to go fill it again. By the end of the day, I'm half convinced he's out to get me.

"Marshall." He comes up to me as I'm about to start lugging the ball bags back to the gym. "No hard feelings, right?"

"Uh. Okay."

"You're a good player," he says. "And a good sport, too."

"Great. Hope I don't drop the ball." I proceed to let the ball bag slip through my hands and fall to the ground, then look at him with an exaggerated grimace.

"Funny," he says. "Michael was always cracking jokes too."

My smile falls. It's the first day of practice, and already I'm being compared to Michael.

"I'm not my brother," I say firmly.

"I know," he replies. "You know why I know?"

I wipe off the hair that's sticking to my forehead and wait for him to tell me.

"Because Michael had confidence on the field," he says. "You've got great control, and a powerhouse kick, but when it comes to passing and intercepting, you're too timid. It's like you're afraid to take the ball away from other people sometimes."

My instinct is to get mad, to clench my fists and tell him that he's wrong—that he's a jerk. The problem is he's *not* wrong. Passing has always been my weak spot.

"If you want to be great," he continues, "you have to be a fighter. Show everybody why you deserve to be on that field."

I try to think of something smart to say but decide it's no use. He can see right through me.

"How do I do that?" I ask.

"Stick with me," he says, and then gives me a pat on the shoulder that reminds me of something Michael would do. "I'll help you."

Over the next couple of days, Elijah takes special interest in my game, partnering with me during passing warm-ups and helping me fine-tune my technique. I'm not really sure why— maybe it's a favor to Coach, or a favor to Michael, or maybe it goes deeper than that. Maybe he sees something in me. Maybe he thinks I really *could* be great.

On Thursday, Coach Berotti comes back, and I finally get a chance to play striker against Elijah. It's the brightest, hottest day of the week so far. It's hard to look up without getting the sun in my eyes, so I don't. I keep my focus on the ball, and it's surprising how easy it is to block out the rest of the world. When I'm in the game, I'm in control.

I get the ball from Serge and dribble it down the center of the field, cutting left just as the opposing midfielder closes in. I pass the ball to Liam, who runs it a few yards and then fakes right when Elijah tries to intercept him, passing it back to me. I hear Elijah's words in my head: *Be a fighter*. So instead of running it farther, like they expect, I take a chance, shooting into the top right corner of the net. I score.

"Nice, Marshall. Good instincts," Coach Robbie shouts from the sidelines. "Whitehouse, where's that aggression?"

I use the bottom of my shirt to wipe the sweat from my face, then get back in starting position. I see Elijah, across the field, nodding his approval.

Monday morning, the first day of school. Immie gets into the back seat of Carrie's car with a huff.

"My new boots are squeaky."

"Should've broken them in first," Carrie says, putting the car in reverse and backing out of the driveway.

"I didn't want to risk getting them dirty!" Immie says. She's wearing a light blue shirt that matches her eyes. She looks really pretty, but that's nothing new. "I was saving them for the first day."

"You don't have to wear them to break them in," Carrie replies. "Just bend them in your hands a bunch of times."

"Too late now," I say, turning in my seat to face her. "How you feelin'?"

She shrugs. "Excited. Nervous. *Annoyed* about my boots."

"Nobody is going to notice," I say. "The halls are so loud."

"How are *you* feeling?" she asks me. "Are you ready for the social studies quiz?"

"Yeah." I turn back around in my seat so she can't see my face. "I'm gonna ace it."

"A test on the first day?" Carrie looks disgusted. "That is seriously messed up."

"I warned him the class was going to be a lot of reading," Immie says. "He wanted to take it."

"Why?" Carrie asks.

"Because . . ." I hurry to come up with something other than the truth. "Because I love our country, and I want to learn as much of its history as I can."

Immie snorts. "Because he wanted to have a class with me. He couldn't *bear* to be away from me all day."

I force a laugh—keep it light. "Yep. Who else is going to appreciate my Wet Willy doodles?"

"Wet Willy is a whale he draws in my notes when he borrows them," Immie explains. "Usually he's jumping out of stuff."

"You two are nauseating," Carrie says.

"Thank you," Immie replies. I turn around to look at her, and she grins at me.

We get to the student parking lot, and Carrie pulls into

her assigned spot. Three spaces down, Andrew is getting out of his Honda. I notice Elijah in the passenger seat.

We get out of our cars at the same time, but he's scrolling his phone, so he doesn't see me right away. It's only when I shut the door that he finally looks up. I raise my hand in a wave, but his eyes are drawn to something behind me. I turn around.

Immie slams the car door closed.

"Hey, Incredible Hulk," Carrie says from the driver's side. "Not so hard, huh? She's delicate."

"Sorry." Immie looks at me, tucking a strand of hair behind her ear. "Ready?"

I glance back at Elijah, who seems to have forgotten I exist. What bothers me isn't just that he's looking at Immie—everyone looks at Immie—but the *way* he's looking. Like she's the last blue raspberry Jolly Rancher.

I turn my attention back to her, trying to push the worries out of my mind. Elijah may have the starting striker spot, but Immie is *my* best friend. She's the one thing he can't take from me.

"Ready."

I bomb the social studies quiz, but other than that, the rest of the day actually goes okay.

A lot of that is because of the guys on the team. I figure, because I'm new, that the upperclassmen will ignore me, but they don't. The opposite happens. They treat me like we're friends already. They say hi to me in the halls, sit by me in classes, and even save me a seat at lunch.

When I get out of line and scan the cafeteria, I see Ben, my teammate, waving me over to a table in the center of the room. There's an empty seat between him and Serge. I take a breath, relieved. It's not lunch with Immie, but it's the next best thing.

". . . remember his face when you made that shot?" Liam is saying when I sit down with my tray. "He wanted to kill you. If the refs weren't there, I bet he would've."

Across the table, Elijah laughs. "He would've had to catch me first. The guy couldn't keep up if his life depended on it."

"We get it," Andrew says, his mouth full of sub. "You're the fastest one on the team. Next?"

"Maybe not anymore." Elijah gestures toward me with his elbow. "Marshall here is giving me a run for my money."

"True," Ben says. "He almost beat your mile time."

"Not *surprising*," Andrew adds. "Considering who his brother is."

I clench my jaw. I've been at this table thirty seconds, and already, Michael is one-upping me—and he's not even here.

"I'm faster than Michael," I say, and then look directly at Elijah. "And soon, I'll be a better striker than you."

A round of *oohs* sweeps the table. Serge widens his eyes at me, surprised, or maybe impressed—I can't tell.

An amused smile slips over Elijah's face. He takes a long swig from his water bottle and then says, "Guess we'll see."

"Guess so," I say.

Wednesday afternoon, the first game of the season. I'm walking to the locker room with my earbuds in and my pump-up playlist on, the volume cranked way up. Loud music has always been the best way to drown out my thoughts.

Yeah, I'm nervous. Both of my parents are going to be there—Dad pushed his evening house showings to tomorrow morning, and Mom got Carrie to watch the twins. Immie is going to be there too, with a sign she made for me. She texted me a picture of it last night. I can't stop thinking about how good it would feel to score a goal, look up at the stands, and see Immie holding up my name in glitter. I want it so bad, I can hardly breathe.

In the locker room, I change into my uniform. The rest of the guys are talking and joking around. They all seem relaxed, even Serge, which makes me ever more nervous. Why aren't they freaking out like me?

I keep my earbuds in. When "Animal" by Miike Snow comes on the queue, I turn the volume up until it's maxed out. The lyrics hit extra hard today—*"I change shapes just to hide in this place but I'm still, I'm still an animal."* I try to lock in, to remind myself that I've got this. I can stay calm. I can stay in control.

Coach Berotti walks into the room with Coach Robbie, and everybody's talking dies down. I take off my earbuds, sit down on the bench. All of a sudden, I feel kind of sick. I drink some water and take deep breaths to calm down.

Serge taps on my arm. "Jack, man. You good?"

I nod, keeping my eyes fixed on the floor. I'm afraid if I look up, the room will start to spin. "Yeah." I drink some more water. "Yeah, fine."

Coach begins to list off the names of the starting players.

I hear Elijah's name, Serge's name, a few other names . . . and that's it. I blink, look up. Did I miss something?

"Don't worry, dude." Serge claps me on the back. "I'm sure he'll sub you in."

I'm too stunned to say anything. I just stand up in a daze and follow the team out onto the field.

Why isn't he starting me? Haven't I proved myself enough? Even if Coach didn't want to give me Elijah's striker spot, he could've made me midfield or winger, and I still would've had a shot at scoring points.

What did I do wrong?

I glance up into the stands. Right away I see Immie, bouncing up and down with the sign she made, and man, it cracks my heart in half. She put all that effort into a sign she might not even get to use, and it's all my fault.

Right next to her, I see my parents. When my mom notices me looking, she waves with both hands, a proud smile on her face. My dad is sitting to her right, predictably stone-faced in his sunglasses. A lump forms in my throat, and I have to look away.

The next eighty minutes are a blur. I'm on the bench the whole time, which is even more embarrassing than if I'd played a bad game. While I sit there, I'm just thinking about Immie and my parents, imagining the looks on their faces. Immie, with her pity, Dad clenching his jaw in frustration, Mom's fidgety discomfort. I know they're all wondering why I'm not on the field—I'm wondering too. I know Dad's comparing me to Michael. I think about the proud look on his face when

Michael made the assist in his first game—can't get the image out of my head, actually—and I know I've disappointed him. This is just one more way I've failed to live up to his expectations.

We lose the game 0–2. After we line up to shake hands with the other team, I head straight for the locker room. I don't want to talk to anyone, or even look at anyone. This was my shot to prove that I could be something special, and I ruined it.

I duck around a corner, into an unused row of lockers, and sit down on the bench. I put my head in my hands. What's wrong with me? I've been working hard on passing drills, trying to be confident in scrimmages, like Elijah said. But it isn't enough.

I squeeze my eyes shut and wish, for the millionth time in my life, that I could be a little more like Michael.

The door to the locker room opens, and I hear voices trickle inside.

". . . with the long black hair?" It sounds like Andrew.

"Yeah." This voice belongs to Elijah. "She's friends with Marshall."

I freeze in place. They're talking about Immie.

"She's hot, dude. You should go for it."

My heart starts to pound. *Go for it?* What is *it*?

"I don't know. She's a freshman."

"Even better." A pause. "Mint condition."

I clench my jaw. I want to jump over the lockers and tackle him to the floor.

"You're an idiot," Elijah says.

The door opens again, followed by more voices, and the subject of Immie is shut down. They start talking about the game, about who missed what pass and which player was talking smack about somebody's mom. I don't move.

Elijah likes Immie. *That's* why he's been so nice to me. He knows we're friends, and now he's using me to get to her. It will probably work, too. Why wouldn't it? He's older, taller, and more experienced. He's the star of the soccer team. And I'm just . . . me.

I stand up. I need to get out of here, to get away from people. My heart is pounding so fast it feels hard to breathe. I stagger over to the showers and close myself in a stall, where I can be alone.

I sit down on the bench and lean my head back against the wall. I'm a failure. That's what I keep thinking. Today was my chance to impress Immie, and instead, I just embarrassed myself. Why can't I ever do anything right?

The thoughts circle around and around in my head, going a thousand miles a minute. It feels like an invisible weight is pressing down on my chest, like I can't breathe.

I can't breathe.

My hands start to tingle, my wrists, my arms, my legs. What's happening? Am I having a heart attack? My vision goes blurry at the edges, and then black, until the rest of the room is far away. I *am* having a heart attack. There's a high-pitched ringing sound coming from somewhere. From everywhere. I'm dying. I *have* to be dying.

And then everything goes dark.

TRACK FOUR

"Nothing's Gonna Stop Us Now"—Starship

You probably don't remember this song, or that cheesy commercial about the couple in the grocery store, but I do. I've thought about it a lot, actually. How nice it would be to buy groceries with the person you love, who also loves you back

Immie: I know we were gonna carpool to the movies but I'm already at the mall. Can we meet here instead?

I'm in my room on Sunday when I get the text, lying in bed and blasting some music in my earbuds. It's where I've spent a lot of my time this weekend. I haven't been getting great sleep since what happened after the game on Wednesday.

I woke up on the floor of the shower stall, confused, but alive. I figured I must have just gotten dehydrated and passed out—it was a hot day, and I wasn't drinking water on the bench. So I left the stall. I joined the rest of the team in the main area of the locker room and chugged my whole water bottle. Nobody even knew that anything had happened.

But that night, I couldn't sleep. I stared at the ceiling while my thoughts raced. I kept replaying what had happened, remembering how I'd felt right before I'd passed out, like I was suffocating and on fire. I thought about my parents, and Immie, and how I'd let everybody down, and I couldn't stop reliving the shame.

I *can't* stop reliving it.

I get out of bed and run a hand through my hair to try to tame it—I don't have to see it to know I've got major bed head. I search through my drawer, trying to find a pair of socks without a hole in them. Then I make my way into the hallway, to the bathroom, but find the door closed. I knock.

"What?" It's Carrie.

"Are you almost done?"

"No," she says. "Go away."

I go downstairs. Dad is sitting on the recliner, watching ESPN with Tina on his lap. Carter is on the couch, gaming.

"Where's Mom?" I ask.

"She took the twins to the park," Carter says without looking up.

I groan. "Do you know when she'll be back?"

Carter makes a face. "What do I look like? Her assistant?"

"I need a ride to the movies," I say, glancing at Dad. "Immie and I have tickets for four thirty."

"Ask your sister," Dad says, his eyes on the TV. "She's not doing anything."

"She's gonna say no."

"Tell her I told her to," he says, and then throws up his hands when a batter strikes out, making Tina jump up in surprise. "Oh!"

That's about the extent of our interactions these days. After the game, when I met my parents by the gate, my mom gave me a hug and said, "Next time, huh?" My dad didn't say anything. He didn't really even look at me.

My thoughts turn to Immie. Yesterday she told me she might want to start looking for her real dad. I felt conflicted—I still do. Her life is perfect as it is. Why would she want to do anything that might change it? Why doesn't she realize how lucky she already is?

"Dad." I try to keep my voice casual. "You coming to my game on Wednesday? It's at home."

Now he does look at me. "I can't, buddy. Gotta work late." He turns back to the TV.

I nod. That's what I figured.

I go back upstairs to find Carrie. She's still in the bathroom.

"Hey." I knock again. "Can you give me a ride to the movies in like fifteen minutes?"

"No," she says through the door.

I roll my eyes. "Why not?"

"Because I'm busy."

"Too bad. Dad said you have to."

A few beats of silence. Then the door opens. Carrie is standing there in sweatpants and a tank top. She's got a lot of makeup on.

"Dad doesn't care whether I take you to the movies or not."

I look into the room behind her. The counter is covered in makeup, and her ring light is propped up. "What are you even doing in there?"

"Why do you want to know, perv?"

I raise my hands in surrender. "Never mind. Can you please just take me to the movies? Nobody else will."

She leans against the doorway, crosses her arms. "What's in it for me?"

"What?" I furrow my brow. "God, Carrie, can't you just help me out?"

"I want an Icee," she says. "Blue raspberry. Large."

"You're going to drop me off and then wait in the parking lot for me to get you an Icee?"

"That's right." She smirks. "Take it or leave it."

"Fine," I say. "Fifteen minutes."

"Fine," she repeats, and then slams the door in my face.

When I get to the movies, Immie is waiting for me in the lobby with Carrie's blue raspberry Icee. Carrie was late getting out of the bathroom—it's a mystery, what girls do in there—so I texted Immie on the way to ask if she could get it for me.

"Thanks." I take it from her. "One sec."

I run the Icee out to Carrie and hand it to her through the driver's-side window. She mutters a quick thanks and then drives off. At least I got a thanks, I guess.

Inside, Immie is looking at the upcoming-movie posters. She's wearing a light purple sweater—she always wears sweaters to the movies—and her dark hair is pulled back in a braid. I like it when she wears her hair like that. It's like drawing back the curtains on a sunny day.

"Thanks again," I tell her. "I'll pay you back."

"Don't be silly. It all evens out." She bumps her shoulder

into mine. Or really, her shoulder into my bicep. We used to be the same height, but now I've got five inches on her.

At the concession stand, we buy Swedish Fish and an orange Fanta for Immie, Milk Duds and Sprite for me, and a bucket of popcorn to share. We take it all into theater 6 and get seats toward the top. Immie likes to sit up high.

"So what's going on?" she asks when we're settled. The lights are still on, and there's an ad for a local jeweler on the big screen. The theater is less crowded than usual for a Sunday afternoon. "What did you do after our emergency meeting yesterday?"

I practiced my dribbling a little and then spent the rest of the day in bed, listening to music. I don't want to tell her that, though. "Not much. Played soccer, hung out."

"With the guys from the team?"

"Yeah," I lie.

She slurps her Fanta. "You look tired."

"Yeah." I look away from her. "Didn't get much sleep last night, I guess."

She continues to study me in that thoughtful way of hers, like I'm one of her butterflies pressed in glass.

"What about you?" I say, eager to change the subject. "Did you break out the deerstalker and start looking for your dad?"

She makes a face. *"Deerstalker?"*

"You know. Sherlock Holmes's hat."

"I didn't know," she says. "I'm surprised *you* know."

"Hey, I know things." I toss a piece of popcorn into the air and catch it in my mouth. First try—*nice.*

"Apparently." She takes another sip. "What's next? The official name for Santa's hat?"

"It's because of my dad," I say. "He loves Sherlock Holmes. Don't know why. Must be a dad thing."

She looks away. "I wouldn't know."

"So you're not going to look for him?"

"I don't know yet." She looks at me with hard eyes. "Let's talk about something else?"

I recognize the same defensive tone she gave me yesterday, when she first brought it up. Maybe that means she knows, deep down, that I'm right, and looking for him is a bad idea.

"As you wish. How was the mall?"

She shrugs. "It's not really my thing, to be honest. Just walking around for no real reason? And with no windows." She makes a face. "But Hannah and her friends do it all the time."

"You've been hanging out with them a lot." I open the box of Milk Duds.

"Yeah, well. I need someone to hang out with while you're at soccer." She holds out her hand for a Dud. I pour a few into her palm. "I do really like Hannah. I mean, I like them all, but sometimes Zoya can be a lot. And Alex is . . . shy."

"She seems more quiet than shy." I pop the candy in my mouth.

She gives me an accusatory look. "How do you know that?"

"She's always in the stands with Zoya during practice," I say. "We talk sometimes."

Now she looks surprised. "You *talk* sometimes?"

"Not like *that*," I say, feeling nervous for some reason. "I just mean—she says hi to me, and stuff."

Immie relaxes into her seat. "Well, that's because you're easy to talk to. You can get along with anyone."

I exhale, relieved. Even though I don't want Immie to know how I feel about her, I don't want her to think anything is going on with Alex and me either. Both things would ruin our friendship in their own way.

"Only because I hate uncomfortable situations." We pull our legs in to let an older couple walk past us. "Which reminds me. You don't have to come to the game on Wednesday."

"What?" She puts down her soda. "Why not?"

"I'm probably just gonna be riding the bench again." I focus on the big screen instead of her face. I know she's going to be giving me that pitying look, and I don't want to see it. "I don't want to subject you to torture."

"Oh," Immie says. I can hear in her voice that she's conflicted. "Are you sure?"

I look at her. I don't see pity on her face as much as I see concern. That's even worse, somehow.

"Yeah. Don't worry about it."

We both look at the big screen. It's showing trivia questions over cheesy background music. *In which classic children's story does the protagonist only eat cabbage?*

"*Winnie-the-Pooh,*" I guess.

Immie looks at me in disbelief. "He's literally a bear."

"So?"

"Bears eat honey. That's kind of his whole thing."

The answer pops on the screen. *Charlie and the Chocolate Factory.*

"Oh well." I grab a fistful of popcorn. "You didn't get it right either."

"Yeah, but you're the one who *knows things*."

The next question appears on screen. *What flavor of Pop-Tarts does Buddy the elf use in his spaghetti?*

"Hey." Her voice is soft. "You know it's not a big deal, right?"

"What, getting the question wrong?"

"No," Immie says. "That you haven't gotten to play yet."

There's an ache in my chest. It's been happening more and more, every time I think about soccer and all the ways I'm falling short. I keep my eyes on the screen, and the answer pops up: *Chocolate.*

"It's just a couple games," she continues. "It's not like the coach is going to bench you all season."

"I know, but . . ."

"But what?"

"It's hard to explain," I say. "It's embarrassing."

"Monty, come on. It's me. I've seen you do way more embarrassing stuff."

I snort. "Like what?"

"We met because you fell on your face! Sorry, buddy. Our whole friendship is founded on you being embarrassing."

"Great. Thanks. I feel a lot better now."

"Come *on*." She shakes my arm. "Just tell me what's wrong. It's obvious something is."

"It's just . . ." I sigh. "Michael played in his first game."

"So what? You're not Michael."

"Yeah, that's the problem. I've never been as good as Michael at anything. And my Dad—I feel like, when he looks at me, that's all he sees."

She looks at me sadly. "Monty, you know that's not true."

"No I don't," I insist. "My parents have always been so proud of Michael, and it makes sense. He was great at soccer, an honor student, now he's going to be a doctor . . ." I trail off. "He's done stuff that's easy to be proud of. But me? I haven't done anything that he hasn't already done before me."

"You're younger than him." She takes another sip of her soda. "You still have tons of time to prove yourself."

I shake my head. At my age, Michael was already doing more, and I never hear the end of it. Just yesterday Dad was reminiscing about the time Michael struck out five batters in a row when he pitched for his middle school baseball team. I only played baseball for one season, because I couldn't catch a ball to save my life.

"You don't understand what it's like to have a perfect older sibling that you're always being compared to." I eat a handful of popcorn.

She sits up a little straighter, sucks in her cheeks, and I can tell right away I said the wrong thing.

"I just mean that there's a lot of pressure, and I can't ever escape it," I say quickly. "Not at home, or school, or on the soccer field. It feels like I'm falling short everywhere."

She picks at her thumbnail. "I get it. I know you don't

think I do, but I do. I know how it feels to worry that you're not good enough."

I want to ask how she could possibly know—she's a straight-A student, a great artist, and so beautiful, I saw a sophomore walk into a wall last week because he couldn't stop staring at her.

"That pressure you feel to be perfect? You're putting it on yourself. Nobody else expects that of you. Trust me—there's no such thing as perfect. Not even when it comes to Michael."

Wrong, I think. *You're perfect*.

"I don't need to be perfect," I say instead. "I just want to prove that I can be something other than Michael's little brother, you know? I want something that's mine."

She wrinkles her nose and lightly flicks my cheek. "But you already have that! You've got me."

I can't help but smile. It's not really the point, but it's nice to hear, anyway.

Up on the screen, two people have a meet-cute in the cereal aisle and spend the rest of their shopping trip in a sort of music video montage of romance and groceries, soundtracked by that "Nothing's Gonna Stop Us Now" song from the eighties. I watch the woman gliding toward the man on the back of a shopping cart, and I realize that the tightness in my chest is gone.

I look over at Immie, and she smiles at me reassuringly. Then I hear the lyrics in the song. I think they sound about right.

> *Want so much to give you this love in my heart*
> *That I'm feeling for you . . .*

TRACK FIVE

"Paprika"—Japanese Breakfast

I like this song because it's got two parts. The epic high of the first half, when the singer is getting attention, followed by the crushing low of the second half, when she's alone. I could definitely relate to that.

I try to go into the game the following week with Immie's words in mind. The pressure isn't real. It's all in my head. It doesn't matter what happens, because she'll be by my side no matter what. Still, when I'm benched right away, *again*, it stings. I just want to play. I don't even care if I play well. My parents aren't here to see it, and neither is Immie. I miss being out on the field.

I look up into the stands. It's even more crowded than usual, because it's our rivalry game against Greenfield. I see a lot of kids from school here, and I'm hit with a fresh wave of embarrassment. Soon the whole school will know that I'm nothing but a benchwarmer.

And then I see her up at the top, next to Zoya and Hannah. Her hair gives her away, blowing in the wind like a shiny black flag against a pale blue sky. She waves at me with a smile on her face, and I wave back, amazed. She came, even though I told her she didn't have to. Even though she knew I'd be sitting on the bench.

The game starts, and right away Elijah almost gets in a fight on the field. I don't blame him. A few of Greenfield's players make a game out of heckling us, especially this one guy who supposedly stole Elijah's girlfriend last year. When we walked onto the field, he actually got some of the crowd on his side to start chanting "Thundercraps." Our Thundercat mascot had to be physically restrained.

Coach tells Elijah not to do it again or else he'll bench him, but we all know it's an empty threat. He hasn't been benched yet this season.

"Jack!"

I turn my head. Alex is walking toward me holding blue and purple Gatorades.

"Hey." I stand up, walk over to her. "What are you doing here?"

She holds the purple Gatorade out to me. "I remembered this was your favorite flavor."

"Wow, thanks." I take it. "Gotta replenish those electrolytes from all that running I've been doing."

She laughs. "My dad is just fueling you up. When you finally get out there, you'll have so much energy that you can kick the ball from one end of the field to the other."

"That's right," I say. "I'm the secret weapon."

"I don't doubt it." She smiles. She's got a perfect smile, the kind you only get if you had braces for years. Not like Immie's smile—one of her front teeth slightly overlaps the other. It's still perfect, but in a less conventional way, which is even better, if you ask me.

"Okay," Alex says. "I guess I'll let you get back to it."

"Right. Thanks again for the Gatorade."

"Of course," she says. "See you later."

I sit down on the bench, crack open the Gatorade, and take a big sip, settling in for another long night.

It all happens so fast.

It starts when Elijah picks another fight with the same Greenfielder. This time, to everybody's surprise, Coach actually punishes him. One minute I'm on the bench, waiting for the clock to run out, and the next I'm on the field, taking Elijah's place as striker. The score is tied 3–3 with just two minutes left in the game.

I'm shaky at first. I miss a pass, fumble a couple of kicks. When the ball is nowhere near me, I take a deep breath and try to relax. The pressure is all in my head. I look at Immie in the stands, and I repeat it like a mantra: *All in my head.*

Eventually, Greenfield's striker goes for a goal but ends up kicking the ball out of bounds, and we get possession again. That's when the ball finally comes back my way. I keep my eye on it, tuning everything else out. I hear Elijah's words in my head: *Be a fighter.*

What happens next is all instinct—the details are fuzzy around the edges. All I know is that the ball gets to me, and I dribble it down the field. I fake a pass and dribble some more. I shoot, and the ball flies through the air, sailing past the goalie's outstretched arms and into the back of the net.

I score.

The crowd erupts, but the sound is far away, like it's happening somewhere else, to someone else. When they don't stop, and the team rushes the field, I realize that we won.

We *won*.

Our first win of the season. The team gathers around me, shaking me and shouting my name and yelling and laughing. I'm still so shocked that I don't know how to react. None of this seems real. I look at the bleachers, where I know Immie will be, and only when I see the gigantic smile on her face does it sink in: my goal broke the 3–3 tie. *I* won us the game.

And she saw the whole thing.

I start laughing, not because anything is really funny, but because I've never felt like this before. Up in the stands, Immie is laughing too. It's like she's right here with me, feeling what I feel, and I'm glad—I want to share this with her. She's the one person who has always seen me, even when I had nothing to show. And now that I'm being seen by *everyone*, I can say without a doubt that it pales in comparison to how it feels knowing that the girl I love is proud of me.

The next day at school, people I don't even know come up to tell me I played a great game. It happens once when I'm with Immie, which is cool. I want her to be impressed by me.

After second period, when I'm standing at my locker, a girl from my math class comes out of nowhere and gives me a piece of paper with her phone number on it. I show it to Immie in social studies as proof that other girls are into me, thinking maybe it'll plant some ideas in her head. But she just laughs and says, *Okay, Fabio,* so I throw the number in the trash. I don't even know who Fabio is.

I'm not sure why I even bother getting my hopes up. Immie doesn't care about soccer. So long as my achievements are soccer related, she's not going to see me any differently. Maybe I should've joined a more intellectual club, like Latin or the debate team.

On Friday, I get to start at our game. Not as striker—that's Elijah—but in a position where I can still score. And I do, two goals. We win the game, and the way everybody reacts in the locker room, you'd think I won us the Olympics or something.

After the game, I go to the diner with Serge and some of the other guys from the team. Everybody is in a great mood, cracking jokes and reliving the highlights from the night. I'm about halfway into an ice cream sundae when it dawns on me. That feeling I was chasing when I saw Michael play for the first time—the feeling of belonging, of wanting to be part of something bigger? Well, this is it, right here. I picture the look on my dad's face when Michael made that very first assist, and realize I saw it again today, only this time, it was directed at *me*.

That was one heck of a match, Dad said after the game. And then?

He gave me a hug and told me he was proud of me.

It feels great to get so much attention, from him and

everyone else. I'm happy about it, I *am*. But there's something underneath the happiness too. Something like . . . worry?

I put my spoon down, stare at the cherry poking out of the melty vanilla ice cream. Yeah. I feel worried. Because getting all this attention comes with the condition that I continue to be the best. The best soccer player, the best son, the best friend—I need to be at the top of my game if I'm going to stay on top of the world. How long until I disappoint someone, and everything comes crashing down?

Serge drops his fork on his plate, and it makes a loud clink. I look up, tune back in.

". . . next week during her lunch period," he's saying. "They're singing Alicia Keys, bro!"

"Huh?"

"Asking Z to homecoming," Serge says. "I got a whole thing planned with some kids from concert choir. Gonna get her flowers and everything."

"Wow." I totally forgot homecoming is in a couple of weeks. Guess I've been a little preoccupied. "Look at you. Boyfriend of the year."

"Don't hate because I know how to treat my girl right."

"I asked Jessi with a card I made," Ben says, smiling proudly across the table. "I spelled out 'Homecoming?' in macaroni noodles."

Greg swallows his bite of burger and shakes his head. "Why do you have to ask your girlfriends to homecoming at all? Like, you're together. Isn't it implied you're already going with them?"

Serge laughs. "Greg, brother. You clearly have a thing or two to learn about girls."

I snort. "You the expert on girls now, Serge? What's it been, four months?"

"I once wore a pair of underwear longer than the two of you have been going out," Greg says.

"And that," Serge says, "is why you don't have a girlfriend."

Ben looks at me. "Who you going with, Marshall?"

I take a bite of my ice cream—or more like, I slurp it. It's pretty melted.

"He wants to go with Immie Meadows," Serge says. "But he won't ask."

"Thanks, man," I say, keeping my head down. "Thanks a lot."

"What? I'm just telling the truth."

"You afraid she'll say no?" Greg asks with his mouth full.

"I'm not afraid of anything," I insist. "I'm not asking because I never had any plans to ask in the first place. We're just friends."

It's a lie. Of course I want to ask her for real, and of course I'm afraid she'll say no. Also, I'm afraid she'll say yes. Then we'll have to dance together, and I'll make a fool of myself, and she'll never, ever see me as anything more than her dorky best friend. We'll be finished before we even start.

"Keep telling yourself that," Serge says.

Behind Ben, at the next table, I see Elijah's head turned in our direction.

— — —

I spend the next week figuring out the best way to raise the subject of homecoming with Immie. Should I bring it up casually—*the dance is next weekend; are you going with anybody?*—or should I ask her, officially, to be my date? We used to talk about homecoming as kids, and how we'd wow everybody on the dance floor with our version of the election routine from *Napoleon Dynamite*. *That* ship has definitely sailed, but what about the part where we'd be there together?

It doesn't help that we don't see each other much outside school. Soccer keeps me busy—we have three practices, two away games, lifting every other morning—and then Mom makes me go to Marigold's ballet recital on Thursday. Not to mention my homework has sort of been piling up. Especially social studies. On Friday, I fail another pop quiz because I didn't do the reading.

"How'd you do?" Immie says in the hall after class. "I think I got the second question wrong. I put C, but now I'm thinking it was B. I kind of skimmed that part of the reading. I didn't *mean* to, but it was such a snooze-fest. . . ." She trails off. "Are you okay?"

"Totally," I say. "I agree. *Bo*-ring."

She gives me a knowing look. "You didn't do the reading at all, did you?"

"I did some of it," I say, avoiding her eyes. Technically, reading the chapter headings *does* count as reading some of it.

"Monty, you can't fall behind. If you fall behind, you'll never catch up." She shakes her head, and her hair falls in her eyes. "See? *This* is why we should be doing the homework together."

"I know, I—"

"I know you're busy with soccer, but you need to make time for me," she says, stopping at her locker and starting on the combination. "I mean—you need to make time for the homework. *With* me." She glances up. "You know?"

I can't help but smile. She's so cute when she cares.

"I know, Outie. Trust me. I'd be nothing without you." I lean in a little closer. "With-*outie* you."

She opens her locker, stifles a laugh. "Monterey Jack, you are *so* cheesy."

"You love it," I say.

"I *love* getting As." She starts swapping her morning books for her afternoon ones. "Which is why we need to study for the Revolutionary War exam next week. Can you get together on Tuesday?"

"Nah. We've got an away game," I say. "And Monday is no good, either. How about Sunday?"

She nods. "I'll bring the brains; you bring the snacks."

"Unless I turn into a zombie before then," I say. "Then *you'll* be bringing the snacks."

"If you turn into a zombie, we've got bigger problems than the exam." She slams her locker shut.

We walk to the end of the hallway, where we have to part ways—she goes left, to the art wing, and I go to the basement for Spanish.

"By the way," I say. I don't want to walk away from her yet. "Are you still coming tomorrow?"

"Obviously. We haven't hung out in forever."

"Good. It will suck way less with you there."

"I think it will be fun," she says, hugging her books to her chest. It occurs to me that maybe I should have offered to carry them. But no, wouldn't that be sexist? Suggesting her puny girl arms can't carry a few textbooks?

I shove those thoughts aside. "Really?"

"Yeah," she says. "I've always wanted to go apple picking."

The next day, an opportunity finally presents itself. We're at the apple orchard, separated from my family, when we find a yard sale next door. I'm looking at a Furby, one of those creepy-looking owl things Elise used to have, when Immie brings up Serge's homecoming proposal to Zoya. She's got her typical Immie cynicism about it all—homecoming proposals are embarrassing, love is for losers, yada yada—but I take my shot anyway. It might be my only chance.

"So nobody's asked you?"

She gives me a confused look.

"To homecoming," I say, messing with a Mr. Potato Head. If I look at her, I might chicken out. "Nobody asked you to be their date?"

She practically cackles, like she can't believe I'm asking her such a thing. Awesome. Off to a great start. "No! No way."

"Crazier things have happened."

"No, I know. I just mean . . ." She hesitates. "I wouldn't go with a date. Nobody's asked me, or anything, but even if they *did*, I'd say no." And then she looks right at me. "I'm going with you. Obviously."

242

"Me?" I laugh, but my heart is pounding. "Outie, you're gonna have to buy me dinner first."

I regret it the second it comes out of my mouth. I don't know what happened—I just panicked.

"Not like *that*," Immie says, and she sounds a little annoyed, which makes me feel strangely stung. Why couldn't it be like that? Is it so crazy to think we could go to the dance not *just* as friends, but on a date? "It's our first high school dance. We *have* to go together, you know—as friends. Unless . . ." She pauses, and the look on her face is suspicious. "You were thinking of asking someone else?"

"Well, now that you mention it." The idea of me going with anybody other than the girl I've loved for seven years is so ridiculous that I can't help but turn it into a joke. "I *was* going to ask Margot Robbie, but turns out she's busy that night."

Then, without any warning, she sees something and wanders off. I wince. Maybe the joke wasn't such a good idea.

"Oh my gosh." She picks up a small object, holds it close to her face. I walk over to get a closer look. It's blue and encased in glass. A butterfly.

Aw man.

She runs her fingers lightly over the glass, which is when I realize her nails are painted light pink. I don't think I've ever seen her with painted nails before.

The butterfly is marked at forty dollars, which Immie says is too much. I have a different idea. I've been to enough craft shows with my mom to know a thing or two about the art of haggling. I once saw her talk a woman into giving her a sixty-dollar basket for twenty dollars by making up some sob story about how Tina passed away. *Everything is negotiable if you want it badly enough,* Mom says. That's why the cat has probably been killed off five or six times at this point. I look around until my gaze falls on the woman in charge.

Challenge accepted.

The woman sees me coming. "Hi, there," she says from her chair. "Find something you like?"

"Yes, ma'am," I say. "But there's a little bit of a problem."

"Oh no." She looks concerned. "Has something broken?"

"No, nothing like that." I glance back at Immie. She's standing by a table full of books, browsing the stacks of spines and pretending she's not trying to eavesdrop.

"You see that girl over there?" I say to the woman, keeping my voice low.

She smiles. "Oh, yes. She's lovely."

"Yeah, she is." I feel a little nervous. "Um. She really wants this taxidermy butterfly you have, and I'd like to get it for her, but, uh—it's a little out of my price range."

She nods, leans forward in her chair. "And what is your price range?"

"Um." I only have five bucks in my pocket, and *only* because these are the same pants I wore yesterday, when Greg bet me five bucks that I couldn't chug his whole root beer float. "It's less. A lot less. But I thought, maybe if I explained the situation to you, you'd consider selling it to me anyway."

"All right." She waves her hand in a *go on* motion. "Explain."

"Okay. Well first, this girl, she collects taxidermy butter-flies. I know you might think that's kind of weird, but they used to belong to her grandma—who she's named after, by the way—so they mean a lot to her. Like, *a lot*. She's got them all displayed in her room, right by the door, so you're basically forced to look at them when you walk in."

The woman stays quiet, waiting for me to go on.

"Second . . ." I sigh. Here goes nothing. "If I got this butter-fly for her, I think it would make her happy. And I'd *really* like to make her happy. When she's happy, it's like, I don't know—the world is a better place, somehow?" I run a hand through my hair. I don't know if I'm explaining this right. "She's my best friend, and we haven't been spending as much time together lately, and I want her to know that I still . . ." I trail off, searching for the right words. "That even when we aren't together, I'm always thinking about her."

The woman gives me an amused look. I can't tell, at first, if she appreciates my honesty or thinks I'm pathetic.

"What is your price range?" she asks again.

I grimace. "Five dollars."

"All right. Five dollars."

"Really?"

She nods.

"Wow." I smile wide, kind of amazed it worked. And I didn't even have to lie! "Thank you." I give her my five dollars and shake her hand. "She'll be so happy."

She puts her other hand on top of mine and looks me right in the eye. "*You* be happy. All right?"

My smile falters. What makes her think I'm not happy?

"All right," I say. "I'll try."

I step off the porch and walk back to Immie. She's got her arms crossed, and she's frowning at me, and I think I've never seen something so beautiful in my whole life.

TRACK SIX

"Black Dog"—Arlo Parks

I didn't know what was happening to me, but it felt like a cruel and unusual punishment. This song pretty much sums it up.

I swear, I've never, ever heard some of those names before!" Immie says with a huff. We're filing out of Ms. Wendt's classroom on Wednesday after the big Revolutionary War exam, and she's fuming. "John Paul Jones? Who *is* that?"

"Isn't that the actor with the really deep voice?"

"That's James Earl Jones," Immie says briskly, like she doesn't have time for my incompetence. "*Ugh.* This is all my fault. We should've studied the earlier battles more."

"It's not your fault," I tell her. "I'm sure we didn't do that bad."

At least, I'm sure she didn't. I, on the other hand, definitely failed. I didn't even get to the essay question.

We walk into the hallway, and there, waiting outside Ms. Wendt's room, is Elijah.

"Yo, Elijah," I say. Out of the corner of my eye, I see Immie make a face.

"Marshall!" he says. "Ready for tonight?"

After school, we're playing against an undefeated team. We've been on a five-game winning streak, so the stakes are high.

"Definitely," I say. "I went home after practice and did another hour of cone dribbling."

"Nice," Elijah says. "Hey."

"Yeah?"

Then I realize it. He's not talking to me.

"Hi," Immie says.

Elijah's looking at her like I don't even exist. "Can I talk to you?"

I glance from Immie to Elijah and back again, see the recognition on her face, and get a little dizzy. She knows him. *How* does she know him? I never told her about him, because I didn't *want* her to know him.

"I gotta get to Spanish," I say, and then walk away.

I try to take some deep breaths, to calm down. Immie and Elijah know each other. So what? Lots of people know each other. That doesn't mean there's anything going on between them.

I think about what Andrew said to Elijah in the locker room. *She's hot, dude. You should go for it.*

Well, here he is, going for it.

My heart is pounding. I should've been more prepared. I should've warned Immie about what I heard. Why was he waiting for her there anyway? What does he want?

My thoughts jump to a couple weeks ago at the diner,

when I stupidly told everyone I didn't want to go to homecoming with Immie, and Elijah overheard. Is it possible *he* wants to ask her to homecoming? But he wouldn't do it here, *now*, would he?

I shake my head. Even if he does, it doesn't matter. Immie and I are going to homecoming together. We talked about it at the apple orchard.

Then again . . .

What if she changed her mind? What if she only wanted to go with me because she thought she wouldn't have any better options? Maybe she thinks Elijah is a better option.

She wouldn't be wrong.

When I get to Spanish, I hide my phone under my desk and send Immie a text.

Jack: How do u know Elijah

Immie: I don't really know him

Immie: We have study hall together

Jack: You didn't tell me that

Immie: ?

Immie: Was I supposed to?

Jack: Idk

Jack: What did he want?

I stare at my screen, watching the dots appear and disappear, waiting for a response that never comes.

I channel my frustration into the game, and I leave the field drenched in sweat and gasping for air. In the locker room, Coach pulls me aside.

"Nice job on the offensive," he says. "But man, your passing was rough today. You don't need me to tell you that you gotta pay attention to where you're kicking the ball."

"It wasn't my fault," I say. I'm exhausted and feeling instantly defensive. "Elijah kept passing to me when I wasn't even open, so I had to get rid of—"

"Elijah did what?"

I turn around. Elijah has just come around the corner with his bag slung over his shoulder and a puzzled look on his face.

I stand up straighter. "Your passing totally sucked."

He laughs. "Mine? Dude, who were you passing to? Your imaginary friends?"

"Your mom, actually."

"Whoa, hey." Coach turns to look at me. "Bottom line, Marshall, your passing was sloppy. You better tighten that up before next game."

I clench my jaw. I know he's right. I was being too aggressive and didn't retain proper control of the ball. A rookie mistake, letting my feelings get in the way of my game. The kind of mistake Michael would never make.

"Yes, Coach."

"Let's pack this up," Coach says. "I'm ready to get home to my fiancée." He taps the locker to his left enthusiastically. "See you boys tomorrow. Be here, dressed, at three o'clock sharp."

"Yes, Coach," we say, along with a few other guys who have been lingering around. Coach goes back to his office, leaving Elijah and me to stare at each other.

"Sorry if my passing sucked," Elijah says. "But if you've got a problem, just come to me. Don't go ratting me out to Coach."

His words make me feel about five years old. I don't know why I'm acting so immature. It's not Elijah's fault that I haven't made my feelings known to Immie, any more than it's his fault my passing sucked. This one is all me.

"Sorry," I say, my insides burning with shame. "I'm just having an off day."

"Happens to all of us," he says. "I've definitely been distracted today."

"Yeah?" I say. "You got a test or something?"

"Nah. Girl stuff." A small smile creeps over his face. "You know how it is."

His phone starts to ring, and he picks it up. "I'm heading out now," he says, instead of hello. He adjusts his grip on his gym bag, gives me a wave, and walks away.

I walk over to the next row of lockers and find Andrew there, packing his bag.

"What's going on with Elijah?" I ask. "Is he dating somebody?"

"Why, you want his number?"

I grit my teeth. "No. I want to know if he's been talking to Immie Meadows."

"Uh." Andrew zips up his bag. "I don't know. I think he's taking her to homecoming."

My chest tightens.

"You think?"

"Yeah, *I think.*" He hoists the bag over his shoulder, already looking bored by the conversation. "He said he was. Or that he was going to ask her."

"Well, which is it?" My heart is pounding. "He said he was going *with* her, or he was going to *ask* her?"

He gives me a weird look. "You good, man? Your eye is twitching."

I don't realize that I'm squeezing my water bottle until the cap bursts open from the pressure. The loud noise makes Greg, Ben, and a few other guys turn their heads.

My phone buzzes in my pocket. I can tell by the vibration that it's a text from Immie. She's finally answering me.

"Forget it," I say to Andrew. "It's not a big deal."

That's a lie, of course. It's the biggest possible deal in the world, but I can't let him know that. I'm pretty sure Elijah already suspects my feelings for Immie. If he hears about my pathetic attempt to get information from Andrew, then he'll know for sure. And what if he tells her? What if they laugh about it together?

I read the text from Immie, and my stomach drops.

Immie: Something . . . unexpected. I'll tell you tonight

"So what happened out there?" Dad asks, pulling out of the parking lot. "Do I need to tell that coach of yours to work in more passing drills?"

I roll my eyes. My dad has been coming to watch my games more and more. I liked it at first. Now, it just adds even more pressure.

"We already do pass and moves, like, every day," I mumble, pulling my phone out of my pocket and opening the text from Immie. I still haven't responded.

"Mm." His eyes are hidden behind his Oakleys, so it's hard to tell what he's thinking. "Well, you were off today. Is anything the matter? You stressed about school?"

"No, Dad. I just messed up," I say, a little louder. "The sun was setting right in my eyes, and I couldn't see. That's all."

He doesn't reply, just nods, so I clench my jaw and look out the window. The fields are empty and flat, and they blur together in a blanket of dull brown as we drive past.

"I'm sorry," I say. It comes out quiet, almost a whisper. I don't know if he hears it.

When I get home, I shut myself in my room and lie down on the floor beside my bed, so that if anyone comes looking for me, they'll think I'm not here. I want to disappear for a while.

I text Immie back.

Jack: I'm kinda tired

Immie: Too tired to see me?

Jack: Kinda. Sorry

Jack: See you tomorrow?

It takes her a few minutes to write back.

Immie: Sure

I feel bad canceling our plans, but at the same time, I don't think I can be who she wants me to be tonight. She wants the goofy guy she can joke around and have fun with. The laid-back guy who doesn't sweat the small stuff. She wants her best friend, and I *want* to be him, but it's like there's something missing. I just feel . . . off.

I put my earbuds on, open up my music library, and press shuffle play. A song by Arlo Parks comes on. I love this song—I *feel* this song. The pretty melody is like a mask for the darker lyrics underneath.

> *It's so cruel*
> *What your mind can do for no reason*

I put my hand on my chest where it feels tight and think, *Yeah. That's exactly right.* Then I turn the volume all the way up, close my eyes, and lose myself in the sound.

TRACK SEVEN

"There'd Better Be a Mirrorball"—Arctic Monkeys

I told myself over and over: don't get emotional. But it was no use. Do you see, now, that it really didn't have anything to do with you? That I would have stayed in that moment with you forever if I could have?

At the football game on Friday night, Immie is her usual self. She doesn't say anything about going to homecoming with Elijah, and I wonder if she's purposely trying to hide the truth because she suspects it'll bug me. I don't really blame her—I'm not exactly in the best mood. Between the sucky game I played the other day and this big secret hanging over my head, I've been feeling more stressed than usual.

"What's up with you?" She nudges me. We're up in the bleachers with Serge, Zoya, Alex, and Hannah. The excitement of homecoming weekend has them all giddy.

"Nothing. I'm great." I force a smile.

"My man is still beating himself up about missing that pass," Serge says, clapping me on the back.

"Why?" Hannah looks up from her phone. "You still won the game."

"Right? I keep telling him it's not a big deal." Serge takes a sip of his slushie. "He's still the MVP."

Zoya grabs the slushie out of his hands. "You shouldn't be so hard on yourself, Jack. You tried your best, and that's all you can do." She takes a big sip and Serge frowns.

"Bruh. I asked if you wanted your own."

"Yeah, and?" She glares at him and takes another sip.

"*And* I knew this would happen." Serge takes the slushie back. "You always do this, Z."

While they start to argue, Immie leans into me. "Want to take a walk?"

My heart starts to pound. This is it. She's going to fess up.

"Yeah." I stand up. Might as well get this over with. Also, I don't need to hear another one of Serge and Zoya's arguments. "Let's go."

We climb down the bleachers, onto the track, and fall in with the crowd that's walking around the football field. A few people say hi to me as we walk—Ben and Greg, two girls from my gym class, a girl I've never met before. After that one, Immie groans.

"It's like hanging out with a celebrity," she says bitterly. "Should we find you a trash can to sneak around in?"

"Trash can? No." I spot Nick, a junior on the soccer team, and fist-bump him as I walk past. "Now, find me, like, a ball that you can bounce from place to place in, and we can talk."

"I'll be on the lookout."

Our team scores a first down, and the bleachers on both sides erupt into cheers and boos. Immie takes a step closer to me, letting her arm brush against mine while we walk. Frustrated as I am with her, I don't pull away.

"So what's really going on with you?" she asks. I want to laugh. *What's really going on with* you, *Immie?*

"Is it soccer?" she continues. "Because if it is, you shouldn't be so hard on yourself. It's just one game."

I sigh. I should just tell her. Just *say it.* "It's not really about that."

"Okay. Then what—"

"I thought we were going to the dance together," I force out. "You know, as friends. I thought that was the plan."

She furrows her brow, seemingly confused. *She's good,* I think. *Really good.*

"We are."

"Then why is Andrew saying that you're going with Elijah?"

Her mouth falls open. "*Pardon?* Who's Andrew?"

Somebody walking the opposite direction bumps into her. She turns around, shoots them a glare. It almost makes me smile. She's always sticking up for herself, even in small ways.

"Come *on.*" I'm getting impatient. "Is it true, or not?"

"No!" She whips back around, looks at me in disbelief. "Jeez! Is this really why you've been acting all huffy?"

Yes, I think. *I'm a pathetic loser. Don't you know that by now?*

"Jack." Her using my name instead of Monty tells me she means business. "It's not true. He asked me, but I told him no."

"When?"

"The other day," she says, annoyed. "You'd know that if you hadn't blown off our plans last night. *Again.*"

I wince, feeling guilty. After practice, I went to the mall with some guys from the team to get some stuff for the dance. I tried to have fun with them, but I was distracted. I had the same weird feeling in my chest as I did the day before. I can't explain it. It felt like . . . like I was losing my grip on everything that mattered to me, and the bad game was just one more example of all the ways I'm screwing up. I got home, put on some loud music, and cried in my room, which is so embarrassing. I didn't want her to see me like that. I could barely stand to see myself.

"Sorry," I say. "I just—" I start to come up with an excuse that doesn't make me sound so pathetic. Then the full weight of what she said sinks in. He asked, but she told him no.

She told him no.

"You *really* told him no?" I say, still not convinced it isn't just wishful thinking.

"Yes!" she says, like I should already know. "I didn't want to go with him."

We're on the other side of the field, by the away team bleachers. I don't remember walking so much. That's what happens when I'm with Immie—she makes time speed up and slow down all at once.

"Why not?"

The crowd picks up. Immie grabs my arm and presses her body close to mine.

"Because, you goof. I'd rather go with you."

A bunch of people around us start booing because the ref made an apparently questionable call. I hardly notice.

Immie had the chance to go to homecoming with Elijah, and she turned him down.

For *me*.

She tugs on my arm and pulls me down the path, through the crowd. The whole time I'm thinking that I can't believe this is happening. She could've gone with Elijah and his popular upperclassmen friends, probably ridden in a limo, but no. She picked me. I'm not just her default.

She picked *me*.

My heart starts to pound. *Why* did she pick me? I don't know anything about taking girls to dances. What if I do the wrong thing? What if I embarrass myself?

We make it through the crowd, and she lets go of my arm. I feel a little colder without her.

"You want to go to homecoming with me," I say. "Even though I'm a horrible dancer and will probably step on your feet?"

She gives me a playful smile. "I'll wear steel-toed shoes."

I try to laugh, even though what she said doesn't really make me feel better. I don't want to be a joke. I want to be cool.

"Come on." She nudges me. "We've shared, like, every single milestone together since third grade graduation. Did you really think we wouldn't share this one too?"

We stop walking at the end zone. There aren't a lot of people over here—all the action is happening at the other end of the field. It feels weirdly intimate, like we're alone.

"I didn't know what to think," I say, leaning over the fence. "But I'm glad I was wrong."

She leans into the fence next to me. Our arms almost touch, but not quite.

"You've been spending too much time with your soccer friends," she says, tucking a strand of hair behind her ear. I notice that the tip is red from the cold. "You're starting to forget about me."

"Forget you?" I can't help but laugh. "That's the most ridiculous thing I've ever heard. Even more than the snack bar charging fifteen dollars for a small popcorn."

Immie gasps. "Fifteen? It's usually twelve."

"They inflated the prices for the homecoming game." I shake my head and raise my fist in the air. "Darn you, PTA president Beverly Stringer!"

"Darn you, Bev!" Immie yells out into the field, making several people nearby turn their heads. Then she looks at me, and we both laugh. It feels so good to crack up with her. So right. Like nothing has changed, and no time has passed at all.

The next night, Serge comes over, dressed for the dance in a purple vest. My dad has a showing, so Serge's dad is the one who helps us tie our ties. When my mom sees us, she starts to tear up. "My little baby," she says wistfully, wrapping me up in a hug. I roll my eyes but let her do it anyway.

We all walk over to Immie's together to meet the girls. When I first see Immie come down the stairs in her sparkly blue dress, it's like the rest of the world dims. Her dark hair is piled loosely on top of her head, so I can see her whole face—

something that almost never happens. When she sees me, she grins, and I feel so much that I have to look away.

"Monty," she says when she gets to the bottom of the stairs. "You don't look cheesy at all."

I smile nervously at her. I want to tell her that she looks beautiful, that the sight of her literally took my breath away, but my heart is going a mile a minute.

"Cool dress," I say, and then immediately hate myself.

Next to me, Serge does a wolf whistle when Zoya appears at the top of the stairs. "Everybody back up!" he says. "The most beautiful girl in the world is coming through."

Immie and I both make a face. Then we glance at each other and laugh.

We pose for pictures, with the parents snapping us from all angles like paparazzi. I don't know why it feels so awkward—Immie and I have been photographed together a thousand times before. Maybe it's all the posing—so stiff and formal, so *not* Immie. When she eventually breaks the line and does a goofy pose, I'm glad. It totally lightens the mood. Soon we're all laughing and making funny faces and taking pictures we'll actually want to remember. It feels nice, like belonging.

The six of us pile into my mom's van. As we're backing out of the driveway, I see Carrie and her girlfriend Lucy walking to Carrie's car in their black dresses. It's weird that I'm old enough to be going to the same dance as my sister. She's always seemed so much more grown-up than me, the kind of grown-up that felt untouchable, like I'd never get there myself.

Now here I am. In *high school*. I don't know why, but I thought it would feel different from this.

That's when the nerves kick in. I look over at Immie and realize something huge. Tonight she's not just my best friend—she's my date. I don't really know what that means. All I know is I can't screw it up.

By the time we get to the dance, I'm sweating. I keep using the paper towel I have shoved in my pocket to wipe my forehead when nobody is looking. Immie seems kind of nervous too. I can see it in the uncertain way she looks at me before we go onto the dance floor.

She takes a deep breath. "Ready?"

She's pushing through her nerves—of course she is. She's brave. I want to be that for her, too. No matter how impossible it feels.

I can pinpoint the exact moment everything changes.

We're dancing—*slow* dancing. My hands are on her waist, someplace I've never touched her before, and my heart feels like it's going to pound right out of my chest. *Don't do anything weird,* I silently tell myself over and over. *Just relax. Be cool.*

"It's just that you've been so busy lately," she's saying. Couples are dancing all around us, so she's talking kind of quietly. "I'm happy that you've got this good thing going with the team, but I really miss you."

She tilts her head down, the way she does when she likes to hide behind her hair. But since her hair is pinned up, she's got nowhere to hide. I can see her emotions written all over her face, and I feel a funny mix of excitement and nerves at the fact that they seem to match mine.

"You don't have to miss me." My voice comes out as a whisper. I try to swallow, but my throat feels like sandpaper. "I'm right here."

I pull her closer. I want her to know that I mean it. That no matter what happens, or where I go, in my heart we'll always be this close. I think she can feel it, because she leans into me, wraps her arms around my neck, and rests her head on my shoulder.

I love you, she'd said earlier. It was a slip of the tongue— just friend love, not the kind of love I feel for her. It couldn't be. Right?

But what if . . . ?

We stay like that for a while, swaying back and forth, not talking, just holding each other. I feel so right, so at ease, that I think it must be a dream. And so what if it is? Dreams are safer. They have no consequences. If this were a dream, I could tell Immie that I love her. For *real*. Better yet, I could *show* her. I'd look into her eyes, tilt her chin toward mine, and kiss her right on the lips. And she'd kiss me back, and there'd be absolutely no weirdness at all. Nothing would change. It would all be perfect.

I turn my head toward her, let my lips almost brush her ears. She doesn't pull away.

And then the song ends, and a much louder, *much* less romantic one takes its place. I fall out of the dream, back into the real world. Here, I can't let my guard down so easily. If I'm not careful—if I feel too much—I could scare her away.

Immie takes a step back, looks at me with wide, wondering eyes. Right away, I'm embarrassed. What was I thinking, nuzzling into her like that? Who do I think I am—her boyfriend? A caveman?

I become very aware of all the people around us, pushing in, jumping around to the beat of the song, and I start to feel suffocated. I need to get out of here now.

"Sorry," I say, trying hard not to give anything away. "I just need to . . . um . . ." What? Run away because I'm pathetic? Because I can't get through one dance without freaking out? "I'll be back."

I leave the dance floor without looking at her. I don't think I could stand it. I push through the crowd, out the doors, and into the hallway, and don't stop walking until I get to the bathroom. There's one guy in there, washing his hands, but he leaves after a second, and I'm alone.

I turn on the sink and splash some water on my face. *It's not a big deal,* I think. *You got caught up in the moment, and she probably did too.* I turn the water off, look in the mirror. The water drips down my face, and I don't wipe it away.

What's wrong with me? I grip the sides of the sink and stare into my own eyes, like a dare. *The girl you love is out there, waiting for you. What are you doing, hiding in here?*

I replay those final moments. The way she put her head on my shoulder. The way she hugged her body to mine. We were so close together, I could feel her heartbeat. We were *connected.* Maybe that's why, for a second, I wasn't worried about hiding my feelings. I knew, at least for that one second, that she felt the same way.

And then . . . I freaked out.

See, when you hide a crush for seven years, you get sort of comfortable with the secret. Sure, you fantasize about what it would be like to send them cute texts or hold their hand in the halls or *kiss* them, but you never expect any of it to actually happen.

I *never* conceived of a world where Immie Meadows would like me back, and I was mostly fine with that, because at least I knew how to navigate that world. I knew how to be me.

What do I do now?

Run away and hide in the bathroom, obviously.

I shut myself in a stall and lean against the door, so full of self-loathing, I could explode. I screwed this all up. It should be simple. Immie and I were having fun. I should be out there with her, having even more fun. But I can't. Because I'm scared.

Scared of what?

I loosen my tie, undo the top button of my shirt. I try to catch my breath, but the tightness in my chest makes that impossible.

I'm scared I won't be enough for her. I'm scared I'll be too much. I'm scared I'll do the wrong thing and push her away. I'm scared I already *did*. I'm scared of losing her. Of having an Immie-shaped hole in my heart forever.

My mind is spinning, spinning, spinning, and I wish it would stop—I would do anything to get it to stop. I just keep thinking about how there's something seriously wrong with me, and that if Immie knew the truth, there's no way she'd ever like me, and I hate myself.

I sit down on the edge of the seat, put my head in my hands. *Make it stop.* I squeeze my eyes shut, silently begging the bad thoughts to go away. *Make. It. Stop.* I start hitting myself in my head with my fists because I don't know what else to do. It doesn't help. It just makes me feel like a baby throwing a tantrum, which makes me hate myself even more.

I start to cry. I hear the creak of the bathroom door opening, followed by footsteps. Somebody goes into the stall next to me, but I don't care. I keep crying. If I don't cry, I might scream.

I take my phone out of my pocket, put in my earbuds, and press shuffle play on my music library. I hear the opening notes of "There'd Better Be a Mirrorball" by Arctic Monkeys. I try to focus on the words: *"Don't get emotional, that ain't like you . . ."*

I'm not sure how much time passes. All I know is that eventually, the tears dry up, and my emotions come to a crashing halt, and I feel numb, like nothing can faze me. I turn off the music, leave the stall. I splash some more water on my face and then go back to the cafeteria, where I know Immie will be waiting for me.

I find her sitting with Elijah. Weirdly enough, there's a part of me that feels relieved. Elijah is the better guy. He's confident. A *fighter*. He'll be able to make Immie happy, much more than I ever could. Seeing them together like this is like seeing pepperoni on pizza. It just makes sense.

I tell her that I'm sick and I need to go home. I know she doesn't really buy it, but she doesn't pressure me to stay, either. I wonder if that's because she secretly wants me to go. She danced with me, realized it was a mistake, and now wants to spend the rest of the night with her arms around Elijah instead. Me leaving early is probably doing her a huge favor.

I find my sister on the other side of the cafeteria with Lucy and a few more of her hipster friends. They're just standing around, probably making fun of the music or something.

"Can you give me a ride home?"

"What?" She looks at me like I'm insane. "No way. The dance isn't over for another hour."

"Carrie," I say, and my voice cracks. I've never felt so desperate for her to stop being evil and just be my sister for once. "Please."

The corners of her mouth turn down. She steps away from her friends.

"What's wrong?" she asks, grabbing my arm and tugging me off to the side. "Did something happen?"

I shake my head. "I just really need to go home."

She gives me a long, hard look, her forehead creased with concern. She looks like Mom when she does that, but I'd never tell her so. I worry she's going to ask me to explain—I really don't have the energy for that—but instead, she surprises me.

"Okay." She puts her hand on my back, and I feel like crying all over again. "Let me get my bag."

TRACK EIGHT

"Feel the Pain"—Dinosaur Jr.

I listened to this song a lot in the weeks after the dance. I liked the noise—I NEEDED the noise—but I related to the lyrics, too. See, my mood only went one of two ways: pain or nothing.

After the dance, it's like something inside me breaks. That suffocating feeling starts happening more and more, and I don't know how to stop it. It goes like this: my chest aches, my heart beats fast, and my mind starts spinning out. All the bad thoughts start pummeling me like soccer balls to the gut, knocking the breath out of me. My arms and legs start to tingle. My vision goes black at the edges. Sometimes I genuinely think I'm going to die, and the thought scares me so much I feel paralyzed. I can't move or talk or breathe; all I can do is feel. And I feel *everything*.

And then it ends.

Nowhere is safe. At school, at home, even on the soccer field—I never know when the feeling is going to hit me again, which means I'm constantly waiting for it. I'm paranoid it's going to happen when I'm around Immie, so I start canceling plans. I blame soccer, because it's easier than telling her the truth. I don't even know what the truth *is*. All I know is that something is wrong with me.

Once, maybe, I could've tried to explain it to her. But things are different now. *We're* different. Our friendship isn't just the two of us anymore. There's high school and soccer and other people to consider.

Lately, it's like we have to try extra hard to make things feel just as easy as they did before. So yeah, I'm scared to let my guard down. What if I do, and she realizes actually, I'm not easy at all—I'm a mess? Especially compared to Elijah, who's all perfect and stuff. Next to him, I'm damaged goods.

But I don't want her to know all that. I'm *so* close to being the person I want to be. I just have to get this feeling under control.

In my room one night, I type *can't breathe, fast heartbeat, tingling limbs* into Google. The first thing that comes up is heart attack. I keep scrolling. Unless people can have heart attacks every day, I'm pretty sure it's not that. Then I see the second result: panic attack.

A brief episode of intense anxiety, which causes the physical sensations of fear.

Panic attacks. Could that be what's happening to me? And if so, how do I stop them? The internet says things like refocus my attention, change my environment, remind myself the feelings will pass. But how can I do any of that when I'm literally being suffocated by my own thoughts?

Loud music is the only thing that helps, so I start listening to it constantly. Unless I'm in class or on the field, I've got at least one earbud in my ear. The effect of this is that it starts to feel a little like I'm sleepwalking through my life, but I don't mind. It's way better than spiraling through.

After practice one day, Coach pulls me aside. He says he can tell I'm off my game; is everything okay? Am I nervous about qualifying for playoffs? Am I getting enough sleep? Yes, I'm nervous, and no, I'm not getting enough sleep. But I don't tell him that.

"I guess I'm just stressed about school," I say, which is partly true. "I'm not doing so hot in one of my classes."

"Which class?"

"Social studies." I glance at him awkwardly. "With Ms. Wendt."

Coach nods thoughtfully. He and Ms. Wendt are engaged. "I'll talk to her, see if there's anything I can do to help you out."

The next morning, Ms. Wendt gives me an extra credit assignment. I have to write a thousand words on a major historical event in the 1920s, due at the beginning of next month. On top of the class's already heavy workload, and how hard it is for me to concentrate on reading anything lately, I have no idea how I'm going to pull it off.

"Ooh, that's such a fun assignment," Immie says in the hall after class.

"Yeah? Wanna do it for me?"

"Nice try. You could do Prohibition. Or the Nineteenth Amendment. Or the flappers!"

"Which one is the nineteenth, again?"

She frowns at me. "Maybe you *should* do that one."

We walk past Elijah. He gives her a nod, and she waves back.

I clench my jaw, put in one of my earbuds, and turn my music all the way up.

The following week, two things happen.

The first is that we win our away game against Lakeville and qualify for playoffs. No thanks to me—I play my worst game maybe ever. I'm sloppy with my dribbling, I second-guess myself before every kick, and instead of intercepting the ball, I let it get taken from me. I start thinking, *Why am I even here?* I clearly don't deserve to be here. After a while, Coach seems to be thinking the same thing, because he benches me. The only silver lining is that it's an away game, so nobody in my family, or Immie, is there to see it.

The second is that, on the bus back to school, the team starts brainstorming ways to raise money for new uniforms. Elijah comes up with the idea to throw together a haunted house at the Halloween carnival next weekend. Some people are against it—how are we supposed to get a haunted house together in a week and a half? Greg says he can get his hands on an inflatable structure—his mom is in the party planning business—if we can figure out how to fill it with creepy stuff. Somebody else suggests the junkyard, and that's all it takes for the majority to get on board. I stay quiet the whole time, listening to everyone talk with one ear and listening to music with the other.

At home that night, I tell my dad we made it to playoffs, and he gives me a hug. Instead of making me feel good, it makes me feel worse. I played a horrible game—I don't deserve the hug. But I take it anyway, because when is the last time he hugged me?

Then I realize something. Immie has never gotten a hug from her dad. As jealous as I am of her small family, I think I'd miss these hugs. They're how I know he loves me.

I try to hold on tight, but he lets go. I watch him scoop up Tina, sit on his recliner, and turn on the TV to ESPN. I could sit with him, watch sports, pretend like everything is fine. That's what Michael would do. It's probably what Elijah would do too.

I go up to my room, lie down on the floor, and listen to music. "Feel the Pain" by Dinosaur Jr. is the first song on the queue.

> *I feel the pain of everyone*
> *Then I feel nothing*

I don't move for two hours.

On Thursday after practice, I text Immie that I'm on her front porch, and she opens the door a second later.

"Monty!" She throws her arms around me. I hug her back and breathe her in, feeling instantly calmer.

"I can't stay long," I say when she lets go. "Mom's got dinner ready. Also, I came right from practice, so I probably stink." Then I wince. Maybe I shouldn't tell her things like that.

"Don't worry. Our whole house smells like chili powder."

I follow her inside, and she shuts the door behind me. Right away I can smell the chili, and my stomach growls. I miss Nora's cooking. I haven't had it in forever.

"We'll have plenty of leftovers if you want to come back tomorrow," Immie says, looking at me hopefully.

"I wish," I say. "But Coach is working us so we're at the top of our game for quarterfinals. The next couple weeks are going to be tough."

It's partly true. The part I'm leaving out is that I'm also nervous to be alone with her. The panic attacks are happening almost every day now, and I live in constant fear of what would happen if I had one in front of her. I don't think I could take it.

I follow her down the hallway, toward the kitchen. "That doesn't make sense to me. Shouldn't you guys be resting so you have maximum energy?" Immie says.

"Try telling him that. He'll probably make you run suicides just for bringing it up."

She makes a disgusted face. "Suicides? Is that the name of an exercise?"

"Kind of. More like a punishment."

She scrunches up her nose. "Sports are so weird."

I turn the corner to see Nora standing over the stove, stirring a pot. She looks up and smiles. "Hey there, stranger. I was wondering when we were going to see you again."

"I know." I lean into the island and reach for the open bag of tortilla chips. "I've been really busy with soccer."

"I heard! Playoffs, that's awesome. Immie and I are both very proud of how hard you're working."

"Yeah, yeah." Immie takes a seat at the island across from her mom. She's clearly been doing homework. Her science textbook is open, and her notebook page is covered in her round, swirly handwriting. "Now what's my surprise?"

"Oh?" Nora says. "There's a surprise?"

"Well." I drum my fingers on the countertop. In the car on the way home, I texted Immie that I had a surprise for her, and she insisted I come tell her immediately. "Kind of. I mean, only if it's okay with you, Ms. M."

She puts a hand to her chest. "Are you asking for my daughter's hand in marriage?"

My stomach drops.

"Mom!" Immie picks up a tortilla chip and throws it across the island at her. "You're so embarrassing."

Nora laughs. "Oh *relax*, it's just a joke." She picks up the tortilla chip and eats it.

I try to laugh too. Nora jokes with us all the time. This isn't any different. Right?

"My family is taking a trip to the cabin in a couple weeks," I tell them. "The whole family, even Michael and Elise. And my parents said Immie can come too if she wants."

Immie gasps. She looks at Nora. "Can I go, Mom? Please?"

"We're leaving early Saturday morning, coming back late Sunday night," I say. "No school will be missed."

"Please please please!" Immie begs. "I'll start my art project before then, I promise."

"Sure," Nora says. "Why not?"

Immie smiles wide. "Thank you!" She jumps out of the

chair and runs around the island to give her mom a hug. "You're the best mom ever."

Immie looks over her mom's shoulder at me, and her eyes are bright with excitement. I can't help but think about how peaceful it would be if I went to the cabin with Immie and Nora, instead of my gigantic, loud, messy family. We'd spend the whole weekend relaxing and laughing and cooking good food, and I'd never feel like I had something to prove. I could live in the moment and just be happy.

Unless, of course, I had a panic attack and ruined everything.

"I have to go," I say, already feeling the tightness creeping in. "See you tomorrow?"

I walk out of the kitchen and into the hallway. Immie calls out after me, clearly confused.

"Uh, bye?"

I stand there for a second, my hand hovering by the doorknob. I could go back. I could push through the pain and pretend like things are normal, the way they've always been. But that would be a lie, and Immie has always been able to see right through those. Maybe it's because she knows me better than I know myself. That used to be a comforting thought. Now it scares me.

I turn the knob and walk out the front door.

TRACK NINE

"Soda Can"—TOLEDO

I love this song. The soft music is like a mask for the heavy lyrics underneath. That's how I felt all the time, like I had to hide from everyone.
Even you.

On Halloween, we get out of eighth period early to start setting up for the haunted house. The carnival is in the field behind the school, and when Serge and I get there, construction is already underway. I walk past U-Hauls and delivery trucks, people unloading food and games, a pumpkin patch and carving station, and a half-constructed hay bale maze.

I've always known that Storm Valley does not mess around with this carnival. I've been coming to it since I was four, when Elise was a student here. So I take my time looking around. I like to see how the sausage is made.

We get to the haunted house to find it already blown up. I do a double take when I see it. It's huge and colorful and way cooler than I thought it would be.

"Not bad, huh?" Greg says, appearing in the doorway.

"Bro, it's sick." Serge leans in to inspect a spiderweb draped over the fake iron gate. "Your mom just had it lying around?"

"Oh yeah. Her company has a whole bunch of stuff like this in a warehouse."

"Wow," I say. "You must have had the best birthday parties growing up."

He crosses his arms triumphantly. "Sixth birthday. Blow-up pirate ship. Enough said."

"Yo, boys," Elijah calls from the front door. He's been bossing us around all week. "We got a lot of furniture to get out of the truck. Once we're all set up, we'll break to get ready. Then we'll regroup in costume and go over where everyone's supposed to be."

"What time are people getting here?" Ben asks.

"Everything opens at six," Elijah says. "We have four hours."

It takes us two to get everything unloaded and unpacked. Serge and I are assigned to set up the lab because it's the room we'll be in tonight. I'm dressing up as a mad scientist, and he's a creepy clown.

"We're gonna fill these with water," Serge says, putting a box of glass jars on the operating table. "Then we're gonna add green food coloring. And *then* we're gonna put stuff inside."

"What kind of stuff?" I say, arranging cloudy beakers on a scratched-up old bookcase.

"Anything that will look creepy," he says. "Fake eyeballs. Stuffed animals. Baby doll heads."

"Yeah, let me just go decapitate one of Marigold's dolls."

"Hey," Serge says. "It could just mysteriously go missing. She doesn't have to know."

"How about, like, gummy worms?"

"That could work." Serge takes his phone out of his pocket. "Z's at CVS right now. I'll tell her to get some."

"Cool." I move two beakers that don't need rearranging. I just want something to do with my hands when I ask, "Is Immie coming with her?"

"Immie? Nah. Alex."

"Right," I say. "Should've guessed that."

"You know she's got a thing for you."

My chest tightens. "Immie?"

"No," Serge says. *"Alex."*

"Oh." I take a breath, try to relax. No. I didn't know that. But I guess it explains all those Gatorades.

"Why do you think she comes with Zoya to watch our practices? It's not to see me."

"I don't know." Now my mind is racing. Is Serge really telling me that Alex has been watching me, specifically, every time she comes to practice? As if I wasn't already self-conscious enough. "Her dad is the coach. I guess I just figured she didn't have anything better to do."

Serge throws his head back in laughter. "Man, you really haven't got a clue."

I walk to the operating table and pick up another box of empty jars. I wonder if Immie knows that Alex likes me. I wonder if she cares.

--- --- ---

"Okay, gents." Elijah has us all gathered in the front room of the haunted house. It's a minute until opening, and there's already a line of people outside. "You've all got your places. Remember, we're breaking on a rotating schedule so there's no more than one empty room at a time. Also—don't touch anybody. Got it?"

"Not even our friends?" Greg asks underneath his *Scream* mask.

"Someone who looks like your friend from the back is going to end up being a mom who takes spin classes, and then we've got a harassment case on our hands."

"So . . ." Ghostface Greg looks around. "No?"

"No!" several guys say in unison.

Serge and I go to the lab room. He lies down on the operating table, and I stand above him and pretend to do experiments that make his guts fall out. When people walk past us, Serge reaches out like he's asking for help, careful to never actually touch anybody. It gets a jump or a scream almost every time.

A few minutes into it, a high-pitched shriek comes from the baby's room. "Oh you *idiot*!" a familiar voice says. "Do you know these drinks are like ten dollars now?"

Serge looks up at me. "Now *that's* scary."

Zoya bursts into the room. She's got bunny ears on her head, and something wet and dark has been spilled all over the front of her white dress. Alex follows a few seconds later.

"Whoever is dressed up like a baby jumped out right in front of me and made me spill my Frappuccino!" Zoya says.

Serge sits up on the table. "Why do you have a Frappuccino in a haunted house where you know people are gonna be jumping out at you?"

Her jaw drops. "Excuse me? The guy was like an inch in front of me. It's called personal space."

"Hey," Alex says to me. She's dressed up in a shiny green skirt and a tight purple tank top. "You look great."

"Uh, yeah, you too," I say. The words come tumbling out. "Are you . . . an eggplant?"

She laughs quietly. "No, I'm Ariel. From *The Little Mermaid*."

"Ahh, right. Because of your red hair."

"Yep."

There's an awkward silence, or maybe it's just awkward to me. Now that I know she likes me, I kind of forget how I used to talk to her. Don't get me wrong: she's great—she's nice, and easy to talk to. She just isn't Immie. And I don't want to say anything that could give her the wrong idea about how I feel.

My phone vibrates in my pocket. It's Immie's signature buzz—she just pounded on the button as aggressively and for as long as she could.

Immie: omw

I feel another tightness in my chest, and I freeze.

No. Please. Not here.

The three of them leave, and I say I'll catch up with them. I sit down in the chair and try to breathe deeply, to remind myself that it's okay, that I'm in a public place, that I *can't* break down, or else everyone will see. A group of people come into the room, and I don't even acknowledge them. When they see me sitting there with my head in my hands, they'll just think it's part of the act.

My phone buzzes again.

Immie: Here

I take a deep breath. *Be confident. Be a fighter. Be the person you want to be.*

Inside the haunted house, Immie's eyes go wide. She seems more impressed by what I've done here than anything I've ever done on the soccer field. I show her around, pointing out cool pieces of scavenged furniture and joking around like we always do. It's so much fun that I forget, for a minute, how worried I was that I'd have a panic attack in front of her. How could I ever feel anything around Immie but completely at ease?

It helps that she's wearing my soccer sweatshirt. It's got my last name across the back for everyone to see, including Elijah. He might have a cutesy nickname for her—*Picasso*, how unoriginal is that?—but she's not wearing his sweatshirt. I'm still winning.

We get to the nursery, where Danny, a senior dressed up as a scary doll, jumps out from behind the door at Immie. She screams and jumps back, and when I put my hand out to make sure she doesn't fall, she grabs it.

Immie grabs my hand.

"Oh." She looks down at her hand like she's surprised to see it there. She starts to let go of me. "Sorry, I—"

Maybe it's the shock, or the fact that Immie can make even a haunted house feel like home, but for once, I don't over-think it. I do exactly what I want to do, and I hold on tight.

I remember the last time we held hands. It was three summers ago at Hershey Park. We were on the Wild Mouse, one of those rides that makes you feel like you're going to fly off when you go around the bends. Immie hated it. I knew she was really scared because she wasn't screaming, just squeezing her eyes shut like she was waiting for it to be over. So I reached for her hand. She took it and held it tight.

"It's okay," I say, wrapping my fingers around hers. "Right?"

She looks down at the floor, and I realize I don't know if I've ever seen her look shy before.

"Right."

We walk into the hallway and make it about fifteen seconds before we come face-to-face with Andrew and Nick, hiding out behind an old picture frame.

"Oh no," I mutter. I thought they were on break too.

"Marshall!" Andrew smiles wide. With his ghostly makeup, he actually looks creepy. "Is this your girlfriend?"

I drop Immie's hand. I don't want to give them any more ammunition.

"Andrew, look, they're having a date night," Nick says. He winks at me. "Don't do anything I wouldn't do."

"You'd kiss a snake if it put on a skirt," I say, which makes Andrew burst out laughing. "And she's not my girlfriend."

Next to me, I feel Immie stiffen. My heart starts to pound. Did I say the wrong thing? I only said it because I didn't want to embarrass her. But I can feel her discomfort like it's my own.

"Is this your first date?" Andrew says, looking back and forth between us. "Geez, man. You could've sprung for some flowers, at least."

I want to tell him that it's not a date, and to shut up, because they're ruining everything, but my chest feels tight. It's getting hard to breathe. I need to get out of this cramped hallway.

"Great catching up, guys," I say, and then walk away.

In the science lab, I try to catch my breath while my head spins. I shouldn't have held her hand. I knew it would be a bad idea. This was my chance to be confident, to be the guy I *want* to be, but I completely blew it. I'm not confident. I'm a coward.

Immie catches up to me, and we walk through the rest of the haunted house in silence. I want to say something, but I can't think. I'm too focused on trying not to have a complete breakdown in front of her. When we're out of the house, and I've mostly got my heart rate back to normal, Immie says my name and turns to me with a serious look on her face.

"I miss the way things used to be. Back when we could disappear under the tree for hours, and nobody would care."

I picture it: Immie lying on her stomach, sipping lemonade and sketching a dead spider. I loved the way the summer breeze lifted her hair off her neck, making the air smell, just for a second, like peaches. All of a sudden, I don't feel panicky anymore.

"Yeah. Me too."

We haven't been to the tree in a while. Part of me feels sad, knowing that those simpler times are gone, but the other part feels weirdly hopeful. We've moved our relationship out from under the tree, into the real world, where it has more room to grow. Who knows what could happen next?

"But at least we can disappear next weekend," I say, looking at her. "You're still coming to the cabin, right?"

TRACK TEN

"Running"—Kate Bollinger

*I've learned my lesson about playing it safe.
And, maybe more importantly, I learned that
Michael gives crap advice. At the time,
though, I didn't know. I really thought I was
doing the right thing.*

Thundercraps Group Chat

Monday, 10:46 a.m.

Greg: Popcorn chicken for lunch today LETS GO

Ben: Do they have mac and cheese too

Greg: It says potatoes

Ben: Aw

Greg: But you know how sometimes they like to get a little wild and deviate from the menu

Jack: You're the only one who knows that

Serge: Still can't believe you get notifications sent to your phone

Greg: Hey. The next time you want to know if it's square pizza day, you can walk down to the cafeteria and find out yourself

Ben: Do the mashed pots have gravy

Greg: Yeah boi

Ben: Sweet

Greg: I'm gonna be all up in those tatoes

Greg: Sorta like how Jack was all up on Immie at the carnival

Jack: ?

Jack: That's a reach

Serge: Like how you REACHed for her hand

Jack: Hilarious

Jack: You guys should take this stuff on the road

Ben: I can't believe your parents are letting you bring her to your cabin

Ben: My mom would never let me take Jessi on a family trip

Jack: Taking Immie isn't like taking Jessi

Jack: Immie and I are just friends

Greg: Lol

Serge: Ok

Ben: Andrew said you were getting hot and heavy in the hall

Serge: How do you get "hot and heavy" holding hands

Greg: Excessive thumb-stroking?

I'm typing my reply with a small smile on my face when a new text from Immie pops up on my screen.

Immie: Look up, genius

I do what she says, and my smile immediately falls. Ms. Wendt is standing over my desk. Even worse, the whole class is looking at me.

"Hand it over," she says, holding out her hand.

I give her my phone without a word, then glance at Immie. She's frowning at me, disappointed or annoyed or some combination of the two. I slouch down in my seat so the guy in front of me blocks her from my view.

At the end of class, I walk up to Ms. Wendt's desk to ask for my phone back.

She's about to hand it over but stops herself. "Wait a minute. Do you have something for me?"

It takes me a second to realize what she means. "Oh, right. I'm sorry. I shouldn't have been texting during class. It won't happen again."

She blinks, unfazed. "No. Not an apology. Your paper?"

My stomach drops. The extra credit assignment is due today.

"I . . . um. I'm not finished with it yet."

Technically I haven't even started it. Between soccer, preparing for the haunted house, and living in constant fear of having a panic attack in the wrong place, I've been a little preoccupied.

She looks surprised. "Not finished?"

I shake my head.

"Are you going to be finished by the end of the day?"

"Honestly . . . probably not."

She sighs and leans back in her chair. "Jack, buddy. This was your chance to raise your grade."

My heart starts to beat faster. "I know, I screwed up. I'm really sorry."

"You don't have to say sorry to me," she says. "If you fail this class and wind up in summer school, it won't be me who put you there. It will be you."

Summer school? Nobody ever said anything about summer school.

"I can't do summer school," I say. "That's when club soccer happens. If I miss the season, I'll fall behind."

"Sorry," she says, though she doesn't really sound it. "You should've thought of that before."

I get my phone back and meet Immie in the hallway. She's got that same sour expression on her face.

"What?" I ask. We start walking.

"It was the group chat, wasn't it?"

"No," I say. "It was Colonel Mustard, in the library, with the candlestick."

"Seriously, Jack. You're always on your phone lately. It's like it's glued to your hand."

"What? That's not true."

"It took you a full thirty seconds to notice Ms. Wendt watching you!"

I wince. "That's embarrassing."

"Not just embarrassing. *Idiotic*." She shakes her head. "You're not going to get your grade up if you don't pay attention. When's your extra credit paper due again?"

My chest tightens. "Uh, it was due today. That's what I was doing in there. Handing it in."

I feel bad lying to her, but if I tell her the truth, she'll just worry. Not to mention she'll be furious at me. *This is exactly what I was talking about,* she'll say with an *I told you so* look. Just the thought of disappointing her like that makes my stomach turn.

It's settled. Until I can figure out how to fix this, I'm keeping it quiet.

"Good," she says, none the wiser. "That should at least get you up to a C."

"Yeah," I reply, my voice flat. "I hope so."

"So about this weekend." She tucks a strand of hair behind her ear. Now that I can better see her face, I realize this is what she's been wanting to talk about all along. "Is there anything I need to know?"

"Like what?"

"I don't know," she says. "Like . . . something specific I should pack?"

I shake my head. "You've been to the cabin before. It's just going to be like every other time."

"Oh." She looks down at the floor. "Right. Okay."

Did I say the wrong thing? Was she expecting something special?

And why *would* she be expecting something special?

It's been three days, and we still haven't talked about the whole hand-holding thing. After we walked through the haunted house, Immie went off with Zoya, Alex, and Hannah. They ended up leaving early, so I didn't see her the rest of the night. Then I had Saturday practice, and she went to the mall with her friends on Sunday afternoon, and when she texted me Sunday night to come over and do some homework, I was in the middle of a panic attack on my bedroom floor and didn't respond. What would I have even said? *Have you ever been so scared that you lose feeling in your limbs and pass out?*

Every time I think about telling her, I chicken out. I don't think she'd understand, anyway. It seems like the kind of thing you can only really understand if it happens to you.

We walk past a girl in our grade who smiles and waves at Immie. I smile at her, too, even though I can't remember her name.

"Vanessa looks pretty today," Immie says. "Doesn't she?"

On Saturday morning, the drama starts as soon as we get to the cabin.

Noah sobs and screams because he left his sleeping stuffed animal at home, and Carrie freaks out because her girlfriend wasn't allowed to come on the trip. It's hard to say who throws a bigger fit.

Then we all eat breakfast, and for a minute, things calm down. This is the first time I've seen Elise and Michael since the summer. Elise lives in Philadelphia with her fiancé Brad, and Michael is at Penn State. Elise is eight years older than me, so we were never super close, but Michael and I used to share a room. We went from being around each other a lot to not at all. That's probably why I agree to go fishing when he suggests it—not because I want to fish, but because I miss hanging out with my brother.

"You hate fishing," Immie says to me in the bunk bedroom right before we leave. Tina is in her arms, purring contentedly.

"No I don't," I lie, focusing on Tina instead of Immie's

face. I don't want to tell her the truth, because she's just going to say I always do what Michael wants to do.

I walk out to the van where Dad, Carter, Michael, and his friend Garth are loading up. I help tie the gear on the roof and am about to get in the back seat when Mom walks outside with the twins. They're both wearing their little life jackets.

"They want to come with you," she says to Dad. "And I'd love a couple hours to myself."

He gives her a look like she just said she's going to the moon. "Deb, c'mon—"

"Frank." She says his name like a warning.

"Daddy, are there sharks in this lake?" Marigold asks, pulling his shirt.

"No, dummy," Noah says. "There are alligators."

"Hey." Dad raises his voice. "Don't call your sister names." He looks at Mom like he's already tired. "Fine." He shifts his gaze to Michael. "We gotta put the car seats back in."

"Thank you," Mom says with a wave, already turning to go back inside.

The fishing spot is just a few minutes from the house, and the twins, still energized after breakfast, spend most of the car ride talking about what it would be like to live in the lake as merpeople. When we arrive, nobody else is there. Right away Dad sets up a beach chair and cracks open a beer. He stays on the beach with Carter and the twins, while Michael, Garth, and I take our fishing rods out to the end of the dock. It's a sunny day, but it's cold on the water. I zip my jacket all the way up to my chin.

"You fishing, bro?" Michael says to me.

"Yeah," I say. "Bet I can catch a bigger fish than you."

I don't know why I say it. I feel nervous for some reason, and it comes out of my mouth like word vomit.

Michael and Garth exchange an amused look. "That so?" Michael says. "Okay, then. You're on. What does the winner get?"

"Oh!" Garth looks excited. "The winner gets to push the loser in the lake."

I laugh. "No way! It's like fifty degrees out."

"Sounds like your little bro is scared of losing."

"Obviously I am."

"Dad would be pissed if one of us rode in the car soaking wet," Michael says, and I exhale. Thank god. He looks at me. "Five bucks?"

I don't have five dollars, but I don't want to give Garth the opportunity to come up with another bright idea. "Sure," I say. "Deal."

It takes me a minute to attach the lure to the line. Michael offers to help me, but I wave him away. It's important that I do it myself. When I finally figure it out, we all cast. Garth holds his rod for all of two minutes before he says he needs to pee and runs off to find the perfect tree. Then it's just me and Michael.

"So, semifinals," Michael says to me. "That's huge."

"Yeah. It is."

"You know I took us to finals my freshman year, right? You've gotta carry on the tradition."

I snort. "Oh, I know." As if I had any other choice *but* to know. Storm Valley lost the finals that year, but Michael still played a great game. I hear the highlight reel from my dad whenever he and Michael are together. I want to be a part of that, to have moments to reminisce about, but it also weirds me out, the idea of always living in the past. Isn't life supposed to get better as you get older? What does it mean that Dad is always looking back?

"Good." He holds his rod in one hand and claps me on the shoulder with the other. "Proud of ya, bud."

It's the first time he's said that. I look out at the water, embarrassed about how much it means to me.

"And you and Immie? What's up with that?"

My body tenses up a little. "What do you mean?"

He gives me a look that says *get real*. "You've had a thing for her forever."

I try to arrange my face in a way that looks shocked by this accusation. "No, I haven't."

He laughs. "We shared a room. I can read you. You might have been able to hide it from everyone else, but you were never hiding it from me."

I sigh. What's the point in lying?

"We held hands." I smile a little. "On Halloween."

He raises his eyebrows. "Well, would you look at that. All those years of pining finally paid off."

"Ha-ha," I say, sarcastic.

"So then what?"

"Nothing." I shoot him a glance. "What do you mean?"

He kind of laughs. "Nothing has happened since then?"

I feel a little pressure on my rod, and for a second I think I have something. When I reel the line in, nothing is there. I sigh. "No."

"Aw." He gives me a pitying look. "Don't worry. She'll come around. Just keep playing it cool."

I frown. I don't think I've ever played it cool in my whole life.

"Uh. What do you mean?"

"You know. Don't seem too eager. Act like it doesn't really matter to you, whether she likes you or not."

I furrow my brow as I cast my line out again. "But if I do that, she'll think I *don't* like her."

"Exactly," Michael says. "Girls like guys that are hard to get."

"Really?" I say, uncertain. "Even Immie?"

"Especially Immie," he says. "She's smart. Smart girls need a challenge, or else they get bored and move on."

Is that why Immie and I have always been *just friends*, because I'm not enough of a challenge? When you spend every day with someone for years and years, it's kind of hard to stay mysterious. Maybe that's why she's been more interested in me lately—because we've been spending less time together, and I'm suddenly more mysterious?

Or what if Michael is wrong? What if I act all aloof, Immie sees a side of me she doesn't like, and it ruins our friendship forever?

"I don't know," I say finally. "I don't want to lose her."

"The only way you'll lose her is if you come on too strong

and scare her away," he says, reinforcing one of my biggest fears. "Trust me. Girls can sense when you have a secret, and it will draw them to you."

I nod. It actually makes sense. The reason Immie and I are such good friends in the first place is because I kept my crush on her a secret for so many years. If she had known, it would've changed our whole dynamic. She might not have bothered to get to know me at all.

Sometimes secrets *are* for the best.

I see Garth walk out of the trees and onto the end of the dock.

"Thanks," I say, before Garth is in earshot. "I haven't been able to talk to anybody about this."

"Any time. Just give me a call."

Garth comes back, picks up his rod, and casts out. The three of us spend the next hour talking about sports or college or nothing at all. We don't catch any fish, but I don't mind. That was never the point.

I think about Michael's words for the rest of the day. Is he right? Do I need to play hard to get to make Immie realize her feelings for me?

At dinner, I watch her across the table. Everything she does is cute to me. The way she ties her hair back before taking her first bite. The way she eats all her veggies before moving on to her chicken. The way she jokes with Michael and asks my dad questions about his boring job and talks to the twins like they're real people, not little kids. Every now and then she glances at me, and when she catches me staring, she looks down at her plate and tries to hide a smile.

It gives me hope.

But then I completely ruined everything during the board game. I lie awake thinking about it, agonizing over the fact that I basically called her gross. Stupid Michael getting in my stupid head. I was so worried about looking too eager that I went *way* too far in the other direction. What's wrong with me?

My racing mind keeps me awake long after everybody else goes to sleep. I need to get out of bed, away from the dark bedroom and the silence that turns my thoughts into echoes. Doing my best not to disturb Tina, who's sprawled out on the end of the mattress, I grab my phone and walk to the kitchen.

I put in my earbuds and shuffle-play my music. "Running" by Kate Bollinger comes on the queue. It's dreamy and sad—perfect for the mood I'm in. I turn the volume all the way up and listen to the lyrics while I heat some water for hot chocolate.

Play it safe or not at all . . .

My mind shifts to what happened after the game. After my attempt at playing it cool backfired, they tried to get Immie out on a technicality. When I stuck up for her, Carrie accused me of *protecting my girlfriend*. Nobody seemed fazed—it's far from the first time Carrie has made a comment like that—and I know I should just let it go. But I can't. I keep seeing the look on Immie's face when Carrie said the word "girlfriend."

Her smile flickered; her eyes fell. It wasn't just a passing jab. It *bothered* her.

And *why* would it bother her?

Could it be because Carrie was onto something?

I'm not sure when she comes to the kitchen, but eventually I turn around and Immie is standing there, looking adorably sleepy. She's wearing my sweatshirt.

"Sorry." I pull out my earbuds. "Did I wake you up?"

In the living room, Immie settles on the couch with our hot chocolates while I light the fire. I remember when my dad taught me how to do this. I was eleven, and I thought it was amazing, the way I could make flames appear out of thin air. It was the closest I've ever come to feeling like a firebender, which was a big deal to eleven-year-old me.

I can tell Immie is still mad about what I said during the murder mystery game. As much as I want to pretend like it never happened, I know the only way to get over it is to address it head-on. That's how it is with Immie. She doesn't like to brush things under the rug.

I sit next to her with a blanket and apologize again for the whole gross-garbage fiasco. She asks why I said it, and I want to tell her the whole truth. Part of it is what Michael said: if I come on too strong, I'll scare her away. But it's more than that, too. Sometimes, I feel like I have to act a certain way when I'm around my whole family. I have to try extra hard to be funny, or shameless, or shocking, or else I'll just fade into the background.

I open my mouth to say as much but then decide not to. She wouldn't get it. Immie is always the center of attention in her family. She can't help it—she's her mom's whole world.

Then my thoughts shift, for some reason, to Immie's dad, whoever he is. I remember what Immie said about him in the woods: What if his music isn't enough? I wonder if she's started looking for him yet. I hear Michael's voice in my head: *Girls can sense when you have a secret, and it will draw them to you.* Does that work the other way around too?

"I'm sorry." I say. I look her in the eye because, even though I can't tell her the whole truth, I want her to know that I mean it. "I really am."

She doesn't say anything right away, she just picks up the bag of mini marshmallows and pours them slowly, deliberately into her mug, like she wants to make me suffer. Not that I blame her. Finally, after what feels like a million years, she looks at me and her expression softens.

"You're off the hook this time, but you better watch yourself, punk." She gives me a small, forgiving smile, and I feel like I can breathe for the first time all night.

She relaxes into the couch, pulls the blanket up to her chin. "I hope your siblings don't hate me for ruining the game."

"They could never. They love you," I say, like it's obvious. I'm so glad she isn't mad at me anymore that I don't really think about what comes out of my mouth next. "And I do too."

My heart practically stops.

I just told her that I loved her. How could I be so thoughtless? I showed all my cards, came on *way* too strong, and now she's going to be scared away. I think about what Michael would say if he was here to see this. *Nice going, Jackie. You totally blew it.* I want to sink into the couch and disappear forever.

But Immie doesn't seem weirded out. She's smiling, laughing a little, like what I said was no big deal. "Duh. I know that much."

She leans into me, and now I'm really confused. I told her how I felt and it didn't scare her away. Just the opposite: it brought her even closer. I breathe in, get a whiff of her hair, of peaches and smoke, and my heart, which nearly flatlined a moment ago, starts to pound.

I hear Michael's voice in my head again: *Don't seem too eager. Act like it doesn't really matter to you, whether she likes you or not.*

I shut him out. *Sorry, Michael.* I'm not very good at playing hard to get, anyway.

"I don't think you do." I force myself to look at her instead of shying away.

"Jack," she says abruptly. She's looking at me intently with her wide, Jolly Rancher eyes. "Why did you hold my hand in the haunted house?"

"Because." *Be confident.* "I wanted to."

"Why?"

The lights are low, the rest of the house is asleep, and Immie's face is just a few inches from mine. *Be a fighter.* Be the guy Immie thinks I am.

I put my mug down on the coffee table and turn to face her. Her dark hair hangs over her face, and I reach out, carefully, to brush it away. Immie doesn't move. I lean forward a little. *I can do this.* I lean forward a little more.

I've thought about kissing her so many times. What her lips would feel like. If she would still smell like peaches, or if she'd have moved on to something more perfumey and mature. Where she'd put her hands. Where I'd put mine. It was one of those fantasies that didn't have a beginning or an end; it existed only in the middle, like a dream. That's all I ever thought it could be.

She closes her eyes. I close mine—

"You are so busted."

I jump back, shocked into high alert by Carrie's voice. Immie spills her hot chocolate all over my sweatshirt.

Carrie is standing in the doorway with one hand on her hip and a smug look on her face. We lock eyes, and then she turns and walks out of the room.

Panic sets in. I don't have time to think, so I act. I leave Immie where she is and follow Carrie into the kitchen.

"Please don't tell Mom and Dad," I say, keeping my voice low.

She gets a hot chocolate packet out of the cabinet and pours the rest of the hot water into a mug.

"I knew you guys were together," she says. "You think I'm such an idiot."

"We're not," I say. "We're still—that was our first, um. Or it would have been."

"Ah," she says, emotionless. She tears open the hot chocolate mix and dumps it into her cup. "Whoops."

"Yeah, *whoops*. You walked in at the worst possible time. Now it's going to be weird between us."

Carrie snorts. "If you ask me, I did you a favor."

"What?"

"Immie is way out of your league." She stirs the mix with her spoon. "I know for a fact that she's caught the eye of a few upperclassmen."

"She doesn't like Elijah."

"Not just him. There are others. Popular guys, and some girls, too. There's no way you're going to be able to compete."

A voice inside my head tells me not to listen to her. Immie cares about me. She *wanted* me to kiss her in there, I know it. Carrie is just trying to get into my head.

She's right about one thing, though. Immie *is* out of my league. I've always known that. It's why I've never made a move, isn't it?

"You're a hopeless romantic," Carrie says. "But Immie is practical. She knows you two aren't soulmates. Better to realize that now, before you're in too deep."

Joke's on you, Carrie. I'm already in too deep.

"Under Control"—MJ Lenderman

It seems ridiculous now, but I really did think I had it under control.

The next morning, I want to get Immie alone, but it never happens. My family is everywhere we are. And in front of my family, nothing is out of the ordinary. She talks to me normally, cracking jokes and telling me all about whatever dead queen's biography she's been reading lately. By the time we're packing up the car to go home, I start to think maybe the almost kiss didn't mean what I thought. Maybe she wasn't even leaning in to kiss me. Maybe she was just leaning toward the fire and blinking really slowly. That's a thing people do, right? Maybe?

Then Monday comes, and I've got bigger problems. At the end of social studies, Ms. Wendt calls me over to her desk. I gesture to Immie across the room that she should go on without me.

Ms. Wendt hands me a piece of paper. "This is a letter to your parents informing them that you're failing this class."

"I'm . . . failing?" I haven't looked at my grades in a while. I guess I've kind of been avoiding them.

"This can't be a surprise to you," she says. "You told your coach that you were worried about your grade, so I offered you extra credit, which you then chose not to complete."

I skim over the letter. "Wait. You're telling them I should drop your class?"

"It's just a suggestion." Students in the next class start to trickle in, so she lowers her voice. "Jack, I know you're struggling here. If you drop honors and move to general social studies after midterms, you'll have a better chance at averaging out your final grade. That way, you avoid having to take the class over the summer or repeating it next year."

I start to feel a little sick. "I can get my grade up. I'll study extra hard for the midterm."

"It's up to you," she says. "There's a spot at the bottom for a parent's signature. Bring it back to me, signed, by the end of the week."

I walk out of the room in a daze, passing by Elijah's desk on the way. Great. I wonder if he heard—he probably did. In the hallway, Immie is there, clutching her books to her chest. I know it's not fair, but I feel a surge of annoyance. I told her not to wait for me.

"Everything okay?" She sounds worried. My annoyance evaporates.

"Yeah." I do my best to sound convincing. "She just wanted to talk to me about the extra credit."

"Oh. How'd you do?"

"Good." I don't look her in the eye. "I got an A."

She smiles. "I knew you could do it."

I try to give her a smile back, but I know it doesn't reach my eyes.

I wait until Thursday night to give the letter to my mom. When she reads it, she sighs and starts rubbing her temples.

"Oh, Jack." She shakes her head.

"I'm sorry."

"How did this happen? I didn't know you were struggling so much." She puts the note down on the kitchen counter, walks over to the junk drawer, and starts rummaging around for a pen.

"I don't know."

"You don't *know*?"

I sigh. "I guess because the tests are really hard. There's a lot of information to know, and sometimes I fall behind on the reading."

She closes the drawer, looks around the counter. "You didn't do the extra credit."

"I know. I was . . . I had a lot going on with soccer. And it was such a big assignment, I just—"

"This is exactly what we talked about when you made varsity. You promised me you wouldn't let it get in the way of your grades."

"It's not like I did it on purpose."

She walks over to where Tina is lying like a loaf on the counter. She picks her up, and, lo and behold, Tina was on the pen. "You didn't try hard enough."

She's right—I could've made more of an effort to sit down and do the reading, instead of skimming it in homeroom. I could have focused more on studying when I was with Immie, instead of just pretending that's what I was doing. I thought I'd be able to coast by in this class the same way I've always done.

"I'm sorry," I say again. "I'm a screwup."

She puts Tina back where she was. "Don't say that—you're not a *screwup*. You screwed up."

What's the difference, I want to say, *when I make mistakes all the time?*

"But it's not hopeless." She returns to the paper and signs on the line. "We'll get you into general social studies next semester, and that will hopefully be more manageable."

"I don't want to go to general," I say immediately. Then I won't have any classes with Immie at all.

"You're going." She gives me a stern look. "You need to do what's best for you. And this class clearly isn't best for you."

"You don't think I can do it," I say, feeling my heartbeat pick up the pace. "You don't have any faith in me."

She frowns at me. "Why is this class so important to you? You've never been very interested in history before."

I try to think of a response she'll believe. Before I can come up with anything, a look of realization crosses over her face. "Oh."

She gives me a smile that's part compassion, part pity. I want to be swallowed up by the ground.

"You don't need to take a class to impress her, you know."

I feel my face get hot. Still, I don't say anything.

"She's your best friend. She loves you no matter what."

Suddenly Marigold runs into the room with a red, tearstained face and a Barbie doll in one hand. "Noah cut Barbie's hair!" she wails.

"Oh no, honey." Marigold holds up the Barbie. Her hair is a hack job, short and spiky in some places and long in others. "I'm so sorry."

Mom folds the letter and hands it back to me. "By the way, you're grounded for the weekend."

"What? Mom, it's playoffs. The team is having a bonfire tomorrow night to celebrate."

"Sorry." She shrugs.

"Mom!" Marigold tugs on her shirt. "Please make Noah be in trouble!"

"Okay, okay. Shh." She follows Marigold out of the room.

I sigh to no one. I guess we're done with my thing already.

Friday. Semifinals. In the locker room, the team is buzzing with energy. I stay quiet and listen to my music. When an MJ Lenderman song comes on the queue, the lyrics stop me in my tracks. *"I had it under control. And then it snowballed . . ."*

I skip the song. I *have* control. And I need to be calm if I'm going to keep my head in the game.

It's been raining on and off all day. There's some debate among the coaches about whether the game will need to be postponed. Part of me hopes it does—the dull weather isn't doing much to help ease my nerves. What if I slip in the rain and get hurt, or miss a pass? I'm not sure which one is worse.

Twenty minutes before game time, the rain subsides into a drizzle, and it's official: semifinals will go on.

Coach gives us a quick pep talk in the locker room. Give it your all. Tune out the noise. If we win, we're going to the finals. That's when a tightness in my chest hits me like a slab of concrete. I need to play the best game I've ever played and lead the team to the finals. Then I'm going to *win* the finals, the way Michael never could. Otherwise, what has this whole season been about?

Right before I put my phone in my locker, I get a text from Immie—Good luck!!!! I'm about to reply when Coach claps his hands and tells us it's time to go. I put the phone away, leave the locker room, and walk onto the wet field to the cheers of the crowd.

Immie and my parents are in there somewhere, probably with Carter and the twins. Elise said she was going to try to make it if she could get off work in time. I tell myself not to scan the crowd for their faces, but I do it anyway. That's when I see him.

Michael. He drove in from Penn State to watch my game. Instead of feeling happy, I feel panicked. Now I definitely can't screw up.

Stay calm, I tell myself. *Stay in control.*

I start the game by sitting on the bench. I knew it was coming—Coach told me I was going to be first sub. He said it's because he doesn't want his two top scorers to get burned out in the first half. Also, because Elijah and I haven't exactly been playing nice lately. It's his fault, though. *He's* the one who doesn't pass to me even when I'm open, so I have no choice but to intercept him. It's the only way I get to see any action.

The other team scores in the first two minutes. The drizzle is more of a mist now. It hangs over the turf like a heavy cloud, making it hard to see what's going on down the field. Coach gives us another pep talk. Trust your instincts. Never take your eye off the ball. If you can't see the ball, listen for it. I don't ask him what to do if we can't hear it.

I get on the field a few minutes before halftime, when Andrew slips and hurts his arm. It's hard to see the stands through the mist, which I'm glad about. It makes it easier to pretend nobody is there. I can focus all my energy on the game.

The ball whizzes past me, over the touchline, and out of bounds. I didn't even see it coming. I hear Coach's frustrated shouts, and the concrete slab on my chest gets heavier. *Stay calm, stay in control,* I tell myself again, but there's an urgency to it. It's not a mantra anymore—it's an order.

At halftime, we're tied 1–1. I redeemed myself just before the buzzer, when I passed to Elijah and he scored. Good, but not good enough. Not like any of Michael's epic assists. I go into the locker room with the team and have a hard time listening to anything Coach has to say. I keep imagining Dad's disappointment when I missed that kick. Michael's wince when I slipped on the turf and let the other team intercept. Mom, straining to see if I got hurt. If I don't walk out of this with a win, how am I going to face them?

Back on the field. The rain is coming down harder. *Stay calm.* Serge passes the ball to me. I dribble down the field. The

308

ball slips out of my grip, but I recover it just in time. *Stay in control.* I pass to Elijah. I overshoot. The other team intercepts.

My hands go to my knees as I struggle to catch my breath. The concrete block is still on my chest, and my heart is pounding like mad. *Stay calm.* The other team's striker runs the ball toward our goal, and I try to catch him but I can't keep up. It's so hard to breathe. *Stay calm.* A pass gets intercepted, and the ball is kicked my way again. *Stay calm.* Instead of running it down the field, which is what I'd normally do, I pass to Elijah right away. It gets intercepted.

"NO!" I hear Coach on the sidelines. I'm letting him down, over and over. I can only imagine what my family must be yelling.

What's going on with me? It's like I've never played a game of soccer before. I knew semifinals would be a big game that would come with a lot of pressure. But it's a lot of pressure for *everyone*, not just me. So why am I the only one who can't handle it?

That's when it hits me. This whole time, I've been pretending to be somebody I'm not: Michael. I started playing soccer because I wanted to be like him, and then I stuck with it because I thought I could be better than him, but the truth is, I'm not a soccer star. I'm not a star at all. I'm a fraud. A nobody. Now my family, my teammates, and all the other people in those stands are going to realize it too—if they haven't already.

And then it really hits me.

The ball comes out of nowhere and smacks me in the face, sending me down to the ground.

TRACK TWELVE

"Iris"—Goo Goo Dolls

After the game, all I wanted to do was hide. I didn't think anyone would get how I was feeling. Ironic, since, when I heard this song, it made me feel understood. Isn't it funny how music can do that?

I never make it back onto the field after my ball to the face. I sit on the sidelines and hold a towel under my nose until the bleeding stops, at which point the trainer tapes it up with gauze in front of everyone. It's so humiliating. We lose semifinals 2–1.

Coach is furious. When we get back to the locker room, he's already hard at work trying to dispute the ref's decision to make us play. Meanwhile, Coach Robbie tries to cheer us up. It was a tough game, but we gave it our all. We had a great season, the best Storm Valley has seen in years. He's proud to be our coach. Blah blah. The whole time I stare at my screen, looking at Immie's last text. Good luck!!!!

I still haven't responded. What do I say? Sorry you had to sit in the rain just to see me get hit in the face?

"Yo, don't forget. Bonfire at my place," Elijah says to the

room once Coach has wrapped up. "There'll be lots of food. Bring friends."

Serge looks at me. "You want to ride over together? I'll tell Zoya and them to meet us there."

"Nah," I say, zipping up my bag. "I'm kinda tired. I'll probably just go home."

"What? No way." He's looking at me like I'm nuts. "You're going."

I'm too embarrassed to tell him I'm grounded, so I don't say anything. I just clench my jaw and sling my bag over my shoulder.

Serge sighs. "Dude, I know you're bummed. We all are. That's why we gotta stick together."

Suddenly Ben claps me on the shoulder. "See you boys there?"

"Yeah," Serge says, and then gives me a pointed look. "You will."

I tell him that I have to go say hi to my parents, and that I'll meet him there. I figure by the time he realizes I'm not coming, he'll be having too much fun with everybody else to care.

I find my dad and Michael waiting outside the locker room. Michael is in the middle of a story I've heard at least twice before.

"Their striker was dirty," he's saying. "He got away with everything, and then we found out later that he was the nephew of one of the refs. Completely bogus, isn't it?"

"You were robbed, buddy," Dad agrees. His eyes land on me.

"Ayy, Jackie!" Michael throws an arm around me and pulls me in for a hug.

"Hey," I mumble into his jacket, careful not to bump my nose. "Sorry you had to drive all the way down here for that."

"Don't be hard on yourself," Michael says, patting my back and letting me go. "They should've called it. It was *way* too foggy." He shakes his head. "The tradition of crooked refs continues."

"My game wasn't so great either," I say. "Where's Mom?"

"Back at the car with the twins," Michael says. "I told her I'd bring you home."

"Your dribbling was sloppy," Dad says out of nowhere.

"Dad . . ." Michael starts.

"Thanks, Dad," I say. "For your always appreciated constructive criticism."

"I'm just saying. It wasn't like you."

"That's because it was *slippery*."

"I'll bet," Michael says, obviously trying to smooth things over. "They're lucky nobody broke an ankle."

"You were always good at keeping control of the ball in the rain," Dad says to Michael. He turns to me. "Your brother could help you out if you let him."

"I'm good. I've got a coach."

"A coach who just lost your semifinals," Dad replies, matter-of-fact. "Michael took his team all the way to finals when he was your age."

"Yeah, I *know*. We all know."

"Speaking of finals," Michael says. "My final for my psychology class is really interesting. We have to—"

"Don't you want to be the best?" Dad interrupts Michael.

"Dad," Michael groans, exasperated.

"No, it's an honest question." Dad looks at me. "Do you want to be the best or not?"

I want to laugh. "You're not seriously saying that Michael is the best at soccer, are you? He doesn't even play anymore."

"Ouch," Michael says. "Thanks for reminding me."

"When did I say that?" Dad replies. "He has experience, and you could learn from him. That's all, my god." He shakes his head like I'm being impossible.

"In case you haven't noticed," I say, my heart pounding, "we just lost a pretty big game. Any normal parent would have a little bit of sympathy before pointing out all my mistakes."

"Oh, here we go with the attitude," Dad says. "I forgot I can't say anything without you making some sort of smart remark."

I look at him, taking in his square jaw, going soft at the edges, the deep wrinkles in his brow, his cropped, graying hair. Time has made him less intimidating. He's not some almighty, untouchable force anymore. He's just a person, like anybody else. Like *me*.

I thought things would be different between us when I made varsity. Finally, I'd know what it felt like to matter to him. I was *so* close. Or at least I thought I was.

Turns out, I never could be.

How many hours have I wasted wishing I had a dad whose love wasn't conditional? Who was proud of me not just for my achievements, but for the mere fact that I'm his son, and I'm trying my best?

"You know what, Dad?" I say, holding his gaze. I see his jaw muscles tighten, like he's bracing for impact. "I'm sorry you're disappointed in me. I'm sorry I'm not Michael."

His brow softens—he actually looks a little surprised. He opens his mouth to respond, and I prepare for the worst. It never comes.

"I'm going back to the car," he says. "See you both at home."

He walks off. Michael looks at me, and I see something like guilt on his face.

"DQ?" he says. "We can get burgers and Blizzards."

"I'm grounded," I say, looking past him. I feel too ashamed to look him in the eye.

"We'll go through the drive-through," he says with a shrug. "Mom was pretty clear. Car, then home. We technically wouldn't be breaking her rules."

I crack a smile at that. Man, sometimes I really miss having him around.

"Hey." I turn around, and there's Alex. Her red hair is damp, and strands of it stick to her face.

"Hey," I say, trying to sound like I'm not totally dead inside. "Alex, this is my brother Michael."

"Nice to meet you," Michael says. "Some game, huh?"

"Yeah." She winces a little. "I've never seen my dad so mad.

He's on the phone right now, practically screaming at some-body from the athletic league. This might be his villain origin story."

I laugh. To Michael, I say, "Her dad is Coach Berotti."

"Good man," Michael says with a nod.

Alex looks at me. "Are you coming to the bonfire? We're all over there, figuring out carpools. . . . I think Immie is wait-ing for you."

She points across the parking lot, where I see Immie standing with Serge, Zoya, Hannah, and Elijah. She's wearing my sweatshirt. My chest tightens.

I can't face Immie like this. She's going to say a bunch of nice things to try to make me feel better, but it won't work, and then I'll feel guilty that it doesn't work, that I can't put on a smile and pretend everything's fine for her. And then I'll picture her standing there with Elijah, smiling at him, talking about happy things, and I'll think, again, about how much more sense it makes, the two of them together, and I'll remind myself of the cabin kiss that never was, because it was never meant to be, because Immie is everything and I'm just me, and I can't be what she needs.

"I'm going to ride back with my brother," I say. "Thanks, though."

She gives me a hug and tells me I played a good game. When she says the words, my dad's face pops into my head. *Don't you see?* I wish I could tell him. *It really is that easy.*

Alex walks back to her friends—our friends. I watch her go for a second and then turn to Michael.

"Want to say hey to your friends?" he says, looking over at them.

"No," I reply without hesitation. "Let's go."

We go through the DQ drive-through, as promised, and I get a burger and snickerdoodle Blizzard, even though I'm not very hungry. It feels impossible to eat with this weight on my chest.

Michael pulls out of the drive-through and into a parking spot. We take our time unwrapping our burgers, our spoons, our straws, just listening to the song on the radio, "Iris" by the Goo Goo Dolls. The lyrics are right on point.

> *I don't want the world to see me.*
> *'Cause I don't think that they'd understand."*

Michael is the first to speak. "So why don't you want to go to the bonfire? Seems like it would be a good time."

"I can't go," I say, looking at my burger. "You know. Grounded."

He makes a face like that's ridiculous. "You deserve to celebrate the end of a great season. You worked hard. You earned this."

I snort. "Yeah. Try telling that to Mom."

"I will," he says with a mouthful of burger. He chews, swallows. "I'll tell her I forced you to go because I want you to have experiences."

"I have experiences," I mutter.

"Okay," he says. "So then, why not have one more?"

"Because," I say, and then instantly regret it. He's just trying to help. "The guy who's having it."

"Somebody on your team?"

"Yeah," I say. "Elijah Whitehouse."

Michael nods. "The other striker. The one who asked Immie to the dance."

"He's just so arrogant," I say, wrapping my burger up in the foil. "And Immie will probably be there, and I don't really feel like seeing him try to flirt with her."

"Jack." Michael looks at me. "Immie picked you. Who cares about this other guy?"

"She didn't *pick* me," I say. "I mean, yeah, she went to the dance with me, but that's it. It's not like she's my girlfriend or anything."

Michael takes a long sip of Coke. Then he says, "Carrie told me about the kiss."

My heart starts to pound. *Thanks, Carrie. Thanks a lot.*

"There was no kiss."

"Sure, fine. The *almost* kiss." He takes another sip. "My point is, did she almost kiss Elijah last weekend?"

I wince. I kind of wish he'd stop saying "kiss."

"No, she didn't," he answers for me. "If you want my advice, I think you should go to this bonfire and finish what you started. Do it right in front of him, if it'll make you feel better."

"I don't want your advice," I say. "And I don't want to go to Elijah's party."

"But—"

"You don't get it. I have to deal with him *constantly*. At practice, at school, at the diner. He's always there, showing me up, acting like he's the greatest thing on earth. And everybody lets him do it."

Michael is quiet. He just sips his Coke and looks at me thoughtfully.

"Huh." He tilts his head.

"What?"

He puts the Coke in the cup holder. "This isn't about Elijah at all. It's about me."

"Oh come on." I don't know whether to laugh or roll my eyes. "What?"

"Yeah. What you said to Dad earlier. *Sorry I'm not Michael.*" He imitates me, making my voice all grumbly. "You're obviously feeling some pressure to live up to my legacy—"

"Your *legacy*?" Now I do roll my eyes.

"—and Elijah is standing in the way of that. That's why you see him as a sort of nemesis. *Yeah*, it makes sense." He pauses, considers. "If you beat him, it's kind of like you're beating me."

I shake my head. "You've taken *one* psychology class."

"Two," he corrects, and then gives me a knowing look. "Listen. I'm sorry that Dad's been putting the heat on you. If it makes you feel any better, he did the exact same thing to me."

"He did?" I guess I've never thought about that before. I was so busy being jealous of Michael's relationship with Dad that I forgot to consider what he had to go through to get it there.

"You've just got to tune him out and do what makes you happy," Michael finishes. "If you're happy, he'll be happy too."

I look out the windshield at the mostly empty parking lot. It's the best time of year to go to DQ. In the summer it's always packed with baseball teams and cheerleading squads. They take all the tables and yell over one another and make it impossible to enjoy a good Dilly Bar in peace. Winter DQ is a much more contemplative place.

"Soccer makes me happy," I say.

"Okay, then." Michael nods. "There's only one thing left to do."

He buckles his seat belt and puts the car in drive.

♥ TRACK THIRTEEN

"Pale Blue Eyes"—The Velvet Underground

Carrie used to play this song in her bedroom all the time, and I'd listen through the walls and think of you. When I saw you at the bonfire, I thought about it again, but not the part about your eyes. I thought about how you weren't mine.

Michael pulls up to Elijah's house and puts the car in park. Before I get out, he helps me take the gauze off my nose.

"Oof." He makes a face. "It's starting to bruise."

Great. Guess it's only fitting that I look the way I feel on the inside.

"Have fun," he says. "I'm hitting the road later tonight, so I don't know if I'll see you."

"I'd rather just hang out with you."

He shakes his head. "If you don't go to this party, you're going to regret it," he says. "Trust me. One day, you won't be playing soccer anymore, and these memories will be all you'll have."

I nod. I don't know what to say. All of a sudden I become extremely aware of the fact that I'm reliving Michael's glory days right in front of him. I feel sort of guilty.

"Okay. Well, thanks for the talk, I guess."

"Anytime," he says. "Like I said. Just call."

I get out of the car and Michael drives off. I hear music and voices drifting from the backyard, so I follow the sound, walking up the driveway and around the side of the house. When I see the gate, my heart starts to beat faster. I feel a little woozy and realize I didn't eat a single bite of that DQ.

I wonder if Immie is here yet. Who she'll be with when I walk in. I haven't responded to any of her messages, and I feel nervous about seeing her.

I take a breath and push open the gate.

A quick scan of Elijah's backyard: people by the fire, people on the patio, people milling around the yard. I spot Alex, Zoya, and Hannah by the snack table. Serge and Greg on lawn chairs. But no Immie.

I walk over to the fire, confused. Did she leave already? Maybe she got here, thought I wasn't coming, and then went home. That would be just my luck. I wonder how long I have to stay until I can leave too. Maybe I can sneak out now, before anybody sees me.

"Marshall."

It's Andrew, sipping from a red Solo cup and walking toward me. This night keeps getting better and better.

"That looks gnarly," he says, gesturing to my nose with his sprained wrist. It's wrapped up in a sling.

"You should see the soccer ball. I mean, the other guy," I say, my voice flat.

Andrew chuckles. "You know, you're not so bad, Marshall. I'm glad we had you on the team this year."

I look at him, skeptical. I wonder if that's really fruit punch in his cup.

"Uh, thanks," I say. "You're pretty much just as bad as I thought."

Now he lets out a big, bellowing laugh that makes a few people turn their heads. "Funny."

I don't respond, just look into the fire and wait for him to say what he came over here to say.

"So," he starts. And even though I was expecting it, my chest tightens. "Sorry to hear about you and Immie."

My expression darkens. Whatever I was expecting him to say, it definitely wasn't that.

"What are you talking about?"

"I know you guys had something going on at Halloween," he says, casual as ever. "What happened?"

"Nothing *happened*," I say, defensive. My mind starts racing. There's no way he could know about the almost kiss, right? What does he have over me? "I literally have no idea what you're talking about."

"Huh," Andrew says. "Then why did I see her go inside with Elijah a while ago?"

Dread washes over my whole body.

"She's here?" I look back at Elijah's house. All the lights are off. "In there?"

"Yup."

"I don't believe you."

"That's fine," he says with a shrug. "But I'm not lying. She was wearing your sweatshirt."

The breath is knocked out of me. I feel like I might pass out or puke or both.

"Messed up, if you ask me." He shakes his head. "But that's Elijah. He can get anyone to do anything."

My heart is pounding, my insides swirling with confusion and rage. Immie went inside with Elijah. Why would she do that? What could she possibly need to do inside that she couldn't do out here?

I clench my jaw. I want Andrew to get away from me. *Now*.

"Jack!"

My stomach drops. It's her voice.

"Later," Andrew says, walking away.

I turn around, and before I can even say anything, she tackles me into a hug. I hug her back, dazed.

"Immie. Hey."

"I've been waiting for you," she says, still squeezing me. I want to ask why she was waiting for me in Elijah's house. "Didn't you get my text?"

"My phone is sort of broken."

My phone is in my pocket, and it's fine. I don't know why I lie. I guess I just don't feel like telling the truth, which is that I've been ignoring her because I didn't know what to say.

"Oh, weird. How'd you break it? You know what, tell me later, it doesn't matter. Better your phone than your nose," she says, taking a step back but still not letting go of me. She's talking fast—almost frantic. "Does it hurt?"

"It's fine." I look down at her sweatshirt. It's not mine. It's a light blue one that says STRAWBERRY LAKE AND BEACH on the front. I've seen it before.

On Elijah.

"It's Hannah's," she says without missing a beat. "I was wearing yours, but it got soaking wet at the game, so she let me borrow it."

I try to turn away from her, toward the fire, but she's tucked herself under my arm like a fly in a glue trap. She wants to be close to me, which would usually be a good thing, but not now. I can't bear to look at her face. All I can think is that she's lying to me. *Why* is she lying to me? I can only think of one good reason.

Maybe there really is something going on between her and Elijah.

And isn't that what I always expected? Immie was never going to settle for me, not when Elijah has been right there this whole time. He's always been the confident one, the cooler one, the one who goes after what he wants. I mean, he knew Immie for all of five minutes before he made his feelings for her clear. I, on the other hand, have known her for seven and a half years, and I've never said a word. Not one.

I don't deserve her. *Elijah* is the one who deserves her. This whole time, I've been playing for second.

And it's okay. The realization comes with a sort of peace.

Now I can stop trying to be something I'm not.

TRACK FOURTEEN

"Unforgettable"—Natalie Cole and Nat "King" Cole

I thought I was dying, and I was still thinking about you.

*I*t takes me a little while to piece it all together.

Somehow, for some reason—was she taking pity on me?—I remember she tries to kiss me. She leans in, closes her eyes, gets *so close* to pressing her lips to mine.

And then, all of a sudden, I can't breathe.

Not in a *she took my breath away* kind of way, but in a *something's not right* kind of way. An *I accepted that you were meant to be with Elijah, not me, and now you're about to kiss me and I'm so confused* kind of way. This is *Immie*, the girl I've dreamed about kissing for as long as I *dreamed* about kissing. I should feel good. I should feel *sure*, the way I did at the cabin. Instead, I feel like I'm suffocating.

"I can't breathe," I try to say between shallow breaths, but I don't know if she hears me. I'm trying really hard not to cry. "I'm sorry."

I remember she looks at me like she doesn't even recognize me. And then, without another word, she walks away.

I remember walking to the tree.

I don't plan it. I'm walking home, thinking that I want to be with Immie but I can't be with Immie, and how scary and unfamiliar that feeling is, when I consider the tree. It isn't Immie, but it's the next best thing.

I walk around Immie's house and crawl underneath the roots of the tree. I remember thinking I haven't been here in months, since Immie called that emergency meeting about her dad's CD collection. That was back when she told me everything.

I remember it starts to rain.

Lightly at first, but then, gradually, it turns into a full-on shower. It pounds into the ground, the leaves, everything in between. It's so loud it feels overwhelming. I can't hear myself breathe. Instead of drowning out my thoughts, it amplifies them, and they sound like screams. I close my eyes, try to feel the breath moving through my body, but it turns out I can't feel anything.

I remember pulling my phone out of my pocket. I unlock it, find Michael's name in my favorites and press call. It rings and rings, until finally I get his voicemail—the generic lady who says, "You have reached the voice mailbox of seven one seven . . ."

I think about going back home, but it feels so far. Instead, I lie down on the cold ground, hug my knees to my chest, and listen to the rain until all sound fades away and I don't hear anything at all.

I remember coming to as I'm being lifted up. It's dark, and I don't have any clue where I am or how I happen to be rising through the air. I just know I'm soaking wet and so cold. And then I see my dad's face.

I remember my parents' voices as I'm being wrapped in a blanket and ushered into a car. My mom's high-pitched panic offset by my dad's low, even commands. I rub the fabric of the blanket between my fingers, focusing on the soft, downy feel of the fibers.

I remember the song on the radio when Dad drives onto the highway. That old, sad song with the piano and strings, where the guy sings, "Unforgettable, that's what you are," and the girl replies, "Unforgettable, though near or far." It makes me think about Immie, which is the last thing I want to be thinking about. I pull the blanket up over my head.

I remember the hospital, the blur of bright lights and the papery bedsheets. A nurse poking me with needles and hooking me up to a machine to test the strength of my heart. I want to tell her that my heart is fine—if anything it works too well, I feel too much. It's my head that's the problem. A doctor asks me what I mean by that, which is when I realize I must have said it out loud. She asks me questions and then pulls my parents into the hallway.

I remember what time we get home from the hospital: 12:17 a.m. I see it on the stove clock before going up to my room. My mom tells me to get some rest, we'll talk in the morning, and that she loves me, and she's sorry. I feel bad for making her sad and want to say she has nothing to be sorry for, but I'm not sure that's true. So I don't say anything. I lie in bed, in the dark, with the words to "Unforgettable" swirling around in my head.

TRACK FIFTEEN

"Lost Cause"—Beck

I know I made a lot of mistakes, and I'm not denying that. But I did try to tell you the truth in the hall, and you didn't want to hear it. You'd already made up your mind.

*H*ere's what happened. After Immie left, I sort of lost track of time. I stayed in the woods for a while, spiraling, until I had such a bad panic attack that I passed out.

My mom let me stay at the party for an hour before she started calling me, trying to track me down. After a while, when I still hadn't answered, she checked the location of my cell phone. Imagine her surprise when I wasn't at the party, but in the woods. She sent my dad out to get me, and when he came back ten minutes later, he was half carrying me.

Anxiety disorder. That's what it's called. In a lot of ways, it feels like a relief to know what's wrong with me—that it's something diagnosable and not just a problem I'm making up in my head.

My parents sit me down after breakfast the next morning to talk about it. They ask how long the panic attacks have been going on for, what it feels like when they happen, things like that. It's humiliating, talking to them about this, and when I say as much, Mom tells me that the doctor recommended a therapist.

I look at Dad when she says this. His eyes are on the floor, his facial expression stoic. I think about the way he looked at me when he found me in the woods, because it was nothing like this—it was wide open. He didn't bother to hide the fear in his eyes, or the love. I wonder what he's thinking now.

I agree to see the therapist next week. Mom hugs me, and Dad hugs me too, and I go back to my room and lie down in bed, feeling numb and exhausted, and, strangely, a little lighter. Finally. I might not be who they thought I was, but I don't have to hide this feeling from them anymore. That's something, at least.

Monday morning before school, I find Carrie in the kitchen, eating a banana.

"Hey," I say. "Don't tell Immie, okay?"

She frowns at me. "About your trip to the ER? Why would I?"

"I don't know. Just . . . in case you were planning to bring it up, don't."

"Why not? Are you embarrassed?"

I focus on packing my notebooks into my book bag. "Obviously."

"Well, that's stupid. You shouldn't be embarrassed to talk about your mental health. Especially with your friends." She

330

throws the banana peel in the trash and picks up her phone. "Are you ready to go?"

I zip up my bag. "Yeah."

"Look at that," Carrie says, her eyes on the screen. She holds it out to me. There's a text from Immie: hey, I don't need a ride today.

My heart starts to pound. We didn't talk over the weekend. I didn't know if she'd want to hear from me, and even if she did, I had no clue what to say. *Sorry I've been MIA. I was in the hospital. Why? Oh, because I passed out under the tree behind your house.*

"What's that about? Are you fighting?"

I don't know if we're fighting. We've never really fought before. The maddest Immie has ever been at me was the Macaroni Incident of '18, and that was resolved in a day. This is more uncharted territory.

"Whatever you did," Carrie says, "you need to fix it."

"Why do you just assume I did something?"

She frowns. "Because you're you." She picks up her oversized purse and slings it over her shoulder. "And Immie is good for you."

"I know, okay? I know she's too good for me. You said that before."

"No. I said she's good *for* you. She makes you more confident. And we all know you need help with that."

I look out the window, toward her house. Carrie is right—Immie does make me more confident. That's probably why this weekend without her has been extra horrible.

"Let's just go." I leave the kitchen and walk out the front door.

Immie doesn't want to talk to me. It's like a punch to the gut. Standing here in the school hallway, seeing the disdain in her eyes, I feel anxious and nauseous and full of regret. I should have told her. I just didn't know *how*. How was I supposed to explain something I didn't understand myself?

"I need space," she's saying. She rolls her shoulders back and stands up as tall as she can, trying in vain to match my height. "From you. To figure things out."

The late bell starts to ring. I don't move. I just look at her, trying to memorize every single detail of her face. She looks tired and grumpy and a little unkempt, but it's her. It's *home*. I feel such an intense surge of longing for her that I want to scream, to tell her that this has all been a huge misunderstanding, that I love her, and to please, *please* not give up on me yet, but it's pointless. I waited too long.

I lost her.

"Fine," I say. "If that's really what you want."

She nods. "It is."

Then it's like all the energy leaves me at once, and I feel numb, dead.

"Okay, then."

I walk away from her. I know I'm going to be late to Spanish, but I don't care. I take my time, and I wonder. Is this how it feels at the end of the world? Like nothing matters? Like nothing could ever matter again?

— — —

I sleepwalk through my classes. My mind stays fixed on one thing, like a frozen computer screen. *I lost her.* How am I supposed to conjugate verbs or solve for *x* when I lost her? It feels huge, all consuming. It drowns out everything else.

Not even music helps. Every song that comes on the queue feels like a sick joke from the universe, a cruel reminder of the state of things. As if I needed reminding. When I hear "Lost Cause" by Beck, it's the last straw. *"Baby you're lost. Baby, you're a lost cause."* I yank out my earbuds and put them in my pocket.

At lunch, I take my usual seat next to Serge. He, Ben, and Greg are having a heated discussion about Formula 1, about whether Daniel Ricciardo should've left Red Bull back in 2019. I'm glad—I don't want to talk. I don't even know if I remember how. I look at the square pizza on my tray and feel instantly nauseous.

"Marshall."

I look up. Elijah is standing there with a folded-up green sweatshirt that says STORM VALLEY THUNDERCATS. He holds it out to me.

"This is yours."

I take it without a word. I don't need to ask why he has it.

"Immie gave it to me to put in the dryer," he explains anyway. He's kind of fidgety, like maybe he feels uncomfortable. That makes two of us. "But she left before I could give it back to her."

I nod, already turning back around in my seat.

"At the bonfire," he adds.

"Got it."

A sigh. And then: "Listen . . ."

I look back at him, annoyed. He's already got Immie. What more could he possibly want?

My mind flashes back to what Michael said in the car. *This isn't about Elijah at all. It's about me.* I look at Elijah's annoying, entitled face and push the thoughts away.

No. It's *definitely* about Elijah.

"I'm not trying to get in the middle of anything. Just so you know."

I stay silent. If that's true, then he's doing a really terrible job.

"She's a cool girl," he says. "I'm not denying that. I like talking to her."

I roll my eyes. "Does this little speech have a point?"

"Just that, if you guys are together, I'll respect it. No hard feelings."

"We're not," I say. "And we never were. She's all yours."

Elijah shakes his head. "You've got this awesome girl who likes you, and you aren't even doing anything about it?"

Suddenly my interest is piqued. Same goes, apparently, for Serge, Ben, and Greg. They're all quiet, watching us.

"You get so in your head," Elijah continues. "It's the same with soccer. You've got to learn to let go, you know? Trust your instincts."

"Preach," Serge says, his hands cupped over his mouth like a megaphone.

Let go. Trust your instincts. I have to admit, I like it a lot better than Michael's advice to keep everything hidden inside. I sigh, frustrated. Why did I ever think it was a good idea to listen to Michael? He's never even had a girlfriend.

"How do you know she likes me?" My heart is pounding, waking me up. "Did she say that?"

His expression is hard to read. "Not exactly."

Not *exactly?* I want to shake him, to make him tell me what he means *exactly.* But it's Elijah. You can't make him do anything.

"She was wearing your sweatshirt," I say, when what I mean is *she chose you.* Didn't she?

He laughs again, and the sound is grating. "Because hers— yours—was wet. I just gave it to her to wear in the meantime, so she wouldn't be cold."

I size him up, trying to decide if he's telling the truth. He could be lying to make me look like a fool. He'll probably go laugh about it with Andrew right after this.

"Come on, dude," he says. "It's just a sweatshirt."

When he goes back to his seat, my head starts spinning. If it's true, and nothing happened between Immie and Elijah in his house, then why did she lie to me about his sweatshirt? Could it be that Elijah's right—that it's *just* a sweatshirt? It didn't mean anything, and the paranoia was all in my head?

It wouldn't be the first time.

A glimmer of hope cracks through the tension in my chest. Maybe it's *not* the end.

TRACK SIXTEEN

"Saturday"—Dazies

Giving you space was the hardest thing I've ever had to do. You can be mad at me for hanging out with Alex if you want, but the fact is, I never would have done it if you hadn't told me to stay away. I just wanted someone to talk to. Can't you understand that?

The next day after school, I show up on her front porch with a weird-looking purple flower I picked from the woods. Beautiful, mysterious, unique—the perfect flower for Immie.

I pull my phone out of my pocket to pause my music. The lyrics in this song by Dazies perfectly capture what I wish I could tell Immie: "*There's so much I can't say, but I still need you.*"

I pocket my phone again, take a deep breath, and ring the doorbell. I probably only have one shot, so I've got to make this count.

I messed up. I miss you. You matter to me, of course you do. Recently I've been suffering from these crippling panic attacks that make it hard to say how I really feel. But this *is how I really feel.*

Nora opens the door. She's in a suit, and her hair is pinned up. She must have just gotten home from work. "Hey there."

"Hey, Ms. Meadows. Is Immie here?"

Nora glances down at the flower in my hand. I quickly hide it behind my back, but it's too late.

"She's not. She's over at Hannah's."

"Oh." My shoulders slump. "Uh, okay. Thanks."

"Did you try her cell?"

I shake my head, even though it's not true. I texted her this morning telling her I wanted to talk to her after school. That means she stayed away on purpose. "Not in a while. I'll text her."

She tilts her head in the same way that Immie does when she's trying to figure you out. It's kind of eerie, the resemblance.

"I know something's going on between you two," she says. "She hasn't been sharing much with me lately, but I can tell it's affecting her. I think it's affecting you, too. That's what the flower's about, right?"

I nod, not surprised by her powers of perception. Immie is her daughter, after all.

"It's all my fault," I say. "I messed up, and now Immie won't talk to me."

"She'll come around," Nora says. "Give her some time."

"How much time?"

She smiles sadly. "You know how she is." Which is to say, *a while*. "But eventually, she'll forgive you."

I nod, crestfallen. More time apart sounds like pure misery, but if it's the only way to get Immie back, then I'll do it. I'll do anything for her.

"I really hope so."

She starts pulling the pins out of her hair one by one. "You're a good kid, Jack. You've always been a great friend to

Immie, which I've appreciated. Before we moved here, she had a hard time making friends. You know—she always kept to herself. But then you brought her out of her shell."

"I didn't do anything," I say. "I liked her for exactly who she was."

Nora smiles. "Exactly." She pulls the last pin out, and her hair comes tumbling down. She breathes out a sigh of relief. "Do you want me to tell her you came by?"

"That's okay," I say. I look down at my hands and then offer her the flower. "Thanks, Ms. M. For everything."

When I'm crossing the street back to my house, my phone buzzes in my pocket. It's a text from Serge.

Serge: What u up to

Jack: Nada

Serge: Going to the mall with Z and Alex. Wanna come?

Alex. I've been so focused on Immie, I haven't really thought about what Serge said at the haunted house. *You know she's got a thing for you.*

Jack: I'll meet you there

"How lucky was it that both the top *and* pants were available in my size?" Zoya says as we're walking out of another clothing store.

"So lucky," Serge says, his voice flat as Zoya hands him yet another shopping bag. He looks at me, raises the bags in the air like he's lifting weights. "At least I can skip arm day."

"Can we go get pretzels now?" Alex asks. Zoya has dragged

us to three different clothing stores and somehow still isn't satisfied. Now I understand why Immie complained about this so much. "I'm starved."

"Same," I say. I can smell the Auntie Anne's, and it's making my stomach growl.

"I just want to hit one last store," Zoya says, pointing across the walkway.

Serge groans loudly. "Seriously? All this isn't enough?"

"I'm looking for a specific pair of white leather boots, Sergio. I need them to match my new top."

"Fine." He sighs. "You guys go. We'll be right behind you. And I mean *right* behind you. If it's longer than ten minutes, send a search-and-rescue party."

"Come on." Zoya grabs his wrist and drags him off.

"Um." I glance at Alex. I wasn't expecting to be alone with her. I hear Serge's voice again: *She's got a thing for you.* "Ready?"

She nods. "Cinnamon pretzel sticks, here I come."

"Ooh, nice." We start walking, and I do what I do best—talk through my nerves. "I don't know yet if I want cinnamon or regular. It's going to be a game-time decision."

"Well," Alex says. "Are you more in the mood for salty or sweet?"

Salty or sweet? I always pick salty. Maybe it's time for a change.

"I think sweet."

She smiles. "Good choice."

We get two orders of cinnamon pretzel sticks with the

icing dipping sauce and grab a table with four chairs. I sit down across from her.

"So." I pick up a pretzel. "Do you have any plans for Thanksgiving break?"

"Not really," she says, dunking her pretzel in the icing as far as it will go. "We're going to my grandparents' house for Thanksgiving dinner. They've got horses, which is my favorite part."

"Horses? Like, on their property?"

"Mm-hmm. They've got a barn and two horses. I always ride Marshmallow. The other horse, Phoenix, doesn't like me. He doesn't like anyone except my grandpa."

"You ride horses." I nod, impressed. I can't even picture Immie on a horse—she'd fall off in two seconds. "That's cool."

"My whole life." She smiles bashfully. "I'll probably be there for most of break, so I can ride every day. What about you? What are your plans?"

Normally, I'd spend my Thanksgiving break eating a ton of food, then going over to Immie's house to watch movies. This year, though, things are different.

"To be honest . . ." I pause, debating whether I should say it. Then I realize—who cares? I don't have anything more to lose. I might as well tell the truth. "The only thing I have planned is a therapy appointment."

"Oh?"

"Yeah. It's my first one."

She nods thoughtfully. "How are you feeling about it?"

How *am* I feeling? I haven't really thought about it. I've

had a few more pressing things on my mind. "I don't know. Weird, I guess."

"Yeah. It's definitely weird at first."

I raise my brows. "You've been to therapy?"

She looks down at her pretzel. "I went for a year after my brother died."

"Oh." I feel awkward suddenly. "I'm sorry, I didn't—"

"No, it's okay." She gives me a reassuring smile. "I used to not be able to talk about him without breaking down. But then I realized that I have to talk about him. That's how I keep him alive." She sort of laughs. "See? I've got therapy to thank for that one."

I return her smile. "So you feel like it helped you?"

"Yeah. I mean, not overnight, or anything like that. But after a while, it wasn't so hard to get out of bed in the morning. I stopped feeling so terrible all the time."

I can't even imagine what it would feel like not to constantly worry about everything. To just be in the moment, or even enjoy it? What a concept.

"Thanks for telling me," I say, meaning it. It's cool to hear her talk openly about something so tough. That's bravery too. And it's nice, talking to someone who gets what I'm going through. I don't have to hide my anxiety from Alex. I don't have to hide anything at all.

I take a deep breath. "At the beginning of the school year, I started getting these . . . these panic attacks," I tell her. "I tried to hide them, but they kept getting worse. Then, last week, I wound up in the hospital."

"That's awful," she says. I don't hear judgment in her voice or pity—just understanding. "So that's why . . . the therapy?"

I take another bite of pretzel, feeling strangely at ease. I'm not trying to be cool or charming or anything other than myself. "Yeah."

"It's normal, you know," Alex says. "I used to get panic attacks too."

"Really?"

"Yeah. And if it makes you feel any better, therapy really helped with those. I haven't had one in a year."

"How—I mean, if you don't mind telling me. How did it help?"

"I don't mind at all," Alex says. "I learned about mind-fulness exercises. It's basically just forcing your brain into the present moment when your thoughts are flying all over the place. Have you heard of the three-three-three rule?"

I shake my head.

"Okay. So when you feel yourself starting to panic, you should try to name three things you can see, three things you can hear, and then move three different parts of your body. It sounds corny, but it really does help."

"Wow," I say. "You know so much about this stuff."

"Yeah, well. When you go through something hard, you don't come out the other side without learning a few things."

I nod, knowing she's right. I'm not on the other side of my anxiety—not even close—but since the diagnosis, I already feel like I know myself so much better. Things that seemed impossible to grasp now feel like they're within reach.

"Thanks for talking to me about this," I tell her. "You're the only person I've been able to talk to about it, really."

What I don't say hangs in the air—that I haven't talked to Immie about it. That she still doesn't know a thing.

"I won't say anything to anyone," Alex says, as if reading my thoughts. "And you can always talk to me. Do you have my number?"

I shake my head and give her my phone so she can add it. When she gives it back, I look at her contact and see she's added emojis next to her name—a strawberry, a smiley face, and a green heart.

"Should I Stay or Should I Go"—The Clash

I guess I got my answer.

*D*ays go by without any word from Immie. She ignores my texts, refuses to look at me in class, and takes the bus to school. Alex, on the other hand, texts me constantly. She sends me pictures of her breakfast cereal, wishes me good night, and tells me basically every single thought she has in between. I start to think the reason she doesn't talk a lot is so she can save her words for text.

I don't mind so much. The attention is kind of nice. It means I don't need to try so hard to win her over. She's always giving me compliments and laughing at all my jokes, even the ones that aren't that funny. *What do you call a fish with no eyes? A fsh.* Immie would have roasted me for that one, but Alex laughs so hard she snorts.

Friday afternoon, Alex and I are leaving school together, following the current of the crowd, when she asks me about my weekend plans.

"Tomorrow I'm hanging out with Serge," I say. "We'll probably just eat pizza and play video games."

"Nice," she replies, both hands gripping the straps of her backpack. "What games?"

I shrug. "*Rocket League. Smash.* The ones where you hit stuff."

"Fun." She giggles. "I'm bad at those games."

Immie's not, I think. In fact, she's freakishly good at *Smash*. "What games do you like to play?"

"Game," she corrects. "*Sims.*"

"I've never played," I say as we cross the lobby. "Too involved."

"Got that right. I have a lot of mods, too." She looks down at the floor. "So, um. What about tonight?"

"Therapy. My second appointment."

"Oh." She nods. I think maybe she sounds disappointed. "That's great. I hope it goes well."

I reach for the door and hold it open wider, gesturing for her to go. She smiles and walks through.

"So what about you?" I ask, following the crowd down the steps. "Got any tomfoolery planned for this weekend?"

"Ha!" She throws her head back. "You're so funny."

I force a laugh. I didn't think it was *that* funny.

Out of the corner of my eye, I see a break in the current of bodies. I turn around and spot a head of long black hair running up the steps, pushing through the crowd. She keeps running until she's back inside, and I can't see her anymore.

— — —

"It was Immie," I tell my new therapist, Oliver. "She took one look at me and ran. That's how much she hates me."

"What makes you so sure it was her?" Oliver asks. He's from Tennessee and has a little bit of an accent. "It could've been anyone with black hair."

"No offense, but I've spent a lot of time looking at the back of her head," I say, and then wince. "Not in a creepy way."

"Okay. Well, why do you assume she was running away from you? Maybe she forgot something."

I shake my head. "Immie doesn't forget things. She hates me."

He looks at me, a little amused. "You're very sure of her intentions, and yet, you still haven't had a conversation."

"That's because I know her."

"But this is uncharted territory for both of you, is it not? So maybe, in this instance, you don't know her."

I lean my head against the back of the couch and stare at the ceiling. It's possible he has a point. Every fight we've ever had ended fast, but that's because the fights themselves have been insignificant. This fight is, like, the opposite of that. It's the most significant it could possibly be.

I'll probably have to try a little harder to fix things.

"So what does that mean? That I should try reaching out again?"

"I'm not saying what you should or shouldn't do. I'm saying don't assume how she feels based on past behavior. There's only one way to know how she really feels, and that's to ask her."

The timer on the table goes off. He jots something down on his clipboard and then smiles at me warmly.

"That's our time for today. I'll see you again Tuesday?"

My dad's car pulls up to the curb in front of me.

"I thought Mom was picking me up," I say when I get in.

"Hello to you too."

He's listening to an eighties rock station on the radio. It's playing "Should I Stay or Should I Go" by the Clash. When we get on the highway, he turns it down.

"How was it?"

"Fine."

He nods. "Does it . . . do you feel like you're getting something out of it?"

"I guess? It's only the second time."

"Yeah, but . . ." He drums his thumb on the steering wheel. He's clearly struggling to figure out what he's even trying to ask me. "Can you tell if it's working?"

"Two therapy sessions aren't going to magically fix me, Dad."

"That's not what I mean." He sounds frustrated. "I just—I want you to be okay, Jack. I'm new to all this stuff. I don't know how it works."

I take a breath. I shouldn't be so defensive. It's not his fault he doesn't know how to talk about his feelings. The important thing is that he's trying.

I guess, in that sense, I could learn something from him.

"He's nice," I say. "It's mostly just been me talking about

my life, and my panic attacks. Turns out they don't just come out of nowhere and are usually triggered by something."

He nods. "Any ideas?"

I glance at him, and I think, *Yeah. A few.*

"I put a lot of pressure on myself," I say. "I have a hard time disappointing people."

"Aw, you mean with your social studies thing?" He makes a face like it's no big deal. "You're not disappointing anybody. We didn't expect you to be a history buff."

"That, and other stuff." We stop at a red light. "Soccer stuff."

"Soccer stuff? What are you talking about? You helped take your team to semifinals. As a freshman. Not many people can say that."

"Michael took his team to finals," I say, echoing his words from the parking lot, not meeting his eyes.

A heavy silence hangs in the air for a while, until the light turns green.

"Buddy," Dad says, easing us through the intersection. "You haven't disappointed me. I'm really proud of everything you've accomplished this year. Not just the soccer stuff, but this therapy stuff too."

I blink, too stunned to respond. Did I hear him right?

"It takes a big man to admit he needs help from other people," he continues. "It took me a heck of a lot longer to realize that than it took you."

"Thanks," I say. "That actually means a lot to me."

"I love you, kid." He shakes his head, lets out a breath.

"Not such a kid anymore, though. You're growing up. How'd that happen?"

"The same way your beard is starting to go gray," I say, like a reflex. He reaches out and ruffles my hair.

When we get home from therapy, it's almost dark, and Dad pulls his car into the garage. Just as he's about to close the door I say, "I need to go see Immie. I'll be ten minutes, tops."

Dad nods. "Ten minutes."

I run out of the garage and down the street, past the two houses that divide us. I only stop running when I get to Immie's front yard. I hear loud music—just the beat at first, but as I cross her yard and climb onto the front porch, I can hear instruments and lyrics.

> *. . . you and I know*
> *How the heartaches come and they go . . .*

I hesitate by the front door, thinking about what I'm going to say. Then I see a flash of movement through the window.

I can't help myself—I lean a little to the left and peek inside.

Immie and her mom are dancing around the living room. Nora is singing along to the song, using the TV remote as a microphone, and Immie is jumping on the couch, laughing. It makes me smile. Here's a glimpse of the Immie I know and love. The Immie I miss.

My smile fades. She's already happier without me.

I should have told her what I was going through instead of pushing her away. I know that now. I can't go back and change it—if I could, I would—all I can do is try to learn from it.

Here's my first lesson. I can't make her happy. Not like this, not right now. I've got my own stuff to figure out first. But in the meantime, I can do what she asked of me. I can give her space.

What's that proverb people say—if you love something, set it free?

I take one more look at Immie, standing on the couch with her arms in the air and a smile on her face.

And then I turn away.

I walk back to my house in no hurry. It's a cold, silent evening, and for once, my thoughts aren't screaming at me. They're calm, at ease. That's how I know I'm doing the right thing.

TRACK EIGHTEEN

"Yes I'm Changing"—Tame Impala

I'm trying to learn from my mistakes. I want to be a better person, and a better friend to you, and that means I need to tell you the truth. Even if it's hard. Even if it hurts. Just like you said. You're not going to believe this, but it all started with your art project.

The last Friday before winter break, I'm packing up my books at my locker when Serge and Alex come walking toward me.

"I just feel like it's going to be so many people," I hear Alex say.

"Yeah," Serge replies. "That's the point. Who wants to be alone on New Year's Eve?"

"I'm not saying *alone*. I'm just saying, a small party might be more fun. Traffic is going to be terrible."

I close my locker and pull my book bag over my shoulders. "What are we talking about?"

"New Year's Eve," Serge says. "Alex is trying to get out of the bologna drop."

"What? Come on." I nudge her. "It's gonna be fun."

She shrugs. "I don't know. I just don't get it."

I feel a wave of annoyance toward her. This is a typical

response from Alex, I've come to learn. There's a part of her that likes to be contrarian. Sometimes I think she underplays how much she actually enjoys things because she wants to seem cooler. It has the opposite effect on me, though.

"I have to stop at my locker," Alex says, looking at me in a way that suggests she wants me to come with her.

"I'm meeting Z," Serge says. "I'll catch up with you guys later. Seven thirtyish."

We have plans with Zoya and Serge to watch a movie at his house tonight. I'm looking forward to it a lot less now than I was when the plans were made. Alex has been coming on strong lately, and I'm scared she's going to expect me to make a move. There might have been a time when I wanted that, but now, I don't know. Her constant attention is getting over-whelming.

"Sounds good," Alex says brightly. I nod in agreement. I can't think of an excuse off the top of my head.

I walk with Alex to her locker. It's a long walk—her locker is on the other side of the school from mine, near the art wing—and she spends the whole time telling me about some drama happening in her favorite reality TV show.

". . . cheated on her with her best friend. Can you even imagine that?"

"Yeah, that's wild."

She looks shocked. "Yeah, you can imagine it? Seriously?"

"Oh, no—I meant no."

"Good. Because I . . ."

Something catches my attention at the end of the hallway. It's in the display case the art classes use to showcase their projects. Alex stops at her locker, but I keep walking to get a better look.

". . . be friends with someone like that. Hey, where are you going?"

I stop in front of the display case, where a sign that reads WHO AM I? hangs front and center. My eyes are drawn to one project in particular. I know, without looking at the label on the left, that it's Immie's. It looks like a big version of one of her taxidermy butterflies, only this one appears to be mid-flight. Its bottom wing has started to bust through the glass.

I read the label.

Papier-mâché butterfly emerging from acrylic box
By Imogen Meadows

My grandma and I shared a love of butterflies. When I was little, we'd spend Saturdays at the butterfly garden while my mom worked her second job at the gas station. The first time, I stood perfectly still while a swallowtail landed on my nose. I remember the tickling feeling of its feet, the way they felt like Grandma's eyelashes on my cheeks when I was little. Butterfly kisses. From that moment on, I was convinced that my grandma was once a butterfly, and I was too, and that we came from a long line of strange, gentle creatures who can't help but spread their wings.

When my grandma died, I inherited her taxidermy butterfly collection. Most people who see it think it's weird, but I know they just don't understand. To me, the things pressed inside the glass aren't dead butterflies. They're memories. That's all anything is, if you really think about it. Even me—who am I without my memories?

Out of all the butterflies in my grandma's collection, the black swallowtail is my favorite. Not because it's the biggest or rarest, but because it chose me that day in the butterfly garden. That is the butterfly I tried to re-create here, made from recycled paper and coated in paste to form the papier-mâché base. The paper in question? My memories, including: My grandma's cinnamon roll recipe. Old ticket stubs from the butterfly garden. Scrap paper from my mom's lesson plans, which I used when I played Teacher. Newspaper clippings, diary entries, handwritten notes from my best friend. My dad's obituary. The signature spots on the swallowtail's wings are pieces of his CDs, shiny side up, that I smashed with a hammer.

When I was putting the butterfly inside the acrylic box, it fell on the floor and cracked. Instead of constructing a new box, I decided the cracked one felt more fitting. These memories are part of me, but they aren't the whole story. I'm growing, evolving, pounding my wings against the glass. Soon, I'll be too big for this cocoon.

"Is this Immie's project?"

Alex is next to me again. I don't look at her. I can't tear my eyes away from the words *my dad's obituary.*

"Did you know her dad died?"

"Yeah," Alex says. "Zoya told me. Immie and I haven't really talked since she totally blew up after semifinals." She glances at me. "You didn't know about her dad?"

I shake my head. So she was looking for him after all. "She didn't tell me."

"She found out a while ago," Alex adds. "Right around semis, actually."

I think about what I said to her that day under the tree.

What if you don't like what you find out about him? What if you're disappointed? This is more than disappointing. This is earth-shattering—and I wasn't there for her. I didn't know about any of it.

For a second, I really think I might be sick.

"Poor Immie," Alex says, oblivious to it all.

My eye falls on my own handwriting on a piece of notebook paper, just a little sloppier than it is now. I can make out a few random phrases: *taco is not a sandwich, but a hot dog is . . . the best song of all time . . . the tree after school.*

"Do you want to get some food before we go to Serge's?" Alex asks. "We could do pizza. Or Hearth's."

I turn to look at her. She's got a hopeful smile on her face, and it makes me feel so guilty, because I know, in that moment, I'll never be able to give her what she wants.

"Actually, there's something I have to do."

Her smile falls.

"And, um. I'm not sure if I can make it to Serge's."

"Oh." She lowers her eyes. She doesn't have to ask me why not.

"I'm sorry," I say. "But maybe I'll see you over break?"

She looks up at me, and now her gaze is sharp. "No. I don't think so."

And then she walks away. I don't know if she expects me to chase after her, but regardless, I stay where I am. I turn back to Immie's butterfly, and I start to think.

— — —

When I get home from school, I toss my book bag into the foyer and head right back outside. It's freezing—it snowed an inch yesterday—but I don't mind the cold. I zip my jacket up all the way, walk across the street and into the woods.

I thought staying out of Immie's life would be the best thing for her. When I saw her dancing with her mom, smiling and laughing, I was overcome with this feeling that I was holding her back. Turns out, I didn't have the whole story.

Now, when I look back, all I can see is how hard she was trying to be okay. And it tears me up inside, because if I had known, I would have knocked on her door. I would have wrapped her up in a giant hug and told her how much I cared about her. That we were both keeping things from each other we didn't know how to deal with. That actually, we could help each other.

I get to the tree and I hesitate. I don't know why I came here. To feel close to her maybe. To feel close to myself. I haven't been here since the night I passed out in the rain and almost got hypothermia. I nearly laugh at the thought of it, even though it's not funny at all. It's just that I've made so many mistakes, and even though I could've *died*, I still haven't learned from them.

I still haven't told Immie the truth.

The woods are coated in a light dusting of bright snow, but the ground underneath the tree is dark and dry. I climb under the roots and am about to sit down when I notice loose dirt.

I lean back, study the ground. Someone dug a hole and then filled it back up.

I don't hesitate. I kneel down and start furiously brushing the dirt away with my hands, and it's not long until I hit something solid. I clear away the rest of the dirt and pull a shoebox out of the ground. It's from a woman's black boot, size seven. Immie's squeaky boots.

Immie.

My heart pounds as I remove the lid from the box. Inside, there's a CD player—Immie's CD player, I recognize it immediately—and a folded-up piece of paper.

I unfold the paper. It's Immie's loopy handwriting.

I take a deep breath.

I start to read.

PART THREE
Immie & Jack

BONUS TRACK

"The Dress"—Dijon

HAPPY NEW YEAR!" Zoya blows a pink party horn from the passenger seat of her mom's SUV.

Immie climbs in the back seat next to Hannah. She pulls her phone out and sends her mom a text. There's a package on the porch.

"Save it for midnight," Hannah says to Zoya.

"Still an hour and twelve minutes to go," Alex adds, on Hannah's other side.

Zoya blows her party horn at Hannah disapprovingly. She turns back to Immie. "Did you dress up?"

The four of them made a pact to wear their fanciest outfits to watch the bologna drop. After serious intervention from Hannah and Zoya, Immie and Alex called a reluctant truce. They're still not best friends—they might never be—but they both agreed that a new year is no place for old resentments. The group has been mostly back to normal since then.

Immie opens her long black coat to reveal a sparkly silver dress with tassels hanging from the skirt. "I found this in my mom's closet, if you can believe it."

"I can," Zoya says. "Your mom's a babe. I bet she had some real fun in her day."

From the driver's seat, Zoya's mom looks at her disapprovingly.

"Do you think they'll have the bologna toss this year?" Hannah says. "Or the hot chocolate stand?"

"I think it'll be exactly the same as it always is," Alex says without looking up from her phone.

"Oh, boo-hoo," Hannah says. "You didn't *have* to come, you know."

"Yes she did," Zoya insists. "I wasn't about to let her sit at home all night just because she wants to avoid—"

She stops herself just in time, silenced by Alex's wide-eyed stare.

"What?" Immie says.

"More like *who*," Hannah mutters. The car goes silent.

"You can say his name," Immie says. "We're all thinking it, anyway."

Alex told Zoya that she broke things off with Jack because he was obviously in love with Immie. Then a game of telephone ensued: Zoya told Hannah, who told Immie, who didn't believe it. Why would it be true? She hadn't spoken to Jack in over a month.

"I don't want to think about him," Alex says. "I just want to have a fun night with my friends."

"Well, he'll be there with Serge," Zoya says. "But we can ignore him."

A song by Dijon comes on the queue, and Zoya turns it up loud. "I love this song!"

Her mom immediately turns the volume back down. "You're going to blow your eardrums out!"

Immie looks out the window, watching the snow-capped trees rush past. She likes the song too. The lyrics describe two people who are seeing each other for the first time in a long time. Maybe ex-lovers, or maybe just old friends, who knows? It doesn't matter either way. Zoya and Hannah both sing along: "'I'm happy to be catching up. No, we don't have to patch things up.'"

Immie's phone buzzes in her hand. It's her mom, texting back.

It's for you.

She locks the phone, resumes looking out the window. Her thoughts drift, as they often do, to Jack.

In a different car, listening to the same song, Jack looks out the window and thinks about Immie.

Serge is sitting next to Jack in the back seat of Carrie's car. "Zoya says Alex is in a mood. And she's sorry, but she's going to have to ignore you in solidarity." He turns his phone screen so Jack can see it. Tell him sorry, the text reads. And happy new year!!!

"Why is she ignoring you?" Lucy asks from the passenger seat.

"Because my little brother is a player now," Carrie says, nodding along to the beat of the song. "He's juggling two girls."

"Ew." Lucy turns to frown at him. "Seriously?"

"No," Jack says. "Shut up, Carrie."

"He's right," Carrie says. "It's more like he was stringing one along while still being hung up on the other."

"Shut *up*, Carrie!"

"Ooh." Lucy turns back around. "That one struck a nerve."

Jack, clenching his jaw, looks out the window again. He never meant to lead Alex on. He liked her—he really did. The problem was he loved Immie. No amount of ignoring it or denying it was ever going to make it less true.

He takes a deep breath and tries to swallow the lump in his throat. Immie is going to be there tonight. What if she doesn't talk to him? What if she doesn't even miss him?

He listens to the song and to Serge singing along. "'I'm happy to be catching up. No, we don't have to patch things up.'"

Downtown, three blocks of Main Street are draped in string lights and sectioned off for the bologna drop. It's crowded by the time Immie and her friends arrive.

"I'm telling Serge to meet me by the funnel cake stand," Zoya says, typing on her phone.

"Perfect," Hannah says. "That's where I wanted to go, anyway."

Immie's heart rate picks up as they push through the crowd. She knows Jack will be with Serge. What she doesn't know is how she'll react when she sees him.

"Bologna toss!" Hannah points to the right, where the toss is currently taking place in front of the butcher shop.

"Priorities," Zoya says. "First funnel cakes, then bologna toss."

"But what if the line is long and we miss it?"

"Go watch the bologna toss," Alex says. "I'll get your funnel cake and bring it over to you."

Hannah throws her arms around Alex. "You're my favorite!"

The line for funnel cakes *is* long. Immie and Alex spend the first few minutes in awkward silence while Zoya talks to Serge on the phone.

"Funnel cakes are past the bologna toss, to the right of the bologna drop," Zoya shouts over the crowd. "No, bologna *drop*. The big wiener!"

"Wieners are sausages," Alex says.

"They're the same thing," Immie replies. "Or bologna is sausage. I'm not sure about the other way around."

"Thanks for the history lesson," Alex mumbles.

"How is that history?" Immie says. "If anything, it's a home ec lesson."

"*Ugh,*" Zoya groans into her phone. "Sergio, where are you?"

— — —

"We're almost there," Serge says on the other end of the line. He and Jack are walking past the bologna toss. "Apparently there are two funnel cake stands, and we went to the wrong one first."

Jack is a bundle of nerves. He keeps thinking he's about to see Immie, and then he doesn't. First there was a different meeting spot. Then they went to the wrong funnel cake stand. And now the tight crowd is making it nearly impossible to cross to the other side of the street fair. It's starting to feel like the universe is against him.

"Well, how am I supposed to know that?" Serge groans. "Do you *really* have to pick a fight right now? It's New Year's Eve!"

He holds the phone away from his ear. Jack can hear the faint sound of Zoya's voice yelling.

"I'll see you in a minute," Serge says when she quiets down. She starts to speak again, but he cuts her off. "Okay, love you, bye!" He pockets his phone, shakes his head. "It's like she expects me to find a way to magically get through this crowd. Like I'm that freaking dude who parted the Red Sea."

"There are worse things in the world than the girl you like wanting to see you," Jack points out.

Serge raises his eyebrows. "Immie's still icing you out?"

Jack sighs. "Yeah."

Serge gives Jack a reassuring pat on the shoulder. "Maybe you'll have some luck tonight. It's New Year's Eve! New beginnings, and all that stuff."

"Maybe," he says. "Nothing like flying bologna to raise everybody's spirits."

"And appetites," Serge says. "Z better have gotten me some funnel cake."

In the distance, Jack sees Alex's bright red hair. Next to her, a little harder to see, is a girl dressed in black. Long dark hair, pale face, eyes the color of blue raspberry Jolly Ranchers.

His heart starts to pound.

Immie sees Jack at the same moment she takes a big, powdery bite of funnel cake.

"Finally," Zoya says. "Twenty minutes until the bologna drop! That's playing with fire."

Serge kisses her on the cheek and then takes a piece of funnel cake from her plate. "Just keeping you in suspense."

"I'm going to give this to Hannah before it gets cold," Alex says, holding up a plate. She avoids Jack's gaze, brushing past him and moving into the crowd.

Jack looks at Immie. Her jacket is open, and her sparkly silver dress reminds him of a disco ball. She's got powder in the corners of her mouth, which is cute. She sees him looking and wipes it away with the back of her hand.

"Hi," he says to her.

"Hi," she replies.

Zoya and Serge exchange a glance.

"We're going to catch up with Alex," Zoya says. She grabs Serge's hand and pulls him into the crowd.

Jack puts his hands in his jacket pocket. "And then there were two."

Immie cracks a smile. "Or maybe just one. I haven't decided yet."

"Ouch. I deserve that."

A beat passes in silence. They're both not sure where to look, what to say, each overwhelmed with the other's presence after such a long time apart. Finally, Jack speaks up.

"Do you want to take a walk?"

They move into the street and fall into the natural flow of foot traffic. They walk side by side but stay a comfortable distance apart.

"I'm sorry about your dad," Jack says. "I saw your art project."

Immie looks down at the funnel cake but doesn't take another bite.

"What did you think?"

"Of the project?" Jack says with a raised brow. "You could ask Alex what I thought. It's basically the reason she hates me." He clears his throat. "I couldn't look away. It, like . . . hypnotized me."

She snorts. "You've always been too nice about the stuff I make. From the very first butterfly doodle you saw in my sketchbook."

"Maybe." Jack nods. "But it's all been true."

They walk past a hot chocolate stand. Both think about that night in the cabin, but neither will admit it, so the memory goes unspoken.

"Do you want any funnel cake?" Immie holds out the plate in front of his face. "I don't think I'm going to be able to finish it all."

He takes a piece and pops it in his mouth. "Seriously, though," Jack says. "About your dad. Are you okay?"

"I'm better now," Immie says after a moment. "It was rough for a couple weeks. My mom and I were in a fight, and you . . ." She glances at him. "Well, you weren't there."

"I should have been," Jack says. "I wish I was."

They walk in silence past the bologna toss, which is down to its final two teams. On the other side of the road, Hannah, Alex, Zoya, and Serge are enraptured by the match. None of them notice Jack and Immie walking by.

"I messed everything up," Jack says, his voice strained.

Immie shakes her head. "I should have told you about my dad. And about, um, Elijah."

Jack nods. Immie and Elijah have been going out for a couple of weeks now. It hurt when he found out—of course it did. But it wasn't all that surprising, either. After all, when they got together, he was already going out with Alex.

"Where is he tonight, anyway?"

"Skiing," she says, not quite looking at him. "In Vermont, with his family."

Jack nods, trying to appear neutral. Secretly, he's relieved.

They walk until they finish the funnel cake and the flow of bodies comes to a halt. Jack and Immie look up. There it is: the giant papier-mâché bologna, tied to a rope and hanging from a crane. Back in the day they used real bologna. Someone would just go up on the roof of the butcher's shop and toss one over the edge. Then one day, some brave soul dared to ask the question: *What if we made it giant?*

"So listen," Jack says, looking up at the bologna. "I got your letter."

Immie blinks. Part of her thought *maybe* Jack might find it someday, years from now, when he'd grown up and moved away and then come back with his wife and kids to reminisce about old times. She hadn't expected it to happen so fast.

"You . . . got the letter? And the CD?"

"Yeah."

She crosses her arms. "When?"

"A couple weeks ago," he admits. "Some of the music was a little too angsty for me—"

She kind of laughs and rolls her eyes.

"But the letter." He looks at her. "The letter was good. I mean, it was hard to read, but I'm glad I read it. And I wanted to say that you were right. About all of it. I mean, I didn't mean to hurt you, but it happened anyway. You *should* be angry."

But Immie isn't angry anymore. She got all that out in the letter. She packed up her memories and buried her pain with the box in the woods.

"We both did things to hurt each other," Immie says. "Maybe we can call it even."

He looks at her hopefully. "Yeah?"

She smiles. If she's learned anything this year, it's that sometimes, people do strange things in the name of love.

"Yeah."

"Good." Jack's heart is racing. "Because I wrote you a letter too."

"You did?"

He nods. "I left it on your porch. And just like yours, it comes with its own playlist."

The box on the front porch. Immie had ignored it, assuming it was a late Christmas present, or something her mom had ordered. Now, she wished she hadn't.

The spotlights on the bologna change from plain white to dramatic multicolor. The mayor comes over the loudspeaker to start the countdown from ten seconds.

Immie and Jack look at each other. They're both thinking the same thing, which is that they've been through so much together. All the scraped knees, bruised arms, and broken hearts are no match for the bond they formed all those years ago, when they were just a couple of lonely kids longing to be seen and loved for exactly who they were and who they wanted to be. They're still figuring out that second part, but maybe that's okay.

In fact, maybe it's the point.

The giant bologna starts its descent. Jack and Immie look up.

"That's one big wiener," he says. "I hope they have enough mustard."

"If not, we could always call whatever town does a giant mustard drop on New Year's Eve."

"Oh, yeah. Ketchup, Oregon."

Immie gasps. "Seriously?"

"Nah," he says. "I just made that up."

She laughs, and the sound is music to his ears.

"Missed you, Monty," she says, leaning into him.

He smiles his small, secret smile, only it's not a secret anymore. It's out in the open for the world to see.

"I missed you too."

The countdown reaches zero, the big bologna touches the ground, and Immie and Jack hug. It's an awkward hug at first, but after a moment, it feels right.

"By the way," Immie says, still holding on tight while the crowd celebrates all around them. "I heard the coolest song in the car."

ACKNOWLEDGMENTS

This book would be nothing without my amazing editor Jessi Smith Dobies. If you told me eight years ago that one day we'd get to work on books together for a living, I would have laughed and then turned into a bird and flown away, because surely such a thing could only exist in a dream. Thank you for your invaluable insight, for helping me turn my jumbled mess of words and feelings into a manuscript worth reading, and for everything else. Love you so much. Jazz and Liz forever.

Thank you to my agent Uwe Stender for taking a chance on me, for your unwavering determination, and for always keeping it real. Here's to many more years and many more books together. #H2P

Thanks to Heather Palisi for the incredible cover design, and to the rest of the team at Aladdin for bringing this book to life. I feel so lucky to be on your roster.

To my mom, Maura Hobson. There aren't enough words to thank you for everything you've given me over the last 29 years, but hopefully this book is a start. I love you. I appreciate you. I hope I've made you proud. In the words of Lorelai Gilmore: friends first, mother/daughter second.

Thanks to my family for your love and support, especially Grandma, Aunt Missie, Ken, Andrew, and Morgan. And to Laurie, Eddie, Oliver, Alison, Greg, and the rest of my Gore family: thank you for letting me brag, letting me vent, and making me feel like I belong. Special thanks to Hadyn for your insight on all things soccer and all things teen.

A huge thanks to all my friends for keeping me sane during the whirlwind that was the drafting and editing process for this book. To Brigid: love you in case we die. To Betsy: you're the Sonja to my Luann. And to Kat: here's to many more years of texting about Zelda and talking books behind the merch table. Thanks also to Ricky, for your soccer expertise and a mullet so good it made it in the book.

I wouldn't be here without the English teachers who saw something in me, who inspired me, and who challenged me to be a better writer and reader. Siobhan Vivian, Craig Bernier, Jeff Martin, Jon Shank, and Jennifer Yohn Stumphy: thank you for helping me and so many others find our voices. Your work is invaluable.

Finally, to Eddie. You're my guiding light through the darkness, my best friend, my forever muse. Thank you for believing in me and always making me laugh. All my love stories are for you.

ABOUT THE AUTHOR

BRITNEE MEISER grew up in rural Pennsylvania where there was little to do but get lost in a book. As a kid, her most prized possession was her Junie B. Jones boxed set. Today, it's her typewriter. When she's not writing, she's probably crocheting or spending time with her partner and their dog at home in Brooklyn. *All My Bests* is her debut novel.